Nothing But the Bones

Also by Brian Panowich

Hard Cash Valley
Like Lions
Bull Mountain

Nothing But the Bones

BRIAN PANOWICH

MINOTAUR
BOOKS
NEW YORK

First published in the United States by Minotaur Books,
an imprint of St. Martin's Publishing Group.

NOTHING BUT THE BONES. Copyright © 2024 by Brian Panowich. All rights reserved.
Printed in the United States of America. For information, address
St. Martin's Publishing Group, 120 Broadway, New York, NY 10271.

www.minotaurbooks.com

The Library of Congress Cataloging-in-Publication Data
is available upon request.

ISBN 978-1-250-83524-6 (hardcover)
ISBN 978-1-250-83525-3 (ebook)

Our books may be purchased in bulk for promotional, educational, or business use.
Please contact your local bookseller or the Macmillan Corporate and Premium Sales
Department at 1-800-221-7945, extension 5442, or by email at
MacmillanSpecialMarkets@macmillan.com.

First Edition: 2024

10 9 8 7 6 5 4 3 2 1

For the misfits.
There are more of us than them.

God loves you, but not enough to save you.
—Ethel Cain

They thought I had guts. They were wrong. I was only
frightened of more important things.
—Charles Bukowski

Nothing But the Bones

Intro

1989

Chapter One

Buy the sky and sell the sky and bleed the sky and tell the sky . . .
—REM

"*. . . Don't fall on me,*" the boy sang out loud, not realizing it. He did that sometimes and he hated that about himself. But that was just one thing. There was a lot to hate.

Nelson spent most of the morning walking the railroad tracks that cut through the northern tip of McFalls County. He'd never actually seen a train come through here, and the foot-tall skunk weed that grew up through the brittle wooden ties made him believe the tracks were now a relic of the past, but at night sometimes from his bedroom he'd hear the whistle blow. Or maybe that was his imagination. He bent over to pick up a glass Coke bottle and hurled it several feet down the tracks. It shattered against the iron rails and echoed out into the morning, spooking a flock of nesting swallows that took to the sky in an inky swirl. He kept walking awhile, stopping to toss crushed soda cans and chunks of rock against the concrete embankment under Slater Street Bridge. Eventually, the boy slid the wire headphones down to his neck and made his way to the pond. After a short hike through the woods, careful not to disturb any of the early morning spiderwebs, the boy emerged through the tree line and crossed the clearing until he reached the water's edge.

Nelson dropped his Walkman and his backpack onto a smooth chunk of limestone and sat down. The breeze sweeping off the pond was cool this time of day and it felt good blowing around the boy's shirt collar. It also helped tame the dull ache of his blackened left eye. His father, Satchel, had popped him pretty good at supper the night before and left a doughy pink welt that had morphed into a patchwork of violet and yellow bruises. It hurt like hell. Nelson rubbed at his face. He'd never been fond of the way he looked, even when he wasn't toting a black eye. The kids at school told him all the time that his eyes were too close together. He reckoned that was true. In fact, all of his facial features pooled together in the middle of his face, making his forehead and cheeks appear swollen.

He felt a sudden urge to jump into the pond. He did that sometimes to try and wash the salt out of his wounds, but he decided against it. Instead, he reached over, unzipped his backpack, and began to rummage through it, looking for the cathead biscuit he'd snatched up before he left the house. When he found it, the smell of fresh churned butter and mashed blackberries made his mouth water. He unwrapped the paper towel and took a bite. He closed his eyes and chewed slowly to make it last. He knew this was most likely all he'd get to eat today. He swallowed hard, set the biscuit down on the rock beside him and then reached back into his pack and slid out a shiny, flat comic book.

Batman—number 428.

The cover gleamed in the morning sun and Nelson handled it as if it were made of spun glass. The boy loved comic books. Most people dismissed them as drugstore garbage, just picture books for little kids. But for Nelson they were much more than that. Comics had helped him learn to read way better than any schoolbook. The way the words came in short bursts along with pictures to help him understand, instead of just rows of letters all lined up in a black-and-white jumble on the page. They allowed him to concentrate—to enjoy the story more. He'd tried to explain that to his teachers at school several times, but they never understood—or they didn't care. But he loved those comics regardless. They were his most prized possessions. His mama used to buy them and hide them in his room to keep Satchel from finding them and tearing them up out of spite. That was the type of love Nelson had come to know from his folks. It came folded down the middle, like a stash of one-dollar bills cupped into a handshake, like a bribe. And now Nelson's mama was gone so these comics were all he had.

Nelson flipped through the pages but couldn't stop rubbing at his swollen eye. He heard the echo of his father calling him a retard as he hit him. He called Nelson that all the time. Especially without Mama around. The boy snorted and rubbed some more at his sore eye before hoisting a middle finger up at the clouds. The common belief among most of the people residing in the Blue Ridge foothills is that God never gives someone more weight than they can carry, but by the time Nelson McKenna was sixteen years old, he'd abandoned that ration of nonsense and took to his own belief—that sometimes God just likes to have a fucking laugh.

He felt a bug sting hard at his neck and shooed it away with a mangled left hand—another blessing from the good Lord. His hand was twice the size of a normal person's hand—all curled and swollen—with shortened, fused, and stubby fingers. It made holding flimsy things like comic books difficult, but he'd learned to manage. He balanced the book on his bad hand and turned the pages with the other. He felt something else graze the back of his head and swatted at the air before picking up his biscuit and taking another bite.

"Oh shit," he said, as he read. "Are they really going to kill Robin?" Nelson thumbed back another page. "No way." For the first time that day, he forgot his monochrome existence and began to get lost in the four-color world playing out panel by panel at his fingertips.

He felt another bite on the back of his head and this time Nelson smacked himself hard enough to hurt his hand. "What the hell?" Nelson whipped his head around to look behind him—and his heart sank.

Chapter Two

Daryl Cliett and Jeter Thompson roared with laughter. "Holy shit, Jeter. I beaned the waterhead three times before he finally noticed."

"Dumb fucker got a thick skull."

The two older boys stood several feet behind Nelson, both holding a handful of river stones. Daryl had another one cued up and ready to throw. Nelson began to stand and fumbled his comic book into the sand. When Daryl chucked the rock, he and Jeter laughed again as Nelson flinched and covered his face. He managed not to get hit and quickly stuffed his deformed left hand into his jacket pocket and out of sight.

"Don't try to hide that thing, McKenna. We all seen it before." The boys made their way closer to Nelson and the water. Daryl was a thick-necked bruiser with a crew cut short enough to see the scars he had cut into his scalp from some ATV accident a few years back, and the other boy, Jeter, was a wafer-thin punk with a barely-there goatee that looked drawn on with a Magic Marker. Both boys had abandoned school last year in favor of working for the Burroughs Clan up on Bull Mountain. That happened around here. Once kids like these got a taste of how it felt to have a little money in their pockets, slinging weed or passing along unmarked paper bags became their new career path.

Jeter stepped up, pressed a finger into Nelson's left temple, and pushed. "What happened to your face, Nelly? Your drunk-ass deddy try to straighten out them crooked eyes of yours?" Jeter looked to Daryl for approval and both boys erupted with laughter a third time.

"Just leave me alone." Nelson took a step back and reached down to pick up his comic. Daryl shoved him back. Nelson wasn't small, and he wasn't easy to knock over, but he lost his footing in the sand and Daryl swooped down and grabbed the book. He also kicked Nelson's half-eaten biscuit into the pond.

"Give it back," Nelson said, without much authority.

"Oh, that's right." Daryl spoke as if Nelson was a toddler. "You wanna find out if Robin gets killed, right?"

Nelson felt a familiar confusion. Had he done it again? Had he been talking to himself out loud again and not realized it? The soft skin of his cheeks and forehead began to flush. "Just give it back. It's mine."

"Oh, I think it's mine now, Nelly. And you know what else I think? I think you're right. I think your little homo superhero does die. Watch this." Daryl dangled the comic out in front of him by the corner, letting the pages fall loose, and then pulled a Zippo from the pocket of his jeans.

"Don't," Nelson said, but made no attempt to stop him.

"I think the Boy Wonder dies by fire. Right, Jeter?"

"Hell yeah he does."

Daryl lit the Zippo and held the long blue flame up to the paper. It caught fire immediately. Daryl tossed it toward Nelson, who slapped the burning book to the ground and stomped it out with his boot. Black flakes of ash floated on the breeze. Nelson didn't know how to process the right words. That happened a lot when he got upset or confused. He balled his good hand into a fist, but the two boys just laughed. Daryl bent down again and picked up Nelson's backpack. "Hey Jeter, how about I see how far I can chuck this into the pond?"

Thompson gave a thumbs-up and let out a ridiculous howl. Nelson wanted to say something, but he couldn't. The words—they just got lodged in his throat. *Because you're stupid*, he thought.

Daryl faced the water and drew back to throw the bag, but a new voice rang out across the clearing.

"Hey—asshole."

Every head turned to watch Kate Farris make her way across the grass. She was one of only three people in school who treated Nelson like a human being, and she was quickly making her way across the field with the other two—her best friend, Amy, and a lanky redheaded kid. "Put that down and leave him alone," Kate yelled, pulling her cocoa-brown hair back into a knot. Amy had to break into a jog to keep up, her braided blond ponytail bouncing over her shoulder. Nelson felt a wave of relief to see his friends, but it was fair to say he felt something entirely different when he saw Amy. She was the prettiest girl he knew. He adored her, and he hated that she had to be out here coming to his rescue. He rubbed at the bruise over his eye again as if his fingers could magically erase it. Daryl shielded his face from the sun and dropped the backpack to his feet. "Who the hell is that, Jeter?"

"That there is Kate Farris. Miss high and mighty thinks her shit don't stink. Her folks got money. Don't worry about her. She's just some twat with a big mouth." He squinted to make out who was trailing Kate and recognized the redheaded kid. Jeter straightened out his posture and smacked Daryl in the arm. "But hey," he said. "Come on, D. Let's get outta here, anyhow."

"Why? You just said not to worry about that bitch."

"She ain't the problem. C'mon. Let's just go."

By then, Kate had stepped between the two boys and Nelson and firmly planted her hands on her hips. "What the hell is wrong with you, Daryl Cliett?"

Daryl looked. "Take it easy, girl. We're just having a little fun with the retard here."

"He's not retarded, you jackass. But if you're looking for dumb, go find a mirror."

"You best shut your mouth."

"Or what, tough guy? You going to throw my books in the water, too? Prove how cool you are?"

Daryl's eyes sank back in his skull and he lifted the front of his T-shirt. A long pearl-handled folding straight razor poked out of his jeans. It looked like the type you'd see on the counter of a barbershop. He let the image of the blade have the desired effect on Kate before he spoke again. "Now, you wanna shut that pretty mouth or do you want me to cut you a new one?"

Kate just glared at him as her redheaded friend stepped between her and Daryl. "I think that's enough, man. No need for all that. Just leave Nelson alone and we can all go our separate ways."

"Maybe I don't want to leave him alone." Daryl took a step toward

Nelson and slapped him in the back of the head. The sound of the hit echoed over the pond and Amy saw the embarrassment in his eyes. She didn't think. She just turned and swung. The slap connected with everything she had, but Daryl was barely fazed. He caught her wrist on the follow-through and spun the tiny blond girl around, pulling her tight into his chest. He held her against him with one arm circled around her neck as she struggled to get free.

Clayton held his hands out in front of him. "Daryl. Let her go. This is getting out of hand. Just let her go and walk away."

Daryl tightened his arm around Amy's neck and shoulders, keeping her pinned in place, and he used his other hand to slide the straight razor out of his jeans. He popped his wrist and the blade sprung out. He stared holes in Clayton. "I know who you are, Burroughs."

Clayton spoke slowly. "Then you know you don't want to do this. Put the blade away and let her go."

Daryl yelled to his friend. "Look at this, Jeter. Little Burroughs thinks he can talk shit because of who his deddy is. Jeter, is that a hoot or what?—Jeter?"

Jeter Thompson had slowly put several feet of distance between himself and everyone else. Especially Daryl. "Hey, man. I gotta go. I'll holler at you later." Although the boy was talking to Daryl, he was looking directly at Clayton.

"Looks like your buddy over there has the right idea. Put the razor away and let her go, Daryl. We can act like this never happened."

Daryl's eyes began to widen and twitch. "I'm not scared of you, Ginger. I know who your people are. Who your deddy is. But see, I'm an earner for them boys. They got respect for me. And you best believe they don't give one shit about you." He moved the dull side of the razor up Amy's hip and brushed her shoulder with the blade. "And they damn sure ain't gonna care about what I do to this uppity bitch."

With that, Nelson had heard enough. He pushed Clayton aside and swung his oversized left fist into Daryl's face. His nose exploded like an overripe tomato. Amy broke free as he fell backward, swinging the razor blindly out in front of him before he landed flat on the huge chunk of limestone. Amy fell into Clayton and Kate, knocking all three of them into the dirt and sand. Nelson grabbed Daryl's wrist and banged it into the rock, until the blade dropped into the water. Once Nelson had Daryl pinned under his weight, he hit him again—and again—and again—and again.

It took all three of his friends to pull Nelson off, but by that point it didn't matter. It felt like only a few seconds had passed, but in that time Nelson nearly demolished Daryl's face. No one said anything. Clayton pinned Nelson to the ground as both girls crept slowly toward Daryl, his body twitching on the rock. His teeth were broken and jagged. Both eyes had already begun to swell shut and his left cheekbone had collapsed. But the biggest concern was the growing pool of glossy blood seeping onto the stone from under his head. Kate dry-heaved into the sand. "Jesus," she said as she glanced back at Clayton and Nelson. "What are we going to do?"

Chapter Three

Clayton finally let Nelson sit up. His eyes were still wild and filled with something none of his friends had ever seen before—something feral—cold and distant. Kate noticed something shiny lying in the dirt between her and her friends. She slid toward it and picked it up. When she realized what it was, she held it out to Amy. It was her braid—a nearly two-foot-long length of frayed rope. Daryl must've sliced it off with his razor when Nelson rushed him. Kate felt a chill shoot through her. Amy could've been killed. They all looked down at the length of twisted blond hair, now slightly pinkened with blood, dangling from Kate's palm. Amy reached up and felt at the jagged stump of hair behind her ear, lopped off right below the neon green elastic hair-tie. Just inches from the pale skin of her neck. She hadn't even noticed. She lightly touched her neck and face with the tips of her fingers. Her eyes began to water. She also became aware of the pain in her scalp. She'd been too scared to feel anything inside the moment. It happened so fast.

Kate rushed over to examine her, too. She ran her hands over Amy's neck and shoulders, making sure there weren't any wounds. She found nothing. "Oh, thank God," she said. "You're okay. It's just your hair. You're okay." Without thinking, Amy spun her head around and glared at Nelson. He'd already been watching her and he recognized the look on her face. People stared at him like that all the time. She was looking at a monster.

"I'm sorry, Amy. I—"

She shook her head. "It's not your fault," she said before she broke into a full sob. Kate wrapped her arms around her and dropped the tangle of blond hair in the grass. Nelson began to say something else, but it came out like a grunt.

"Hey, man," Clayton said. "Just give her a minute. This wasn't your fault. Do you hear me? This isn't your fault."

Nelson heard that for the lie it was. This was all his fault. If not for him, none of his friends would be getting razors pulled on them. Amy wouldn't be crying like that. Kate wouldn't be looking so damn scared. Why did he always have to mess things up so badly? He wiped at the blood on his bony knuckles, not able to get them clean, smearing it around on his skin. Sweat poured off him, too. It had gotten so hot so fast. God, how did it get so hot out? He wanted to scream. He wanted to tell Amy how sorry he was. But, as usual, he couldn't speak.

"Clayton," Kate said, still holding Amy. "We need to call for help."

Clayton looked confused.

"The CB in your truck. Go call the sheriff or an ambulance or something. We need to help him or we are going to be in a lot of trouble."

"Help him? You saw what happened, Kate. That asshole could've killed somebody. Nelson had every right to—"

"I know that, Clayton, but we can't just do nothing and let him bleed to death."

Clayton knew she was right, but he didn't like it. Who was going to believe them? That beating didn't look like self-defense. It looked more like Daryl was mauled by a goddamn tiger. Clayton also didn't want to leave them there alone. Nelson still had something weirdly wrong in his eyes and what if that other kid, Jeter, came back—with more of their crew? "Let's just think about it a second," he said.

"Please, Clayton. We don't have a second. Go call for help. Go now."

"Okay. Okay. I'm going." He gathered himself, brushed the grass and dirt off his bloodstained Levi's, and squatted down next to Nelson. "I'll be right back. You just breathe and stay here. Watch out for the girls. Nelson? Just nod if you can hear me. You good, man?"

Nelson said nothing. He wasn't good. This was bad and he knew it. He felt far away, outside himself. Clayton asked him again and this time Nelson nodded.

"Wait," Amy said. Everyone turned to look at her as she wiped tears off her face with the back of her hand. "Maybe Clayton's right. Maybe we should take a second."

"Amy . . ."

"No, Kate. Listen. The sheriff isn't going to believe anything Nelson says."

"But he'll believe us. Look at your hair. We can just tell him what happened."

Amy yanked the neon elastic out of her sheared hair and let it fall free around her face. She stood up, walked over, and took a seat in the grass next to Nelson. Even he didn't understand what was happening.

"You saved my life, Nelson. If you hadn't done what you did, he might've killed me. I'm not going to let you be punished for that."

"Amy, we don't have a choice here. Nelson is my friend, too, but we can't just do nothing."

"I'm not saying that we do nothing, Kate."

"Then what are you saying?"

"I'm saying maybe we shouldn't call the sheriff."

"I don't understand."

"I'm saying maybe we get help from someone else." Amy looked up at Clayton. He already knew what Amy was suggesting. "I'm saying we call Clayton's father."

Kate was stunned. "Are you fucking kidding me?"

Amy stood up. "No. I'm not." She faced Clayton. "Your dad can be down here in half the time it would take the sheriff coming from Waymore. And he can fix this, can't he? He can make this all go away. I mean, he can help, can't he?"

"Maybe. But, Amy. For real. I don't know what his help will look like. He's not the law up here. He's . . ."

"Please, Clayton. He'd do it for you. C'mon. How many times are we going to let the world screw Nelson over?"

Clayton scratched at his neck. Everything his father did came at a price. Not even his family members were let off that hook. And this would be no different.

"You're not seriously considering calling that psycho are you?"

"He's not a psycho, Kate."

Kate lowered her voice and spoke slowly. "You need to call the sheriff,

Clayton. Not your criminal father. Do you hear me? You call the sheriff or give me your keys and I'll do it myself."

"Okay," he said. He glanced at Amy and squeezed Nelson's shoulder before he walked to his truck. Kate watched him cross the field and climb into his truck. She watched him make the call, step out, and head back toward them. She let her chin fall to her chest. She knew by the way he kept staring at his boots that he hadn't listened to her. At least she tried.

Chapter Four

After Clayton returned from the Bronco, they all waited in silence. Everything felt wrong and upside down. At least it did to Kate. She might not have agreed with the choice they made, but she was loyal and she held Clayton's and Amy's hands anyway. They sat huddled in a group around Nelson, while they waited for *help* to arrive.

They heard an engine first, and then an old Ford step-side pulled up next to Clayton's Bronco. Everyone watched as four men unloaded from it. Two of them jumped out of the truck bed. They carried rifles and double-checked their payloads before walking in opposite directions to the left and right of the clearing. Another one, an enormous Black man dressed in a red flannel shirt and overalls, stepped out and leaned against the driver's side of the truck. He slapped on a ball cap. The fourth man was Clayton's father, Gareth Burroughs. He took a moment to survey his surroundings and then slowly began to walk toward the water. He wore a brown canvas coat over a gray collared shirt tucked into a loose pair of work pants, and he slipped a plug of tobacco into his cheek from a foil pouch as he walked.

"Jesus Christ," Kate whispered. "Is he smiling?" She felt a chill run a lap down her back as she watched him get closer. "What the hell did we do, Clayton?"

Gareth went to Daryl first. He spit a long stream of glistening tobacco juice into the sand and took a closer look at the broken boy.

"Deddy, Nelson did what he had to do. That guy was about to hurt Amy real bad and—"

"That's enough. I don't need to know all the details. The less you say to me, the better. I'll take it from here." Gareth nudged a boot into Daryl's ribs. He glanced around at the kids, all of them standing silent, and then looked down at Nelson, still sitting at Clayton's feet. As everyone held their collective breath, Gareth held a hand up over his head and signaled something to the men standing sentry around the pond. They both disappeared into the thick cover of loblolly pine, birch, and maple trees that surrounded the water. The big Black man in flannel, who'd stayed back by the trucks, whistled and held a hand up, spreading all five of his fingers wide and then balling them into a fist. Gareth watched, nodded, and sighed. "Clayton, get these girls outta here. Put 'em in that fancy truck of yours and bring 'em back to Waymore."

Kate spoke almost against her will. "Wait a minute. Do we just go home now and act like none of this happened? What's going to happen to Nelson? We can't just—"

Gareth didn't even look at her. He kept his cool gray eyes on his son. "Tell your girlfriend there not to worry her pretty little head about any of this. Your friend will be fine. But Val over there just let me know that the sheriff is five minutes out. And I can't clean this mess up with all of you here. Clayton, you are covered in blood. I can't let you be seen like that. And those two girls? They were never here. End of story. Now, do what you're told. Get them out of here—now."

Clayton nodded and began to usher the girls toward his truck.

"Take the Summer Branch fire road out of here instead of McDowell," Gareth yelled behind them. "I don't want you passing any cop cars on the main road."

"Yessir," Clayton said.

Gareth listened to the mumbling begin once they were several feet away. The sound of some entitled little Waymore brat giving his youngest son an earful of lip irritated him to no end. He absentmindedly rolled his wedding ring around on his finger, then spit, shook his head, and waited until the kids were out of earshot before he kneeled next to Nelson McKenna. The boy seemed to be the only person out there capable of looking the mountain-born shot-caller directly in the eye. Gareth took that as a good sign.

"You're Satchel McKenna's boy, ain't 'cha?'"

Nelson didn't speak. He wanted to, but as always, his words were still gummed up in his head.

"You know how to talk, son?"

Nelson nodded.

"Then get to it. I asked if you were Satchel McKenna's boy?" Gareth already knew the answer. He was just trying to gauge the boy's state of mind for what was about to happen. "Okay. You don't wanna talk. Fine. How about you listen instead. The sheriff down there in Waymore heard Clayton call me on the radio, so inside of about four minutes you're going to see one of those shiny white and brown sheriff's cars roll in here next to where my friend Val over there is standing by that truck. You see him?"

Nelson looked and nodded.

"Good. And then next, a sloppy-looking idiot with a tin star pinned to his shirt is going to walk down here and start flapping his gums. But don't you worry about him. I only want two things to happen once he gets here. One, I want you to keep your mouth shut. Just like you're doing. That don't look like it'll be too hard for you. I can see that you're the quiet type already. You tracking?"

Nelson nodded again.

"Good. Number two. I want you to trust me. You think you can do that?"

Nelson held his head as still as his tongue.

"Okay boy, the clock is tickin' and I need your word that you're not gonna spin out on me. Do you know who I am?"

Of course he did. Everyone on the mountain knew who Gareth Burroughs was. Nelson nodded again without any hesitation this time.

"Well good. And if you know me then you know I don't like being owed to nobody. And right now I'm owed out to you."

That made Nelson raise an eyebrow.

"That's right. See, that sack of junkie garbage over there is a real piece of shit. I know that, because he used to work for me—when he was upright—and you, my boy—you just saved me from the unpleasantry of having to put him down myself. So, I'm saying that I need to return the favor. So we can call it square. That way we can both be eating some hot supper in no time. My oldest boy, Halford, is cooking up some catfish stew back at the house. You like catfish, don't you, son?"

"Ye . . . yes, sir."

"Atta boy. So, I'm going to ask you again if you think you can trust me?"

"Yessir. I trust you."

Gareth spit in the dirt. "All right then."

Just as Gareth predicted, he and Nelson watched as a white and tan Crown Victoria wheeled into the gravel and parked in the same place Clayton's Bronco had been just a few minutes earlier. A chubby man with mirrored sunglasses in a tan button-up shirt with a shiny star pinned to it got out of the car. He offered a chin tip to Gareth's friend Val, and then cocked a stiff county-issued sheriff's hat on his brow. Everyone watched as the McFalls County sheriff, Sam Flowers, made his way toward the pond.

"He looks like a goddamn fool. Don't he, boy?"

Nelson had no true gauge for what a fool looked like, but he'd found his voice and he didn't want to lose it again, so he spoke. "I reckon."

When Flowers saw the extent of damage done to Daryl, he grabbed for the radio on his belt.

"Don't touch that radio, Flowers."

"Now look here, Gareth. If this young fella is still alive, I need to radio in for a medic or some shit."

"Take your glasses off, Sam."

"Huh?"

"I said get your hands off that goddamn radio and take off those dip-shit sunglasses before you talk to me."

"Now, Gareth, c'mon and be reasonable here. This kid looks bad and as a representative of the law in McFalls County, it's my responsibility to—"

Gareth cut him off with a high-pitched whistle like the one they'd heard the Black man sound a few minutes ago. Another whistle rang out from the tree line. And then another. The two men with rifles that Nelson had watched create a perimeter earlier were suddenly present. Nelson had forgotten they were there. He guessed that was the point. The two men lifted the barrels of the long guns. The message was clear. Sheriff Flowers removed his mirrored aviators and hung them from his shirt pocket. Gareth spit in the dirt, pulled the plug of wet tobacco from his cheek, and tossed it in the water. "Now, you were saying? Something about your responsibility?"

"Gareth, I've got the right to know what went on here. And I've got a responsibility to try and help that young man over there before it's too late."

"It's already too late for that one. He's done. And honestly, there ain't all that much to tell you about what happened. My boy Clayton and his buddy here, come out to the water to cool off, maybe get some use of that tire swing over there."

Flowers wiped at his salt-and-pepper mustache. "To get some use of the tire swing?"

"Yup."

Flowers looked around. He didn't see a tire swing.

"Then they come up on ol' boy over there all worked over, probably by some fellas he owed money to, and so Clayton called me out here to help, seein' as I was closer. But as you can tell by looking at him, there ain't no help to be offered."

Flowers looked down at Nelson, who tried to hide his scraped-up knuckles in his lap.

"Don't look at him, Sam." Gareth snapped his fingers. "You look up here at me."

Flowers did. "Gareth, the boy's got blood all over him—"

"Yeah, bless his heart. He tried to help. Clayton did, too. That's why I sent him home—to clean up." Gareth spit again, just inches from Flowers's patent leather shoes. He licked his front teeth and took a step toward the sheriff. "That's all that happened out here, Sam. And my word is as good as the Gospel of John. Unless you're calling me a liar."

The air went thin, and Sheriff Flowers had trouble stringing together the next sentence. "No, Gareth. I ain't. Wait. I ain't saying that. Not at all. I'm saying. I mean . . ."

"What, Sam? What do you mean?"

"I mean, what is it exactly you want me to do with this?"

"Well, if I was you—and thank God I ain't—I'd mosey on back to that office in Waymore and wait for a missing person's report. Because when you get it—lucky you—you'll know right where to look."

"Now, Gareth, what you're asking is—"

"I ain't asking, Sam. I'm telling you what's what. This ain't Waymore Valley. This is Bull Mountain. So it's my call to make. Not yours. That's the arrangement. Now, go on back to Waymore. Answer your phone. Fill out some forms. Do whatever fat-ass police do on a Tuesday because your investigation here is over."

"All right. I get it. I understand. I'm going." The sheriff backed away with his hands in plain sight for the gunmen in the trees to see, and then began to fumble for his sunglasses.

"No, Sam. You leave those right where they are until you get back in your car."

Flowers didn't understand why that mattered but he didn't argue. He took one more backward step before turning on his heel and breaking into a brisk pace back to his cruiser.

"Oh, yeah, and Sam? I ever find out you been monitoring my son's CB channels again, I'm gonna break every bone in your gun hand. You'll never jerk off again."

Gareth waited until the dust settled from the sheriff's Crown Vic leaving to signal his men. He twirled a finger in the air, indicating to bring the perimeter in and then took a seat in the grass next to Nelson. "You know why I love it when shitbird police wear mirrored sunglasses, boy?"

Nelson did not. He shook his head.

"Because it makes the shiniest target." He spit. "And I just love it when he hangs 'em there right over his heart. You get what I mean about being a fool, now?"

"Yessir."

Chapter Five

Gareth held his hand out to one of the gunmen who'd come down to the water from the trees. This man had a headful of rust-colored hair, too, like Clayton. Nelson even thought that he looked a bit like his friend but a few years older and he carried a squirrelly kind of crazy in his eyes—like a ferret. The young man pulled a blued steel .45 caliber pistol from a military-style rucksack and laid it in Gareth's open palm. Burroughs made a show of the gun's weight and shape until it garnered enough of Nelson's interest. The intended result. "You ready to make all this square, son?"

Nelson was confused. "I thought you said if I trusted you with the sheriff then we'd already be square."

Gareth let a small grin ease across his lips. "What I said was I'd handle Johnny law in exchange for you putting down a dog. Well—that dog over there ain't all the way down." Gareth held out the .45. "You know how to handle one of these?"

Nelson nodded, indicating that he did, but he didn't reach out to take it. Gareth sighed. "My boy said that punk over there tried to hurt one of your friends. That true?"

"Yessir."

"Would you be surprised to hear that ain't the first time that junkie piece of shit ever roughed up a lady?"

"He done it before?"

"Several times. See, boy, there's a misconception in the world that took me a long time to come to terms with. Something that took me until

I was almost grown to completely understand. But it's something that you could learn right here and right now. And looking at the beating you put on that fella over there tells me you really need to hear it. You see, most folks believe that you're either born a hammer or a nail. Meaning that if you're born a hammer, you tend to see other people as nails, and you just want to bash on them. Good intentions or not." Gareth reached down and pulled Nelson's clubbed fist out of his lap. He held it up despite Nelson's resistance. "Why, the good Lord even saw fit to build a hammer right into your hand." Gareth held Nelson's deformed and bloodied fist up a few moments, finally allowing the boy to pull it away. The boy stuck his hand back into his jacket pocket and stared into his lap.

"It's almost like the world already decided your fate. But I don't believe in that shit. I don't think the world is that simple. It ain't that black-and-white. You see, hammers are a dime a dozen. Anybody can be a hammer. Just like that fool on the ground over there. A hammer's just a tool. And it's too damn easy to dismiss somebody like you as just another tool in the shed. Hell, that's what most people are going to expect from you. But the truth is, it's the nails that matter. The steel. The bite. The precision. They work in unison. By themselves they don't seem like much, but together—together—they can hold up an entire house—or even an empire. But that choice is yours to make. You can just be another tool, good for one thing and one thing only, or you can be one of the nails that help hold something together—something important. You can belong to something much bigger than just you alone, son. You can be what everyone on this mountain expects you to be, or you can be one of us. One of the *nails* in the house of Burroughs. But you need to earn it."

Gareth paused to see if the boy was picking up what he was laying down. But by the faraway look in Nelson's eyes, he wasn't sure, so Gareth opted for a different approach. He knew this boy's history. He knew his father, Satchel. So Gareth used what he knew to taunt him. "Or maybe I'm wrong about you. Maybe you're just another dumbfuck like everybody says—somebody like him—" Gareth used the pistol to motion toward Daryl. "Just someone that beats on people because they can—somebody like your deddy. Maybe you're just another Satchel McKenna."

That did it.

Nelson puffed up inside his secondhand jacket and his voice rose enough to surprise Gareth. "I ain't nothing like him, Mr. Burroughs. I hate him." He rubbed the bruise under his eye. "I hate that bastard."

Gareth wasn't sure which *bastard* Nelson was talking about, Daryl or his father, but he didn't really care. He took the opportunity to hold out the gun a second time and this time Nelson took it. Gareth stood up and helped Nelson to his feet by his forearm. The boy walked over to where Daryl lay on the rocks. He pointed the revolver down at the boy's ruined face.

"Not too close, son. I ain't got another set of clothes for you to wear and Val don't want all that blood in his truck."

The big Black man in red flannel, who'd made his way down to Gareth from the truck, came over and stood next to him. "All that is news to me, Gareth."

"All what?"

"All that shit about Cliett. I didn't know he'd fallen off the deep end like that. Hell, Gareth. That kid made a few runs for me just last week. Seemed all right to me."

Gareth cocked his head, genuinely confused. "Who you going on about, Val?"

"Cliett. The kid. The hamburger man over there on the ground."

Gareth chuckled and watched Nelson standing over Daryl's body. "Shit, Val. I never even heard of that Cliett kid before today."

Val raised an amused eyebrow. "You mean you made all that stuff up? His history with dope, being a junkie, beating up on women?"

"I'm sure there's some truth in it somewhere."

Val laughed quietly into his hand. "You reckon little 'Nails' over there has it in him?"

"Let's see," Gareth said, and held a finger to his lips. They didn't have to stand there very long before Val got what he thought was the answer to his question. After holding the gun on Daryl for what seemed like an eternity, Nelson eventually dropped it to his feet. Val sighed but the grin never left Gareth's face. They both watched as Nelson fell to his knees on the limestone and straddled the bloodied bully. And then he swung on him. One hit after another. He yelled out over the pond as he pummeled the boy. To a stranger, the echoes would've sounded like madness. To Gareth Burroughs it was more like music.

"Okay, Val. Go pull him off. Get him out of here. Take him to the house and clean him up. Fill his belly. We're done here."

Val didn't understand, but he'd also learned not to question Gareth. So the big man did as he was told and pulled Nelson off the boy and did his best to calm him down.

"You did good, son," Gareth said. "That piece of shit is gone, and good riddance. You did a good thing out here today. You made the mountain a safer place. Now go with Val to the truck. Let's call it a day and go home."

Nelson's rage was subsiding and he allowed Big Val to walk him toward the truck across the clearing. Once they were far enough away, Gareth squatted down next to Daryl's broken body. He tucked the gun in his pocket and used two fingers to check the boy's neck for a pulse. He felt one before wiping the blood off his hand on his coat. That tough little bastard was still alive. Gareth leaned in closer to the boy's ruined face. "I almost envy you, son. It's about to all be over. No more pain." And then Gareth covered the boy's mouth and nose and held his hand in place until he saw the life finally fade from Daryl's eyes. He felt a chill run through him—because that was the part he enjoyed. Once he was sure the boy was just a husk, he stood up and wiped more blood across his coat. He looked down at himself and all at once he felt a swell of sadness rise up from his chest. He loved that damn coat.

1998

Side One

Chapter Six

"Ow, man, shit. C'mon, Nails—take it easy."

The man Warren Dixon called Nails twisted the fry cook's left arm even further behind his back and slammed him into the cinder block divider wall for a second time that night. Dixon yelled again. "Fuck, man. Stop it. I'm working . . . I'm pulling double shifts. I'm doing my best to get the money. I just need a little more time."

Nails held Dixon in place against the wall with his shoulder, keeping his arm anchored to his back and his cheek pressed flat against the raw concrete block. "You're going to break my arm, man."

Nails reached around Warren's hip and began to rummage through the pocket of his dirty white apron.

"Oh, c'mon, man. I just told you—"

"You just told me you were doing your best." Nails felt around until he found what he was looking for and yanked his hand out of Warren's apron. He held up a golf-ball-sized plastic baggie of crank and spun it like a top under the buzzing electric light that lit up the side porch of the club. "This ain't your best, Warren. This shit cost money. Money you could be using to pay off your debts. How the hell is this your best?"

"Put that away, man. C'mon. You're going to get us shot out here." Warren strained to try and peek over Nails's shoulder from the uncomfortable position he was in to see if anyone else was eyeballing the entirety of his last paycheck, now that Nails was putting it on display for the world. He only saw more of the big man's shoulder. Nails thought about it and looked as well. He scanned the parking lot and didn't see anyone worth notice. Only a skinny blond girl in cutoffs using her hip to balance and search through a huge floral handbag. He stuffed the baggie of dope into the pocket of his coat and lingered on the girl for a moment. She was pretty, an almost fuzzy presence, and way out of place at a shithole like this. For a split second she looked directly back at him, but quickly realized that wasn't a good idea and turned her head down. Nails lost interest and returned his attention to Warren.

"This isn't cool, Warren. If Freddy knew you were using while you were on the clock he'd be really pissed. And how do you think it looks to Burroughs?"

"Damn, Nails, please. Please don't tell Freddy. And tell Gareth I'm sorry. I am, man. Really."

"He knows you are, Warren. I am, too." Nails pulled up on Warren's arm and the snap of bone breaking was followed by Warren's bellow of pain. The damage to his arm stole all the fight Warren had, so Nails let go and helped the cook ease down the wall into a crumpled heap. His left arm dangled out to his side like a stretch of chewed-up saltwater taffy. Nails took another brief survey of the parking lot. The girl was long gone now. Nails leaned down and tapped Warren on the cheek a few times. "Warren? Warren? Don't black out." Finally, he slapped him.

"Jesus Christ, Nails. Enough. Stop it."

"Okay. That's it. But you need to get your shit together. Please don't make me have to do that again after you get it all patched up." He lifted Warren's chin off his chest. "Do you hear me?"

"Yes, fuck, I hear you."

"Okay. Try to have someone look at that arm tonight. Go ahead and I'll cover you with Freddy."

Warren just held his ruined arm and watched the big man take the sack of dope back out of his coat. He cut it open with an overgrown thumbnail. Warren wasn't sure what hurt more, his newly fractured arm or watching three hundred dollars' worth of yellow cake-mix crank disappear into the night breeze.

Chapter Seven

The Chute wasn't just any bar in the middle of the North Georgia woods. There were plenty of moonshine shacks to choose from, but this one was a landmark of sorts. It was unique and sought out by a wide variety of deviants and fetish-chasers in the tristate area. The place was operated by a drag queen named Freddy Tuten, hence the full name of the establishment, Tuten's Chute. That's what it said on the flickering neon sign above the front door. Most people thought the name was some kind of explicit vulgarity, and maybe Freddy Tuten even encouraged the double meaning, but Nails knew the real story. Freddy and his brother, Jacob, had been paratroopers in the U.S. Army. An airborne company out of Fort Benning in Columbus. After they both served tours of duty in Korea, Freddy finally came home. His brother did not. The bar and the moniker was Freddy's way to cope with the pain of losing him. Nails felt more at home here at Tuten's Chute than he ever had in Satchel McKenna's house.

He pushed open the front door and was immediately immersed in the bass-heavy music and the smell of sour beer, cigarette smoke, and sweat. He moved through the flood of red light and bits of diamond reflecting off the disco ball. He only had to push two people out of his way. One of them was an older man wearing a tweed blazer and a low-rider UGA ball cap, and the second, his apparent guest—a kid half his age with an identical hat—worn the same way. The headgear was probably bought at the same time, for exactly the same purpose—to help the two men not be recognized. Nails took an open seat at the bar and slid his fanny pack around to the front. It didn't take any time at all for Freddy to walk over and set down a bar napkin—a luxury reserved only for The Chute's regulars.

"Nails."

"How you doing, Freddy?"

"I'm not falling, but I'm damn sure leaning. How about you?"

"Another day." Nails unzipped his fanny pack and pulled out a small paperback novel. *The Postman Always Rings Twice* by James M. Cain. A few years ago, Nails had grown to love the old pulp fiction noir novels that read just as quickly as the comic books he grew up on. Short bursts of simple words. Short chapters that got to the point. Freddy set down an ice-cold mug of apple juice, and Nails opened the paperback to a dog-eared page. A wave of urine stink washed out from the swinging bathroom door to the right of the bar and Nails sneezed into the book. "How the hell does this place always smell like piss? Somebody needs to fix the plumbing."

Freddy stared blankly at Nails. "You do realize you just said that directly to my face, right?"

"I did?"

"Yeah, you did. And if the stink is too much for you, I can get you a mop and some Pine-Sol."

"Sorry, Freddy. I didn't mean no harm. Just thinking out loud."

"You do that a lot, you know."

"I know. Sorry."

Freddy dismissed it and turned toward a thin Latina woman waving a twenty like she was tipping a stripper. Freddy snatched it without a word and mixed something red in a hurricane glass. He set it in front of the woman and returned to Nails.

"You think I could get an order of onion rings?"

Freddy let out a half-ass chuckle and tucked his long graying hair behind his ear before leaning down on the bar. His eye shadow was bubble-gum pink. "Is that a joke, Nails?"

"No. I'm starving."

"Are you?"

"Yeah, what's wrong with that?"

Freddy turned his head up briefly to yell over the music at some

Goth-looking dickhead who'd just spilled his beer on the jukebox and then returned to Nails. "Yeah, um, I'd love to get you an order of onion rings, Nails. But you broke my fry cook's arm outside a few minutes ago and the only other guy I got working the kitchen had to leave to take him down to Waymore Memorial to get it fixed." Freddy looked annoyed but not angry.

"You know about that?"

"I know everything that happens in this place, Nails. You know that."

"Sorry, Freddy. It was work."

"Well, work or not. You're out of luck on the onion rings."

Nails lowered his head back to his paperback. "Out of luck. Of course. Stupid." He wasn't sure if he said that out loud or not, but either way, he got no argument from Freddy.

Chapter Eight

Nails guessed the blonde from outside was about nineteen now that he could see her up close. She'd just managed to squeeze herself between Nails and the Latina woman sipping her second glass of red diabetes. Nails tried to steal a better look at her, but she caught him and he looked away. He had never learned how to handle himself in close contact with a pretty girl. He mostly just scared them off. He stared down at his book feeling a little embarrassed that his arm was forced to mash up against hers, but he figured she was just as uncomfortable and would soon move anyway. He was wrong.

"Hey there, handsome."

Nails didn't respond.

"Hello? Big man to my right reading a book at a bar?"

Nails side-eyed her. "What?"

"I'm saying hi to you."

"Okay."

"Whatcha reading?"

"What?"

"What. Are. You. Reading?"

Nails looked down at the book again. He hadn't read a damn thing since she'd walked over. "It's a . . . story . . . a novel . . ." And that was all he was able to say about that. He went silent.

"Well, that sounds fascinating," she said.

Freddy made it over to her and tipped his chin. She slid a five-dollar bill toward him across the bar. "I just need some quarters for the jukebox if that's okay?"

Freddy picked up the five and popped the drawer to the register. The girl turned back to Nails.

"I saw you outside earlier."

That surprised him, so this time he looked directly at her. "So? What are you saying?"

"I'm just saying I saw you is all. Did you see me?"

Nails felt his head gumming up. Freddy put a stack of quarters on the bar. She winked her appreciation and looked back at Nails. "I asked if you saw me out there, too?"

Nails still wasn't sure how to process what she was getting at.

The girl swiped the cash from the bar and stuck it into the pocket of her cutoffs, lifting just enough of her cropped black Nirvana T-shirt to show a sliver of pale belly and the right amount of sharpened hipbone. Nails watched as a reflex and didn't like that he did. She waited for his eyes to lift back up to hers. "Never mind," she said. "That was a stupid question." She eased herself out of her position at the bar using Nails's shoulder to push herself free. She twirled herself around a complete three hundred and sixty degrees and faced him. "Of course you saw me. I don't think you saw anything else."

Nails felt flushed. A grind of guitars and electronic drums poured out of the jukebox and Shirley Manson's sultry voice filled the bar. The blond girl's eyes lit up with what looked like pure joy. "Oh my God, this is my song." And with that she spun again and headed toward the jukebox. Nails watched her walk the entire length of the dance floor before turning back around in his seat. Freddy stood behind the bar with his arms crossed wearing a wide toothy smile.

"What?"

Freddy laughed. "Damn, son. That one there got you all worked up. I didn't think that was even possible seeing that you're all mister badass and all."

"Shut up, Freddy."

"Hell, Nails. Go over there and dance with her."

Nails shook his head and returned to his book. He tried to focus, but he couldn't. It was like trying to solve a crossword on the beach in the middle of a typhoon. But he kept his head down anyway. He'd been dizzied by women before. It would pass. And it almost did. He'd taken in about three more pages of the James Cain novel before she showed up next to him again. Her wide-necked tee hung loose over one bare shoulder, showing off a thin black bra strap, and her skin looked hot and damp. Nails kept his face forward as she ordered a round of rattlesnakes for her and her circle of friends—which included the punk dressed up like Robert Smith who'd spilled his beer all over the jukebox earlier. She didn't speak to Nails this time. It took Freddy a long time to make the multi-layered shots, so Nails sat in the uncomfortable hot zone next to a girl who could've easily gotten a better spot at the bar if she wanted to. But she chose to stand right there next to him. She rattled his cage. He didn't understand exactly why but he knew he didn't like any of it. Maybe it was because she didn't act like she was afraid of him.

Freddy finished making the shots and lined them up on the bar. He yelled the total out over the music. The blond girl laid some cash on the bar and Freddy took it. She put a delicate hand on top of the barkeeper's callused knuckles. "Hey, mister? You think I can buy my big friend here a drink while I'm at it?"

Freddy smiled at her. "Your big friend there doesn't drink."

The girl smiled back. "Is that right?"

"That is right."

"Does he know that he's in a bar?"

"Why don't you ask him?"

"I don't think he's much on talking."

"Not to strangers he ain't."

Nails had enough. "Stop. I'm right here. Don't talk about me like I'm not right here." He tried to be genuinely angry, because anger was an emotion he could understand, and he could navigate that water without much effort. Freddy put his hands up in the air as if to say "my bad" and walked off. The girl picked up the four shots. "I didn't mean any harm, handsome. I was just trying to be friendly."

"Friendly really ain't my thing."

"I can see that. I'm sorry. I won't bother you anymore."

Marcy Playground faded in the background and for a moment while the CD changed, there was an eerie silence in the room. Nails lowered his voice down from the yell-talking they'd been doing to compete with the noise. "It's . . . it's okay. I'm . . . *stupid,*" he thought as he fumbled over just a few simple words. The chime of an acoustic guitar accompanied by a sweeping slide eased out of the jukebox and the honey-soft melody of Mazzy Star's "Fade into You" floated through the air. The girl's eyes lit up again. "Ooh. Ooh. I gotta go. This is my song." She turned to go.

The words arranged themselves in his head and Nails yelled out to her. "I thought that other one was your song?"

She stopped, smiled, and yelled back. "They are *all* my songs."

She zigzagged through the thick crowd of people on the dance floor and handed three of the shots to the Gothy asshole. He was talking with a group of people Nails had never seen in there before, but he figured him for the boyfriend. That tracked. Assholes like that always ended up with pretty girls. The blonde downed her own shot, handed the vampire boy her empty cup, and moved slowly and confidently onto the dance floor. The breathy vocals of the Mazzy Star tune ached along through the air almost like a cool breeze, and the blond girl's hips caught the rhythm. They swayed in time.

"I want to hold the hand inside you."

She closed her eyes, leaned her head back, and lifted her hands into the air as she slowly twirled, lost in the song. Raising her arms also raised her shirt, again exposing a pale flat belly and her subtle curves.

"I want to take the breath that's true."

Most of the people on the dance floor had moved out of the way to give her space—to allow her all the red light in the room. She bathed in it and her body moved like silk falling in the wind.

"I look to you, and I see nothing."

She swayed with a gentle grace and Nails didn't think there was a single person in the place that wasn't watching her. She owned the room. She was hypnotic to watch. She certainly didn't look out of place anymore. In fact, she looked more like the single best reason anyone would have for being there.

"I look to you to see the truth."

The boyfriend—the vampire—was even paying attention to her

now. But he must not have been that pleased by her performance because twice he attempted to stop her, and twice, she melted out of his reach, clearly not wanting him to touch her. He finally backed off as she finished seducing the room.

"*Fade—into—you.*"

"*Fade—into—you.*"

When the song finally ended and died away, she opened her eyes as if her soul had just returned from some astral plane. She looked hazy and lost, but when she focused, she was looking directly at Nails. Maybe. He could've been wrong. He most likely was. But it didn't matter. The vampire moved and stood in front of her, cutting off Nails's line of sight. The boyfriend wasn't happy. He began to wave his hands around and motioned toward the group of men he'd been talking to. He pointed his finger in her face and then around the room but the show was over and by the time the next song began, everyone had gone back to not being noticed inside the noise. The vampire grabbed the girl's arm and jerked her toward an adjacent room where all the pool tables were. The group of men with them followed. Nails couldn't see into the poolroom from where he was, and he shifted in his seat. He was about to stand up, but Freddy reached a hand over the bar and popped him hard on the shoulder. "Leave it, Nails."

"Did you see that? Did you see that guy grab her?"

"Yeah, I saw it. But I got people for that. If it gets out of hand, Monk will handle it. That's what I pay him for. You already shut down my kitchen for the night. I don't need you beating the shit out of some ATL punk having an argument with his girlfriend and running out the rest of my paying business. Okay? Nails? Okay?"

"Yeah. Okay. I hear you." The vampire and the blond girl were gone, and Nails spun back around to face the bar. Freddy had already poured him another mug of apple juice. He downed it in two gulps.

Chapter Nine

The rest of the night dragged along. Nails had given up on the girl ever coming back into view and figured she'd either found her bliss with the vampire at the satellite bar in the pool room or they'd left through the side door. By two a.m., Nails was tired, bored, and ready to leave. The bar was packed elbow-to-elbow now and would be until sunup and Nails didn't even know why he was still there. Yes, he did. He'd enjoyed the mild flirtation and couldn't get that dance out of his head. What was that about? He felt like she'd done it for him, and that kind of thing just didn't happen. Not in his world. In fact, tonight was the most interaction he'd had with a woman in years that didn't include a tableful of one-dollar bills and a two-drink minimum. But now, he was almost relieved that he hadn't seen her again. At least this way, there'd be less room for disappointment. "I'm checking out, Freddy."

Tuten offered up a half-ass salute and returned to wiping up an over-turned Jager Bomb from way down the bar. Nails unzipped his fanny pack, grabbed some cash, and laid it on the bar. As he stood up, he felt a tingle in his nose and sneezed into his deformed fist. "Fucking cat piss again." He turned to the source of the rancid smell, the open bathroom door, and that's when he saw her. Maybe. A group of men, three—maybe four—had just walked in, and in the middle of them—a flash of bleached blond. He didn't see her face, or much of anything else, but he didn't feel good about it either. It could have been anybody. And it wasn't uncommon for a woman to go into the men's room with a boyfriend or date, but not with a group of men—alone. He knew he should just leave it be like Freddy had asked him to. Maybe on his way out he could just tell Monk to check the latrine. Nails slid his fanny pack around to the small of his back and pulled his canvas coat in tight over his chest. He took a step away from his stool as two women wearing feather boas swarmed in behind him and filled the vacated seat at the bar. He stood there a moment, thinking he'd just hang out a minute or two longer to see if the crew that had walked into the bathroom would come out, drying their hands, and laughing. Doing normal shit. Not at all taking advantage of a young blonde who had gotten into something over her head. An older man, the one in the tweed jacket and UGA hat that Nails had seen earlier that evening, pushed open the bathroom door and walked in. Nails tried to look past him inside but saw nothing but a flood of fluorescent light.

Just leave, he thought. *Everything is fine. It's none of your business anyway.*

Just as he nearly convinced himself to start moving toward the front door, the bathroom door swung open again and the man in the tweed jacket rushed out. *Or did he get pushed out?* Nails rubbed at the back of his bald head. The old man had come out so fast that his hat nearly flew off his head—and he looked offended. Nails turned back and spotted Freddy, who was busy pouring drinks for a group of gorgeous Black women at the end of the bar. *Fuck it.* Nails easily pushed through the crowd and made his way to the bathroom.

Chapter Ten

The small cement box of a room had nearly every inch of its walls covered in stickers from bands and singer-songwriters that had played at The Chute over the years. If there was any blank space, it was covered in Sharpie scrawlings of cartoon dicks, fuck-yous, and graffiti tags. One urinal hung on the wall filled to the rim with neon yellow. There were two stalls. One of them was narrow and missing a door. It was also empty. The other stall was wide, almost twice the size of the first. It was the kind that came equipped with a stainless steel rail on the wall for handicap access. The door on the wider stall was intact and closed. There was also a single porcelain sink above a padlocked cabinet, a wall-mounted push-button hand dryer, and a large mirror with a spiderweb of cracks spreading out from the center.

A short man in a black Carhartt coat, carpenter jeans, and a well-maintained mullet stood in front of the sink, filling it with running water, with his back to Nails. The man spoke almost immediately after Nails walked in. "Shitter's full, pal. Get the fuck out." Nails opted *not* to get the fuck out. The man also must not have been able to see who was behind him through the broken mirror because after he cut off the faucet and turned, he found himself staring down the barrel of Nails's .45 caliber revolver. The man's superior attitude evaporated instantly.

"Whoa, dude. Hold up." Carhartt put both of his dripping wet hands up, palms out. "I didn't mean . . . I'm saying . . . be cool . . . you can piss if you want . . . all good, man."

"I saw a girl come in here. A blond girl."

Carhartt didn't hesitate. "She's . . . she's in there, man." He used a single finger to point toward the closed stall.

A third voice joined in from behind the locked stall. "What the fuck's going on out there, Zane?"

"Um, there's a dude out here, man. With a big-ass—"

Nails shook his head and held a curled finger from his deformed left hand to his lips to keep the word *gun* from coming out of Carhartt's mouth.

"What the shit?" The sight of Nails's hand disrupted the man's train of thought almost as much as the gun did. "I mean . . . he's . . . a big . . . um . . . a big . . . dude, man. He's asking about your girl, Robbie."

Nails took a step toward Carhartt, who raised his hands higher, closed his eyes, and began to shake. "I saw a girl come in here. I want to know if she's okay."

The main bathroom door began to open again, filling the small room with bar noise. Nails mule-kicked it shut without looking back. The door knocked whoever was trying to open it backward and they must've gotten the point because it stayed closed. Nails kept the gun steady, less than a foot from Carhartt's face.

"Hey, man," the voice from the stall answered. "My girl's just fine. Shit, we're just trying to get a little romance in is all. Nothing to worry about. We'll be out in a sec."

"I want to hear that from her."

Something shifted around inside the stall and a few seconds later a small voice—her voice—minus the confidence from earlier at the bar—spoke up. "I'm okay." More ruffling behind the door followed. Nails thought he heard whispering.

"You're sure?"

"Yes. I'm sure. I'm okay."

"And no one is forcing you to be in there?"

More whispering.

"No. I'm fine. Thank you, but I'm fine, really. You can go."

Nails stared at Carhartt. He wanted to kick the door to the stall in and see if she was okay for himself, but Freddy would be mad. He'd told Nails to let it be. He'd already cost Freddy kitchen money with that whole Warren ordeal earlier and he didn't want to make more trouble by smashing up Freddy's bathroom just to find out he was being stupid—

again. He put the right words together. "Okay. I just wanted to make sure."

"Thank you . . . handsome."

Nails took his eyes off Carhartt for the first time and stared at the stall. *Did she know it was him? Or did she call everybody handsome? Was that code or was he an idiot?* His brain went full static like a detuned radio. He stood there a moment, still training his gun on the man in front of him. "Okay," he said to her. And without looking, or lowering the gun, he back-kicked the bathroom's entrance door again. This time it swung open wide and the noise and music from the bar filled the small room again, but Nails didn't leave. While the music poured in through the doorway, he quietly stepped forward and pressed the .45 into Carhartt's forehead and let the door ease back to a close. Zane didn't move as a dark blue stain bloomed from the crotch of his jeans and spread down his leg.

Robbie called out from the stall, "Zane? Dude, is he gone? Zane?"

Nails nodded and pressed the barrel of the gun hard enough into Zane's head to leave a mark. Zane understood. "Yeah, man. He's gone. He left."

"Good. Now get your shit together out there. Block the door with something or some shit."

"Yeah man. No worries. I got it." Zane did nothing.

Nails sidestepped across the tiled floor, careful not to lower the .45 or let his eye off Zane, and he listened. The smell of urine was making his head hurt and he wanted to sneeze again, but he stifled it so he could hear this *Robbie* asshole talk under his breath from inside the stall. "Okay, now get to it, bitch. Stop acting like this isn't exactly why we're here. I'm not playing. Just do for him what you do for me."

"Please, Robbie. I don't want to."

That was all Nails needed to hear. He swung the .45 into Zane's jaw, spinning him in a circle. Zane hit the sink and then the floor with a loud thud. Commotion started inside the stall as Nails took a step back and kicked the door completely off its hinges. It toppled inward against everyone inside. Nails grabbed the top edge of the busted door and yanked it out, letting it drop on top of an unconscious Zane. Robbie—the vampire— took the brunt of the hit when Nails kicked in the door. The black-haired punk was holding onto the handicap rail, dazed, trying to right himself.

He also held something else in his hand. It looked iridescent. A pipe? A lighter? Whatever. Nails didn't care. He grabbed Robbie by the hair and yanked him out of the stall, barely paying attention to the girl or the other asshole sitting on the commode with his pants around his ankles. Robbie screamed as Nails twisted his grip into the vampire's scalp. Nails bashed him in the mouth with the gun. He shut up. The girl worked the zipper on her shorts and bolted out of the room. Nails watched her vanish and swiveled his head to see that the guy on the toilet had fainted. Then he slammed Robbie's head into the tiled floor. Nails could feel his skin burn.

"You just getting some romance in? Is this romantic to you?" Nails lifted and slammed Robbie's head into the grimy, piss-covered tile again. A good portion of the kid's hair ripped out into Nails's fist, so he reapplied his grip, twisting his webbed fingers into a tighter pull. Someone else opened the bathroom door and the screaming started. There was blood all over the stall and the floor now from Robbie's broken mouth. Nails was peppered with dark red liquid freckles. The girl was gone and Zane still hadn't moved. The yelling from outside in the bar got louder than the music.

"Get up." Nails yanked Robbie upright and used his body to push open the bathroom door. He shoved him out into the bar. The crowd parted and moved off the dance floor. Freddy or Monk must've cut the power to the jukebox. The music stopped cold, leaving only the pandemonium of people scrambling for the door. The house lights popped on, replacing the moody red, and Nails dragged Robbie onto the dance floor. "You like to hurt women?" Nails flung Robbie across the hardwood, and he went sprawling headfirst into the jukebox. Nails heard Freddy call his name but he ignored it. He didn't care. He just wanted to break this asshole in half. The third time he heard Freddy yell, he yelled back. "This guy, Freddy. This guy, he . . ."

"Nails, stop." Freddy held his hands out in front of him. "Stop right now."

"Freddy, you don't understand. This is the guy. From before. He had her—I'm just . . ."

"Nails, just stop and look at me. Put down the gun."

"He—he . . ."

"It's okay. Just look at me and put down the gun."

Nails glared at Freddy. "He was trying to hurt the girl, Freddy. He was hurting her. I stopped him."

"Okay, okay. Fine. But stop and listen to me. We might need to call an ambulance."

"He don't need no ambulance. Fuck him. Just let me get him outside."

"Not for him, Nails—for you." Freddy pointed down. Nails was confused. He followed the old man's finger and looked where he was pointing. He saw the hunk of iridescent metal Robbie had been holding in the stall. Only now it was flapping against Nails's thigh. It wasn't a pipe or a lighter. It was a knife—a butterfly knife. And it was stuck in Nails's thigh all the way to the hilt. He didn't know when it happened.

"He stabbed me?" His anger flashed. "That son of a bitch stabbed me?" Nails went for the kid on the floor again but a pair of thick arms wrapped around him from behind and Monk tackled Nails to the ground. With Freddy's help, they pinned him on the floor and Freddy slapped the gun from his hand. He felt the coolness of the stone on his cheek under Monk's weight and he allowed himself to stay there and take a breath— until he caught the eyes of the mangled kid on the floor in front of the jukebox. He'd seen eyes like that before. They were black and empty. Well, shit.

Chapter Eleven

The pain in his leg felt like someone was holding a blowtorch to it and Monk's fat ass was crushing the wind out of his lungs. "Get off me."

"Are you going to chill, bro?"

"Get the—fuck—off me."

"Bro—I said are you going to chill?"

Nails bucked his chest and swung his fist up at Monk. The hit connected awkwardly with the side of his head, but it was enough, and Monk fell onto his side. More yelling came from the far end of the bar and Nails could see Stan Moody, another Chute employee who tended bar in the poolroom. He was checking the kid Nails threw at the jukebox for a pulse. No luck. He was dead. He'd lost it and killed somebody. The vampire was heaped up on the juke like a discarded Halloween decoration and Nails was going to catch hell for it. He turned to Monk. "Help me up."

"Nails, dude. What the hell, bro?" Monk said, rubbing the side of his head, still laid out on the floor to Nails's left.

"Monk, for real. Help me up."

"Fuck you, Nails."

"Help him up, Monk—now," Freddy yelled from behind the bar. Nails pushed himself up to a seated position and he could see Freddy with the bar phone to his ear—the cord coiled tightly around his forearm.

"Here," Stan said, and slid one of the chairs over from an overturned table near the dartboards. "Sit him down here."

Monk and Stan each got a grip on Nails's armpits and lifted him into the chair. He groaned. His leg hurt like hell now. Stan looked fascinated by the knife sticking out of it. The little man was squatting down now, inspecting the bizarre injury. It did look strange. There was no blood—no clear tear in his jeans—no exposed skin or wound—just a weird-ass piece of space metal folded over against the denim.

"Does it hurt?" Stan said and pushed his newsboy cap up high on his brow. Nails suddenly wanted to laugh *and* slap that awful hat off Stan's head. He did neither. He also didn't answer his stupid question. It was four inches of steel buried in muscle. Yes, it fucking hurt.

"Get away from him, Stan." Freddy held the phone to his chest. "Get away from him and go into my office. In the bottom left drawer, there's a bottle of pills. Big—white—oblong—pills. Go get them and bring them to me."

Stan stood up. "Oblong?"

Freddy sighed. "Just get the pills."

Nails tried to swivel in his seat toward the bar. "I don't want any pills, Freddy. I just—"

"Don't—tell me what you want, Nails." He held up a finger. "You just . . . just sit." He moved that same finger to his lips and put the phone back to his ear. Nails didn't push it. Freddy would fix this.

Monk sat heavy on a bar stool. "You didn't have to hit me, bro." He was still rubbing his head.

"I'm sorry," Nails said, as if the definition of *I'm sorry* had somehow changed recently to mean *eat shit*.

"I was only doing my job."

Nails felt a muscle in his cheek twitch. "Your job? Keeping people safe in this place is your job." He pointed at the dead kid on the floor. "Keeping someone like that from molesting women in the bathroom is your job."

"I'm only one dude, bro."

"Are you, bro? Are you only one dude, bro? Come here so I can hit you again, bro."

"All right," Freddy yelled. "Enough." He hung the phone back in the cradle on the wall, leaned on it for a minute, and then scribbled something down on a notepad. He moved the framed picture of him and his brother off the back bar to get at the safe behind it. He spun the combination lock and Stan poked his head in from the poolroom. "I didn't see no pills in the left drawer, boss. Just a bunch of papers and shit."

Freddy sighed again and his chin fell to his chest. "Try the other left bottom drawer, Stan."

"Right, okay. Like stage-left, you mean."

"Yeah—Okay . . ."

Stan disappeared a second time.

"Monk, sweep the bar and check everywhere. Make sure there's no stragglers or drunks in the back rooms, and then lock both doors. Double-check the side exit as well and lock this bitch up, tight."

"Okay, boss."

Freddy took a first-aid kit out from under the bar, set something from the safe on top of it, and then grabbed a jug of apple juice from the beer cooler. He walked out from behind the bar, set everything on the floor, pulled another chair over directly in front of Nails, and took a seat.

"I'm sorry, Freddy."

Freddy's face tightened at the word *sorry*. "No," he said. "We're not doing that right now."

"But I am, Freddy. I know I fucked up."

"Nails. Seriously. We are not talking about that right now. I just need you to listen."

"Was that Mr. Burroughs on the phone?"

"You know that already."

"Is he pissed at me?"

Freddy ran both hands back through his hair. "It doesn't matter who's pissed at who, Nails. What matters is what we're going to do now considering that you just killed some random asshole in front of an entire bar full of witnesses."

"I didn't mean to kill him, Freddy."

"It doesn't matter what you *meant* to do. Only what you did do."

"Yeah, I know. But can't we just get rid of him? Can't we just dump him in the woods somewhere? You know, no body, no crime? Mr. Burroughs does it all the time."

Freddy looked around the bar frantically as if they were being recorded. Nails had never seen Freddy look nervous before. "Jesus, Nails—shut up. And no, that's not the way it works. Not here."

Monk returned and gave an all-clear. Freddy picked up the first-aid kit and unlatched the lid. "Listen to me, Nails. I know you think Gareth can come in here and make all this go away. And maybe if you were up on the mountain—where things can be controlled—and people can be trusted—maybe he could. But that kid over there?" Freddy turned and motioned to the vampire. "That asshole walked in here with *other* people. People we don't know. People I don't know. People that are now gone. Along with about fifty other people who are also gone. In a few minutes, I won't have any choice but to call the cops and report this shit because I can't spin it." Freddy squeezed the bridge of his nose to hold back the headache that was brewing under his painted eyelids.

"But, Freddy, we don't need to tell them nothing."

Freddy held up a finger and Nails stopped talking. "And when the sheriff gets here, me and Monk and Stan are all going to say the same thing. That we didn't see shit. We've got zero idea what happened. But this isn't just a bar fight, Nails. Someone is dead. A kid is dead. A kid that ain't from around here, and the goddamn law is not just going to take my word on what happened. They can't. So, they are going to start sniffing. They are going to want to talk to people. All the people who were here. That kid's people. And eventually, somebody somewhere is going to tell them about you. They are going to describe you because, let's face it, you are easy to describe. Next, they are going to find out your name and where you live and what you do. And when they find you, because everybody gets found eventually, you are going to be given an option. Burn for this or burn somebody you know. And we all know who that somebody is."

Nails shook his head defiantly. This didn't make any sense. He was just protecting a girl. He didn't mean for it to get out of hand. This was bullshit. "He stabbed me, Freddy. I'm still stabbed." They looked at the rainbow metal dangling from Nails's leg. "I'll just explain."

"No, Nails. That idiot must've stabbed you before you even came out of the bathroom. Everybody saw it hanging there but you. By the time you bashed his head into my jukebox, he was already beaten, and he was already unarmed. A far cry from self-defense. Too many people saw it that I can't control." Freddy took a large wad of gauze out of the first-aid kit and set it in his lap.

"So, what am I supposed to do, Freddy?"

"You're going to do what Gareth just told me on the phone for you to do. And trust me, considering what this whole shitshow does to expose him, I'm surprised he even gave you an option here. He must be softer on you than I thought."

"What option?"

Freddy picked up a canvas bag from the floor next to his feet and held it out for Nails to take.

"What's this?'

"It's eight thousand dollars and a phone number."

Nails opened the bag and looked at the cash. He pulled out a folded sheet of notepaper and saw the number that Freddy had written down—and the name *Wilcombe*.

"Who is that?"

Freddy didn't answer.

Stan returned from the office with an orange medicine bottle as big around as a Coke can and he shook the pills inside like a maraca. He handed the bottle to Freddy, who set it in his lap along with the gauze.

Nails held up the note. "I don't understand, Freddy. Who is this? What's the money for?"

"I don't know who that is," Freddy said through his teeth. "But Gareth said you need to call that number and do whatever that guy tells you to do. He's trusted and he's apparently high enough up the food chain to be able to keep you off the radar until we can figure all this shit out. The money is to get you where you need to go since you don't have the time to go home. That's Gareth's entire take of this place for the month. It's a good thing he hadn't collected already or else you'd be even more fucked than you are. So buy some clothes. Gas. Food. Whatever. Use cash only. That cash. I wish it were more, but that's all I've got here, and Gareth said you need to get gone—now."

"Wait." Nails's brain was spinning like a piñata that just took its first solid hit. He tried to stay focused—to keep his thoughts right. "The money is to get me where? Where am I supposed to be going?"

Freddy pulled in a deep breath and eased it out slowly. The answer to that question tasted like a mouthful of spoiled cheese. "Jacksonville."

Nails went completely blank. "What?"

"That's all I know. I'm just supposed to patch you up. Give you the cash and tell you to call *our friend* . . . in Jacksonville."

Nails was quiet for several beats. He looked at the cash in the bank bag and then at his leg, and then over at the dead kid on the floor. "Jacksonville? As in Florida?"

"Yeah."

"Mr. Burroughs just told you to tell me—to go to Florida? Right now?"

"Yeah."

"Freddy, I've never even been out of McFalls. I can't go to Florida."

Freddy was done with this conversation. The clock was ticking and there was a dead kid's blood turning into strawberry Jell-O on his dance floor. "Put that cash away and hold this." He handed Nails the gauze. Nails stuffed the bag of money and paper with the phone number into a pocket inside his coat. He took the gauze and held it as if it were a Magic 8 Ball that was about to offer up a fortune better than a midnight run to Florida. Freddy opened the medicine bottle. He shook out six ten-milligram hydrocodone footballs. He dry-chewed two of them and then handed the other four to Nails. "Put those in your mouth and wash them down with this." He picked up the jug of apple juice. Nails popped the pills and took the jug.

"Okay, now in about ten minutes, you're going to feel those kick in and then I'm going to pull that blade out of your leg. You hear me? Ten minutes. That's all we got. Okay?"

Nails nodded. Still holding the gauze in his bad hand, he lifted the jug to his mouth with the other to wash down the chunky pills. Freddy waited until he saw Nails swallow the painkillers and then he gripped the handle of the knife and yanked it out. Nails screamed and dropped the jug. Apple juice exploded all over the floor. Freddy handed the bloody knife off to Stan. "Get rid of that. You know where. I don't ever want to see it again." He leaned over and pushed Nails's hand, full of gauze, into the oozing wound. "Keep pressure on that."

"You said ten minutes." Nails bounced in his chair. "Ten minutes, Freddy."

"Yeah? Well, you said you wouldn't cause any trouble in my bar tonight. So, suck it up, asshole." He reached back into the first-aid kit and
took out a roll of bandages. He tossed it at Monk. "Once the bleeding is
under control, I want you to wrap that leg, give the man his gun back,
and get him out of here—now." Freddy walked back behind the bar and
washed his hands in the sink.

Chapter Twelve

Twenty minutes ago, Nails was sitting at a bar debating whether he was going to eat a frozen burrito or some leftover mac and cheese when he got home. Now he was on his way to goddamn Florida with a bank deposit bag full of cash and a phone number for some asshole he didn't know. He felt like he'd just been dismissed from his own life. Tossed out like a bag of trash after the night shift. He didn't mean to kill that kid, so he didn't understand why he was being punished for it. Yes he did. This wasn't something he'd been ordered to do. He'd acted on his own. That's not how things got done up here. He knew that, too.

Nails's head hurt almost as bad as his leg, and the cold night wind was chapping his cheeks. So he rolled up the window of his '71 LTD and turned up the heat. That's when he heard it. At first he thought he was still confused, one last bumblebee still bouncing around inside his head. But the second time he heard it he knew it wasn't in his head. He drove another mile or two down the state road and ran a hand over his .45 before he pulled the car over to the soft shoulder of the road. He cut the engine and got out. Standing there in the darkness, his gun in hand, Nails opened the back door.

"Get out," he said to the pile of laundry spilled over the seat. Nothing happened. No movement. No sound. He clicked back the hammer on the revolver. "I heard you moving a few miles ago. So, I'm only going to tell you one more time to get out of my car before I unload into that seat."

The laundry shuffled and a small voice spoke. "Wait. Please, don't shoot."

"Get out—now."

"Okay. Okay." After an awkward couple of seconds, the pile of clothes and spare coats began to shift enough for the white skin of a woman's leg to appear—followed by another, and then two small hands, palms out. Next Nails could see a familiar black T-shirt with NIRVANA printed in yellow above a drunken smiley face. Finally, he saw a messy head of bleached blond hair. A stack of Batman comics spilled from a box on the floorboard onto the shoulder of the road.

"Please don't shoot me, handsome. I just needed a ride to—"

Nails grabbed one of the girl's wrists and yanked her out of the car a little rougher than he needed to. He let go and she landed hard on the asphalt.

"Ow, shit, man. Take it easy. You nearly pulled my arm off."

"What are you doing in my car? I could've killed you."

"I'm sorry. I just needed a ride. Can you help me up?"

"Get yourself up." Nails kneeled over and grabbed the comics, tossing them back into the car. The girl stared up at Nails with the same pout and bashful eyes she'd used on him at the bar, but this time it looked like what it was—a practiced expression. It pissed him off and he was ready to go. It didn't even occur to him to wonder how she knew that this was his car.

"I said get up and get your ass over there." Nails tossed the last book through the door and used the .45 to motion toward the back of the car. The girl slowly got to her feet and brushed the dirt off her cutoffs.

"Look, I'm sorry. I just—"

"Just nothing. Move." Nails nudged her with the gun until he'd pushed her back behind the LTD.

"Wait, please. Just wait a minute."

"Sorry, you're on your own." Nails nudged her even further back. Once she was completely out of the way, he backed up to the car's open back door.

"My bag, damn," the girl yelled. "Can I at least get my bag? It's still in there."

Nails didn't drop his aim but leaned over and fished an oversized handbag out of the backseat. He tossed it over the trunk of the car. Some of the contents spilled out into the dirt at the girl's feet, some makeup, a leather wallet, a disposable camera. "Oh, c'mon, man." She bent down and clawed around to put her things back in the bag before hooking it over her shoulder and clutching it tight to her chest. It looked big enough for her to crawl inside it. "You can't just leave me out here like this."

Nails stood at the open car door and stuck the gun back in his pocket as he tuned her out.

"Please, mister. How long do you think I'll last out here like this?"

"Somebody will stop and give you a ride."

"Oh I bet *someone* will. And what are the chances of that someone not being a drunk redneck? Look at me. Look where we are." She swiveled her head in the red glow of the LTD's taillights. "I don't even know where we are."

Nails gave her a once-over. "Not my problem."

"So, it's okay to save me when I ask you not to, but you have no problem leaving me out here to get raped or killed or whatever when I'm actually begging for your help?"

Nails glared at her. "You," he said. "You were in trouble. I was . . . It's not . . ."

"I'm in trouble now. Please. I'm begging you. Don't leave me out here. Please."

Nails tried to shake away the confusion in his head. It felt like a swarm of houseflies had entered the inside of his skull. "No," he said, not even sure why or to what. He got into the car and closed the door. The girl banged on the trunk like a toddler. He could see her in the rearview mirror, clutching her bag, bathed in the red light. For a moment she didn't look frail and scared. The red light and the dust floating around her made her look like she did in that smoky bar—when she danced. But that only lasted a moment before he saw her for who she was right now. Alone and half dressed on the side of the road. She was right and he knew it. The only people out traveling at this hour would be bad news. He laid his forehead on the steering wheel. "Fuck."

He rolled the window down and waved her to come on. She wiped at the fresh tears on her face after she climbed into the passenger side and closed the door.

"Thank you," she said. Nails said nothing. He just reached over into the backseat and grabbed one of the heavy canvas coats from the pile of clothes. He tossed it over her, and she immediately covered herself up. He'd give this girl a ride to the closest town and that was it. Whatever happened to her after that was her problem.

Chapter Thirteen

Clayton Burroughs put down the axe, hit the pause button on the small boom box he had balancing on the woodpile, and picked up his thermos. He unscrewed the top and the coffee puffed a swirl of steam into the morning air. He breathed in deep, and he drank even deeper. The mountain was chilly this morning, but he'd worked up enough of a sweat on the woodpile to keep the frigid air at bay. He liked getting out to the property first thing, cutting wood, drinking coffee from a thermos. He felt like a man out here on his own land. He loved the idea of building a house on this land. Building a home to start a family in. *Family*, he thought. It was a complicated word for a member of the Burroughs Clan. The idea of him being a father someday, a figurehead of something brand-new yet timeless and ancient. It was scary as hell. But he welcomed the idea. He'd been treated like the runt of his father's tribe for so long that the thought of sitting at the head of the table—his own table—filled his chest with something he wasn't used to—pride, maybe? No matter, he liked it. He also liked the idea of what this house represented. He wasn't surprised when his father offered to fund it. Money meant nothing to Gareth. But when he offered to physically help Clayton build it—now that was something he didn't see coming. His father had never offered to help Clayton with anything, ever, but whatever his reasons for choosing this landmark to bond over, Clayton didn't question it. These past few months, working on this house, had been the most time he'd spent with his father since he was a kid in single digits. Sure, the old man just growled at him half the time and criticized damn near everything he did, but he showed up—

every day—ready to work—on Clayton's first home. And the showing up was the part that mattered most. He could be as critical as he wanted. Clayton was just happy he was there.

The sound of an engine purring up the mountain caused Clayton to set down his thermos and reach for the shirt he'd hung from the side mirror of the Bronco. His deddy was here early. Clayton hadn't pulled all the tools from the barn. He was sure to catch a first-light ass-chewing for that. Gareth wanted things a particular way. Clayton hustled toward the barn as he buttoned up his shirt, but he slowed when he realized the engine he was listening to most definitely wasn't his old man's Ford step-side. And it wasn't Kate's Ranger either. Clayton watched until a small Toyota hatchback finally appeared and parked in the gravel next to the unfinished porch. Clayton didn't receive many visitors up here. The place didn't even have a mailbox yet or an official address on record with the McFalls County Clerk's Office, so the small shiny car looked both odd and out of place. He tucked his shirttails into the waist of his jeans and picked up his hat from the hood of his truck.

He saw Kate first. He smiled when she appeared from the passenger side of the Toyota. The sight of her always made him smile. Today was no exception. A moment later the driver emerged, a petite woman with short blond hair that framed an almost perfectly rounded face. She slipped her car keys into the pocket of a long wool coat. The two women moved to the front of the car and Kate offered a small wave. Clayton held his hand up as well. He was happy to see her but it did strike him as strange to see her out here—at least at this time of the morning. Her being here meant she was taking the risk of running into Clayton's father, and that wasn't something she'd normally do. She was equal parts frightened and disgusted by the older Burroughs. In fact, she felt that way about Clayton's entire family. He felt lucky sometimes that she just didn't give up on him—or this thing they had—because of those intense feelings she harbored about his outlaw family. Without even realizing he was doing it, Clayton began to start entertaining ways to get out of the day's work ahead—to get Kate back in the car and down the mountain before Gareth showed up and purposely said something that the two of them would argue about for the next few weeks, but just as that thought crossed his mind, the blond woman offered a delicate little wave of her own. The recognition set in.

"Amy?" Clayton said to himself and moved toward the car. He hadn't seen her in years. She'd left McFalls County right after graduation. She was never one for small-town life. And the minute—the second—she had the opportunity—she was gone. He thought he remembered Kate saying something to him about Amy living in North Carolina somewhere—Chapel Hill maybe—working for a newspaper or something like that. "Wow," he said as he got close enough. "Damn, Blondie—you done got all fancy."

"I've always been fancy, Clayton. I've just been waiting patiently for all you hillbillies to finally see it."

They embraced, Amy standing on the tips of her patent leather boots to reach Clayton's neck. "Well, you look great, girl. What brings you home?"

"Mama. She had a birthday yesterday. I've been back for a few days, but the family has had me tied up. I should've called y'all when I got here. I'm sorry."

Clayton swiped at the air. "No way. Stop it. Family first. I get it."

Kate waited patiently for the small talk to end before slipping her hand into Clayton's. He squeezed it like he always did. Her hand was both cool and warm at the same time. "Hey, you."

"Hey." Clayton kissed her on the cheek. He pulled back and saw that Kate's smile was a bit sideways, and then she exchanged a brief glance with Amy.

There wasn't much about the way Kate moved her face that Clayton hadn't memorized over the years. And that little twitch of her nose and the tight bottom lip meant there was a storm brewing somewhere behind that polite smile. "Everything good, babe?"

"Maybe we could go talk inside. Is the kitchen about finished?"

"No electricity yet, but the main plumbing is nearly finished up, so there's water . . . but I can't put on a spot of tea for you ladies yet." The faux-British accent and the joke both landed flat, so Clayton let his attitude pivot. "Okay, what's going on?"

Kate and Amy both looked around at the land that Clayton and his father were building his house on. It was beautiful country up there. Almost at the crest of the mountain, surrounded by acres of pastureland and a backdrop of blue-green forest. A magnolia tree stood about thirty feet from the house. It was Kate's favorite part of the landscape. But neither of the women was looking to admire the beauty of Clayton and Kate's future home. They were both making sure that Gareth wasn't there. That it was just the three of them. Clayton immediately offered some reassurance. "My deddy's not here yet, Kate. It's just us. And seriously, what's going on?"

"Amy's mother may be the reason she's home, but there's another reason she's here—why we're here. We need to talk to you."

"About what?"

"Can we just go inside?"

"Yeah. Yeah. Of course. Follow me." Clayton let go of Kate's hand, walked to the porch, and pulled a cinder block out from underneath. Since there weren't any steps built yet, he held out his hand and guided both women up as they stepped on the block. "Y'all head right in the door and to the left. Just be careful of all the tarps or any loose nails on the floor." Within seconds the three of them were standing around the island in the middle of the kitchen. Clayton leaned on the marble top.

"This house is going to be beautiful, y'all," Amy said as she ran her small hand over the smooth stone counter.

"Thank you," Kate said.

"It's a work in progress for sure," Clayton added. Kate took his hand again and gave it another squeeze. "Does somebody want to tell me why you two lovely ladies are up on the mountain at the crack of dawn? I mean, I know that Kate loves to show off my master carpentry skills every chance she gets, but this ain't about that, I'm guessing."

Amy and Kate were both now sliding their fingers over the marble counter.

"Anybody?"

Amy steeled herself, leaned forward on the island, and caught Clayton's eyes. "I'm here about Nelson."

"Nelson?"

"Yeah. Nelson McKenna."

Clayton rubbed at the fresh beginnings of a beard on his chin. "Oh, you mean Nails."

Amy shook her head. "I hate when people call him that. His name is

Nelson and he's a sweet man. He doesn't deserve that awful nickname. Why do you and everyone else up here insist on calling him that?"

Clayton held his hands up, letting go of Kate's warm grip. "Whoa, take it easy. I don't mean any disrespect. He just goes by Nails now. He told me to call him that. So take it up with him."

"I can't take it up with him . . . he's gone."

"What do you mean, gone?"

"When was the last time you saw him, Clayton? When he insisted you call him by the name your father gave him?"

"Hold up." Clayton stood a bit taller and began to take the visit a little more seriously. He wasn't clear on the hostility, and he wasn't sure he liked it. "It's been a while," he said. "Maybe six months or so. Why?"

"So you know he's changed. He's almost a different person now."

"Yeah, I know. But for real, what do you mean he's gone?"

"I mean, something happened last night, and he was told to leave Mc-Falls County, maybe to never come back. And I'm worried about him and what is going to happen to him next."

"Amy, you've been gone a pretty long time. Trust me. Whatever you might've heard, nobody tells Nails—I mean Nelson—where he can and can't go."

"No one but your father, Clayton. Nelson does whatever that man tells him to. You of all people should know that." Amy was getting increasingly upset, and her eyes never shifted away from Clayton's. They were a little red, too, like she hadn't slept all night. He wasn't completely sure, but he felt it coming. Something bad had happened.

"All right," Kate cut in. "I understand why you're upset, Amy. I am, too. But I brought you up here so the three of us could talk about it. Getting angry isn't going to help anything. Just breathe a second and tell him what you told me."

"For real. It's me, Amy. Tell me. What is going on with Nelson?"

Amy did take a breath. A slow inhale and an even slower exhale while Clayton waited.

"Okay. Have you ever met my uncle Stan? My mama's brother?"

Clayton thought about it and then finally nodded. "Yeah, I think so. Little guy. Always wears that big floppy hat."

"Right. That's him. Well, for the past few years he's been working as a bartender at some place out by Prouty Hollar. I forget the name, just that it's a dingy old converted barn or something."

"Yeah, The Chute," Clayton blurted out. "I know the place."

Kate narrowed her eyes a bit at Clayton. She wasn't all that pleased that her fiancé was knowledgeable about a place like that. She filed that conversation away for later. Amy continued.

"Well, my uncle has been sleeping on my mama's couch for the past year or so because he's a degenerate mooch. That's beside the point. But last night he showed up there at almost three in the morning with a story to tell. Me and mom were up playing Mario Kart, otherwise I wouldn't even know any of this, but apparently Nelson was at that bar last night while my uncle was working and there was a, I don't know, a disturbance."

"A disturbance?" Clayton repeated.

"He hurt someone. Nelson hurt someone."

Clayton nearly shrugged but thought better of it and stayed still. "Amy, like I said. You've been gone a long time. I hate to be the one to tell you this, but it's kinda what he does now."

"At the behest of your father."

Clayton didn't see the point in arguing that fact. It was common knowledge. He nodded. "Yeah. For my father. Is that what this is about? My dad? You're angry at me because of Nelson's relationship with my father?"

"I'm not angry at you, Clayton. I'm angry at us." It was obvious that Amy wasn't happy with Clayton's nonchalant attitude. She took another deep breath. "Nelson didn't just hurt somebody last night. I don't know all the details about what happened, because my uncle was wasted when he was telling us this story. But somebody died. Nelson killed someone."

Clayton nearly dismissed that right away but took a beat before he said anything. He tried to sound comforting. "Listen, I don't know anything about my father's shit. I'm not part of that life, or my father's business dealings, but I will tell you that I've known Nelson McKenna just as long as you have. And he may not be the man he used to be. But he's not a murderer, Amy. I live up here. I see Val, and Scabby Mike, Jimbo and all those guys, all the time. So, I'd know if Nelson ever crossed that line.

NOTHING BUT THE BONES • 61

Even if it was just a rumor floating around Deddy's house. So, I seriously doubt he just up and killed someone just because my father told him to."

Amy's whole face filled with a profound sadness. "He didn't do anything for your father, Clayton. That much of the story I did get from Stan. Nelson was protecting someone. A woman. A blond woman. A woman that my uncle said could've passed for me." Amy's words got stuck in her throat, but she kept herself from tearing up. "Some dirtbags were doing something terrible to her and Nelson stepped in. And apparently, *he stepped in* a little too hard."

Clayton leaned back on the counter and rubbed at his stubble. "Well, Amy, protecting a woman sounds exactly like something Nelson would do."

"You know what else it sounds exactly like?"

Clayton knew what she meant but said nothing. Amy's words hung in the air between them, and Kate used the uncomfortable silence to fill a few Styrofoam cups on the counter with water from the main sink beside Clayton.

"It sounds exactly like what happened out at Burnt Hickory Pond, Clayton," Kate finally said as she set the three cups of water down on the island. Clayton drank his in one gulp and then crushed the cup and tossed it onto the counter. Amy didn't even look at hers.

"It sounds exactly like what happened when that same man stood up and protected me from another one of the psychopaths that live up here—or I should say, lived." She picked her cup up from the marble and sipped at it. "Right before we made the worst decision of our lives."

"Amy," Clayton began to say.

"No, Clayton, listen. I know I was the one that asked you to do it. To call your father that day instead of the sheriff. I was wrong and I'll live with that for the rest of my life."

"But, Amy—"

"But no. Listen. The truth is, we all made that decision together. Jesus, Clayton, we didn't even ask Nelson what *he* wanted to do. We just decided his fate for him. And because of what we did, look at what happened to him after. We allowed your father to dig his claws into one of the kindest people I've ever known and infect him like a virus. And then we all lied about it. We're still lying about it. And Clayton, it looks like you might even have started to believe the lie."

Clayton pushed back. "Amy, you just said my father wasn't involved with whatever happened last night, so I don't understand how one thing has anything to do with the other."

Kate put her hand on top of Clayton's. "We allowed it, Clayton. We allowed your father to mold Nelson into what he is and we didn't do anything to stop it. We had the chance to let him tell his side of the story about what happened that day, and who knows, maybe if we had, he'd have been with *us* last night, instead at of that club."

"That's an awfully big maybe, Kate."

Amy finished off her water. "It's fine, Kate. It's clear that Clayton doesn't want to take any responsibility for what we did."

"I didn't say that, Amy. I just don't know what you expect me to do about it now."

Amy took her car keys out of her pocket. "Nothing, Clayton. I don't expect anything. Kate, I'd like to leave."

"What the fuck?" Clayton said.

Kate squeezed his hand harder. "All right, Clayton. Calm down." She crossed the floor to Amy. "Why don't you go wait in the car. Let us talk and I'll be out in a minute."

"Okay." Amy hugged Kate and said goodbye to Clayton. It sounded indifferent but not hateful. She turned and left, letting the door close behind her. Kate watched from the window until she saw Amy slide behind the wheel of the Toyota and shut the door before turning to face Clayton. She finished the rest of her water and then slid the empty cup across the island. "Will you get me some more, please?"

Clayton turned and refilled the cup from the faucet, still feeling like he had just been attacked for no reason by one of his best friends. He slid the cup back across the marble. "What was that about, Kate? I haven't seen Amy in years and then she just busts up in here and blames me for every bad decision that Nails has ever made. I mean, did I deserve that?"

Clayton waited on a response. He waited for her to agree with him. But she didn't. Instead, she took another sip of water and calmly set the cup back down on the counter. "She isn't blaming you for anything, and that's not what just happened. She said that all three of us deserve the blame. And that Nelson doesn't, and she's worried that he is going to end up dead because of what happened last night."

"Dead? Sounds to me like he's just in the wind, not dead."

Kate moved around the island and took Clayton's hand for a third time. "Her uncle told her last night that your father is the one who ordered Nelson to leave the state. Stan said that he was told to go to Jacksonville, Florida, and not come back."

Clayton threw his arms in the air. "So good. End of story. Nails is resourceful. And with my dad's help, maybe that means he's finally free of all this shit. That should be a good thing. Maybe it means he's finally out from under my family."

Kate sighed. She never understood why it was always necessary for her to remind Clayton of the most crucial things about his own kin. Things that he, of all people, should already know. Sometimes it felt like he was a trauma patient that blocked out the things that caused him the most damage in the interest of self-preservation. She did a terrible job of covering up the disappointment in her voice. "Clayton, who have you ever known up here that got to just walk away? Who retires from working for the Burroughses? Name one."

Clayton gave it some thought, but he didn't have a response. She knew he wouldn't.

"Your father sent Nelson away to get him off the mountain. He sent him somewhere he'd be alone and isolated. Somewhere that no one knew him or would think twice about putting a gun to the back of his head. He's been close to your family for years. So that means he knows entirely too much about what your father and your brothers do up here to just let him go live peacefully in the Sunshine State. I'm not telling you anything you don't already know."

"But Kate, this doesn't have anything to do with us."

"It has everything to do with us. We might not have guided his hand last night, but we definitely helped guide his life into the mess that it is right now. And Amy's right. We need to stop lying to ourselves about it. We are personally responsible, and deep down in that big heart of yours, you know that's true, too."

After a long silence Clayton asked, "And just what exactly am I supposed to do about it? Talk to my dad? Get him to change his mind? You know he's not going to do that. He doesn't even talk to me when he's here—about anything. He's only here helping me with this house because he feels obligated to. I'm not going to be able to change anything."

"I know you can't change his mind. I wouldn't expect you to."

"Then what? What is it I'm supposed to do? Why did y'all come up here and tell me any of this?"

Kate finished her water. "She—we—thought maybe you could go find Nelson and bring him back home."

"You've got to be kidding me."

"I'm not."

He looked at her as if she were a stranger and let go of her hand.

"What good would that even do? If what Amy said is true and Nails did kill someone, he's still going to have to deal with that. He could go to prison, Kate. That's what you want?"

"What we want is a chance to make up for what we did to him—to make it right. We think if you were to bring him back here and give him the chance to tell his side of the story, for once, instead of leaving it up to someone else to decide for him, then he could plead self-defense. You said it yourself. He's not a killer. So people must've seen what happened and know the truth. People might be scared to talk right now, but if he was here, then maybe people would come to his defense. Instead of out of sight, out of mind. He may not face any jail time at all. Maybe he truly can be free of all this. And he can do it all out in the open. You know Nelson would never turn on Gareth; he'd never turn on anyone he cared about. And this way he can prove that to your paranoid father."

"Thinking that a guy like Nails is going to come and take his chances with the law against my father's wishes is pretty naïve, Kate."

"Naïve or not, it's the right thing to do. And at least we'll know that he won't end up in a ditch somewhere in Florida. But you need to bring him home before it's too late."

"I do . . . ?"

Kate smiled at him. "If not you, who else?"

Clayton was still convinced his woman had lost her mind. "And how the hell am I supposed to do that? No one is going to tell me anything. My brothers hate me and no one up here talks to anyone about my father's business, Kate. No one. And I'm not some kind of Magnum P.I. I wouldn't even know how to start."

Kate shrugged. "You know he's going to Jacksonville. Start with that and just figure it out."

Clayton laughed. "Just figure it out, she says."

Kate leaned both her elbows down on the counter. "Do you remember when we met Nelson back in school?"

"Sure, I guess, but what's that got to do with anything?"

"Do you remember how we actually met him? I do. I remember it like it just happened. We were eating lunch. Outside the gym. Remember? Nelson was reading a comic book under that big oak tree next to the track. Ben Skidmore and a few other assholes took his lunch and dumped it on the field. They kicked his food all over the track. I don't remember if you were the first one to see it happen or not, but I do remember you wrapping your sandwich back up in tinfoil and asking me to hold on to it for a second. You told me you'd be right back. Then I watched you get up and walk over to that tree. You talked to those kids for a second and then out of nowhere you swung and popped Ben square in the face. I think you broke his nose. The rest of those boys scattered like crows. You remember now?"

Clayton crossed his arms and looked down at the plywood flooring. "Yeah, I remember."

"Well, you know I detest violence. But I have to admit, cowboy, watching you clock that bully—it was pretty sexy. But that's not the part that made me fall for you. It was after those boys left. You picked up that comic and handed it back to Nelson and helped him up to his feet. You invited him over and introduced him to the rest of us. And once it dawned on you that he didn't have anything to eat for lunch, you took that sandwich wrapped in tinfoil that you had me hold and you gave it to him. You even lied and told him you'd already ate, and it was extra. Now that—that's when I knew you were it for me. Right then and there."

Clayton leaned his elbows down on the counter opposite Kate and took in the whole of her face. He'd been in love with her for several years before that day out in the schoolyard with Nelson, but he'd never really known when she started to love him back until now. "Baby, I still don't see what that has to do with any of this?"

"I need you to be that guy, Clayton. That guy that just saw something wrong and made it right. You didn't think about the how's or the why's. Or the consequences. You just did it. Because that's who you are."

"But Kate—"

She held a slim finger up against his lips.

"Be that guy right now. We let him down once already. Be that guy and figure it out so that we don't make the same mistake again."

Clayton rested his forehead against hers and closed his eyes. After a moment, she leaned back. "I'm going to get Amy back down the mountain and get out of here before your father shows up."

Clayton nodded. "Okay."

"Call me later?"

"Okay."

Kate left and joined Amy in the car. Clayton listened as the small four-banger drove away. He turned to the sink. Poured more water into another Styrofoam cup and drained it. He looked out the window at Kate's favorite Magnolia tree and yelled "FUCK" loud enough to scatter the birds.

Chapter Fourteen

Nails and his young blond passenger had been traveling the two-lane interstate between Blue Ridge and Franklin County for miles before the girl finally said anything.

"So, what's your name?"

He didn't bother to look at her. In fact, he hadn't looked at her once since she'd been in the car. But after a moment he answered her. "Nails. My name is Nails."

A half mile of silence passed.

"Ain't you gonna ask me my name?"

"No."

"Why not?"

"Because I don't care."

"Right . . . Well, it's Dallas. Dallas Georgia."

Nails side-eyed the girl and smirked while she flashed him back a huge smile packed with perfectly white teeth. "That ain't a name," he said. "It's a place."

"Well," Dallas turned to face him in her seat, grabbed her hip, and popped an elbow out in mock dismay. "Nails ain't no name either. It's a thing."

Nails let that small truth sink in while he drove. "Yeah," he said. "You're right."

The conversation ended there, and they rode in silence for several more miles. Finally, she spoke back up, saying his name as if it were something he'd made up. "So, *Nails,* does that thing work?"

"What thing?" He looked down at her hand and noticed a silver ring with a blue stone. A sapphire, maybe. But it was too big, like a man's ring, and it hung loose on her finger. She was pointing to the tape deck on the dashboard. "I don't know. I've never used it."

"What?" Dallas said, stretching out the word. She looked both shocked and annoyed. "Well, we fixin' to find out." She began to rummage through her gargantuan handbag. Nails wanted to tell her no, and to stop. That the tape deck was broken. He wanted to tell her not to touch his stuff. He wanted to tell her that she should feel lucky to even be in his car and not sitting on the side of the road in the dark outside of The Chute. But he didn't say anything. This was one of those times when the words wouldn't come. He didn't understand why sometimes he could carry out a normal conversation and then sometimes he felt like a mute. He just went blank. The words, he couldn't line them up right in his head. And he knew if he said anything at all that he'd just stumble over his own tongue. He'd sound foolish and stupid, and she'd probably laugh at him. So he stayed quiet and just took occasional glances off the road to watch her dig through her bag until she found what she was looking for.

When she did, she held it up with both hands and then turned to show it to Nails. It was a cassette tape. An old generic one, white, with the label peeled off, and the words *R's Mixtape* scrawled across it in black Sharpie. Dallas's whole face lit up as she held it. A whole-face smile that stretched from ear to ear. Definitely not the look of a woman sitting next to a man who had just killed someone—someone she knew—less than an hour ago.

"Can I, please? Can I? Can I?" she pleaded with a child's voice, still holding the cassette just inches from his face. He still didn't trust his brain or his words so he just nodded that she could. Dallas didn't hesitate. She jammed the cassette in the tape deck and turned up the volume knob. Now Nails was hoping that the damn thing did work because he didn't want to see the look of excitement fade from her face. He was beginning to like her face. It was a good face. And the tape deck did work. The scratchy broken drumbeat of Massive Attack's "Teardrop" filled the car. "Oh shit," she said. "This is my jam." Dallas cranked the volume up as far as it would go to an almost distorted level and immediately Nails reached out and turned it down to something a little more reasonable.

Dallas didn't touch the dial again, but she did put on that well-rehearsed pout and playfully shoved Nails in the shoulder. "Come on, handsome. Live a little."

This time the words did come. "I can't think with the music that loud and I gotta think. I need to think."

"Think about what? It's just you and me out here on the open road. That's what music is for. It helps me think—I think." She laughed at her own joke. "We're like Bonnie and Clyde out here, man."

"Bonnie and who?"

"Bonnie and Clyde, silly. Like the movie. With Warren Beatty and Faye Dunaway. The famous outlaws? C'mon. Don't tell me you've never seen that movie."

"I haven't. I don't watch a lot of movies."

"Oh my God, handsome. That has got to change, too. I love movies. And that one is one of the best ever. It's about a situation like this one— like us . . ."

Nails turned the music down some more. "Stop. Okay. Just stop. There is no us. And this ain't no movie. And this *situation* ain't about a couple. Or about you. It's about me. And it's about trouble. A lot of it. So if you want to listen to your music, go ahead. But listen to it like that, or I can let you out right here."

"Okay. Okay. Relax." Dallas took a disposable Kodak camera out of her bag and took a flash-less shot of the waning moon as she played with the ring on her finger and hummed along to the song. Nails thought she had a good voice, too. And oddly enough he did relax—a little—and his frustration eased as they drove, onward, downward, and into the early morning.

Chapter Fifteen

Just as Massive Attack faded into Nirvana's "All Apologies," Nails turned the volume all the way down. "Can I ask you something?"

"Sure?" Dallas answered, never taking her eyes off the following moon or the endless whipping trees outside her window.

"Who's *R?*"

"*R?* What do you mean?"

"On the tape. The tape you're listening to. It said *R's Mixtape* on it. Does the *R* stand for that Robbie guy? The guy that—you know, the guy at the bar?"

Dallas let out a small, unintentional laugh. "No. Robbie was a piece of shit. I couldn't stand that asshole. I'd only known him a few weeks and I'm glad you did what you did." She spoke about it so nonchalantly.

"I didn't mean to go that far."

"Is that the first time you've done that? Gone that far, I mean?"

Nails wasn't comfortable with that question. So he didn't answer. And the fact that none of it seemed to bother her made him a little uneasy. Uneasy was not something he was used to feeling. The whole surreal situation was setting in. He tried to just let the conversation end there, but Dallas didn't let it.

"Well, I wouldn't feel too bad about it. I don't think a soul on the planet will miss that asshole. I know I won't." She stopped talking and then abruptly held up the ring to let it catch the moonlight. "You see this, though? This was his. He told me once that it was valuable, so I slid it off his finger before all hell broke loose back there. I figured he fucking owed me." She went back to staring out the window. She was clearly trying to sound tougher than she was. Nails didn't understand why people did that. You are who you are. Just be that and drop the baggage. He'd seen her face back there. She was scared to death. The story she'd just told him about that ring was clearly a lie, but he left it alone.

The moon was on their trail out the window and Nails realized he still hadn't gotten an answer to his original question. He waited a few more minutes before asking her a second time.

"Then who is *R*? The *R* from the tape?"

A slight but noticeable shift of sadness washed over Dallas, and she pulled the oversized canvas jacket in closer around her thin frame. Nails slid the dial up that controlled the heat. He already felt like he was driving inside a broiler, but she was obviously cold.

"The *R* stands for Riley. He's my brother. He made me that tape."

"Oh. So you—you have a brother?"

"Not anymore. He's dead. He died about a year ago."

"Oh—I'm—I'm—sorry. I didn't . . ."

"No, don't be. You didn't know him. No need to be sorry. It sounds terrible to say, but he's in a better place now."

"That does sound terrible to say."

Dallas looked up at the star-filled night. "Trust me. If you knew our parents, you'd understand."

Nails's brain entered another blank space. He wasn't good with sympathy—or talk of any heaven-type nonsense either—so words failed him again. Instead he turned the radio back up as Kurt Cobain finished up the coda of "All Apologies."

"All we are is all we are."

"All we are is all we are."

Dallas, still intent on talking for the sake of talking, immediately turned the volume back down. "So you asked me a question. Does that mean I get to ask you one, too?"

Nails thought about it. "I guess so."

"Why me?" she asked. "Why did you do what you did for me? Back there at the bar with Robbie?"

"I told you. I didn't mean to do it."

"No, I mean, why did you do anything—for me?"

Nails thought about that, too. "It was the right thing. He was a bad person."

Dallas shook her head. "Nope. I'm not buying that. I saw the way you were talking to the old guy that was working the bar. He's the owner there, right? He's your friend?"

"Yeah. Freddy. So what?"

"So what? So that means you're probably in that place a lot. Enough for your buddy Freddy to know what you drink without asking and that he knew that you always sit in there and read, so you must see that place fill up with bad people all the time. I mean, it's got a history. It's pretty much where bad people go on a regular basis. But tonight. Tonight you stepped over a line that you knew would get you in trouble—at least with your boy, Freddy—so why did you do it? Why tonight? Why for me?"

"That sounds like more than one question."

"Well, it's not. I just want to know why you chose to help me?"

Nails already knew the answer, but he waited nearly two miles before he responded. He wanted to get the words right in his head first. "You reminded me of someone. Someone I used to know a long time ago."

"Ahhhhhh. An ex-girlfriend."

"No," Nails said in almost a growl.

"Okay. Okay. Take it easy. Not an ex. Got it." She didn't press it, but Nails went on to tell her about the other girl. Another girl with blond hair. One he knew back in high school. He told her about a girl named Amy Silver that he scared so bad one day, it was enough to make her leave McFalls County as soon as she was able. He surprised himself at the amount of detail he remembered from that day—and that he was able to say it—to this stranger. He left out the part of the story he was never supposed to talk about according to Mr. Burroughs but now he felt the night's cool air as well.

Dallas put a hand on Nails's thick shoulder. "I'm sorry, handsome. It's her loss."

Nails shook her hand off like a dog shaking off loose dander. Being touched felt wrong. It felt odd and he didn't like it. She took her hand away.

"I'm sorry."

"It's okay. But it's like you said about your brother. She's better off."

That was all he said, but he made it clear that he didn't want to talk anymore, so Dallas turned the music back up—but just a little. She stared back out the window some more and hummed along to Soul Asylum's "Runaway Train." Her moon was gone now, and the sun was beginning to crest over the trees outlining them in orange trim. The adrenaline was also wearing off and the tired was setting in. She let her eyes close under the weight of the heavy night and she fell asleep. Nails only looked over at her a few times—fifty maybe—maybe more.

Chapter Sixteen

The biting wind that cut over the Briar Cliff Golf Course this early in the morning made Alex Price's muscles a bit stiffer than he liked before he set out to play, despite the rigorous stretching regimen he practiced every morning. But on days like this when he preferred only the company of himself, which was most days, it was best to hit the course early. Hours before it filled with the older and slower members who didn't really have any business being out there or a healthy respect for the game. Damn that. This was the time to be out here. During the cool of dawn. Just him and the majesty of the grounds.

Alex held his hand up to shield his eyes from the morning sun as he looked in the direction of the fourth hole, "The Widow Maker," notorious for the lengthy sand traps that flanked both sides of the green. And despite the strategically set flags placed in the distance to indicate the direction of the wind, he still crouched down and yanked out a large tuft of grass and tossed it into the air to call the wind speed and direction for himself. He slid a white leather glove on to his left hand and held it out to the caddie standing a few feet behind him. Without looking back, he simply said, "Three wood." Benji, a man with green eyes and a face full of freckles, slid the club from the bag and placed it in his hand. Alex positioned and then repositioned his footing several times until he seemed to find perfection of purchase. He gave himself one, and then two, and then three practice swings before winding back to take the shot.

"Excuse me, sir?"

Alex pivoted and spun around. "Really?" he said. "Really, Benji? What the fuck?"

The caddie pointed toward a golf cart roughly thirty yards away and moving quickly in their direction. "We've got someone incoming, sir. And it looks like Mr. Gerald."

Holland Gerald was the general manager of Briar Cliff, and it was an odd sight to see him outside the clubhouse, much less on the course, alone in a golf cart. Even tours of the grounds were handled by others down the food chain. Alex shielded his eyes from the sun again. "What the hell am I paying this place for if I can't get any peace while I'm out here?"

"I'm sorry for the interruption, sir. I just thought you should know before the sound of the cart distracted your shot."

"You distracted my shot, Benji. You did."

"My apologies, sir."

"Whatever." He tossed the club back at Benji with just enough aggression for the catch to sting. Benji slid the club back into the bag without complaint as both men waited for Mr. Gerald to arrive. When he did, the large man took a breath before he stepped off the golf cart. He was dressed in a navy blue suit with a white shirt, complete with sweat stains around the collar and a loosened tie. Alex was unforgiving of obesity and poorly fitting clothes. Mr. Gerald happened to be afflicted with both.

"I apologize for the intrusion, Mr. Price. I really do. But there was a message left for you a few minutes ago in my office and I . . ."

"A message?"

"Yes, sir."

"You drove all the way out here and blew my shot to deliver me a message?"

"Yes, sir."

"I thought I was clear that I wasn't to be disturbed this morning. Was I not clear about that? Benji? Was I not clear?"

Benji nodded in agreement.

"Did I not tell you directly, Holland, that any and all calls for me—including any *messages*—could wait until I got back to the clubhouse?"

"Yes, sir. Yes, you did."

"I did what, Holland?"

"You spoke to me directly and you made yourself very clear. But I—"

"But you what? But you can't follow a self-admittedly clear and simple direction?"

"No, sir . . . I mean, yes, sir. I can. And I understood you completely. But again—"

"But again what?"

"But this information comes from Mr. Abdullahi at your father's estate and considering the context of this particular message, I assumed you'd want to have it right away—sir."

"You assumed?"

"Yes, sir. Like I said, my apologies, but under the circumstances, I felt like it was the proper call."

"Under the circumstances."

"Yes, sir."

"The proper call."

"Yes, sir."

"Well, okay then, Holland. What's so important?"

Gerald patted at both pockets of his slacks before reaching into them and pulling out a folded yellow index card. He held out the card and apologized again. Alex snatched it and unfolded it with his thumb, a phone number and a name, *Sheriff Sam Flowers*. He turned the card over, blank. He held it up.

"What is this?"

"It is the name and the direct line to the sheriff of McFalls County, sir."

"McFalls County."

"Yes, sir. That's correct. I believe it would be best, sir, if you were to call Sheriff Flowers immediately."

Alex took another look down at the card. "And how exactly am I supposed to do that out here?" He motioned with both hands around the grounds. "Am I supposed to just yell the phone number into the goddamn air or what?"

Gerald clapped his hands together in front of him as if he had just done something right. "No, no, sir. I took the liberty of bringing one of the club's mobile bag phones out here with me. Here, look. It's in the cart."

Alex peeled off his glove, tucked it into his pocket, and snatched up the receiver.

"Again, I apologize, Mr. Price. I am so—"

"Sorry. You're sorry. I get it. Now please stop talking." Alex punched the number from the card into the keypad and hit send. The phone rang six times. Five more times than necessary to irritate Alex even more.

Finally. "McFalls County Sheriff's Department."

"I would like to speak to . . ." Alex held the index card up to read the name again. "Sheriff Sam Flowers."

"Well, that'd be me. What can I do you for?"

Alex set the card down on the seat of the golf cart and switched the receiver to his other ear. "Sheriff, my name is Alexander Price, Esquire. I understand you have been trying to reach me?"

"Well, I am trying to reach a fella named Alex Price. I don't know nothing about no Esquire, though."

Alex pinched the bridge of his nose. "I am he, Sheriff. And now you've reached me. Would you mind telling me what I can do for you?"

"Are you the same Alex Price of 713 Quaker Knoll? Out in Greene County down by Oconee?"

Alex closed his eyes and pinched harder. "Yes, Sheriff. I am indeed."

"We tried you at the address there first, but a fella by the name of Michael something-or-other said it might be best to go on and catch up with you there at the country club to get you into the mix as quickly as possible."

"Okay." He waited.

"So am I correct in saying that you have a—hold up a sec—that you have a younger brother who goes by the name of Robert Price?"

Now the fog was lifting. *Of course. This was about Robbie.*

Alex's disappointing idiot brother was in trouble again—*again*. And he'd finally decided to reach out. Alex had been trying to find his brother for a few months now. "Yes," he said, suddenly sounding more interested than angry. "I have a sibling by the name of Robert. What has he done?"

"Well, he um—he got himself killed."

Alex went still. "I'm sorry. What did you say?"

"Listen, son." Flowers had the bedside manner of a used car salesman. "Yeah, I hate to be the bearer of bad news and all, but your brother is dead."

Alex waited quietly to hear more.

"Yeah, what we know so far is that Robert Price, age twenty-six, was killed last night at roughly two-thirty in the a.m. Now, I am sorry, I recognize this is a bit of a stinker, having to deliver this news via a phone call, and all, but like I said. He's dead. His body is currently down at the Rabun County Coroner's Office and morgue, and we're going to need you to come and identify the body. Next of kin and whatnot."

Alex slowly eased down onto the seat of the golf cart, crossed his legs, and switched the receiver to his other ear. "How? How did it happen?"

"Well, it seems he was involved in some kind of altercation with another fella at a shine shack out by the county line and, uh, he didn't fare too well."

"He didn't—fare too well?"

"No, sir, he did not. It looks like some kinda blunt force blow to the head. I'm thinking that the injury caused him to bleed out. But I ain't no doctor and I don't have all the details right here in front of me. The coroner is still working up the report. So like I said, I reckon you should just come on up to Rabun and then afterward, I'll need you to stop by my office here in McFalls."

"You said my brother was involved in an altercation—at a shine shack?"

"That's right. But I use that term loosely. It's more of a gathering place for uh, folks that practice, um, alternative lifestyles. If you catch my meaning."

Alex bit at his bottom lip. "Was there anyone with him?"

"With who, son?"

Alex took the phone away from his ear and just stared at it for a moment. "Never mind, Sheriff. I'm leaving now and I'll be there directly. Was there anything else?"

"You mean other than the death of your brother?"

"Yes, I suppose that's what I mean."

"I reckon that sums it up."

"Well then, thank you, Sheriff."

Flowers began to ask if Alex needed to write down directions to the coroner's office in Rabun, but Alex just pressed the red button on the phone and ended the call. He gently laid the receiver back in its cradle and removed a stick of gum from his shirt pocket. He crumpled up the foil wrapper as he chewed and flicked the tiny silver ball out onto the lawn. No one said anything until he stood up.

"A ride back to the club, sir?" Gerald asked.

"No," Alex said. "You can leave." He tucked the index card into his wallet, removed the glove from his pants pocket, and began to put it back on. "Just have Michael waiting with a cart for me outside gate six by the ninth green. He's probably almost here by now. Tell him I won't be long."

"But sir? It's really not a problem. I can . . ."

Alex didn't repeat himself.

"Of course, sir."

"No one is to know about this, Holland. If it becomes public knowledge, I'll know it came from you."

"No, sir. Absolutely not."

"Then run along."

Gerald climbed into the golf cart and quickly headed back the way he'd come. Alex walked back to the tee, positioned his footing until he was pleased, and then, without looking back, he held out his hand to Benji.

"Give me the goddamn three wood."

Chapter Seventeen

The new day's sun stirred Dallas awake. She rubbed at her eyes, smearing her mascara even more than it already was, and yawned. When she realized that Nails had pulled into some backwoods gas station, the type with only one self-pump and zero signage anywhere on the building, she popped open the passenger side door. "I've got to pee like a racehorse. I'm gonna go see if they've got a bathroom. Cool?"

Nails's door was already wide open, but he was still sitting straight-backed in the seat, gripping the steering wheel with both hands, and looking at it like he was trying to understand the purpose of it. He nodded. "Go ahead. We need gas. I'll pump. The gas, I mean. I'll get the gas."

"You want me to go pay? I've got a few bucks. I don't mind."

Nails thought about the deposit bag of cash in the glove box. "Freddy had handed over eight grand at the bar. Why did Freddy give me so much money just to leave the state?" Nails thought it was weird. "Eight thousand dollars is a lot of money for gas and food." But whatever, he didn't need this girl's *few bucks*. And he told her so. After a long silence, he looked at her. She just stared back at him. The look on her face was strange and unreadable. It made Nails feel even more uncomfortable than he already was. "I said I got it, okay? I got it. Just go pee. You probably have to go inside and get a key first."

"Okay," she said, and began to slide out of the car. With only one foot on the ground, she paused and turned. "You're not going to leave me here, are you? My bag is in here. Everything I own is in that bag. Promise me you're not going to leave me here."

"I'm not going to leave you here."

"Promise me."

"I just said it."

"No, you have to promise me. Saying it doesn't count unless you promise. So promise."

"I promise."

"You promise you're not going to drive away and leave me here?"

"I promise I'm not going to leave you here, fuck."

"Okay." Dallas slid the rest of the way out of the car, shuffled out of the canvas coat, and let it fall back on the seat. She shut the door and stretched her back before heading toward the store. When she stretched, her bones popped and her cropped tee rose to show a healthy portion of her lower back. Nails immediately turned away to stare at the steering wheel again. He gripped tight and went back to thinking about leaving her there. She must've felt him thinking it, too, making him promise not to like that. He didn't put much stock in promises. No one ever kept their word. Ever. About anything. But this time, oddly enough, it seemed to matter. Because it was his promise to keep. And his word did mean something, even if no one else's did. He pulled his gun out of his pocket and stuffed it into the glove box with the cash. He also took out the bottle of hydrocodone and dry-chewed four of the chunky white pills. He put the medicine bottle back, stepped out of the car, and reached for the gas handle hanging on the left of the pump.

Parked facing the opposite way, on the other side of the dual-handled pump, was a stunning customized Mustang Mach 1, an original 1968 or '69, he guessed, painted a dark custom green. Nails liked cars. Especially old Fords. And this one was well maintained. A man in his early twenties wearing a bandanna skullcap sat on the hood facing Nails, staring but not talking. He smoked a cigarette pinched tight between his fingers like a joint as a kid, a teenager about sixteen or seventeen, pumped gas in their ride. The kid wore a backward baseball cap and looked like he'd yet to figure out how to properly utilize a razor. His face had several swirly patches of corn silk facial hair. "Hey, dude," he said. "Badass ride." And then he tipped his child-beard at Nails. Nails ignored him. He shut the door to the LTD, removed the handle from the gas pump, and began to fill the tank. The man with the bandanna took a long drag off his cigarette, flicked it behind him, and slid down off the hood of the car. He leaned against the fender, crossed his arms, and repeated the kid's sentiment. "For real, man, that LTD is solid. You don't see many Galaxies looking full-pimp like that these days. Is that a '71, or a '72?"

Nails didn't look at the man, but he did answer him. "It's a '71."

"I fucking knew it." He slapped at the hood of the Mustang. "That thing is badass. You do all the restoration yourself?"

Nails didn't like talking to people he didn't know. He barely liked talking to people he did know, but found himself doing it anyway. He was proud of his car. And the Mustang those boys were driving wasn't nothing to be scoffed at. It was a nice car. "It was my father's. He bought it new. Just kept her up."

"Hell, yeah," Bandanna said. "You gotta keep shit like that in the family. Me and my brother here built this beauty up from bare bones. Bought her as a shell." He ran his hand over the length of the hood. "Everything you can't see, the 302, the transmission, the dual exhaust, the steering column? All that shit is brand-new. Me and Jack did all that. Just me and him. High test, low drag."

Nails looked at the car and nodded. "It's a really nice car."

"And she rides like a beast, too," the younger brother said, as he hung his gas handle back on the pump. He fished some cash from his jeans and Nails watched him walk inside the store as Dallas was walking out. She was holding the bathroom key that the store owner had apparently attached to a sawed-off pool cue. The place had probably lost a ton of those keys. Dallas smiled, waved the pool cue keychain at Nails, and then pointed it toward the side of the building where the bathroom was. Her white teeth glowed in the sunlight even from thirty feet away. Not that the kid paying for the gas would've noticed. He stared down Dallas's ass until she turned the corner out of view. That punk kid just stood there, holding the door handle like a fool until finally swinging the door open and heading inside. Nails didn't like that at all. He suddenly regretted having talked to these two assholes.

The bandanna brother tucked his hands in the pockets of his jeans and stepped up on the concrete median between the cars. It was clear that he was feeling friendly. Nails was not.

"So you take that bitch out? Let her rip? I bet she purrs like a kitten when you drop a hammer on her."

Nails flipped the lever under the trigger for continuous gas flow and took his hand off the handle. He turned to face the man. He let all seven-plus feet of himself loom over his new *buddy*. "Who are you calling a bitch? She is a young woman. And she has a name." He clenched and unclenched his fists, his deformed hand now fully prominent. Bandanna saw the hand, understood the tone of voice, and stepped back. He pulled both of his hands from his pockets and held them palms out in the air. "Whoa, dude. I was talking about your car. The Galaxie, man. I meant your car purrs like a kitten . . . not your girlfriend. I swear to Christ. I meant your car."

Nails took a moment to process that response in his head. He replayed what the man had said in his mind. Nails had gotten confused. It wouldn't be the first time but having this girl around made it worse. He was sorry he snapped at the bandanna man, but he wasn't very good with apologies, so he just said the first thing that popped into his brain. "She's not my girlfriend." As if that was somehow the point. As if his anger had been manifested and brought on by that single detail. He should've known better than to open his mouth in the first place. This is what happened when he engaged with strangers and now he had one buzzing in his head like a horsefly in a jar and Nails just wanted him to shut up.

"Whatever, man. She's your girl. She's not your girl. It's totally cool. None of my business. I didn't mean no disrespect. I was just talking Ford, man. That's it. You know? One Ford Guy to another. It's like a club, man. You know?"

Nails eased back and the other man slowly put his hands down. "I don't want to be in your club," Nails said. "And I don't want to talk to you anymore. About cars or anything. Are we clear?"

Bandanna man looked more insulted now than scared. But he agreed. "Yeah, man. We're clear." He hopped back up on the hood of the Mustang as he waited for his younger brother to come back out of the station. He didn't say another word to Nails, but he never took his eyes off him ei-ther. Nails watched the side of the building, waiting for Dallas to reappear. When he heard the click of the pump he turned and could feel the heat of the other man's stare. He wanted to smack the smug look off the bandanna man's face, but then something else caught his eye. Twenty feet behind the man on the hood of the Mustang, next to a telephone pole by the road, was a pay phone. Finally, some direction.

Chapter Eighteen

The bucket of roofing nails tipped over and a cascade of silver metal shone in the sun and tumbled down the hot black tar of the shingles. Clayton had lost his footing by just a few inches and tapped the bucket with the heel of his boot. He closed his eyes and waited for it. Any second now, Gareth would bark out his disappointment. He would have something shitty to say and that would set the mood for the rest of the day. It was impossible for Gareth Burroughs to accept accidents or simple mistakes from anyone, much less his youngest son. He demanded perfection and for his orders to be followed to a T or he simply had no use for you.

Clayton regained his balance and figured he might as well face his father for the coming tirade. But the insults didn't come. Instead, Clayton turned to see his father, shirtless and sweaty, perched on the roof like a gargoyle, paying no mind to the overturned bucket. Gareth took off his hat and wiped his brow with it before returning it to his head. He scratched a little at his beard and laid his claw hammer down on the roof. Clayton wondered if his father was even aware of what had just happened. Something was off. He stayed silent as he watched his father use his palms to inch himself over to a small cooler he'd tied to the top rung of a ladder leaning against the house. He opened the lid, pulled out two cans of Miller High Life, the champagne of beers, and closed the cooler. He held one to his forehead to feel the chill from the ice and then held the second can out to his son. Clayton was sure something was wrong now. He wondered for a minute if his father was feeling okay or if the sun had somehow scrambled his brains.

Clayton glanced over his shoulder to see if one of his brothers had joined them on the roof. Someone his father respected. He saw no one, so he moved carefully across the pitch on his palms the way Gareth had done and took the beer from his father's outstretched hand. He held the cold can to his own forehead, and then both men, still sitting in silence, popped the tops and killed the beers in seconds. Gareth motioned with his hand for Clayton's empty can, and the older Burroughs returned them both to the cooler. He grabbed two more. He opened them both and again handed one of them to Clayton. The first one had been meant to be hammered. This second one was meant to be sipped. It meant there would be words exchanged.

"Thanks, Deddy." He held up his beer with a half-ass one-man cheer and took a sip.

Gareth nodded and without looking at Clayton, his father said something strange. Strange coming from Gareth anyway. "How are you, son?" His tone of voice was soft. It almost sounded—concerned. Clayton couldn't remember the old man ever asking him about his life, but he sipped his beer and decided to roll with it. "I'm good, Pop. You all right?"

Gareth leaned back, rummaged through the pocket of his work pants, and pulled out his ever-present foil pouch of chew. He set a plug, rolled up the pouch, and stuffed it back in his pocket. "This is a good spot," he said. "Pretty country."

"Yessir, it is," Clayton agreed.

"What's that pretty little girlfriend of yours think about it?"

"She loves it up here. And she loves the house."

Gareth sipped at his beer. "I bet she loves that it's free, too. Seeing that it comes connected to you, huh. She love that, too?"

Clayton shook his head. That rare father-and-son moment he thought they were about to have had just been shattered. He almost laughed for allowing himself to think such a thing—such a normal thing—would ever happen between his deddy and him. He chugged on his beer, taking down nearly half the can. "Deddy, if there's a price, just name it. Kate and I have our own money. In fact, if you don't want us here, we can find somewhere else to live."

Gareth sucked tobacco juice through his teeth. "Just calm yourself, boy. And watch your tone. This land comes with the blood in you. That's price enough."

The sun had already warmed the rest of Clayton's beer, and he didn't want it. He just wanted to get this chat over with and get back to work on the roof.

"She like the marble we laid in the kitchen?"

Clayton studied his father. They'd just installed that countertop yesterday. How the hell did he know Kate had been out here? He shook his head. Because nothing happened on Bull Mountain without Gareth Burroughs knowing it, and Clayton knew that. But why did it matter? "Yeah, she does. She loves it."

Gareth spit over the ledge. "Yeah, I heard she'd come up here early morning—way early."

"You heard?"

The old man didn't explain; he just kept on. "I figured you might show her the work we did in the kitchen. Women just love their kitchens."

Clayton could see it now. His father, this talk, it was all bullshit. Gareth was playing a game. Clayton just couldn't see the angle yet. "Well, Katie ain't the type of woman to be spending all her time in the kitchen, Deddy, but yeah, she liked it just fine."

Gareth nodded a few more times. "I heard she brought some company with her. A friend of y'all's from back in school. What's her name again? Mary? Something like that?"

"Amy," Clayton said, but he was sure that his father knew that already. "Her name's Amy Silver."

"That's right. Silver. She's Gene Silver's little girl, right?"

"I suppose that's her deddy's name. I wouldn't know."

"Well, I reckon you would know that girl packed up and moved out of this county years ago."

"She did. She's in town for her mother's birthday. I don't know her name either, but I'm sure you do. Kate just brought her up here to show her the house. No big deal."

"Amy Silver." Gareth dragged her name over his teeth. "She's kin to ol' Stan Moody, too, yeah?"

Clayton was done with the small talk. "What's this about, Deddy? What do you care about Amy Silver, her parents, or anyone she may or may not be related to?"

Gareth allowed a bit of mock surprise to spread over his face as if he was offended. "I don't give one good goddamn about some girl you used to know who ran away from our way of life. In fact, it's probably for the best, if you know what I mean."

Now they were getting to the heart of it. "No, Deddy. I don't know what you mean."

"I'm just saying this life up here ain't for everybody. These mountains? This land? It's not just rock and dirt. It's a living, breathing thing. And when it gets hungry? It eats the soft meat and leaves nothing but the bones. Son, there are bones all over this mountain, all around you, as far as you can see. There's probably more bones in the dirt out here than there are worms feeding off 'em. Hell, even some of the people born and raised this far up in the hills find themselves in the jaws of the beast. That's life. It just happens. Ain't nothing no one can do to stop it. Some folks, they take this place for granted. They just end up over their heads. And then some folks, well, they just have accidents."

"Accidents," Clayton repeated.

"Yep. Happens all the time. Like take me and you for example. Here we are, just two fellas with mountain blood pumpin' through our veins. Up here just laying down some tar and shingles." Gareth hunched forward and looked toward the ground. "What would you say, we're about fifteen feet up right now? Maybe higher? And here we are drinking beers. Some folks might say that's normal. But—some folks might say that's not so smart. Impairs your judgment. Slows your reaction time. Makes you sloppy. Might even be enough to make one of us fall—like that bucket right there." Gareth kicked at the overturned bucket, and it went sailing over the edge of the roof to the ground. "And that right there—that—would be a damn shame, you know?"

"Yeah, Deddy, it sure would." Clayton tossed his can of warm beer over the edge as well, while Gareth tucked his empty one back into the cooler. Clayton began to inch his way back to where he'd stopped working. The message he thought he just heard had been delivered and he was done with this charade his father was trying to disguise as something other than it was. But Gareth put a hard-knuckled hand on his son's shoulder. He finally looked at his youngest boy. Clayton knew that look. And for good reason he still feared it

"Do you understand what I'm telling you, boy?"

"Yeah, Deddy. I understand exactly what you're saying."

Gareth tightened his grip. "So I don't need to tell you in any other specific terms to stay out of any, and all, of my business, right?"

"No, Deddy, you don't. Those terms were specific enough."

"So we're clear?"

"As creek water."

"Well, all right then. That's that." Gareth removed his hand, inched himself closer to the ladder, and positioned himself on it. "I reckon you got it from here. I've got some shit to handle. I'll see you tomorrow morning. And make sure you pick up that empty High Life can you tossed out in the yard before you leave. You've got a respect problem."

"Yessir." Clayton watched his father descend the ladder, the small cooler hanging over his forearm. He watched the old man crack open the last beer in that cooler before he cranked up the rusty step-side and headed off toward whatever *shit he needed to handle.*

Gareth had whupped his ass plenty growing up, but he'd never signaled his intentions before. Clayton sat on the roof in the heat feeling equal parts terrified and furious. Eventually he climbed down the ladder as well and walked over to his Bronco. He changed into a less dirty T-shirt from the backseat and then sat behind the wheel for another twenty minutes before turning the key in the ignition and slowly making his way down the mountain.

Chapter Nineteen

Nails all but forgot about Dallas and the asshole sitting on the car across from him as soon as he saw the phone. He hung the pump handle up, opened the car door, reached across the seat, and pulled the canvas bag of cash out of the glove box. He fished out the sheet of paper with the name and number Freddy had written down, tossed the bag back in the box, flipped the lid closed, got out of the car, slammed the door, and made for the phone.

Please let the damn thing work.

He repeated it over and over in his head until he was standing in front of it. He picked up the receiver, wiped the mouthpiece off with his shirt, and held it to his ear. There was a dial tone.

Finally, he thought. *Maybe now he'd get some answers.*

He held the phone between his cheek and shoulder as he unzipped his fanny pack and scooped a handful of loose change out from the bottom. He dumped the change on the metal shelf beneath the phone, flipped open the paper, and punched in the Florida number. A prerecorded female voice came on the line and asked for $1.75 for the first three minutes. Nails began to pump quarters into the slot until the voice thanked him and the phone began to ring. Another woman's voice answered, deep and sultry like a late night radio announcer. "Wilcombe Exports," she said. "Oscar Wilcombe's office."

"Yeah," Nails said, as he looked down and double-checked the name written on the slip of paper. "Wilcombe. I need to talk to that guy."

"All right, sir. May I tell him who's calling?"

"I'm Nails. My name is Nails."

"Just Nails, sir? Is that the name you'd like me to give to Mr. Wilcombe?"

"It's my name. I work for Gareth Burroughs. I'm supposed to call this number. I was told to call this number."

"All right, Mr. Nails. Please hold."

Nails endured a few bars of "Slide" by the Goo Goo Dolls before someone with a British accent picked up the line. Nails thought it sounded cool.

"Ah, Mr. McKenna, I presume. I have anxiously been awaiting your call. Our mutual friend informed me of your predicament, and I am more than pleased to offer you my assistance."

No one had called Nails by his last name in years. Mr. McKenna was something other people called Satchel. Nails didn't like being called that at all. "My name is Nails. You can call me that."

"Of course. Nails it is. Well, please then, let us get down to brass tacks, shall we? Do you have a pen and paper available, so I can relay to you an address?"

The man sounded fancy. Nails didn't deal in fancy. He also didn't know what "brass tacks" meant, and he didn't have a pen—or paper. The operator's voice came back on the line insisting that the caller add an additional fifty cents to continue the call for another three minutes. Nails slammed two more quarters into the slot and told the British man to hold on. He let the phone hang by its cord as he unzipped his fanny pack and dug out the paperback copy of *The Postman Always Rings Twice*. He also found a stubby dull pencil inside. So he flipped to the blank inside cover of the book and pressed it down flat against the metal shelf. "Okay. I'm ready."

"Wonderful," the British man said. "All right, I'm going to need you to come to 444 23rd Street in Jacksonville. The establishment is a motel called the Sunshine Palace. Once you arrive, you are to call this number again and relay to me your room number. You will receive a callback with further instruction on how to proceed. By the way, the Sunshine Palace is adjacent to a wonderful little pub called Cues. And yes, it is exactly what it sounds like so if billiards is your forte than I recommend you bring—what do you Americans call it?—your A game."

This fancy man was too pleasant. He sounded fake. And all Nails got out of his speech were the digits 444. Words like *forte* and *billiards* jammed his head up with all the wrong things. "Can you repeat that? I can't hear that well on this phone." That wasn't true, but Nails didn't feel like spilling his issues into the phone.

"No problem." The British man repeated the address, this time much slower, and he stuck to the point. Still, Nails tried for a second time to write it down and failed. He chose another route. He'd go off his memory. "You said the name of the place is *the Sunshine Palace?*"

"Correct."

"And that's in Jacksonville."

"Correct again."

Nails repeated the name of the motel and the city again, and the British voice on the phone agreed again.

"Okay, I'm on my way."

"Outstanding, mate. And again, once you arrive, please call this number again and if all is well, we will see you tomorrow night. My man will be there to meet you with instructions on what is to follow. You won't recognize him, but I assure you that he will recognize you and make contact. But please be punctual. My man is not likely to wait very long."

"Sunshine Palace. I got it." Nails began to stuff the book and the pencil back in his fanny pack when the entirety of what the fancy man just said struck him. "Wait, what? Be there tomorrow night? I'm in Georgia. I can be there today. I'm on my way now—right now."

The British man loosened a chuckle. "Nails, my friend, you must understand. These things take time. Pieces need to be arranged on the board. Plans must be made. If we were to force an early exit strategy, it would simply not allow the time needed to make the proper arrangements."

Pieces on the board? What the hell was this man talking about?

"What the hell am I supposed to do until then?"

"Might I suggest that you enjoy yourself. Jacksonville and the surrounding area can be quite lovely in the fall."

The operator's voice cut in for a second time, demanding another fifty cents. "Hold on a minute. This damn phone." As he finished jamming coins into the slot, he could hear the Mustang Mach 1's engine roar to life.

He was sure the whole county could hear it. The exhaust had been modified to make it as loud as possible. The kid with the ball cap was at the wheel and Bandanna sat passenger. He flicked another cigarette onto the asphalt in Nails's direction as the muscle car screamed out of the parking lot. Nails covered his free ear and had to wait until the Mustang was at least a quarter mile down the road before he was able to hear or continue his conversation. When it was possible, Nails repeated himself. "What am I supposed to do for the next twenty-four hours?"

"Outside of my recommendation that you relax? Nails, from what I understand about you from our mutual friend, you are a very resourceful man. I'm positive that you will think of something."

Nails took a deep breath and turned from the phone to see if Dallas was back from the bathroom yet. He didn't see her. She was taking a long time. He shouldn't have left her alone. It was beginning to bother him. But then he saw something that bothered him more. The door to the LTD. His door. The driver's door. It was open. Not all the way, but slightly. He was sure he'd shut it before he walked over to the phone.

But did you lock it, Nails? Did you lock the car?

The British voice on the phone sounded like it might have been recapping the plans they'd just made but Nails dropped the phone and sprinted back to the car. He could see the open glove box through the window before he even reached the pump. His brain erupted into a chaotic buzz. He snatched the door handle, swung the door open even further, and got in. He rubbed his hand along the smooth plastic of the interior of the glove box. The money was gone. The bottle of pills was still there, but nothing else. He scanned the floorboards. The car's operator's manual, parts receipts, and registration slips were scattered all over the floor mat next to Dallas's handbag. They didn't take the bag. Or the pills. That confused him. Why wouldn't they take a purse or drugs? It was all right there. He turned around and shuffled through the stack of coats, laundry, and comic books in the backseat. Nothing. "Fuck." He repeated over and over. He got out of the car, looked under the car. For what, he didn't know. It was gone. They got it. Those bastards in the Mach 1, they'd taken his money.

And of course they did, stupid. Because you left it in the glove box of an unlocked car.

"Fuck," he yelled again, and noticed the revolver in his hand. How long had he been holding it? He didn't have it on him at the phone. No. He'd put it in—the glove box—along with the money. He must've picked it up from the floorboards. That means those fuckers left the gun, too. They took the bank bag but left the gun, the handbag that could have had even more money in it, and a huge bottle of pills. Like they knew exactly what to steal and where it was. How? Nails hit himself in the head, right about his left temple, hard enough to make himself bleed. "How?" he yelled out into the nothing.

"How what?"

Nails spun toward the voice behind him and pointed the revolver directly at Dallas.

"Whoa, man. What's your damage?" She held her hands up, still holding the pool cue keychain, and stumbled backward, nearly falling over. Nails bent his arms and pointed the gun straight up. "Did you take it?"

"Take what? Jesus. What the hell are you doing? Put the gun away." Dallas scanned the area to see if anyone else was watching this. No one that she could see.

"The money. Did you take the money?"

Dallas went from freaked out to indignant. "No—Nails. I didn't take any money. And you need to put that gun away before someone calls the cops. You look like a crazy person."

She was right. He did. Nails lowered the gun completely and tossed it through the car door onto the seat. "My car was robbed. I went to use the phone. That's what I was supposed to do. Find a phone. And call the number. So that's what I did. But I didn't lock the car. I didn't lock it. I never do. I don't have to. People know not to steal from me. I didn't lock the car."

Dallas listened and then freaked out. "My bag?" She rushed over to the passenger side of the car. "Did they take my bag?" She yanked open the passenger door with both hands and exhaled when she saw her handbag. She took a quick inventory and tossed it back on the floor as she leaned against the fender well and calmed down. Nails got into the car and Dallas got in next to him. He laid his forehead against the steering wheel.

"Did you see who did it?"

NOTHING BUT THE BONES • 95

"No. But I know it was those brothers."

"What brothers?"

"The two guys in the Mustang. They were here when we pulled up. And hauled ass when I went to use the phone. But I just don't understand."

"Understand what?"

"They left your bag. Freddy's pills. And my gun. All that was in the glove box, too. It's like they knew exactly what to take and where to find it."

Dallas sank deeper into the seat and laid her head back on the headrest. "So, two guys in a Mustang parked right next to you, waited until you walked away, and then robbed your car, but only took the eight Gs in the glove box?"

"Yeah." A brief moment of silence passed and then Nails lifted his head off the wheel. He glared at Dallas before snatching her by the arm—hard.

"Ouch, stop it. You're hurting me."

He pulled her closer to him. "How did you know that?"

"How did I know what? Let go of me."

"The amount. You said they only took the eight thousand dollars. How did you know how much money was in there?"

Dallas looked confused but pulled back and managed to free her arm from Nails's grip. It was already starting to bruise. "Are you kidding me right now?" she asked.

"Do I look like I'm fucking kidding?" Nails's whole face was hot red and for the first time Dallas felt legitimately scared of him. "How did you know how much money I had and where it was? Did you know those two guys? Did you plan this?"

"No, Jesus. Nails. We pulled up. I went inside. I got the key. I peed. I washed my face. I came back. And you were freaking out. I didn't even see two other guys and a Mustang. This is bullshit."

"How did you know the amount?" Nails yelled again into her face.

"You told me, you fucking asshole," she yelled back. "Do you not remember that? When we got here. I offered to pay for the gas, and you told me you didn't need my money because you had eight thousand dollars that your friend Freddy gave you. You said you didn't know why he gave you that much and it was in the glove box. Seriously. You don't remember that? I didn't understand why you were telling me, but I just said okay and then made you promise not to leave me, because with that kinda cash, you certainly didn't need me around for anything. Shit. I can't believe you're acting like that didn't happen. Grabbing on me. Yelling at me." Dallas rubbed her arm.

Nails watched her while his brain did cartwheels. He remembered thinking exactly that. Everything Dallas had just said. He remembered thinking it. But did he say it out loud? Did he fucking do it again? Of course he did. He'd told her everything and not even realized it. That's why she acted so weird when she got out of the car. Is that why she was so insistent that he promise her that he wouldn't leave? It didn't matter. It didn't matter that he told her. What mattered is that he also told anyone else who might've been within earshot. Like those two assholes in the Mustang. He smacked his forehead on the doorframe. And then again. "Stupid. I'm so fucking stupid."

"Stop that." Dallas put her hand out, but he slammed his head into the steel a third time. "Nails, please. Stop it."

"I did this. I didn't just tell you, but I told them, too. They were standing right there." A fourth headbutt into the doorframe.

"Nails, stop it."

"That's why they were so chatty. And then as soon as I walked away, I basically handed it to them."

Dallas practically sat herself on Nails's lap, shoving herself between him and the steel frame before he could do any more damage to himself or the car. She grabbed his shoulders. "Listen to me. It's done. It happened. There's nothing we can do about it now. So stop hurting yourself. Damn, you're going to crack your skull open."

"That was all the money I had. And I gave it away."

"You didn't give it away. You got robbed by two rednecks. It happens. It did happen. We'll figure it out."

Nails stared out the windshield at nothing, trying to avoid looking at Dallas, but she put her face in front of his. She forced him to look at her—to look in her eyes.

"We—will—figure—it—out. Okay?"

Nothing.

"Okay?"

"Okay," he conceded.

"So if I sit back down, you'll stop with all the head banging?"

"Yes."

"Promise?"

"Just get off me, Dallas."

She did and slid herself back down onto the seat. She rubbed at her arm some more where Nails had grabbed her, and he watched her do it. The skin was already stained purple.

"I'm sorry I hurt you."

"It's okay. Just don't do it again."

"I won't."

"Good. Your leg is bleeding."

"What?"

She pointed. Nails looked down and saw the sticky red blotch on the gauze Monk wrapped his wound with. He hadn't even thought about it since they left The Chute. The pills were doing their job. "It'll be fine."

They both sat in silence for a while.

"Okay, listen. You filled the tank, right?"

Nailed wiped at the fresh blood on his temple where he'd hit himself with his gun. "Yes."

"Cool, well, I've got some cash. So I'll go and pay for the gas and see if they have any—I don't know—medical shit in there. Maybe some rubbing alcohol or something, okay? Maybe the old man in there knows who those two guys are. If we're lucky, maybe they're local and he knows where they live. But either way, we can at least get out of here just in case anybody saw you acting all Dirty Harry out there."

"Dirty Harry?"

"It's a movie. Never mind. I'll tell you about it later. But what I just said, can that be the plan? Okay? Nails? Does that work?"

"I'll go in."

"Dude, your leg is bleeding like hell, and you were just in the parking lot screaming and waving a gun around. If you go in that store, you'll give that old guy in there a damn heart attack. Just stay here. I got this. Okay?"

It took him a minute, but finally he agreed. "Okay."

"Cool. I'll be right back." She grabbed the bathroom key from the seat between them, snatched her handbag from the floor, and headed back inside.

Chapter Twenty

Nails didn't have time to run through the events of the past few minutes before he heard the shouting. Dallas was running back toward the car, yelling for him to crank the engine. She still had the bathroom key, holding it down by her side in her left hand while clutching her bag tight against her chest with the other. She jumped in the car and slammed the door behind her, tossing the bathroom key on the seat between them. Now Nails could see that it wasn't the bathroom key at all. It was his gun.

"Go, man. Start the car. C'mon. Let's go." Dallas alternated looks back at the door to the store that remained shut and at Nails. She was smiling and excited. "Go, man. Seriously. Crank it up."

"What did you do? Did you pay for the gas?"

She laughed. "Please, Nails. Just drive."

"Tell me what you did in there."

Dallas reached over and grabbed Nails by the chin. It was the second time he'd ever allowed another person to touch him on purpose. And both times had been by her. She held his face inches from her own and removed a pair of sunglasses Nails had never seen on her before, a neon green pair of knock-off Wayfarers. "Listen to me. I just robbed that sweet old man in there, so now we have gas, and we have money, but I'm not sure how long he's going to lie on the floor in there. So, please—will you drive? Right now? Before we both get arrested? Or before that old coot comes out with his own gun and starts shooting at us?"

Nails turned the key in the ignition and peeled away from the gas pump. "I don't think that was a good idea, Dallas. This is my car. We're going to have to ditch my car."

"It's just a car, man. Don't worry about it. I saw this in a movie once. We'll be fine."

"*Bonnie and Clyde?*"

"Well, it was more like Bonnie and Bonnie but similar vibes. Just drive."

Nails pressed the pedal down and Dallas pulled a freshly stolen map of Georgia out of her bag. "We just need to get off this main highway, handsome. And you need to tell me where we're headed."

"Did you hurt anyone back there?"

"No. I swear."

"Do you promise?"

Dallas stared at Nails for a very long time and then smiled. "Yes, Nails. I promise."

Chapter Twenty-One

Clayton wheeled the Bronco into an empty parking place in front of Lucky's Diner. The local eatery had been opened a few years back by a pair of Yankee brothers who showed up in town with a deed for the storefront, money to invest, and their six-year-old niece, Nicole. The two fellas were likable enough but lacked enough intrigue for anyone of any importance to ever ask questions about their lack of physical resemblance—or what happened to the little girl's parents. The simple truth was, if a man could country-fry a steak that melted in your mouth and follow it with fresh blueberry cobbler that consistently tasted like it just came out of the oven, he could basically get away with murder in a town like Waymore Valley. So, Lucky's had rapidly become the most popular place for lunch and dinner in the county. Clayton pushed open the door, listened to the sleigh bells ring, and took a seat at the counter. It was early still, the breakfast rush was over, and the place was almost empty—almost. Little Nicole came running around the bar and greeted him with a smile full of silver braces, her dark hair pulled tight into pigtails wrapped with neon yellow scrunchies.

"Hey, Mr. Clayton."

"Hey there, kiddo. Are your uncles around?"

"Uncle Harvey is down in Anderson, but Uncle Hollis is in the back chopping onions. He wouldn't let me help, though. He says I'm too young and that onions will make me cry. But I don't see nothing sad about onions . . . except maybe the way they taste."

Clayton chuckled. "Well, if I had to guess, I'd say you'd make a champion onion chopper."

"Thank you. I think so, too."

Clayton rubbed the top of the little girl's head, but she backed up and expressed her concern that he might "mess it up."

Clayton laughed a little more. "Hey, Nicole, do you think you could go and get your uncle Hollis for me? I need to talk to him."

"Sure. Be right back." And with that, the little girl disappeared around the bar and through the swinging doors to the kitchen. A minute later, Hollis Peterman appeared behind the counter, his jet-black hair slicked back with half a can of pomade. He wore a white apron that had been stained and bleached at least a hundred times.

"Hey there, Clayton. You here for the meatloaf? Because it's going to be about an hour or so before we start serving lunch."

"No, Mr. Peterman. As much as I love y'all's meatloaf, sadly I'm not here to eat. I was just wondering if I could use your phone to page Kate, and maybe I could have her give me a callback here? Would that be okay?"

The Peterman brothers weren't the type to ask questions. It was an endearing trait. "Of course it is. Hang on." Hollis moved down to the end of the counter, reached underneath, and pulled out a tabletop phone. After wrestling with the cord a little, he set the phone down in front of Clayton.

"Thank you, so much, Mr. Peterman."

"It's Hollis, Clayton. And anytime."

Clayton picked up the receiver and punched in Kate's pager number. While he waited for the prompt, he asked Hollis for the number to Lucky's. Nicole, who'd been standing behind the bar the whole time but out of sight because she was only about four feet tall, belted out the number with pride. Hollis gently maneuvered her back toward the kitchen but nodded that the number she'd just announced was correct. Clayton punched in the callback number, waited for the final beep, and hung up. "She normally calls me right back, so it shouldn't be but a minute or so."

"Not a problem. Take all the time you need."

Clayton pointed back toward the double doors leading into the kitchen. "That kid in there is growing like a weed."

"Who you tellin'? And smart as a whip, too."

"Best be careful she don't get smarter than y'all."

"I think it's too late for that."

Both men laughed as the phone rang. Clayton picked it up. "Kate?"

"Hey, baby. Where are you? I don't recognize the number."

Clayton gave Hollis the thumbs-up, and the thin man in the apron disappeared into the kitchen to allow Clayton his privacy. "I'm at Lucky's. I didn't want to call you from the phone at my place."

"Um, okay. Why?"

"Let's just say I'm feeling a little paranoid at the moment."

"That's a little cryptic."

"I know. I'm sorry. But I need you to trust me and listen for a minute, okay?"

"Okay. Okay, but be quick. My planning period is almost over, and I've got to cover Chloe Hedges's American government class since she's out on maternity leave."

"Middle school kids have to take U.S. government now?"

"It's a new world, Clayton. But really, I only have a minute."

"Okay, first of all, I'm sorry I wasn't more receptive to what you and Amy had to say this morning. I'm sorry if I was an ass."

"It's okay. I figured you'd call me after you thought about it."

"Yeah well. I did. I have."

"And is *that* what this phone call is about?"

"Yes. Kinda. I want you to tell Amy I'll do it. I've got some things to square away on the mountain but I'm going to head out first thing tomorrow morning. I'll try to find Nails and bring him home. She was right. You were right. I'm sorry it took me so long to see that, but I'm going to do my best to find him. We owe him that."

"What changed your mind?"

"My father."

"Really? I didn't think you'd even mention any of this to him."

"I didn't. But I don't know. Something about him today—felt—I don't know—unhinged. He knew you and Amy were at the house this morning and he was being weird about it. But, nonetheless, I think y'all are right about Nails being fed to the wolves."

"Did he tell you that?"

"No, but I've got a feeling in my gut that I can't shake. He basically told me not to get involved. Something is definitely wrong. So, just tell her I'm not promising anything, but I'll try. I'll do what I can."

"Okay. I'll tell her."

"And listen, I don't know how long this is going to take, so if Amy is planning on heading back to North Carolina soon, let her know that's probably not a bad idea. We can keep her informed afterward. She doesn't need to stay here."

"Clayton, do I need to be worried over here? About either of y'all . . . about me?"

"No, no. It's nothing like that. Just let her know I got this."

"Okay. I will. I'll tell her. But Clayton—"

"Yeah?"

"Just be careful . . . and I love you."

"I love you, too. I'll call you as soon as I know more."

Clayton hung up the phone and yelled his thanks back to Hollis in the kitchen. *Be careful,* he thought. He wondered if those two words meant anything anymore. He knew full well that he'd left *being careful* behind him as soon as he'd climbed down from that roof.

Chapter Twenty-Two

Nails and Dallas ditched the LTD in a wooded area off a secluded park in Central Georgia, in a small blink of a town called Tignall. A few miles back, Dallas suggested that they stuff a rag down into the gas tank and set it on fire behind an abandoned grocery store or a parking lot somewhere. But the idea of watching his cherry LTD burn didn't sit well with Nails. So he decided on the woods scenario instead.

Dallas found what looked to be a perfect spot on the map she'd stolen in Franklin, and Nails took a hard left off blacktop onto winding dirt. He turned again onto a pig path, barely wide enough for the '71 Ford to fit on. If the car was going to be found, it would be by a mountain biker, or a family of campers, or better yet, by a group of potheads, much more interested in the price of antique car parts and less likely to take it to the nearest police station. That notion made him feel a little better about what he was about to do. Ditching this car was more upsetting than he thought it would be but, thanks to Dallas, now completely necessary.

Once the Galaxie had begun to get entangled by the thick bramble, he gunned it and pressed the gas pedal flat to the floor, ramming the powerful rear-wheel drive through all the thick vines and low-hanging tree limbs until the car simply couldn't move forward anymore. He cut the engine and sat there. That car was the only thing Satchel ever gave him. The last remaining thread of kinship he felt with his old man. It figured this was the way it'd get left. To hell with him.

"You okay?" Dallas asked.

"I'm fine."

"You know you could've let me out at the road first—before you did all this."

"You're the one who caused me to have to do this in the first place, Dallas. So deal with it."

They both had to roll down the windows and climb out to exit the car. Dallas made sure to retrieve her mixtape from the stereo, and her handbag. She wrapped herself in the thick coat she'd been using as a blanket the night before and used it now to guard herself from the thorns and broken branches as she crawled out. She made it to the safety of the clear space behind the car relatively unharmed. Her ankles got the worst of it, cuts and scratches circling the bare skin above the tops of her red All-Stars. Nails didn't care about anything inside the car except his gun, the bottle of pills, and a change of clothes from the backseat. He saw the box of Batman comics but despite the heartache it caused him to leave them behind, he did it anyway. He tucked the .45 into the waistband of his Levi's, put the pills in his pocket, and climbed out of the window, using the spare clothing to protect his face. He pushed his way through with only a few steps to join Dallas behind the car.

"I'm sorry, Nails. I know that car was important to you."

"I said it's fine."

"I really am sorry."

"Just leave it. Stop talking about it."

Dallas may have been good at a lot of things but not talking wasn't one of them. "I know I messed up but even if we stuck to backroads all the way to wherever it is we're going, driving a big-ass fire engine red car is just begging to get caught."

"Competition Red."

"What?"

"It's called Competition Red, not Fire Engine Red. Those are two totally different colors. Fire Engine Red isn't even a Ford option."

"Okay . . . whatever. You still get my point, though, right?"

He did, but it didn't change anything. She still didn't understand any of this. She still acted like she was living inside one of her goddamn movies. But Nails didn't feel like trying to explain to her how stupid it was to rob that store. Or to cost him his car. So he just said, "Right," as they started the two-and-a-half-mile hike back up to a park they saw by the main road and, more importantly, to the adjacent neighborhood they'd spotted. A perfect place to find a suitable, but much less noticeable, car to steal.

They didn't talk much as they walked back to the dirt road. She knew he wasn't happy about abandoning his car. She didn't know what to say, so she just asked him if he was okay a lot. He didn't answer her about the same number of times. Reality had really begun to set in, and they could both feel the ache of the past twenty-four hours deep in their bones. Dallas had gotten about an hour of sleep in the car before she became wanted for armed robbery, but it was hardly what anyone would call rest. And Nails hadn't slept in going on two days. They were moving slow, but he still outpaced her two to one. Every fifteen feet or so, he'd deliberately slow down, or stop altogether, so she could catch up and wouldn't have to walk alone. At one point, she stopped and squatted to wipe a patch of blood from a scrape on her ankle.

"I should've let you out first," Nails said. "Before I buried the car. That was dumb."

"Yeah, well, I didn't think to tell you until after either. So who's the bigger dummy?"

When they were able to see the park up ahead, she asked him again where they were supposed to be going. What was the endgame? She'd been asking him all afternoon, ever since they left the gas station. It was a little hard to be the navigator when you didn't know where you were navigating to, but all he kept saying was "south" and to "stay off the interstate." She figured he'd have to tell her eventually. Unless, of course, he wasn't planning to keep her around to see his final destination. That thought—of being left behind and alone—was never far from her mind. But this time, as they made their way across a large grassy clearing, he just came out and told her.

"Jacksonville. We're going to Jacksonville."

She laughed, a deep and unsettling laugh. Nails stopped. "Why is that funny? Have you been there before?"

"Yeah, I've been there before. And it's not funny. That place is a shithole."

"Well, you asked. Now you know." Nails started walking again and Dallas trailed him shaking her head. They were going to end up in Florida.

Yes, she had been there before, but she felt bad for telling Nails that it wasn't funny. She did find it kind of funny. Or ironic at the very least. All of it was. Going south, back to Florida, after everything she'd gone through to get out of there.

Chapter Twenty-Three

When they'd nearly reached the main road, Nails pointed at a small playground in major disrepair. There was a lonely swing set, a slide filled with matted leaves and stagnant rainwater at the bottom, and a dome of monkey bars that resembled the skeleton of some prehistoric tortoise. A trio of some strange-looking androgynous sea animals mounted to the ground on thick coils, with handles on their heads and seats on their backs, lined a small patch of sand. They were goddamn fucking weird and they creeped Dallas out. The entirety of the park was also shaded by clusters of towering pecan trees, so the ground was littered with rotten pecans—bitter Georgian ankle-breakers.

"There." Nails pointed to the playground. "Wait for me there. I'll find us a car and I'll be back to pick you up at the road."

"You want me to wait over there?"

"Yes. I want you to wait over there." He pointed again.

"Why can't I just go with you?"

"Have you ever stolen a car, Dallas?"

"No, but . . ."

"It's not a two-person job. Wait over there and I'll be back." He turned to leave without another word.

This was it. This is where she was going to get left—and it was ironically perfect. The playground looked abandoned and sad. And Dallas couldn't think of a better place to be left behind, seeing as her whole life could be summed up as abandoned and sad. She felt hollowed out and sick, but she was also bone-tired and didn't have it in her to argue or play the promise game.

So, she twisted the big silver ring on her finger, hitched the strap of her handbag over her shoulder, and just said, "Okay." He'd either be back or he wouldn't. But she'd seen this same scenario play out before over the last year or so. Promise or no promise. Her likability had waned. Her luster had tarnished. Just like the dull and rusty monkey bars she was currently staring at, that looked more to her now like just another cage to sleep inside. She watched Nails walk toward the neighborhood and fought the urge to follow him. She knew he didn't want her around anymore. She'd been in this position before—many times. She knew she was nothing but deadweight now. That stunt she pulled at that gas station was stupid and impulsive. She might have thought it was cool at the time, but it only made things worse for them both. But whatever. She'd done it for him. She spun the ring again. She'd called this all wrong. Every decision she'd made so far had left her right back where she had started—alone. She could feel the tears start to swell in the deep corners of her eyes. Then she heard Nails call her name.

Dallas wiped at her eyes with her thumbs. He was walking back toward her. When he reached her, he stood very close, closer than he was normally comfortable with, and he scanned the park.

"Take this." He held out his gun, holding it out to her by the barrel. "In case something goes wrong."

"Nails, I don't even know how to use one of those. I almost dropped it back at that gas station."

"You just point it at who you want to hurt and squeeze the trigger. I'd also recommend that you hold it with two hands. It kicks pretty hard."

"Don't you need it?"

"No. I told you. I'm going over there to steal a car. But you're a pretty—" His voice snagged on the words, so he tried again. "You're a—a—girl—alone in a strange place. Just don't use it unless you have to and give it back to me when I pick you up." Nails scanned the park again and then lifted the flap on her handbag and tucked the gun deep inside. "I won't be long—I promise."

She watched him walk away while she held tight to his last two words.

I promise. He knew she needed to hear that. She clutched her handbag with its new heft close to her chest with both arms. He was right. She was a girl in a strange place. But inside that moment, for the first time in a long time, she felt hopeful. She didn't feel alone.

Chapter Twenty-Four

Dallas popped a small white pill and swallowed it dry. She shook the bottle. She was running low but that was a problem for another day. She rocked back and forth slowly in the one swing on the swing set that looked the least likely to give her tetanus. The minutes felt like hours as she waited. She used her camera to take a picture of the blue and yellow cloud formations rimmed in pink and gold that covered the sky, but only one click. She only had a few shots left according to the dial on the back of the camera.

Other than the swirls of color above her, it was a creepy place to be alone. There weren't many, but every car that drove by the park made her heart race thinking it was Nails in their new ride. That feeling turned to crushing doubt every time a car passed without the brightening of its brake lights. A blue Camaro slowed a little as it passed the park and then must've circled back around to get a second look at her. But it wasn't him. It looked like a bunch of kids, and it was the only time Dallas put her hand on the grip of the .45 in her bag. Thankfully the scare didn't last very long. By the third time the pimple-faced vultures had circled around, a black Honda Accord had pulled over to the curb directly across from the park. Nails rolled down the passenger's side window. She nearly busted her ass hopping off the rubber swing as she bolted toward the car. The Camaro decided to move along.

Nails leaned over and opened the passenger door for her. Dallas slipped into the car as if the seat had been custom-made for her. Once she was settled, she filled her lungs with the pine-scented air inside the black sedan. It felt like it was the first full breath she'd taken since he'd left. She wanted to reach over and hug his neck. She wanted to thank him over and over and over, to tell him how worried she was, but she didn't say anything. She just put on her seatbelt at Nails's behest and watched his face as he wheeled out onto the road. The expression he carried wasn't one of doubt or regret. It read like a man who had never even entertained the idea of leaving her behind.

She pulled in another long breath of faux pine air coming from the bundle of cardboard airfresheners shaped like tiny trees hanging from the rearview mirror. She hadn't called it wrong. He was exactly who she thought he was from the start, back at that bar when she saw him break a man's arm and then help that same man to the ground.

They drove for a while, both feeling a little better about themselves, as Dallas marked on the map the easiest way into Florida that avoided interstates. After fifty miles or so, she suggested that maybe they stop and get a motel room or something. The car had a full tank, but they were both running on fumes. Nails insisted on driving straight through. It wasn't until the third time he nodded off and swerved into the median that he finally conceded to stop somewhere and rest. The problem now was that they were in the middle of nowhere, somewhere outside Valdosta, according to the map. But it was miles and miles of residential area. No hotels to be found. Nails suggested they just sleep in the car, but Dallas got him to agree that was a bad idea. Parked cars with foggy windows attracted police. The conversation shifted when Dallas saw the sign for a subdivision under development up ahead. Her face lit up. Under development meant still under construction. The sun was setting, and Dallas had been at this homeless thing for quite a while now. This was something she knew about. And she had an idea.

Chapter Twenty-Five

"Pull down there. Into that cul-de-sac."

"Into the what?"

"There, into that circle, where the streetlights end. Next to those houses still being built . . . and cut off the headlights."

Nails killed the lights and crept the Honda quietly down onto the recently paved road, so new that the fresh tar and rock stuck to the little car's tires. He circled around as Dallas looked at the unfinished houses. All of them were in various stages of completion. A few were only stick frames and some of them were nearly completed. Some were closer to having electrical contractors come out but still needed a ton of cosmetic work done, like paver stones, Spanish windows, and ornate glass doors. Dallas pointed to the one she thought made the most sense—one of the early phase models.

"Okay, park and c'mon. We can crash in there." The houses that just needed pavers and cosmetic work, most likely needed skilled tradesmen. Contractors who didn't take squatters lightly. But the house she picked was still being erected, which meant that mostly undocumented workers would be the only ones showing up with the sun. That meant sympathy if they got caught or at least a longer window of escape time, if necessary. The exposed pink and foil-lined puffs of insulation that showed around the entrances were what to look for. She was sure from experience the house would suit their needs.

"You want us to sleep in somebody's house?"

"It isn't anybody's house yet. Trust me, I've done this a hundred times.

We can get a few hours of sleep and be long gone before any workers show up to cause us any trouble. No one will even notice the car out here. The streetlights aren't working yet."

Nails didn't look pleased.

"C'mon, it's this, or sleeping in the car. And we just agreed that's not going to work."

"I don't know, Dallas."

"Well, I do. Now c'mon." Dallas opened her door, gathered her bag and coat, and silently made her way up the driveway. When she reached the front doorframe, she turned and waved for Nails to follow. He did. Once they were inside, he watched as she began to arrange a pallet under the front room windows from a pile of blue tarps she found. She went to work on making up an impromptu bed as if she knew exactly what she was doing. She had done this before. "Are you going to help me or what?"

Nails grabbed an old tarp and laid it on the plywood flooring, making sure to kick away any debris or loose plugs of insulation. They layered the first tarp with another one, and then used the rest of the pile to create the closest thing they could use for pillows. Dallas lay down on the uncomfortable space immediately, pushed her bag between her and the wall studs, and patted the empty space next to her. "Come lay down. I promise I don't bite."

Nails stood still as if he wasn't sure that was true. "I can—stay up a while. Take first watch."

"We don't need to take watch, Nails. We need some sleep. *You* need some sleep." She patted at the tarp again. "Now c'mon. Lay down."

Nails sat down next to her and awkwardly moved into several different positions before ending up flat on his back, his eyes fixed firmly on the rafters. He was exhausted, but this situation was making his heart pound. It was beating so hard in his chest, he was sure Dallas could hear it.

"Would you hand me that jacket?"

"What?"

"That jacket, by your leg."

Nails grabbed the canvas coat, handed it to her, and went straight back to lying stiff as a board. He tucked some of the piled-up plastic tarps under his neck and arranged them to support his head as she flung the coat over them both. She was almost able to tuck completely inside it, but it barely covered Nails's left arm. He didn't try to adjust it or pull it more to his side. He let her have as much as she needed.

Choosing that spot to arrange the pallet turned out to be perfect, the sun had set completely, and the moonlight kept the house lit with enough indigo blue for them to at least be able to see each other, and multiple ways out just in case. Dallas lay on her side, facing Nails, curled into a ball, her knees pulled up between them with her feet together. She wanted so badly to take off her shoes, but that wouldn't be very smart. If they needed to leave in a hurry, she would end up making the rest of this trip barefoot. Not that it would matter. Like most of the people she'd left behind in Florida, she walked around barefoot all the time anyway. *Grocery Store Feet,* her mother used to call it. It meant when you walked around barefoot so much that the bottoms of your feet stayed ashy black. It was so gross. When she was little, she'd have to sit on the edge of the tub and let the hot water wash all the nastiness off her feet before she could fill the tub and take a bath. Otherwise she'd have been sitting in a tubful of dark gray water. The idea that *"Grocery Store Feet"* was about as close as Dallas had to a happy childhood memory made her feel heavy and even more tired, but she still let out a giggle.

Nails lifted his head from the tarp. "What's funny? What did I do? Did I say something out loud just now?"

"No, hush. Nothing's funny. Get some rest." Dallas closed her eyes and Nails laid his head back down, still focused on the rafters and crossbeams above him.

"Why do you do that?" he asked.

"Do what?"

"You laugh for no reason and then you tell me that nothing is funny."

"I do that?"

"You did it earlier, at the park, before I left to get the car. I told you we were going to Jacksonville, and you laughed. Like you knew something I didn't. Like something was funny. But then you said nothing was funny. And you just did it again. Are you laughing at me? I can get why you'd—"

"No. Stop. I wasn't laughing at you. I laughed earlier when you said Jacksonville because it struck me as funny. I'm from Jacksonville. Well, sorta—I'm from a smaller town just south of there called Petty Branch."

"Petty Branch?"

"Yeah, where real men beat their wives and young dreams go to die."

"It was that bad?"

"Worse." Dallas attempted to lay her head on Nails's shoulder, but he pulled away.

"I told you I don't bite."

Nails sat straight up. "I'm not comfortable," he said, hoping those were the actual words that came out of his mouth and not just a string of grunts.

"Okay. Okay. I'm sorry. No touching. I get it. It won't happen again. Just lay back down. Please. You need to sleep."

"I was asking about your laugh. That's all."

"I know. I'm sorry. Lay back down."

He did. Slowly and cautiously, but he did. He went back to staring at the rafters as his heartbeat leveled out. "What about just now? When you laughed. We weren't talking about Jacksonville, but you were laughing. Was that about your hometown, too?"

Dallas smiled. "No, handsome. That time I was just thinking about my nasty-ass feet."

Chapter Twenty-Six

Nails had no idea how long he'd been asleep when he woke up to a shotgun barrel just inches from his face. He also had no idea who the man holding the gun was. What he did know was if that man pulled the trigger, that would be that. He instinctively showed the man his hands, holding them flat and palms up by the sides of his head. There was light in his eyes, too. A flashlight, maybe. But he still couldn't see anything but a large round figure above him with a lot of upper hand. The cops, Nails thought. Someone had heard them or seen them pull into this neighborhood. Maybe someone had seen the Honda parked where it shouldn't be. Parked where Dallas said to park.

Dallas.

He was suddenly aware of her absence. She wasn't lying next to him anymore. It was just him and this guy with a gun in his face.

"I don't want any trouble. I was just sleeping. I needed sleep. I was tired. But I can just go now."

The barrel of the gun didn't move, but the light in his face lowered allowing Nails to see two people in the room with him. The man with the gun—and someone else with a flashlight—and they were definitely not the police. The man holding the shotgun had a massive belly that exposed itself under a *Van Halen 1984* T-shirt. His face was covered by a thick, unkempt beard and his comb-over hadn't been combed over in a while. The man behind him with the flashlight wasn't as big and had gray in his beard but it was easy to see the family resemblance. Nails figured the gunman for the son of the less sloppy older man.

He repeated himself. "I was just sleeping. I can leave." Then his brain misfired and he added, "I don't steal . . ." He ran out of words.

The older man squatted down close to where Nails was lying. He had to pull at his jeans, and it took him a minute to get all the way down, but he managed to crouch all the way down. He shone his flashlight into Nails's face, again. "Where's your buddy?"

"Dallas? I don't know. She isn't here. I don't know where she is. She was sleeping, too."

The two rednecks exchanged a brief confused look. "I ain't asking about no girl. I'm talking about your boyfriend. Now I'm gonna ask you again. Where's your buddy?"

"I don't know what you're talking about."

Van Halen pushed the shotgun closer to Nails's face. "You need to stop playing games with us, big boy. Y'all faggots think this place is a hotel for fairies or something? Tell my daddy where the other one is before I fuck you up good."

Nails stared up at the face of the man behind the gun. He wasn't sure exactly what was happening, and he didn't know where Dallas was, but two other things became abundantly clear at that moment. He didn't like anyone who talked about people like that, and the threat this asshole just made sounded hollow. Nails had enough guns stuck in his face before now to know which ones he needed to be afraid of. He was guessing this porky bastard didn't have it in him to pull the trigger on an unarmed man, or anybody else. Nails slowly slid himself up to his elbows. Van Halen moved back a few steps. The old man groaned his way back to standing upright.

"I told you. I was just sleeping. I don't know whoever it is you're looking for. But I'm done being here now and I'm going to leave." Nails started to push himself the rest of the way up, but Van Halen leaned in again and pumped the shotgun. Nails stopped moving. Van Halen cocked his head and looked closely at Nails. "Hey, Daddy? Look at this dude. Check out his eyes. I think he's retarded."

The old man didn't answer. Dallas had let him know to shut up right before she pressed the .45 revolver against the back of Van Halen's head. "Call him that again, fat ass. Please," she said, "call him that again so I can paint this whole place with all the dumb inside your skull."

Van Halen froze and Nails thought for a second that the man might piss himself. He'd seen a lot of men like that piss themselves in situations like this one.

"Now hold up a sec . . ."

Dallas thumped Van Halen with the snout of the .45 hard enough to hurt him. "No, you hold up a sec, dickhead. Toss that shotgun behind you. Back and to the left."

"Don't worry, son," the old man said. "It's just a girl."

"You're right, you old bitch, but I'm *just a girl* with a loaded gun and a healthy respect for the Second Amendment, so trust me when I tell you I will shoot this prick and then have zero problem blowing your miserable old brains out, too."

Nails sat up a little more. "Remember to use both hands like I told you."

"I got it, handsome. Now, fucknuts, throw that shotgun behind you. Back and to the left."

Van Halen looked to his father for the final word on what to do and the old man nodded, so he tossed the shotgun back and behind him—to the right. It bounced off the wall and landed right where Dallas had been sleeping earlier. Nails sprang up and snatched the shotgun from the tarp. He moved so fast, Dallas barely saw him slam Van Halen to the ground, lay the shotgun over his left forearm, and stuff nearly a full half inch of the barrel into the soft flesh of the fat man's cheek.

"No, Nails," Dallas yelled. "Don't shoot him."

He turned to her. The look on his face was feral. Like he'd looked back at The Chute with Robbie. Like he'd looked at her in the car in Franklin when they got robbed. He was fucking scary like this.

"Don't shoot him, Nails. You don't have to shoot him. You can control it."

"You heard what he said to me, right? And the other shit. You heard him, right?"

"I did. I heard him, and he's a piece-of-shit bigot. They both are. But it's over. You don't need to kill them." She had begun to shake—wave after wave of shivers started to hit her. Her hands began to tremble so bad she almost dropped the .45 to the floor. Nails spun the shotgun around and brought the stock down hard into Van Halen's left eye. The fat man went to sleep. He was also possibly blind in that eye now, but it would be hours before he found that out, and Nails and Dallas would be long gone by then. He turned to the father and lifted the shotgun in the air.

"Wait, wait, please." He held his hands out to protect his head. "Just listen to me for a minute, please. We wasn't never gonna hurt you. Not after knowing what was really going on. This here is our neighborhood. Me and my boy there was just looking out. We've had some trouble back in here a few times. We caught a couple pillow-biters back here a few weeks back. Had to teach them a lesson. We thought y'all was like that. And you know. We can't have that kinda shit going on. This is a nice community. We had you two all wrong. Please don't hurt me. Please. I'm real sorry it got outta hand like that."

Nails slowly lowered the shotgun. "Pillow-biters?"

"Yeah, you know. Homos."

Dallas was cradling her knees on the floor next to the door. She'd set the gun down on the floor but glared at the old man.

"And I'm real sorry for the way I acted toward you, too, young lady. It wasn't right. I mean, we're really all on the same team here, you know?"

Nails looked down at the man.

"The same team?"

"Yeah, you know, God-fearing folks. Not like the trash we're trying to keep out of this neighborhood."

Nails thought about Freddy. This time he brought the shotgun stock down so hard that blindness would be the least of the old man's worries. He'd probably never talk again. And the world was all the better for it.

Nails helped Dallas to her feet and steadied her. "Are you okay?"

"Yeah. I'm just shaky. I should eat something."

"Where did you go?"

"I had to go pee. They must've saw me outside or something. I'm sorry."

"Don't be sorry. You saved me. I owe you."

"Not even close, handsome. Not even close."

Chapter Twenty-Seven

When Alex Price walked into Tuten's Chute, he stood inside the door and took the place in as if he were the local fire inspector. He stood with his hands in his pockets and examined the painted black plywood walls and the open-raftered ceiling. He studied the bar area, taking careful inventory of all the exits. Alex imagined that the main structure had been a barn that had been later fortified to allow for backwoods parties. From there it was added onto and evolved into an actual business. A business that he assumed thrived only at night, judging from the fact that now, during the day, there were only three people inside other than himself. Of course, that meant only three he could see, but he felt relatively safe since he wasn't there to cause any trouble anyway—and he'd also provided safeguards.

He crossed the floor to the bar, cutting through about half a dozen round tables. He nodded to a white man with massive biceps sitting at one of them eating chicken wings out of a Styrofoam clamshell. "Sup, bro," the man said. A Black man sitting in a booth by himself with a sweaty untouched beer looked as if he might've been having a bad day, so Alex opted out of nodding to him. Besides, the man he'd come to talk to had already taken notice of Alex. He took a seat in front of Freddy Tuten.

"What can I get you?" Freddy said.

"Just a water, please."

Freddy grabbed a plastic cup from a stack and reached for the dispenser gun hanging from its cradle on the bar. Alex stopped him before he hit the button for water. "I'm sorry. Do you have any bottled water? I'd rather not drink anything that comes out of—that."

Freddy set the dispenser gun back in its holder and replaced the cup to the stack. "Nope. No swanky water here. If you want something from a bottle, friend, I suggest you order a beer."

"Friend," Alex repeated the word. "That's an odd descriptive to use on a stranger. Don't you think? We just met. Right this moment. So are we friends already—Mr. Tuten?"

Freddy sighed, not even acknowledging that this stranger knew his name. He yelled over Alex's shoulder to the man eating the wings. "Monk. I think we got us an asshole here."

Monk held up a finger as if to say, "Hold on, I'll be right there," and then wiped at the hot sauce on his mouth with a paper napkin.

Alex didn't want any part of that. He'd forgotten for a moment how far out of his element he was, so he tried to squash it. "No, wait, there's no need for that. I apologize for my lousy manners. It's just been a really hard day. May I begin again?"

"Sure," Freddy said and waved Monk off. "So what can I get you— friend?"

"I'll take whatever local IPA you have."

Freddy set a tallboy of PBR on the bar. "That it?"

"Well, no, actually. My name is Alex Price, and I was hoping that you could help me shed a little light on a situation that happened here two nights ago."

"And what situation would that be?"

"A man was killed." Alex turned and pointed over to where an unlit and apparently broken jukebox stood against the far wall. "Right over there, I believe."

Freddy eyeballed Alex. "You clearly know who I am, but do I know you?"

"No—I'm pretty sure we've never met. But I can understand why you might think so."

"And why is that?"

"The man that was killed, the man I just spoke of, he was my younger brother. We happen to look very much alike."

Freddy narrowed his eyes at Alex and the recognition set in. "I can see that. Minus the whole Sisters of Mercy bullshit."

"Well, my brother has been . . ." He corrected himself. "*Had* been known to be eccentric from time to time."

"Yeah, well, what is it you want from me? I told the sheriff everything I know already. I don't see what help I can be to you."

Alex took a sip of the Pabst Blue Ribbon and immediately decided to never make that mistake again. He slid it away from him and Freddy grinned.

"I was only alerted to my brother's demise yesterday and I just left your sheriff's office after identifying my brother's body at the Rabun County Morgue. I came here, hoping to fill in a few of the blanks in my understanding of what happened that night. Details that not one single person interviewed by your local officials can seem to remember."

Freddy rubbed at the bar with a rag that looked dirtier than any mess he was attempting to clean up. "You say you been to Sam Flowers's office?"

"I have."

"Then, like I said, I'm sure he told you everything I know already."

"I'm sure he relayed to me everything he was *told*—but I thought that maybe you'd be able to tell me more."

Freddy tossed the bar rag into the sink. "Look, I imagine this must suck for you, that boy being your kin and all. I lost my own brother a while back, too. There ain't a day goes by I don't wish I could put my hands around the throat of the man who done it. But I can't. It's a mean world we live in, Mr. Price. It's an every-morning sucker punch I can't avoid. But I've learned to live with it—tolerate it at least—and the simple truth about what happened here the other night is that I didn't see anything. Only the aftermath of your brother on the floor there and I called the sheriff. I can't speak to anyone else's recollection, but as for me, that's all I can tell you. I do know that Sam asked around. Talked to a bunch of folks that were here. And no one else from what I heard seems to know any more than I do. But if someone comes forward with any information, I'm sure that Flowers will be in touch with you. And I hate it for you. I do. But that's really all I've got to say on the subject."

Alex nodded and wiped at the corners of his mouth. "Well, you don't know if you don't ask, right?"

"I reckon. That'll be two bucks for the beer."

Alex slowly rose to his feet and fished a thick wad of cash from the pocket of his khakis. He began to peel off hundred-dollar bills and lay them on the bar one at a time until the row of bills reached a thousand dollars. Freddy was not impressed. "I said the beer is only two bucks."

"Listen, Mr. Tuten. I can assure you that my interest in this matter is not motivated by revenge. It is purely financial. My family is wealthy. And there is a lot more money to dole out here if necessary. But I need to piece together what happened to my brother in order to get those wheels turning. This . . ." Alex motioned to the spread of cash like a blackjack dealer, "is only the beginning of the fountain of money I can send your way for a simple starting point. I can also promise you that no harm will come to the man you're protecting. I have other reasons for finding out what happened here that don't concern any of your people. You have my word on that."

"I have your word?"

"Yes, of course."

"The word of a total stranger that I've never seen around here before in my life."

"But I thought we were friends, Mr. Tuten."

Freddy laughed, leaned on the bar, and shook his head. "Look, I told you all I have to tell. So you're either thinking that a thousand dollars laid out on my bar is somehow going to trigger some unconscious memory, in which case you'd be wrong, or you think you can buy my friendship, which pisses me off. Either way, never mind the two bucks. Let's call it a toast to the dead, and then how about you put all that cash back in your pocket and get the fuck out of my bar. You're officially unwelcome here. You can leave on your own . . ."

"Or you'll call your muscle back over?"

Freddy smiled. "Oh, no. Monk can finish his lunch. I'd be happy to put you out myself." Freddy pushed his sleeves up. "You decide."

Alex stuck his hands in his pockets and exhaled. "All right then." He made no effort to collect the money. "None of that will be necessary. I can find my own way out. But if you'd just allow me to show you some-thing first."

"Nope. Not interested. Just get out and take your buddy over there with you," Freddy said.

Alex looked mildly surprised.

"Yeah, I know he's with you. We might be rednecks up here, Mr. Price, but we ain't dumb. That fella over there, who I also never seen before, and who hasn't touched his drink in over twenty minutes, is a hammer you sent in a little early just in case shit went sideways."

"I can assure you, Mr. Tuten, that Michael is not a hammer."

"Whatever. I don't care if he's your butler. Just make sure you take him with you."

The Black man in the booth stood up and straightened out his pants. Monk stood up, too, his face covered in hot sauce.

"He is not my butler, either. His name is Michael Abdullahi and he's a retired Nigerian police officer. Calling him my butler could be con-sidered an insult. That man can trace his family history back eleven generations."

"Well, then, he shouldn't have any trouble tracing himself out the fuckin' door. His beer can be on the house, too."

"Please, Mr. Tuten, I'm not here to cause any trouble. That's the truth. Just let me have one more minute of your time, and no matter what, af-terward, we'll be gone. And you can keep the money."

Freddy looked down at the spread of bills and eased off the baseball bat he'd been clutching out of sight beneath the bar. He glanced at Monk, who was doing his best to look threatening while wiping bright orange sauce from his face with a handful of napkins. "Okay, Price. One minute. The clock's ticking."

The Nigerian man approached the bar, and Freddy motioned for Monk to stay back. He also made a mental note to replace the big sloppy idiot for someone he could count on not to look like a dumbass in situ-ations like this one. Michael handed Alex a photo, and Price laid it on the bar on top of the cash for Freddy to look at. It was a four-by-four glossy photo of Alex's younger brother Robbie looking a little less Goth and laughing—alongside a girl. She was smiling, but didn't look all that happy. The photo had been taken inside a bedroom or a hotel room and most of the background had been obscured, but there was no question as to who Robbie was—or the girl. She had streaks of pink in her bright blond hair, but it was definitely the same girl. There was no mistaking that smile. She was the reason all this shit was happening right now. Freddy's face stayed true to his look of mild irritation but showed nothing else.

"Do you recognize my brother in that photo? He's the one from the other night?"

"Yeah, that looks like him."

"But have you ever seen this woman before? Was she here the night my brother was killed? Was she with him?"

Freddy picked up the picture and pretended to study it before handing it back to Alex. "Never seen her before."

"Are you sure? Please, Mr. Tuten. Look again." Alex laid the photo back down on the bar, and again Freddy pretended to look at it with a stone face.

"I'm pretty sure I'd remember her if I saw her. And I didn't. We don't get a lot of lookers in here. Especially if they ain't from around here. And your minute is also up."

"This person." Alex tapped at the photo. "She isn't just some hapless cock tease. If she was here, and this entire mess concerns her, I can promise you, Mr. Tuten, it was not an accident. In fact, I'd say that the person who killed my brother was most likely targeted—by her."

"Is that right?"

"Yes. She's a grifter and she's well versed in what she does. But I can't be sure the man no one seems to remember is one of her marks unless I know for a fact that she was here. So again, if there is anything you can tell me . . ."

"I've told you everything I can. I didn't see what happened, and I didn't see that woman. So, again, I'm sorry. But your time is up."

"All right, then. Your patience is much appreciated, Mr. Tuten." Alex began to pick the photo up, but Freddy used his pointer finger to press it back down firmly on the bar.

"Let me ask you something, though."

"Of course. Anything you think might be helpful."

"Who's that?" Freddy tapped on the edge of the picture at a sliver of shoulder that could be seen where the picture had been cut. It had clearly been a standard four-by-six photo before someone standing to the left of the girl in the picture had been sliced out of the shot. "Who's that standing on the other side of that girl?"

Alex was much less trained at keeping his facial expressions to himself. He caught Freddy's eyes. "Does it matter?" he asked.

Freddy lifted his hand. "I guess not."

And with that, Alex handed the photo back to his associate and they both left the bar. Freddy watched them leave before snatching up the grand in cash and putting it into the safe behind him. He was sure to put it in with the money that would be picked up later by someone in the Burroughs camp.

Before Alex was able to get back into the Audi he'd rented to make the trip north, a hushed whistle caused him and Michael to turn and see a short older man in a tweed newsboy hat taking a huge bag of garbage out to a dumpster. The man was waving them over and appeared to be in a hurry. Alex grinned. He was hoping this would happen. The smell of money always brought out the rats. He whispered to Michael about seeing what the little man wanted before climbing behind the wheel of the sixty-thousand-dollar sports car. "Give him whatever he wants, but make sure he sees that photo."

Michael nodded and approached Stan Moody. The little man swung his head from side to side and behind him. "Look, if you got another stack of bills in them deep pockets, I might be able to help you out with some of the shit your boss was asking about."

"Mr. Price is not my boss. I simply work with his family on matters like this one."

"Whatever, man. You got the cash or what?"

Michael reached into his pocket and pulled out a thick fold of hundreds, clinched by a silver money clip. He also took out the photo and showed it to Stan. "Was this woman here the night Robert Price was killed?"

Stan looked at it briefly and nodded. "Hell yeah, she was. Finer than fucking frog's hair, too. She's the reason Nails lost his shit."

"You are sure? This woman. She was here."

"Yeah, yeah, I'm sure, now put that away and chop-chop on the bankroll."

Michael began to count out the requested thousand, but Stan was getting increasingly nervous. "Hurry up, man. Or we could be killed. For real." He hefted the bag of trash into the dumpster and Michael held out the money. Stan didn't bother to count it. He just stuffed it into the back pocket of his pants.

"You said the man responsible is called Nails?"

"It's a nickname. The guy's real name is Nelson McKenna. He just goes by Nails. And last I heard, he was headed to Jacksonville, Florida."

"Where in Jacksonville?" Michael asked.

"Don't know, brother. Never asked. You wanted a starting point. Now you got one."

"Is the woman with him?"

"No fucking clue. I just know she was here with the dead guy and disappeared about the time Nails did, and now you know where he's going. Nice talking to you." Stan opened the side door to the bar and eased it shut behind him. Michael walked back to his own car, turned on the air-conditioning, and left the lot.

When Stan got back inside, he immediately peeked into the main bar to make sure that both Monk and Freddy were still where they had been before he took out the trash. He let himself breathe when he saw that they were. He started prepping the poolroom bar for the night as he thought about turning that fat wad in his pocket into three times that much at Buckley Burroughs's poker game after his shift. Stan was going to be high-rolling tonight for sure. He could already see it. He couldn't wait to clock out tonight. Goddamn, lady luck in some bitch-ass khakis and a fancy car just made his day. The only thing he hadn't considered was the silent alarm light that blinked in the main bar by the phone that let Freddy know every time the side door opened. The Chute was a holdover spot for a ton of Burroughs's business-related cash, so Freddy always needed to know everything. Stan was unaware of this. No one knew all the safeguards Freddy had in place to protect himself and the Burroughses. No one but him and the Burroughs boys themselves. It was the kind of information Freddy held back from degenerate gamblers with dollar signs in their eyes like Stan.

Freddy let his head hang for a moment after he saw the blinking green light. Then he stepped into his office to check the tapes, expecting the worst, hoping for anything else. When he came out, he smiled at Stan like he always did. And then, without all the details, he let Monk know what just happened. Monk tossed his chicken bones into the trash behind the bar. "You want me to go handle it now, boss?"

"No. I won't be able to find another bartender to work tonight. I'll let Gareth know after we close." Freddy stared at the wall as if he could see through it and pictured Stan Moody cutting lemons and stocking coolers, as if he hadn't just decided to kill himself.

Chapter Twenty-Eight

Once Clayton had left McFalls County and the comfort of home, he found himself headed south on Highway 76 wondering just what the hell he was doing. The hubris he'd fed Kate over the phone had all but vanished and he truly did feel like an idiot. Where did he think he was going? And for what? For whom? Was it really because he cared about his friend? Or was it because Kate had sweetened him up back at the house? For Amy, maybe, to try and soothe some misplaced guilt she'd felt after Burnt Hickory Pond almost a decade ago?

It might have been all of that. But the real reason was obvious to him. It was the same thing that had informed all his decisions throughout his entire adult life. He was doing it because of his father. But this wasn't another pointless attempt at gaining favor or proving something to the old man. Not this time. This time, it was *fuck the old man* that bounced around in Clayton's head like a loose ball bearing. Fuck him for constantly telling Clayton he wasn't good enough, or that he wasn't up to the job, or to stay out of his business. He'd been hearing it his whole life. And he was sick of it. And that shit on the roof was next-level fucked up. Did the old man think he was being subtle? What kind of father threatens violence on his own son? Gareth Burroughs did.

But even as this not-so-surprising revelation came over him, Clayton also wondered just what the hell he was supposed to do now. Amy had pointed him south toward Jacksonville on the word of her drunken uncle, but still, Jacksonville was a big place. Bigger than anywhere Clayton ever had to navigate before. Nails could be anywhere, and Clayton was a full day behind him. Nails might already have left Jacksonville by now—or worse. This whole idea was just ridiculous. Best-case scenario, he'd just drive around for a few days, stay at a hotel, maybe eat some fresh seafood, and report back to Kate that he couldn't find anything. It wouldn't be a lie. She'd get over it. And yeah, his dad would be pissed, but he'd get over it, too. None of his *business* got messed with and the only one that suffered was Clayton, who was losing a couple of days of work on the house. Clayton was sure his father didn't want to be there anyway, so no harm, no foul. That was best case. The worst-case scenario would be, by some act of God, he did pick up a trail on Nails, and then what?

Hey, Nails, buddy, please come home. Your friends that you haven't talked to in months are worried. Come home and cop to a murder that will possibly get you locked up for the rest of your life?

That was a genius idea. Clayton didn't think Nails would hurt him—although he didn't rule that out—but at the very least, Nails would tell him to go fuck himself and do whatever he was going to do anyway. This trip was truly up there at the top of all of Clayton's biggest bonehead moves. But he had given Kate his word, so he was still going to try.

He leaned over and turned the radio down low enough that he could listen to the Bronco's police scanner. His father had made him and his brothers memorize all the county police band channels within two hundred miles of Bull Mountain ever since they were kids. Clayton didn't understand why at the time, but he was always better at numbers than both his brothers, so he took a little pride at being good at something. Now, almost on instinct, he switched the dial on the unit as the counties shifted. He figured if Nails was taking a road trip, the odds of his not doing something to trip the law's radar were pretty slim. So, he hummed along to Waylon Jennings and Garth Brooks until that act of God came over the scanner at the edge of Franklin County.

Chapter Twenty-Nine

Clayton turned down "Friends in Low Places" and cranked up the scanner. He wasn't sure what he'd just heard, so he slowed and pulled the Bronco to the shoulder of the road.

An LTD. An early model Ford Galaxie LTD—bright red in color—had been used in a robbery of some gas-and-go a few miles east of where Clayton currently was. It happened yesterday, but there was an active APB out on the car and there was a deputy on the scanner double-checking the make and model. That sounded like Nails's car, but another part of what the officer on the scanner said didn't make sense. If Clayton had heard correctly through the static, there was a woman involved. The suspect wanted for the robbery was a woman. There was no way in hell, Clayton thought, that Nails McKenna would be traveling with anyone—much less a woman. Especially one who would stick up a gas station. None of that sounded right. That was the opposite of low profile, and it didn't fit Nails's MO at all. But still, what were the chances of there being two bright red old-school LTDs within fifty miles of McFalls? That had to be Nails's car.

Clayton eavesdropped on the Franklin County deputies long enough to get the address of the gas station. He looked at the map spread out on the seat of the Bronco and pulled a U-turn back onto the highway. After a series of wrong turns and corrections, he finally arrived at the station about forty-five minutes later, but he just crept by without stopping. The last thing he wanted was to run into the local law he'd just been listening to. His Bronco had a McFalls County tag and if the local cops had that same info on the LTD, he didn't want to end up getting into a conversation he couldn't get out of. His lying skills weren't all that sharp and he was supposed to be out here saving, not snitching. His last name alone would be reason enough to lift a local sheriff's eyebrow. When he circled back around for a second time, he was sure there were no cop cars in the lot. In fact, there were no cars other than a small wreck of a teal Toyota pickup. Clayton pulled up next to the ugly truck, checked his hat in the rearview, and went inside the store.

The inside of the gas station looked like any other. A few rows of chips and candy, some groceries and household essentials, and a spin-rack of comic books and magazines. Everything from *Swamp Thing* to *Better Homes and Gardens*. The whole place smelled like Pine-Sol as if the floor had just been mopped end to end. He stood in front of the register and spun the display of cheap plastic sunglasses. The counter had a locked case of cheaply made knives on it and a gallon-sized mayonnaise jug that had been repurposed into a collection jar. Donations for a local family in need. Behind the counter, an old man in a US ARMY T-shirt kneeled by a set of sliding cabinets and loaded cartons of cigarettes into them from a cardboard box.

"Hello?" Clayton said, and then said it again before the old man heard him and looked up.

"Oh, my goodness. I do apologize." The old man got to his feet and both his knees popped as he stood. He had a kind face and a slow manner. He smiled at Clayton. "Can I help you?"

Clayton took out his wallet and asked the old man for a pack of Camel Lights and a lighter. The old man rummaged through the shelves below him until he found the right brand and asked Clayton if he wanted a particular color from the rack of Bic lighters.

"No sir, dealer's choice."

"Alrighty then." He removed a yellow lighter from the rack and slid it along with the pack of smokes across the counter. "Will that do it for you?" he asked as he punched the prices into the register.

"Well, no," Clayton said, "I was actually hoping you could tell me a little about the robbery that happened here yesterday morning."

The old man picked up a cheap pair of glasses. He put them on and gave Clayton a once-over. "Are you with the police, son? Because I already done told them what I know."

"No sir, I am not."

"Then do you mind me asking what's your interest in all that?" The old man hadn't stiffened at all at the mention of the robbery. The smile hadn't left his face and his tone stayed as warm as the afternoon air. All of that seemed odd to Clayton, considering that the place had just been robbed twenty-four hours ago. And by what he heard on the scanner, it had been at gunpoint. Most people would have at least taken a day off, but for this old-timer, it was just another Monday afternoon. He still came to work, and he still mopped the floor. Business as usual.

"Were you the one working when your store was robbed?"

"I was. This is my place. Ain't got no other employees. It's just me now ever since my Martha passed." The way the old man's eyes seemed to sadden but his smile remained endeared him to Clayton even more.

"Well, you don't seem all that shook up about it."

"And what would be the point in that?" the old man said. "I knew the minute that girl walked in that there wasn't no way she was gonna hurt me. Sometimes you can just tell things about people. You know how you can just tell things about people?"

"Yessir. I suppose so."

"Ain't no supposing. They either are or they ain't worth a damn and that poor thing wasn't nothing I needed to get all riled up about. She was a little lost maybe, but not a lick of bad intention."

"She did rob you, yeah?"

"Hell, son, I would've given her the money if she would'a just asked, but there wasn't no way for her to know that. Not in this day and age. And why would she? I'm just some old geezer. Most old geezers can't stand young people. So I understood it."

"I heard she pointed a gun at you, though."

The old man waved a hand in the air as if he was shooing away a fly. "That girl wasn't going to shoot me. I doubt she'd ever even held a gun before. She could barely hold it up straight. I told you, she seemed like a nice girl, and nice girls don't go shooting old men over a few hundred dollars and some groceries."

"If it wasn't such a big deal, then why even bother calling the police?"

"Honestly, I hated that I had to, but it was the gas. That fuel out there is regulated. Her and that fella she was with drove off without paying for the stuff and the state insists that I gotta keep a log on that sorta thing to keep my insurance and business license. I fail to report a robbery and I could lose my license and then I could lose this place. And it don't look like much but it's about all I have left. Martha and I opened this place together right after I got out of the service and made it work for nearly forty years. Then we lost our daughter, Jenny, to a house fire. A year later, almost to the day, the cancer took my Martha—so I didn't have no choice but call the law. The day I lose this place is the day I lose the one thing I still have left."

Clayton rubbed at his itchy chin. He admired how this old fella was able to keep a genuine smile on his face, although he'd clearly taken some major hits in his life. Clayton imagined that's what a lifetime of content-ment looked like. Even if it was mixed with heartache. He didn't get to see much of the former on the mountain—but plenty of the latter. "Did you get a look at the man she was with?"

"I did."

"Can you tell me what he looked like?"

"Son, you said you ain't the police but you still ain't told me what business this is of yours?"

Clayton ran through a rapid cycle of lies that he could tell the old man but was convinced the old-timer would be able to see through every one of them, so he decided just to tell the truth. "The man driving the car might be a friend of mine. And if it was him, I believe he's in a lot more trouble than he can handle. I'm trying to find him before some-thing worse than this happens. I'm afraid that's about all I can tell you."

The old man studied Clayton for a good long time, peering at him over his crooked glasses. "Are you looking to hurt that little girl?"

"Sir, I don't even know who that girl is or why she'd even be with my friend. He's always been kind of a loner. That's why I'm asking if you could tell me what the man you saw looked like. It might be possible that it was just two other people in a similar car."

The old man looked satisfied with that answer and settled himself onto a stool behind the counter. "He was a big ol' fella. Thick as a Redwood and just as tall. Baldheaded, and there might've been something wrong with his hand. It looked swollen or something. I couldn't really tell from in here. That sound like your friend?"

Clayton nodded and scratched again at his fresh beard. "Yes, sir, it does. That's him."

"Is he a bad man? Is that girl in trouble being with him?"

Again, Clayton went with the truth. "I don't know. But I can tell you that my friend would never hurt a woman. In fact, looking out for one is what got him in the mess he's in right now."

The old man just sat and rubbed at the aluminum counter. He looked content with that answer, too.

Clayton adjusted his hat. "Any idea where they were going? Did the girl mention anything to you? Anything at all."

"Look, I'll tell you everything I told the police. The red car pulled up. I heard the fuel bell ring, so I cut on the pump. The girl come in looking for a bathroom and I give her the key. The customer bathroom's outside to the left. Right about that same time, Jack Comey come in and paid for the fuel he and his brother put in that ridiculous green Mustang of theirs, and I went about my business over there by the coolers." He pointed back to a row of beer coolers that lined the back wall of the store. "A few minutes later, that young girl come back in to return the key. Set it right there on the counter. She put on a pair of sunglasses from that rack right next to you and asked me if we had any medical supplies."

"Medical supplies?"

"That's right. I asked if she was hurt or anything like that, but she said no, that she needed them for someone else. I didn't figure it for your friend, the driver, either. That fella looked just fine out there pumping gas, but I wouldn't swear to it. Anyhow, just after I rang her up and opened the register, she pulled out a revolver that looked like it weighed more than she did. She stood there all shaky-like and tried her best to keep it pointed at me while she told me to please put all the money I had in the drawer into her purse. I told her she didn't have to do all that, but she insisted, and a gun is a gun, so I wasn't about to argue."

"How much did she take?"

"Oh, I don't know. Four hundred bucks. Maybe less. But that ain't what matters. I'll tell you what does, though. After I gave her the money—

she said thank you and that she was real sorry—but not for taking my money—but about my losin' Jenny and my Martha. I must'a been jaw-jackin' about them. I tend to do that a lot, and that girl, well, she must'a been listening. Remembered both their names. Now what kinda criminal does that?"

"She said thank you?"

"Yes, she did. And then she promised she'd pay me back and I believed her."

"The woman robbed you at gunpoint and you're talking about her like she just walked in and asked for a hug."

"Listen, boy, I've got a twelve-gauge back here just a few inches from where my hands are at this very moment. There's also a Beretta M9 tucked under this shirt that I could pull on you before you had time to tip your hat. And my Martha's little .22 is still sitting in there beneath the till. I could've went down the other side of the road with that girl anytime I wanted to, and it wouldn't have been the first time I'd done it that way, either. I told you, I been here forty years and I've seen every type. So, I wouldn't normally think twice about putting a hollow point or a load of rock salt up the ass of a man trying to take what ain't his to take. But the truth is, this was different. I really felt like she needed it. Not that she wanted to take it, but that she honestly needed it. A lot more than I did."

Clayton became hyper-aware of just how charming this old man was. He wasn't just some old fool with a big heart. He had the upper hand on anyone who rolled through that door and Clayton found it disarming that he was just now realizing it.

"Anyway, after all that nonsense was over, she went to looking all around like she was confused about what to do next. That's how I knew for sure that I'd called it right. She wasn't trouble. She was *in* trouble. So, I told her I'd lay down here on the floor and count to a hundred before I got up and called anybody."

"Wait, you offered to get on the floor? She didn't tell you to?"

"Son, I don't think you're hearing me too good. I told you. She wasn't no good at robbin'. It was clear. So I helped her along as best I could. I even used Mississippi's when I counted."

Clayton couldn't help the laugh that escaped his belly. "And that's it?

You laid on the floor and counted from one-Mississippi to a hundred-Mississippi?"

"I did. And when I stood up, they were gone. I figured they'd gotten a decent ways away and that's when I thought about the gas logs an all—and my license—and my family—so I went ahead and called the sheriff. Like I said, I had to."

"And that's all you can remember?"

"That's all that happened, son." The old man took his glasses off and set them back on the register. "Did you still want these cigarettes, or was this just a bullshit reason to come and ask me all this?"

Clayton took a second to pull his head away from the story the old man had just told him. "Oh, right. Yes. Yessir. I'll still take them." Kate hated when he smoked and so he didn't—around her, anyway. But he wasn't going to be around her for a while, so he figured what the hell? He paid the man what he owed, thanked him, and turned to walk out. He stopped short of the door. "Excuse me, sir. Can I ask you one more thing?"

"Not your final approach?" the old man said.

Clayton had no idea what that meant so he ignored it. "You mentioned someone else had come in the store to pay for gas."

"That's right. Jack Comey."

"If you know this Jack Comey fella well enough to know his full name, he must be a local."

"Yup. Him and his brother Melvin live up Fran Farmer Road. Their deddy passed a few years back and now they got themselves a little auto shop business you can find in any phone book. Those two boys can get a little mouthy sometimes but they're harmless enough. Good people. You ain't gonna find too many folks out here that ain't."

"Right. Do you think my friend and these Comey brothers might've talked to each other?"

"It's possible. Like I said, they can both be kinda mouthy, so it's likely they'd chat up a stranger at a gas pump."

"Did you tell the police that? About that possibility?"

The old man gave Clayton a crooked grin. "They didn't think to ask."

Clayton smiled back as he pushed open the door. "I appreciate the help, sir."

"Just do me a favor. If you find your friend. You do your best to look out for that little girl, too. She struck me as someone who could use a few more people in the world on her side."

"I'll do what I can, sir."

The old man nodded and went back to stocking cigarettes and sleeves of Skoal under the counter. Clayton sat in his truck and found Fran Farmer Road on the map, and then he walked over to the pay phone by the road. He flipped through the yellow pages in the phone book until he found what he needed. The address for Comey Automotive.

Florida

Side Two

Chapter Thirty

After tying up the unconscious neighborhood watch duo with a length of electrical cord, Dallas fished out their wallets and car keys. She chucked both sets of keys into the backyard and met Nails at the Honda. He tossed their newly acquired shotgun into the trunk and within minutes they were southbound.

Jacksonville was about a four-hour drive from where they were, and they hoped that adrenaline alone would fuel the trip. No more stops. No more chances or close calls like this one. Dallas went through both wallets and giggled a little to find out that the father was a retired police officer, but this time she explained her laughter to Nails so he wouldn't dwell on it the whole trip. That information didn't seem to bother him that much. Most of the police he knew were scumbags. It tracked.

Dallas reached into her handbag, took out her pills, and dry-swallowed another one. Nails noticed but didn't say anything. She knew she'd have to explain that eventually. She'd been careful so far not to take her pills in front of him but felt that this time she had no choice.

Seeing the awkward expression on her face, Nails reached into his pocket and pulled out his own medicine bottle. He chewed up two hydrocodone tablets and looked at Dallas. They both chuckled.

"Aren't we a pair?" she asked.

"I reckon. I take these for my leg. What are yours for?"

Dallas looked down at the pill bottle in her hand. "My sanity, I guess."

Nails left it at that, and Dallas stuffed her mixtape cassette into the Honda's tape deck. She knew that the Honda having a cassette player didn't play into Nails's decision to take that particular car, but it made her feel good to think so. So she kept the volume at a moderate level and forced him to endure The Sundays' version of "Wild Horses." Nails didn't complain.

They arrived at the Sunshine Palace in Jacksonville just before noon. Dallas got excited because the sign outside boasted FREE HBO AND VCRS IN EVERY ROOM. She knew there would be time to kill before Nails had to handle whatever business he had to handle, so at least she'd be able to keep herself entertained.

Nails pulled the Honda into the parking lot and told Dallas to stay put in the car. He went inside and, of course, she followed right behind him. A leathery woman wearing a green plastic visor and a yellow romper slid the rolling office chair up to the counter. "What can I do you for?"

"I need a room."

"How many nights?"

"I don't know."

"The weekly rate is two hundred plus the deposit."

Nails thought it over. He'd need Dallas's money.

The woman behind the counter gave him a good eye-fucking and then turned to Dallas, who was admiring the wall-sized shelf full of movies on VHS. "Oh, my God," she said. "Are these all for rent?" She snatched a copy of *Pump Up the Volume* from the rack. "I fuckin' love this movie."

"We're on the honor system here, darlin'. Take one and either leave it in the room when you go or return it to the office for another. Two out is the maximum. Just write 'em down here on the list next to your room number." She motioned to a small notebook held to the counter with some duct tape and twine. "You don't return 'em and your boyfriend here is going to pay for them out of the deposit."

Dallas clutched the movie to her chest and went back to searching for her second choice.

"So how many nights was that for, young man?"

Nails repeated himself. "I don't know. Just one, I guess. If I need more, I'll let you know."

"Fair enough." The woman slid a clipboard across the counter for Nails to fill out a registration form. He stared at it for a moment while the old woman watched and began to understand. "You want maybe your friend over there to fill it out for you, sweetie?" She slipped into that familiar syrupy tone of voice that Nails had endured his entire life—as if she were speaking to a five-year-old.

Dallas didn't give him a chance to answer. She set copies of *Pump Up the Volume* and Tim Burton's *Batman* on the counter and then grabbed the pen that was connected to the clipboard by a chain. She filled in the dates and times correctly but wrote their names down as Bruce Wayne and Vicki Vale. She slid it back around to the woman. "How much?"

"How many nights, sweetie?"

"Ummm, let's start with two."

"Okay, two nights plus the deposit is gonna be eighty-five."

Dallas handed over the cash from the roll of robbery money in her bag and told the old woman to keep the change. The old woman adjusted her visor and slipped the entire amount down deep somewhere into the front recesses of her romper. "You'll be in room 129. It's only the one bed, but the sofa is foldout just in case you need it."

"Thank you, ma'am."

"And don't forget the checkout log for your movies."

Dallas scribbled the titles into the tattered notebook, and then snatched up the movies and the key to the room. A few minutes later, she and Nails were behind the relative safety of the Sunshine Palace's four walls. Dallas headed straight for the bathroom. Nails picked up the phone. He double-checked the phone number for Wilcombe in his fanny pack and dialed. He hadn't even finished punching in the digits before he heard the busy signal. He tried again and got the same thing. He smacked the phone against the tabletop.

"What's going on?" Dallas yelled from the bathroom.

"The damn phone is broken."

"Try dialing nine first."

"What?"

"Just dial nine and then wait for the tone and try your number again."

Nails didn't understand the point, but he did it and it worked. He sat down on the bed as the phone rang in his ear.

"Mr. McKenna?" said a British voice.

"Yeah."

"Your room number?" This time the fancy man was all business and Nails was fine with that.

"One twenty-nine."

"At exactly eight p.m., a man by the name of Pinkerton Sayles will be there to pick you up. He will bring you to an establishment I own, and you will be given all the information you need to put this predicament behind you."

"Why can't you just tell me what I need to know right now? Or have your pink friend talk to me here? Why do I need to go anywhere else?"

"Mr. McKenna. I don't conduct business on the telephone, and I certainly don't speak freely in environments I cannot control. My man, Pinkerton, will pick you up at eight p.m. sharp. And we will handle this the way things like this are handled. These are the terms. Do you agree to them or not?"

Nails squeezed the receiver. "Eight p.m. I'll be here."

"Excellent," the British man said, and ended the call. Nails looked at the digital alarm clock next to the phone. It was 11:30 a.m. Less than nine hours until the next part of this nightmare kicked in. But at least he had company.

Dallas wasn't in the bathroom long before the door swung all the way open. Her hair was brushed, and she'd washed all the smeared mascara off her face. Her faded denim eyes were a brighter blue without all the black war paint around them. "Come in here," she said and motioned for Nails to join her.

"For what?"

"Will you just come here," she asked a second time. Nails walked to the bathroom and saw that she had set several fresh packages of gauze and a bottle of hydrogen peroxide on the edge of the tub. "Ta-da," she said. "Now off with those pants, mister, and let's clean up that leg before it gets infected."

"Where did you get all that stuff?"

"From the gas station back in Franklin. That sweet old man hooked me up."

"The sweet old man you robbed."

"Well, yeah, but honestly, I don't think he minded all that much. He was super-nice about it. Besides, that's not the point. Let's have a look at that leg."

"I can do it myself."

"Don't be silly, I can—"

"I said I can do it myself." Nails raised his voice more than he wanted to.

"Okay, okay. Have at it."

Nails turned to leave.

"Wait, where are you going?"

"To the car. I've got some clean clothes out there I took from the LTD."

"Okay, well, at least let me go get that stuff. You handle your leg and get cleaned up. And I'll go get your shit."

Nails didn't look like he cared for that idea either, but Dallas convinced him. "And when you're done?" Dallas picked up the copy of *Pump Up the Volume* from where she'd laid it on a small coffee table by the door. "It's Christian Slater time. We'll start with this one and then we can watch *Batman*. Cool?"

"Okay," Nails said. He shook his head and watched Dallas practically bounce her way out the door. He didn't have the heart to tell her that Burton's *Batman* was total shit or that he had no idea who Christian Slater was.

Chapter Thirty-One

There was no visible signage on the road, so Clayton passed by the address several times. Finally, he was able to read the numbers on one of the beat-to-shit mailboxes. The gravel drive leading down to the Comey place was thin and winding, and the overhanging thicket looked like it hadn't been maintained in years. A sedan-sized car, or something low to the ground, might've been able to make it through unscathed, but Clayton cringed every time he felt one of the sharp limbs scraping against the top and sides of his fiberglass roof. He immediately regretted turning the Bronco in. He'd be buffing scratches from the paint for weeks. The drive opened into a yard of mostly red dirt with patches of sawgrass, weeds, and endless veins of kudzu entangling everything. It turned out that the family auto shop wasn't an actual auto shop by any stretch of the imagination. It was a mildew-covered single-wide trailer about fifty feet off the main road with a faded tin sign emblazoned with the COMEY AUTO logo nailed to the siding. A rust-covered engine lift with heavy chains stood under a rickety carport off to the left of the trailer, and the whole place reeked of motor oil and gasoline. The one odd-looking standout on the property was a gorgeous fully restored 1969 Mustang Mach 1 parked under another small awning. The car had enough metal flake mixed into the dark green paint to make it shimmer in the shade. Clayton parked his truck, got out, and knocked on the front door of the trailer a few times, but no one answered. There was a plastic CLOSED sign behind the small Plexiglass window that looked like it hadn't been flipped to the OPEN side in decades. He couldn't hear anything or see anyone moving inside so he figured he'd wait awhile in the Bronco. He got back in the truck and lit up one of the Camel Lights. The smoke burned his throat and made him gag. He coughed and hacked a good-sized loogie out the window. Next came the head rush, and he felt ill. That's what he got for thinking he'd get one over on Kate. He pinched out the fresh cherry of burning ash and tossed the cigarette out the window. Damn that shit.

He sat in his truck long enough for his stomach to start grumbling and he looked through the console for some of Kate's Nekot cookies. He came up empty, wishing he'd have gotten some snacks back at the gas-and-go instead of the pack of Camels. The second time his stomach rumbled, he decided it was time to leave and find a Waffle House somewhere, get himself a plate of scattered and covered hashbrowns. He'd see about catching these boys at home in a few hours. He didn't know what he was going to find out anyway. And there was no telling if they'd be back here today or ever. Clayton hadn't gotten fifty yards down Fran Farmer Road before he passed a primer gray custom F-150 headed in the other direction. He didn't see who was driving, but he did notice a massive brown box, taller than the cab of the truck, strapped down in the center of the bed. Clayton also watched in the rearview mirror as the truck slowed and turned down the same gravel driveway he'd just come off of. It looked like his dinner could wait. It looked like the Comey brothers had made it home.

He found a place to turn around and headed back. But this time he didn't turn down the drive. His truck had endured enough damage already. He figured he'd rather walk instead of having to pay to get his truck completely repainted. He pulled over to the side of the road by the warped metal mailboxes, grabbed his Stetson from the seat, and walked back down the drive.

By the time he'd gotten to the front yard, the boys had the F-150 backed up directly to the front door of the trailer with the tailgate down. One of the brothers, the younger one, was standing in the truck bed trying to help the older brother unload the big box. The one in the doorway was hollering up into the truck for his little brother to be "fucking careful."

"I am, damn. But this thing is crazy-heavy, dude."

"Just ease it off the tailgate. I got it. When I tell you to, jump down here and grab the other side."

Clayton saw them having trouble with the box from Circuit City labeled *Sony LT50* so he yelled out to see if they needed help. "Hey, fellas. That thing looks pretty heavy. You need a hand?"

The kid in the truck flinched at the sound of Clayton's voice and lost his grip on his end of the box. It slid down and dented a corner on the concrete stoop. "Goddamn it, Jack," the older brother yelled before slowly setting the box down and facing Clayton.

"Damn. I'm sorry. I was just trying to help. What is that? One of those big-screen TVs?"

Melvin ignored the question. "Can we help you with something, mister?"

"Yes, actually. I'm out here looking for Jack and Melvin Comey. Would y'all be them?"

"That's right. I'm Melvin Comey. But sorry, bud, we're closed for the day."

"Oh, I don't need a mechanic. I was just hoping to get some information."

"Information about what?"

"I just left the gas-and-go up the road off Highway 76. And the old man that works there told me you might've run into a friend of mine when y'all were out there yesterday."

"A friend of yours?"

"Yeah, he's a big guy. Bald. Drives a red Ford Galaxie. Him and his car should be easy to remember."

Melvin looked pensive and rubbed at his chin. He finally shook his head. "Nope. I mean, yeah, we was up there yesterday, but I can't say I remember seeing anybody who fits that description. We must'a not been there at the same time."

Clayton slid his hat back. He didn't take that old man back there as a liar, so he supposed that Melvin Comey must be. "Are you sure? Because the owner said you were. He said you paid for your gas, or rather, your brother paid, and then left right before they did."

"Old-ass Owen told you that?"

Clayton shrugged. "I reckon that's his name. I didn't catch it. But he was pretty positive that you were there at the same time. He even described your car." Clayton motioned toward the Mustang but watched for Melvin's reaction. He puffed out his chest.

"Look here, buddy. I ain't got the slightest idea what you're talking about. And Owen's older than dirt and blind as a bat, so I wouldn't doubt he got it wrong. So like I said, we're closed up today. It might be best that you go on now and get off our property."

Clayton glanced over at Jack Comey, still standing in the bed of the truck, unsure of what to do or say. Clayton put his eyes back on Melvin, and then slowly leaned down and set his Stetson on a cluster of sweetgum tree stumps. That hat was pricey—and a gift from Kate. He didn't know what was about to happen, but he did know he didn't want to get that Cattleman dirty. He straightened back up. "Listen, I didn't come out here looking for any trouble, Mr. Comey. I'm just trying to find a friend. Now, I know you were there. So, just be straight with me. Did you speak with him or not?"

"I done told you. I ain't seen no bald guy, no blond girl, or no LTD, neither."

Clayton narrowed his eyes. "I just said it was a Galaxie. I didn't say it was an LTD."

Melvin took a step closer. "I just figured. I'm a Ford man. That's all. I assumed."

"I also didn't say anything about no blond girl."

All pretense melted away, and Melvin knew he'd just stepped in it. He took a clumsy swing at Clayton, who sidestepped it and grabbed the man's hand. He twisted it hard to the left and used the torque of Melvin's own body weight to force him to his knees. Clayton pivoted and twisted Melvin's arm up and behind him, pushing him forward, forcing him to use his other arm to keep from lying facedown in the dirt. That was a move both of Clayton's brothers had used on him growing up more times than he could count. This was also the first time Clayton had ever done it to someone else. He surprised himself.

"Like I said, dickhead. I ain't looking for any trouble, and I'm not sure what the hell is happening here, but I'm damn sure you saw my friend yesterday afternoon. And the only reason you'd lie about it is if you had something to hide. So tell me what went down. And tell me now."

Melvin did nothing but yell for Clayton to let him go. Honestly, Clayton didn't know what to do next. He had the upper hand but felt foolish. If he hadn't seen the shadow of the spade shovel on the ground, he would've felt even worse. He might've gone down. He might've gotten his skull cracked open or even been killed. But he did see the shadow cross over the dirt and sawgrass, so he shifted himself just in time for Jack Comey to hit him in the shoulder instead of his head. Clayton's vision went white, and the pain rushed through his entire right side. He let go of Melvin's arm, lost his balance, and then stumbled a couple of feet to regain it. Jack, who looked scared shitless, took too long before deciding to swing a second time, so this time Clayton was ready for it. He caught the shovel by the handle and yanked the whole thing out of the boy's hands. He drew it back to swing at Jack, but the kid ran and took cover behind the F-150. Clayton turned and managed to stop Melvin as the older brother rushed him. Clayton clocked Melvin in the temple with the concave side of the shovel, knocking off his skullcap. Melvin dropped to his knees like a scarecrow cut loose from its post. Clayton rubbed his shoulder where he'd been hit and then jabbed the tip of the spade shovel into Melvin's armpit and used it to force him down flat on the ground. He pushed the shovel down into the dirt enough for it to cut into the soft flesh of Melvin's arm. He spoke as he struggled to catch his breath. "What do you know about my friend? What did you two dipshits do? Tell me what I want to know, or I swear to God I'll cut your fucking arm off."

"Kiss my ass, Ginger. We ain't done nothing."

Clayton applied more force and sank the spade down deeper in the dirt, cutting deeper into the skin of Melvin's armpit. Melvin screamed and grabbed at the handle with his free arm, but still didn't have anything else coherent to say.

"Hey, Jack? You listening? I'm about to cut your brother's arm off. You hear me? Come out here and show yourself." Clayton knew it was another stupid move, playing chicken with someone he couldn't see. The kid might've been inside loading a rifle or aiming a handgun out the window at that very second, but Clayton was gambling that the kid was even more scared than he was. So he kept up the bluff. "You hear me, Jack Comey?"

The gamble paid off. Jack came back around the truck slowly with both hands in the air. He was holding a canvas bank deposit bag in one of them. "Here man, we're sorry. We should've never took it. It was wrong. We spent some of it on the TV and a little more on a bottle of Johnnie Walker Blue and a bucket of Popeyes. The chicken's all gone but the bottle is in the kitchen if you want that, too. Just please don't hurt my brother no more. Please. Here—take it." The kid crept forward with his head down and held the bank bag out in front of him. Clayton snatched it, adjusted himself for leverage on the shovel and unzipped it. The bag was full of cash. A lot of it. Thousands.

"You stole this from Nails?"

"If you mean the big bald dude in the LTD, then yeah. Shit, man, he was just sitting in the car with that girl talking about all the money he had, all loud and shit, and then he just walked away. It was almost like he wanted us to take it."

Clayton stared at the money. These two idiots had robbed one of the most dangerous men in North Georgia. Did they want to walk with a limp for the rest of their lives? But then he thought about it. *No. Nails was one of the most dangerous men in McFalls County. This was a small town in Franklin, not McFalls. They might have heard of the Burroughses, but would have had no idea who Nails was.* He stared at the money in his hand. *But they did leave him broke.* The pieces fell together like a jigsaw puzzle in Clayton's head. *That's why the girl—whoever she is—robbed the old man. Because these two dipshits robbed them.*

Wait. The girl.

"Who is the girl he was with? What do you know about her?"

"Nothing, man, only that she was foxy as all get-out. They showed up there together and we left them there together. I swear, man."

"Did she look like she was in trouble? Like she was being held against her will?"

Jack looked confused. "Nah, man. We figured she was the dude's girlfriend. I mean, it didn't make no sense to me, him being all— retarded—or whatever he is—but to each his own, right?"

Clayton used his thumb to flip through the bills in the bank bag.

"Listen, sir. We did a bad thing, and we know it, but we ain't bad people. Please just take it and let my brother go."

"Right, you and your brother here are just good country people. Ripping off strangers, calling them retarded, suckering folks with shovels. Got it."

"We're real sorry, mister."

"Whatever. Do you have any idea where they went?"

"No, sir. We didn't talk all that much."

"You didn't hear him mention anything to the girl, or her to him? Anything at all about where they were headed?"

"No, sir, I swear to God. I didn't hear them say shit. Only him talking about his money. He even said that he didn't really need it. Please just let my brother up."

Clayton stood silent and thought about what to do. He looked down at Melvin. "If my friend knew where you were right now, he'd have already come here and hurt both of you for stealing from him. So I'm guessing since that hasn't happened, he doesn't know where you are, so for the moment, you're safe." Clayton eased the shovel out of the dirt and off Melvin. He tucked the bag of cash in his pants. "Unless of course, I let him know where to find you. Then everything goes real bad, real fast, for you both. Nails is not the forgiving type."

Melvin inched away from Clayton on his elbows.

"So here's what's going to happen. I'm going to leave, and you two are going to stay right where you are. If either of you tries to follow me up that drive or decides to take a shot at me before I get to my truck and drive outta this dump, I *will* find my way outta here anyway. And I *will* find my friend. And I will aim him right at this place—like a fucking missile. Do you understand me, Jack?"

The kid nodded. "Yes, sir. We'll make it right. You want me to go get the Johnnie Blue to take with you?"

Clayton almost said yes but didn't. "Nah, y'all keep it. Your brother here is going to need it to numb the pain. What about you, Melvin? We tracking?"

"What about the TV?" Melvin asked from the ground.

Clayton shook his head. This guy was thinking about a TV. These two really had no idea how close they'd come to being permanently crippled. "Good luck getting it through the door," he said and tossed the shovel way out into the yard. Melvin got to his knees but stayed there.

Clayton snatched his hat off the tree stumps and cautiously backed up the drive.

"Hold up," Melvin said, and Clayton quickly took cover behind a thick yellow pine.

"My brother wasn't bullshittin'. We did a bad thing but Jack's right. We ain't bad people. Your friend—and that girl—I think—they are going to Jacksonville—down in Florida."

Clayton stepped halfway out from behind the tree. Melvin was still on the ground holding his injured arm. He didn't look anything other than dirty and defeated. "He's supposed to meet somebody. At a place called the Sunshine Inn. Tonight I think."

"And how the hell do you know that?"

"'Cause I heard him. I heard him talking about it on the pay phone, back at the station—he's kinda loud—and he kept saying it over and over."

Clayton stood in the woods to the side of the gravel drive and studied Melvin's demeanor. He was exhausted, holding his wounded arm like he'd never been hurt before. He was done fighting and Clayton was already leaving, so he had no reason to lie this time. Clayton thought about what the old man back at the gas-and-go had said about these boys, "mouthy but harmless." He called them good people. He said that's mostly who he'd find around here. He decided to believe him but used the cover of the woods to make it back up the road anyway.

Chapter Thirty-Two

Before Clayton rode out of Franklin County, he stopped back by the gas-and-go and got a couple bags of pizza-flavored Combos and a big twenty of Mountain Dew. He also picked up an atlas of the United States and a dusty map of Florida. Clayton thought he might be the first person to ever buy one of these from a gas station in North Georgia. *After all*, he thought, *who goes to Florida on purpose?* The old man behind the counter had mischief in his grin as Clayton laid the goods down on the counter but didn't even bring up their past conversation. He didn't ask about the Comey brothers, or even what the maps were for. It wasn't his business. Clayton admired the restraint in this man, as well. He put sixteen dollars and change for the travel supplies on the counter and then took the time to look at the large plastic container next to the register. The jug had a laminated photo taped to it. The picture was of a woman with silver hair smiling, with her arm around a teenage girl with golden curls that fell over her shoulders. Clayton guessed this was a photo of Owen's late wife, Martha, and their daughter, Jenny. The lettering on the jug said,

"*The Jenkins Family Fund. All Donations for the Atlanta Burn Center and the ACA.—Thank you, Owen Jenkins.*"

The fold of money that Clayton tucked into the jug was just north of six hundred dollars. The old man said nothing. He just nodded and smiled that same warm smile he wore the first time Clayton met him.

"You got a nose for people, old man. I hope you'll consider their debt paid."

The old man put the sixteen dollars and change in the register and made a point of letting Clayton see Martha's little silver .22. "She didn't owe me nothing, son. But you tell her thank you just the same."

"I will." Clayton tipped his hat and pushed open the front door. "As soon as I find out who she is."

Chapter Thirty-Three

Nails sat on the bed with his back pressed flat against the headboard and his legs stretched out in front of him. The knife wound in his thigh was sore and throbbing from the cleaning he'd just given it, but at least now it was wrapped and concealed under a fresh pair of blue jeans. He chewed a few more pills from Freddy's bottle. If he kept his mind right and his weight off that leg, no one he ran into tonight would be wise to the wound. The supplies Dallas thought to get had been a godsend. She lay next to him on her belly, using one of the motel pillows to prop her elbows on as they watched the movie she'd picked out. From what Nails could understand, it was about some nerdy high school kid who secretly operated a short-range radio out of his bedroom. His undercover radio personality was popular at school but the kid himself stayed a nerd. The whole mess complicated his life. Nails didn't get it, but Dallas seemed to have memorized every word of it. She watched and got excited from scene to scene, quoting along with every third line of dialogue. When the credits rolled, so did she, onto her back, propping herself up on her elbows. "So what did you think?"

"It was good."

Dallas looked as if she'd been slapped across the face. "Good? That's it? Just good? It's Hard Harry, man." She pumped her fist in the air. "Talk hard, Harry."

Nails almost allowed himself to smile. It was becoming a habit, fighting back the relaxation. Dallas sat all the way up and Nails realized that he hadn't wrapped his left hand back up. He hadn't thought to. He was becoming too comfortable around this woman. His scarred-up knuckles and webbed fingers were on full display. He quickly shuffled them under the stiff sheets of the motel bed.

"Hey," Dallas said and slid over closer to him, crossing her legs like a child sitting on the floor of a third-grade classroom. "What's the story with that hand?"

Nails didn't want to have this conversation. People who knew him better knew not to ask. And even after these past few days together, the familiarity he was beginning to feel toward this woman still didn't shield him from the unease her constant questions brought on.

"There's no story."

"C'mon. It's me. There must be a story. Don't be embarrassed. Just tell me."

Nails stiffened his back. "I'm not embarrassed. There is no story. I was born this way. There wasn't any accident. I didn't hurt myself. Nothing happened to it. I was just born with it. I was born with it, and I deal with it. Why do you feel like you can just ask me whatever you want to? It's none of your business anyway."

"Damn. You don't need to get all shitty like that with me. So you were born with a messed-up hand. Big deal. It could be a lot worse, believe me, I'd know. You need to start focusing on the positive. You can be the biggest Debbie Downer sometimes."

"I wasn't being shitty."

Dallas rolled her eyes. "Never mind. I'm just saying that you don't need to be such an emotional Grim Reaper, you know? Shit happens. Like your hand being messed up. You could've just said that, and let that be it. I mean, after all the stuff we've been through together, you'd think you'd trust me by now not to judge you."

"Trust you? I don't even know you. I don't know anything about you. You still act like we're in some kind of movie and we're not. I don't even know your real name. I don't know why you're here with me at all."

"Okay." Dallas held her hands up. "Just stop. I'm here because I want to be here. It's the first time in a long time I've ever *wanted* to be anywhere."

"In a motel room in Jacksonville?"

"No, dummy. In a motel room in Jacksonville—with you."

Dummy was not a word Nails allowed many people to call him, but he didn't even focus on that part of what she said. It was the other part. The part he'd never heard anyone tell him before.

"I know you find this hard to believe for some reason, but I like you, Nails. You're not like every other pathetic human being out there who only thinks about themselves. You're just not. And as far as not knowing my name? I know for a fact that two completely sane people didn't sit down one day and decide to name their baby Nails. So in all fairness, I don't know your real name either, but you don't see me getting all shitty with you about it. You said that's your name. I accept it. I accept you. Case closed." She slid back and sat on the edge of the bed and crossed her arms. "I'll tell you what. You want to know who I am? Ask me anything you want. Anything. I'm an open book."

Nails twirled his hand in the sheet. He was hungry. He didn't want to play this game.

"I'm serious, Nails. Ask me anything you want to know."

Nails thought about it and decided he did have a question. "What happened to your brother, to Riley?"

The playful smile disappeared from Dallas's face. "I meant ask me something easy."

"You didn't ask me something easy."

"Fair point." She was quiet for a moment as she allowed herself to be swept away to a place in her mind that she obviously didn't like to revisit. Nails knew that place. He had one of his own. But she pulled it together, tossed her hair back, clapped her hands together, interlaced her fingers, and laid them in her lap. "He died. Suicide. A little over a year ago. First he got sick and then he killed himself."

"Damn. I'm sorry—I mean—you don't have to tell me anything, Dallas. I shouldn't have asked."

Dallas stood up and hit the green reverse button on the VCR. "Be kind, please rewind. No, it's okay. I said you could ask me anything. I don't mind talking about him. He was my brother. I loved him. It's sad and weird, but it's okay. What else? Let's see."

Nails could hear the belligerence in her voice. This kind of loss was something he could relate to. "What kind of sick was he?"

Dallas sat back down on the edge of the bed with her back to Nails. It took her a long time to answer. "I don't know exactly what it was called. Nobody does, I think. My mom called it a brain disorder. They said he had a chemical imbalance in his brain, but despite what the doctors said about meds that could help him, you know, be normal, my mother was positive that *God* was the answer. That God was going to heal him. She actually believed that if she prayed hard enough, some ghost man in the sky was going to swoop down and make my brother better. Can you believe that shit?"

Nails could believe that. More than Dallas knew. He'd experienced plenty of that "God" nonsense when he was a kid. His own parents had tried to pray away his own disabilities. As if that was a thing.

"My dad, though. He didn't buy into any of that Jesus shit. That was my mom's bag. He just went along with it, which makes him worse. And he's a drunk. He figured that he'd just beat my brother better. When I was a little kid, he used to hit my mom a lot. Then he moved on to smacking Riley around, too. But once it got pretty obvious that wasn't going to work, he took another route. Denial. He just started pretending like he didn't even have a family at all. My dad, he owns this bar, a place called Taillights back in Petty Branch. It's a pretty hot spot, so he was there most of the time anyway, but once he found out that Riley wasn't getting any better, he practically lived at that place. He stayed at work later and later until eventually he was barely ever home. He just disappeared. Like the David freaking Copperfield of dads. Because he's a piece of shit. But me and mom, we stuck it out. Damn, I even prayed with her sometimes. She'd bring the pastor over from her church sometimes and a bunch of other pointless head doctors, too, until finally—one morning. That was it. He was gone. I woke up to see my mom sitting on Riley's bed. Crying. He was dead. End of story."

Nails sat up and put a hand on Dallas's shoulder. He fully expected her to flinch, to pull away from his touch, but she didn't. She leaned in and rested her head on his hand—his left hand.

"Is that why you left home?"

"Yeah. That same day. I know that sounds cold. But I had to. I put everything important to me—well, almost everything—in my bag, and all the money I'd made working over the summer at Video Warehouse and I left."

"What did you forget?"

The weight and sadness of telling this story caused her shoulders to slump, and she moved away from his hand. "My brother played piano. He was amazing. My mom played her whole life. She even played at our church, and we had a huge white piano in the den. When she first forced Riley to start taking lessons when he was little, he hated it so much, but he got really, really good at it. Better than mom even. And he began to love it. I swear to you, he'd light up the room when he played. He wrote his own music, too. He had notebooks of songs he'd written. Songs he wanted to—I don't know—play for people someday, like a professional. It was his dream. But after he died, I was so messed up over what happened, I didn't take any of that stuff. It doesn't matter now though. I'm sure my father burned it all by now. It breaks my heart to know that people will never hear that music, but I blew it. I left it all there."

"Maybe we could go get it? You said it wasn't far from here. Where you lived. In Petty Branch?"

"I'm never going back there. Ever."

"I'm just saying . . ."

"Nails, no. Not ever."

Nails didn't press it and quickly changed the subject. "Okay, so how did you end up at Freddy's?"

"I have an aunt who lives in Augusta, some hoity-toity golf town, so I called her and asked if I could stay there for a while. At first, she said I could, but by the time I got there, my mom had gotten in touch with her and told her what happened to Riley and so my aunt insisted that I go back home. That wasn't happening. There was no way I was going back there. So I left Augusta, too. I had zero plan and no idea where to go, so I just bought a bus ticket to Helen. You been there?"

Nails shook his head.

"Well, I'd always wanted to see the little German villages up there. I figured I'd try to get a job or something. Like a beer wench, you know?"

Nails had no idea what a beer wench was but he didn't interrupt.

"But that turned out to be a huge mistake because that's where I met Robbie. He had money, like a lot of money. And after mine ran out, he promised to look out for me. He was sweet, you know? But what looking out for me really meant was that he had a plan to share me with a bunch of his weirdo friends. So yeah, you're hanging out with a freshly minted whore."

"Dallas . . ."

"No, it's fine. No one ever hurt me that much, and honestly, at first, it was a little exciting. It was fun being on my own. Being me for a change. Until Robbie started to get mean about it. It's weird. I mean, he really was sweet to me in the beginning. I really thought he liked me for who I was. But then it all changed. He started doing a bunch of drugs with his creepy brother until they had a falling out and suddenly his money dried up, and I became his new meal ticket. He started bringing me out to clubs, trying to rent me out to strangers he'd meet. That's what led me to your neck of the woods. My job was to dance for the crowd, and he would find someone willing to pay a stack of cash for me. That's what you saw in your friend's bar that night. One of Robbie's 'transactions' and you know the rest. But Robbie slipped up. You weren't supposed to happen—but you did."

Dallas stopped talking and Nails stopped asking her anything else. He really didn't want to hear much more anyway. He was beginning to feel angry all over again with nowhere to direct it. He didn't want to feel that way. When the VCR came to a stop, and the movie ejected from the machine, Dallas slipped out from under Nails's hand and rose to her feet. She turned and faced him as she wiped away the fresh tears on her face. "Bet you didn't expect all that, did you?"

Nails couldn't look at her. He stared at his lap. And it made him feel like a hypocrite. That's what other people did to him. She deserved better.

"But now you owe me one, mister."

"What do you mean?"

"An answer. I get to ask you anything I want next. And you have to tell me without all the trepidation."

"Without all what?"

"Without getting all angry and weird and shit."

Nails didn't want to answer any questions. He didn't want to do anything now except help his friend feel better—and he was hungry, so he thought that maybe some food would help. "Can I go get us something to eat first?"

"Oh, don't worry, handsome, I'm not going to ask you anything right now. I'm going to put some real thought into it first. So you're off the hook for the time being." She wiped at her face some more with the backs of her hands. "And I could definitely demolish a cheeseburger and fries right now."

Nails stood up. "I'll go get some food."

"Okay," she said, and then did something Nails was not expecting at all. She rushed him. The hug came on so sudden that Nails didn't have time to understand and hug her back. She squeezed him tight with both arms. "I'm not a whore, Nails. I swear to you, I'm not."

Nails just stood there with his arms out to his sides. "I don't care about any of that, Dallas. It wouldn't change anything. But I'm hungry. I'm going to get us some burgers."

She laughed a little and then let go. "Take the money out of my bag. I'm going to grab a shower. I smell like a goat."

Nails thought she smelled like cherry cola lip gloss.

"Your thing is at eight, right? I heard you on the phone."

"Yeah, someone is supposed to be here at eight o'clock."

"I thought I saw a Whataburger across the street."

"Is that what you want?"

"More than anything in this world. With extra mustard, jalapeños, and a metric fuck-ton of fries."

"Okay. I'll be back in a few minutes."

Dallas walked into the bathroom and shut the door. Nails stood in the middle of the room before walking to the dresser by the wall and fishing out the roll of cash. He took out a twenty and put the rest back, grabbed the key to the room from the table by the door, and walked out. He sat in the Honda for a minute while he hotwired it, trying to remember the last time he'd gotten a hug—from anyone. He couldn't. When he was little, maybe? From his mom? He should've hugged her back. Why didn't he just hug her back? Why did everything so simple always have to be so complicated? He saw the sign for the Whataburger across the two-lane highway in the rearview mirror. He hated fast food. But that's what she wanted. So that's where he went.

Chapter Thirty-Four

When Nails returned with the sack of greasy burgers and fries, Dallas had put in the *Batman* movie and turned the volume up loud enough to hear it in the shower. He couldn't hear the water running, and the bathroom door was cracked open about an inch.

"I'm back," he shouted, setting the food down on the little table by the door and going back out to the car to get the two large Cokes. He came back in to the room, arranged the food and drinks on the table, and called for Dallas again.

Jack Nicholson bellowed from the TV. *"Have you ever danced with the devil in the pale moonlight?"*

Nails hated this movie but left the TV on high anyway. He wanted to eat but not be rude and start without Dallas. He called for her a third time, sat at the table for a few minutes as the fries began to get cold, and stared at the TV. He really hated this movie. Worse Joker ever. He also hated cold fries. He yelled over the volume one more time. "Dallas, I'm back. I got the food. Come and eat."

No answer.

Finally, he got up, crossed the room, and lightly rapped his knuckles on the bathroom door. "Hey," he said, "come and eat."

Still no answer, but the door eased open on its own, and he could see her through the steam. She stood with her back to him at the sink wearing only her bra and panties. The mirror was fogged up so she couldn't see him as she swayed to the Batdance booming from the TV. He couldn't stand that song, but somehow, at this moment, she made it work. All the curves he'd been trying to avoid looking at for days were fully exposed and on display. Her hair was wet and slicked back out of her face and she had a light sprinkle of summer freckles across her shoulder blades and back. As soon as he caught himself staring, Nails immediately dropped his head and studied the tile. He should've backed away but he couldn't move. She must've felt his presence behind her because she spun her head around and looked completely mortified. She snatched a towel from the counter to cover herself, careful to keep her back to him, before turning and pushing him back through the doorway.

"Oh my God, Nails. Knock much?" She slammed the door just inches from his face.

"The fries are getting cold." He looked at the floor. *Wow*, he thought. *That's all your idiot brain could assemble? The fries are getting cold?*

"Asshole," she yelled from behind the door.

Nails went to the table, sat down, and drank most of the Classic Coke from the large cup all at once. It was a very long time before Dallas came out and joined him. He'd already finished his food. She was wearing a little black one-piece dress that tied behind her neck and hugged the rest of her, stopping at her thighs. After she turned the TV down, she sat opposite Nails at the table, crossed her legs, and picked up a cold fry.

"So that was awkward."

"I did knock."

"Whatever." She took a bite of a fry and tossed it back down on the wax paper in favor of the cheeseburger. Cold fries did suck. In between bites, she tried to make small talk, but Nails wasn't having it. He just kept looking over at the digital clock by the bed as if he could wish it to be eight o'clock any faster. But he couldn't, so he had to face the fact that he still had a few hours left to sit in that room and picture Dallas in her panties. There was no getting around it. He couldn't look her in the eyes. But he couldn't look at any other part of her either. He couldn't think of anything to say. It was torture. Dallas finished about half of the double cheeseburger before wrapping it back up in the wax paper, standing up, and making everything worse.

"I know it's not as hot as me in my skivvies," she said as she spun around in a circle and held her arms up. "But what do you think? I let the steam from the shower iron out most of the wrinkles. There's still a few." She pulled at the spandex fabric clinging to her hips. "But I don't think anyone will notice. Can you believe this whole dress can squish down to the size of my fist? I wish I had better shoes, but I bet we can find some black flip-flops somewhere between here and there." She rummaged through her bag for her camera. "Will you take my picture? I feel pretty."

Nails had zoned out while thinking about eating the rest of her burger and didn't quite understand what she was talking about. Dallas shook her hair like a wet cat. "Should I wear it down?" She then pulled it up in a knot behind her head. "Or up?"

"Up or down for what?" Nails asked, his eyes still avoiding her body, keeping them laser-focused on the half-eaten burger.

"For tonight. For wherever it is we're going."

That jarred him and took his attention away from the food. "*We're* not going anywhere, Dallas. *I'm* going somewhere. *You're* staying here."

"Like hell I am." She turned the TV off just as Michael Keaton was about to rescue Kim Basinger.

"You are *not* leaving me here."

"This isn't some night out on the town, Dallas. This is serious. These are serious people."

"What are you saying? That I can't handle myself? You saw me last night with that fat shit and his redneck dad. I can handle myself just fine."

"No, I'm not saying that. I'm saying this is something I have to sort out by myself. It's not just something I can bring a date—a girl—a friend to." He stumbled over his words. "I need to be on top of this . . . I can't be worried—"

"—about me?" She was angry now. "Some poor defenseless little whore you just met?"

"That is not what I meant."

"Well, what do you mean then? Why can't I go with you?"

"You just can't, okay?"

"No, not okay. I don't know where you're going or what's going to happen to you, and I'm just supposed to sit here and be okay with that?"

"Yes. It's hard enough already for me to focus when you're not around. But when you are . . . I can't stay right. There could be bad people there tonight. Bad people that see you dressed like *that* and act even worse."

"So it's what I'm wearing?"

"No. That's not what I meant either. You're messing with my words."

"No. I'm just repeating them back to you. So there's a problem with your friends seeing me like this, but you can stare at me when I'm naked with my back turned. Got it."

"They aren't my friends. And you weren't naked."

"Fuck you, Nails. Good luck finding someone else to watch your back tonight. Someone else you *can* stay focused around. That you don't have to worry about. Or dresses more appropriately. Goddamn, all of you— every single one of you—you're all the same. What was I thinking?"

"I don't need anyone to watch my back."

"Fine. Neither do I. So maybe I just won't be here when you get back—if you get back." She watched and waited for a reaction, and she got the one she didn't want. Nails stared back down at the table. The distance he put off was immediate. She'd seen him do that before. At the gas station when he thought about leaving her the first time. He couldn't look directly at her then either because he wasn't sure if he'd see her again. "That's it, isn't it? You're not sure if you're coming back here, are you?"

Nails said nothing.

"Tell me I'm wrong, Nails. Tell me."

Nails still said nothing.

"It's still a lie, even if you don't say anything." Dallas stormed across the room into the bathroom and slammed the door behind her. Nails heard the click of the lock. He used his forearm to slide his trash off the table and into a small trashcan, sat on the bed, and stared out the window. She was right. He didn't know what was going to happen tonight. It was better that she stay out of it. Better for her. Better for him. She would have to understand that.

She didn't come back out of the bathroom before it was time for him to leave. At exactly eight p.m., Nails went outside and stood on the curb. A van pulled up to where he was standing, the passenger side window went down, and the driver leaned across the seats. "You McKenna?"

"Yeah."

"Then get in."

Chapter Thirty-Five

Alex checked into his suite at the Grand Hyatt Hotel in downtown Jacksonville. His suitcase sat open and in disarray on the loveseat in the office and he stood in his boxers in front of the parted blackout drapes that hung from ceiling to floor. He stared more at his own reflection in the plate glass windows than out over the city and chewed a stick of gum. Damn this city, damn this state, and damn his brother, Robbie, for making him have to come here. He'd only just arrived from the airport in Atlanta a few hours ago and his driver brought him straight to the hotel but he was already feeling the urge to leave. He shouldn't have come himself. He should've sent Michael. This was more his type of thing. But Alex needed to make sure that it all got taken care of, so there he was, and there he'd stay, until it was done. He'd taken one of the towels from the bathroom to rub the sweat off his neck and chest and then adjusted the air conditioner by the door to its lowest setting. He leaned his forehead against the wall and stood there like that long enough to feel his body temperature come down. He needed a shower and some strong bourbon, but the phone rang, so all that could wait. He peeled himself off the wall, walked over to the bed, stepping over the mangled mess of sheets on the floor, and held the phone to his ear without speaking.

"Mr. Price, it's me."

"Hello, Michael."

"I trust the flight and the hotel are satisfactory for your needs?"

"Yes, everything is fine, thank you."

"And your driver, he was waiting as instructed?"

"Yes. I said everything was fine. I'm in the hotel now."

"And the other thing you requested?"

Alex hung the small towel around his neck and sat down on the bed. He leaned back and rubbed a finger down the thigh of the young woman lying next to him. Her midnight skin was slick with sweat as well. "Half of what I asked for arrived, but I assume the other is coming?"

"Of course, sir. Our trusted source assured me, but it's my fault they didn't arrive at the same time. My apologies."

"It's fine. Accidents happen." Alex put the phone to his chest and instructed the young woman to go take a shower. She nodded and slid from the bed, making a show of her walk toward the bathroom. Once she was behind the glass door, Alex held the phone back to his ear.

"Look, so I'm here. How is everything on your end? Are you at the main house? Are you with him?"

"I am indeed. Your father, for the most part, is still incapacitated, but he does have his moments of lucidity. I will remain here as the barrier between him and the possibility of his finding out about your brother's demise until you return to deliver the news in person."

"Thank you, Michael. I've gotten assurances from the sheriff in McFalls County that he'll continue to hold off any media involvement as long as he can."

"And you trust that man?"

"I trust the amount of money I gave him to keep him complicit, but it won't last. So before he starts asking for more, or before the eventual cracks in the dam begin, do not let my father speak to anyone. Not Maria. Not Francis. Definitely no one from the network. Not even his physical therapist or any of those other parasites and their prayer groups. In fact, call off all that shit this week. No one speaks to him. No one but you. Not until we can spin this mess our way, and I get this handled."

"Understood, sir."

"Fucking Robbie. I can't believe he let this happen. Leaving us unprotected like this."

"Yes, sir."

"And have you found out who our best contact here is to track her down?"

"I've gone through every available resource I have down there and the name that keeps popping up on every radar is a man named Wilcombe. Oscar Wilcombe. He's a British expat who runs a . . ." Michael paused, as if to read something he'd written down. "He runs an export business for motorcycle parts. Mostly for overseas racing vehicles and so forth, but that is only for cover. He's also rumored to be quite nefarious, dabbling in all sorts of nastiness. Guns, drugs, procurement, and most importantly for us, information."

"I didn't come here to consort with a criminal, Michael. I have zero interest in lying with the dogs out here. I am not supposed to be getting mixed in with the garbage. That was my brother's problem and why I'm here cleaning it up. If I don't find what I came here to find, everything our father built—everything I built—is lost. Like it was all for nothing."

"I understand all of that, sir. But if you are there to find a criminal, who better to ask than another one. And a criminal of this Wilcombe's caliber seems to me like the right person to ask. He is also renowned for his discretion. I would never knowingly allow you to walk into a lion's den. You know that."

"I know that. I know. I'm just feeling a little out of my depth here. If any of the network investors catch a whiff of this, Michael, if she makes a move before I can find her. This is the type of scandal that can destroy everything. I expected this to be under control eventually, but with Robbie in the fucking morgue . . . I feel vulnerable. Maybe cutting him off was the wrong thing to do."

"Don't second-guess yourself now, sir. We can salvage this."

"Forgive my anger, Michael. I just feel like a fish out of water here."

"I understand, sir. But if you are uncomfortable, I can be there on the next flight. I can assign someone else to your father and track her down myself."

"No. I need you to be there. You're the only one I trust around the old man. I'm just frustrated. I want this all to be over."

"As do I, sir. And I believe that this man, Wilcombe, will only serve to forward that very agenda."

Alex chewed at the flavorless gum, spit it into his palm, and stuck it to the side of a large crystal ashtray. "All right. Give me his information but keep trying to dig up anything else you can find out here concerning this McKenna idiot—or anything else that can lead me in the right direction."

"Of course."

Alex used the pen and notepad provided by the hotel to take down the information and hung up the phone without saying goodbye. He poured himself a double Maker's Mark from the prestocked minibar and looked out over the sprawling sun-bleached city. He could feel the dread absorbing into his bones. The feeling made him tired and angry. No. That wasn't true. What made him angry was that he allowed himself to be in this position. He let his little brother's games get the best of them both. Alex never really thought Robbie would hurt him, but now Robbie was dead, there was no one to keep the whore in check. A knock at the door broke Alex's train of thought. He saw a sandy-haired boy through the peephole and let him in.

"I'm very sorry I'm late, Mr. Smith. I was stuck in traffic. I'm Jay."

The young man looked enthusiastic enough, but Alex couldn't stand excuses. He sat down in a wide chair opposite the bed and used the glass of whiskey to motion toward the bathroom. "I don't care what your name is. Just take your clothes off, fold them, and put them on the dresser. Then go and join your associate in the shower. Rinse the stink of this city off you."

The young man began to unbutton his shirt. "Will you be joining us, sir?"

Alex knocked back the bourbon and slid out of his boxers. "I'll be watching."

Chapter Thirty-Six

The van was completely empty inside, stripped down to the bare metal flooring. No backseat. No carpeting. No tools or cargo. No frills. There wasn't even a console between the two bucket seats in the front, just an Igloo cooler jury-rigged to the driver's seat with thick rubber bungee cords. The man driving the van was slim and he wore a white T-shirt with a black leather vest. The vest had a bunch of patches on it, but nothing that Nails could make out in the darkness. The driver's hair was black and shaggy, his skin smooth, but his defining attribute was the massive salt-and-pepper mustache curled and crafted into carefully waxed handlebars. Nails couldn't help but stare at it. That mustache was a goddamn work of art. The driver stuck out a hand with silver rings on almost every finger. "Pinkerton Sayles. Most folks call me Pinky."

Nails shook the man's hand, unsurprised that it felt like wilted lettuce. "Nails," he said and pulled on his seatbelt. He couldn't stop staring at the wad of manicured fur dangling from Pinky's upper lip. "You look like somebody."

Pinky side-eyed him. "Yeah, I get that shit all the time. Sam Elliott, right? Because of the 'stache. I don't mind looking like a movie star, but I wish I had his movie star money. You know what I'm saying?"

Nails didn't know who Sam Elliott was. "No," he said. "You look like the cartoon Sam."

"The cartoon Sam?"

"Yeah, Yosemite Sam."

Nails wasn't sure if Pinky took that as a compliment or not but he laughed it off just the same. "Shit. I never heard that one before, but I reckon if I dyed this bitch red, I sure might."

From that point on, they drove up the interstate in an uncomfortable silence. Pinky finally turned off at an exit and stopped at a red light.

"Where are we going?"

"To the club."

"What club?"

"Just a bar that Oscar owns."

"Who's Oscar?"

Now that confused Pinky. He hooked a right when the light turned green. "Oscar Wilcombe. The man who arranged for this meet."

"Right. Wilcombe. The guy who talks fancy."

Pinky laughed again. "Yeah, that's him."

"Is he going to be at this club?"

"Nah, he leaves shit like this up to Bracken and the rest of us."

"Who's Bracken?"

"C'mon. You're fixing to find out."

Pinky slowed the van and eased it into a parking lot in front of a plain gray cement block building adjacent to a small liquor store with security bars covering the windows and doors. From the window of the van, Nails could see a flickering Miller Lite neon sign in a window above the front door of the bar, but there was no other indication of what kind of place it could be. He slowly brushed his fingers over the .45 in his jacket pocket to give himself a small spark of reassurance. He would at least have a fighting chance if he was walking into some kind of ambush. Looking at this shit box in the middle of nowhere made him feel a lot better about having left Dallas back at the motel. Everything about this smelled bad.

Three matte black motorcycles were parked outside the bar next to a few other cars. Pinky parked the van on the left side of the building in an area that looked as if it was supposed to be there. The nondescript van was an extension of this nondescript club—a fetching tool. When Pinky cut the engine and got out, Nails could make out the patches on the back of Pinky's vest. A rocker that spelled out "Jacksonville Jackals" above the head of a badly drawn animal. Pinky slammed the door and drummed on the open window ledge with both hands. "C'mon, Nails. Let's go meet the boss."

Another small car pulled into the lot and parked in front of the liquor store as Nails got out of the van and followed Pinkerton Sayles through the door.

Chapter Thirty-Seven

Pinkerton slammed the door behind them. He led Nails down a hallway decorated with posters of half-naked women sprawled out over
shiny Harley-Davidsons. They passed two doors labeled MEN and OLD
LADIES and then moved out into the main area of the bar. The entirety
of the small club was lit by two fluorescent lamps that hung over a set
of pool tables in the middle of the room and the lights behind the bar.
No natural light at all. Two men in plaid shirts were playing pool with
a blue-haired female in a leopard print miniskirt. She looked about half
their age. Some other men in vests like Pinky's had dibs on the second table. An overly tanned man wearing a blazer and a blond woman
sat at the bar. The woman stared into her empty glass, bored to tears.
Tom Petty's "You Wreck Me" blasted through the bar from unknown
speakers.

Pinky led Nails to one of the high-backed leather booths that lined one
side of the club and sat. He motioned for Nails to sit opposite him and
then waved to get the attention of one of the other bikers playing pool.
The man he waved down couldn't have been any more the polar opposite
of Pinky. He was twice as wide, looked to be built out of cinder blocks,
and stood a near foot taller than everyone in the room. He wore a denim
jacket under his cut of leather, and at first Nails thought the man was bald,
like he was, but after the biker laid his pool stick on the table and got
close enough, Nails could see this big man had a very close crop of hair,
that was every bit as light and faded as the denim jacket he wore. The big
man held his hand out for Nails to shake. Nails was impressed. That didn't

happen very often. He rarely met other people that matched him in size. He took the man's hand and shook it. This man's grip was also completely different from the man who had driven him there. It was a vise grip of solid granite.

"Bracken Leek," the stone man said. "President of the Jacksonville chapter of The Jackals MC. Pleased to meet you."

"Nails." It was clear that he wasn't *pleased* about anything.

Bracken swung a chair around to the end of the table and sat in it backward, resting one forearm across the back. He, too, motioned for Nails to sit. This time he did.

"What are you drinking?"

Nails suddenly felt foolish. He hadn't brought any money with him. He doubted that he had more than a dollar's worth of change in his pocket from the food he'd bought earlier.

As if Bracken could read his mind, he said, "Your tab is on the house, of course, and Pinkerton here would be happy to get you anything you'd like." If Pinky was happy or disappointed by his role as manservant, it was impossible to tell under his walruslike tusks.

"Just apple juice if you have it."

"Apple juice," Pinky repeated. "C'mon brother, have a real drink, it's all-paid—"

Bracken interrupted by sliding a stone hand across the table and letting it rest in front of Pinky. "The man said he wanted apple juice. Bring him some apple juice. I'll take a pint of Newcastle."

"You got it, boss."

Nails understood the pecking order immediately. This guy ran the show, at least the part of the show that the fancy man allowed to be seen publicly. Pinky got up from the booth and walked to the bar. Nails turned and watched as he chatted with the tan man and waited for the bartender. Nails didn't like it that he had to stretch his neck and look behind him to see the bar. He could see the front door, but not the back of the room or the side door he'd come in from. The way Bracken had positioned himself in a chair at the end of the table gave him a perfect vantage point of the whole place. "He's pretty smart."

"What's that?" Bracken asked.

"I didn't say anything." But Nails knew that he had.

Bracken yelled out to the bar over the music. "Pinky, tell Romeo to turn the music down some—for me."

Two thumbs-up from Pinkerton Sayles and a moment later Tom Petty was coming in at half the volume. "That's better. Now, Mr. McKenna."

"Nails."

"Right. Won't happen again. Now, Nails. Oscar has discussed with me in great detail the circumstances of your situation."

"Why isn't Wilcombe here? He's the man I was told to deal with."

Bracken showed none of the normal apprehension or backpedaling that Nails associated with most of the people he questioned. This man's expression stayed as neutral and firm as it had been when he first approached. "The Englishman is the man you were told to contact. You and he will most likely never meet. I'm the man you're dealing with. Am I good to go on?"

Nails looked back at the bar again to see Pinky returning with three drinks balanced in his hands. He set down the two pints of beer and the glass of apple juice, managing not to spill a drop, but still set bar napkins from a plastic caddy on the table down next to each drink, before taking a seat.

Bracken asked again, "Nails, should I continue?"

"Yes."

"All right, then. Due to the nature of the relationship between the man I work with and the man you work for, an arrangement has been made for you to disappear."

"I thought I'd already done that. I disappeared—to here."

"Getting you here was only the beginning, my friend. Let me explain. This state is surrounded by water. And more importantly by ports, a lot of which my organization has control of. We run an export business. Mostly engine parts for rice rockets. But it's not unusual for us to export—other things—if the need arises."

"And you mean to export me?"

Bracken sipped at his brown English ale and wiped the foam from his upper lip with the napkin that Pinky had provided. "Let me put this another way, Nails. You didn't come to Florida to reside. You came here because now you have the means to *really* disappear. Look, as you probably already know, homicide is a federal offense with no boundaries or statutes of limitations. That means that everyone from state police to the Feds will be able to look for you back home, here, or in any state for that matter, with no ticking clock. Having no statute means they could hunt for you until the end of days if they so desired. Your boss is not willing to risk that hunt being a successful one, either now or years from now when someone somewhere finally talks—because in this business of ours, again, as you probably already know—someone somewhere is always going to talk. Luckily for you though, the man you work for also doesn't want to put a bullet in your head and call it a day. So he's gone to great lengths to get you here and called in a large favor with my business partner to get you out. It's not ideal. But it leaves everyone whole— including you. And that's what we all want to see happen."

Nails moved his glass around on the table in a slow circular motion but didn't drink any of it. It was warm—room temperature—Freddy kept it ice cold for him.

"Where would I be exported to?"

Bracken finished his beer almost as if to signal to Pinky that he wasn't privy to this part of the conversation. He set his empty glass down next to Pinky's barely touched glass, and the thin man got up to refill it without argument. Bracken waited until Pinky was at the bar and then leaned down hard with both arms on the back of the chair. "I told you we were in the business of exporting motorcycle parts, among other things. Well, we recently acquired a manufacturing plant in Mexico. The labor is cheap, and the price was right. The laws are also different down there. And we need someone in place for security. Someone that can be trusted. Someone like you. Like I said, it's not ideal, or what you're used to, but it's a solid fit— for everyone, and it's a place where you can not worry about running. You can put this shit behind you and make a hefty profit to boot."

Nails took a minute to process that. "So you want me to go to Mexico?"

Bracken leaned back. "No, I don't want you to do anything. *You* want you to go to Mexico. Listen, don't take this the wrong way, but neither I nor anyone else in my crew have skin in this game. I don't know you. This is your call. You can take the offer on the table, or you can take your chances and do your own thing, but if your answer is no, your protection ends here."

"Protection from who?"

"I believe you know the answer to that question. But at the moment, our friend in Georgia feels like you're more of an asset to us than a threat to him. Look, I've seen men in your position killed before just to err on the side of safety. So, I'd say this is a solid play, Nails."

Nails caught the stone man's cold gray eyes. He saw sincerity. He let the idea of his being smuggled out of the country by people he didn't even know bounce around his brain. How did this happen? How did he let this happen? "Can I talk to Mr. Burroughs first?"

Bracken shook his head. "No. That's not an option. That part of your life is over."

Nails moved the glass of juice around on the table some more until the front door opened and flooded the bar with outside light. That's when Nails felt the ripcord get pulled, and his brain caught fire.

Chapter Thirty-Eight

First it was the blond hair. It wasn't up or down but teased straight out in every direction into an Aqua Net lion's mane. Then it was the black dress. The black dress that fit her like a second skin and tied behind her neck. The same dress she had steamed the wrinkles out of in the motel bathroom.

Dallas? What the fuck? How did she find this place? What the hell was she doing?

He watched as every other set of eyes in the bar, including Bracken's, followed her across the room and to the bar. She was half stumbling as if she'd already been drinking, and Nails wasn't sure if she winked at him as she walked by or if it was his imagination. He wasn't even sure if she was real at all. It didn't make any sense. Once she was seated at the bar next to the tan man and the bored woman, Nails turned back to Bracken, who had already lost interest in the girl. Pinky returned with another pint of English ale and sat back down.

Bracken began to speak some more about the proposed plan. He said that someone would be by Nails's room to pick him up—tomorrow night. At least, that's what he thought he said. But he couldn't keep his mind in the game enough to catch all the details. His head swiveled as his brain swam in battery acid. *How was she here?* He kept looking over his shoulder. She pulled at the tiny dress as she adjusted herself on the stool. She said something to the bartender. The bartender started laughing. Then she was laughing. Nails was spinning.

Bracken tilted his head. "Is there something wrong, Nails?"

"What? No. I'm just . . ."

"Look, I get it. It's a lot to take in. But trust me, this is the best thing for everyone involved."

Nails turned back to the bar again. Now Dallas was talking with the tan man. She also had a tall drink, filled to the rim, and an upside-down shot glass next to her on the bar. The tan man was laughing with her now. She nudged at the man's shoulder as if they were old friends.

"Nails?"

Nails turned his attention back to Bracken. "What?"

"Do you know that woman? The blonde at the bar? You've been clocking her ever since she came in and I've never seen her in here before. Do you know her?"

Nails didn't answer the questions. He wanted to, but his brain was full of glue and he couldn't form the right words. He began to slide out of the booth but Bracken moved his chair and blocked him in. Something frigid and dark washed over Nails. This wasn't an odd or unnatural feeling. This was a feeling he knew well, and his words began to flow perfectly now. "You want to get out of my way."

Bracken didn't budge nor did the expression change on his chiseled face. He remained calm. "I'm not sure what just happened, but this conversation isn't over, Nails. It's the reason you're here."

Nails let his right hand fall to the lump of steel in his jacket pocket. Pinky pressed himself back in the booth. Bracken couldn't see under the table, but he knew. He spoke with the same steady tone. "Don't. Don't do that. You need to take a breath."

"I need you to get out of my way. And I'm not going to tell you again."

"Nails, I need you to understand that other than that woman who just got you all heated up, every person in this room is armed and waiting for this conversation to go sideways. And they are all on the same team. My team. As of right this moment, it's your team, too. But if you pull that .45 out of your pocket, you're going to get mowed down before you can even aim it. There is no other way it plays out. I know your history. I know what you're capable of and I respect you, but I didn't walk in here without knowing exactly who I would be talking to."

"You don't fucking know me."

"I know you are not someone to fuck with and I know that people are going to get hurt if you decide to take this road. Some of my people might even go down. But I can promise you, the only person who *definitely* won't be getting back up is you. That is not a threat. I'm just laying out the facts."

Nails fumed in his seat but he stayed still and quiet. So did everyone else he could see in the bar. Every set of eyes was on him. And every gun hand looked ready to draw. This man, Bracken, wasn't lying. Nails knew when he sat down that they'd sat him here, at this booth, to keep him at a disadvantage. And he'd let them do it anyway. He'd let these people walk him into a cage like a zoo animal—and now Dallas was involved, too. He wanted to scream. He wanted to flip the table. He wanted to bash in this biker's skull and see just exactly how hard the stone man was. But he didn't do any of that. Instead, he did what he was asked to do. He took a breath. That's what Dallas had told him to do back in Valdosta. She said he could control himself. He just needed to breathe. So he did. Now he was doing it again and it was working.

He slowly put his hands on the table. Neither of the Jackals sitting in the booth had seen the deformity in his left hand until then. Pinky slid away further down the booth, but Bracken paid it zero mind as if he'd already known about it. He'd either been incredibly meticulous about knowing who he was sitting down with—or he simply didn't care. By his eyes, it was impossible to tell.

"That's better. Now I don't know what's going on with you and that woman over there, and I don't care. That's your business. All I need from you is a simple answer. Are you going to take Wilcombe's offer or not? If it's a hard no, then you have my word that no harm will come to you from me or anyone in my crew. Your trouble will come from Georgia, not us. My man Pinkerton here will bring you back to your motel, and I'll pass along the information. Again, it's your call, but like I said, you'll be on your own from here on out."

"Can I think about it?"

Bracken lifted a hand to ease the tension in the room as he decided. "I'll tell you what. You have until eight p.m. tomorrow. You'll either be there waiting like you were tonight or you won't. After that, the deal expires, and the ship sails without you."

"So can I get up now?"

Bracken hesitated but finally slid his chair out of the way and both he and Nails got to their feet. The sound of Tom Petty, runnin' down a dream, was in the air now, but before Bracken stepped aside, he had one last thing to say. "Nails, you need to keep in mind that this red carpet rollout?" He tipped his chin at Dallas, who was currently working on her second cocktail. "It's only available for one passenger. Just you. That's it."

Nails nodded. He understood, and the weight of that information slowed his walk to the bar.

Chapter Thirty-Nine

Dallas had managed to order and consume two Long Island iced teas and two sidecars of Cuervo during the time that Nails and Bracken had nearly blown up the bar. The twin hourglasses of melting ice and pair of upside-down shot glasses were quickly whisked away by the bartender. He was also a member of the Jacksonville Jackals. This one looked Latino and too young to be keeping bar. He asked Nails for his order. Nails ignored him.

"Dallas?"

She acted like she didn't hear him and purposely cranked up the fake laughter with her new friend. Up close, Nails could see that the tan man looked more like an orange man. Like he'd been spray-painted with Tang. He had an accent, too, but not as prominent as Wilcombe's. This guy sounded more like some kind of surfer asshole, but Nails couldn't guess his nationality. He did however want to bash his weird painted face into the bar. But that was because of how Dallas was acting. The other woman who'd been sitting with the man had apparently left. She must not have been a fan of this version of Dallas either. The bartender tried getting a drink order again but after being ignored by Nails for a second time, he finally left him alone.

"Dallas," Nails said again, much louder.

This time she turned, keeping up the party-girl charade. "Oh hey, handsome. Here, meet my friend, Bonner. But don't call him Boner. He doesn't like that."

"What are you doing here?" Nails said, not just ignoring Bonner's outstretched hand but disregarding his presence entirely.

"I'm having a drink. What does it look like?"

"I'm not playing games, Dallas. What the hell do you think you're doing?"

First, she turned to Bonner. "I'm so sorry, my friend Nails isn't very sociable." And then she produced a tube of lip gloss out of thin air like a magician. "I love these little things," she said as she applied it. "They remind me of my mama. We used to get them two-for-a-dollar at Kmart when I was a kid, and then we'd always stop and get Little Caesars pizza. That was her favorite. *Pizza, Pizza.*" She rolled the tube of lip gloss between her fingers. "But I'm surprised my mama even bought these back then because of the names. She'd get so flustered." She showed Nails the label on the tube. "This one is called *Kinky*. I don't even think they make these anymore."

Nails fought the urge to snatch the little plastic cylinder out of her hand and toss it across the room. "How did you find me?"

She whipped her head around completely and tried to focus her eyes on his face. She'd had a lot to drink. It was obvious by her struggle to keep eye contact and the slur of her words. "I followed you," she said in a voice softer, but angrier, than before. "In the Honda. You're not the only one who knows how to hotwire a car. I saw the Walrus over there pick you up in that van and I followed you."

"Why would you do that?"

She got even angrier. She poked him in the chest and spilled her drink on the bar. "Why would you leave me there alone?" she growled. "You know being left alone is the thing that scares me the most, but you—you did it anyway." Then just as suddenly as the anger appeared, it waned, replaced by insufferable drunkenness. "But why be angry, right? Anger is just fear in a little black dress. Somebody told me that once. I have no idea what it means, but it sounded cool." She went to take another swig from her drink, but Nails took it from her and set it on the bar. "You've had enough."

The anger came back, full volume. "You don't get to tell me when I've had enough. You don't get to tell me anything. You just get to leave. That's your thing. Who cares who might be looking for me."

"Dallas. What the hell does that even mean? Who's looking for you?"

"Nope. No sir. You don't get to ask me questions anymore." She stood, swayed, and motioned to the door. "You just need to peace out, man. So, go ahead. Leave. The door is right there."

Dallas's new buddy Bonner stood and helped steady her. The bartender came back over as well. "Maybe you should listen to your boyfriend here and let him take you home."

"This asshole isn't my boyfriend. I don't have a boyfriend. I'm as single as it gets," she said.

"Well, whoever he is, he seems to care about you. Whereas I don't, and you're getting kinda loud. So I think it's time to go."

"Fuck you," she said, knocking over her third drink. The barkeep looked ready to dial it up to the next level. Nails didn't want to find out what that was. He saw a five and some one-dollar bills on the bar, so he pushed it toward the bartender. "Look. I'm sorry. She's leaving. Does she owe you anything else for the drinks?"

The bartender picked up the money from the bar and shoved it in his pocket. "Just get her the fuck out of here."

Nails turned back to Dallas and Bonner. They were both giggling and again Nails wanted to bash his teeth in, but Pinky Sayles helped quell that idea. He stepped in between Nails and Dallas. "You gonna need a ride back to the motel?"

"No, I've got it."

"I can take you and your girlfriend both if you need me to."

"I said, I've got it."

"The man said he's got it, friend," Bonner said, and he discreetly pressed one of his business cards into Dallas's hand. "Our secret, yeah?" She smiled a drunken smile and tucked the card down the front of her dress before Nails could see it. He slid an arm around her, and began to walk her out. Everyone took a moment to watch the lumbering ox drag out the drunk blonde. He looked around for Bracken as they left, but he was gone. When they reached the door, Dallas yelled back to her new friend at the bar. "See ya later, handsome. Had a blast."

Handsome. It rang in Nails's ears. She was just being mean. Or she said it to everyone. Either way, that was the first time she'd hurt him.

Chapter Forty

Bracken sat in the small office upstairs where he'd been watching Nails get his drunken blond friend under control on one of the several security monitors. *Who the hell was this, now?* He hated not having all the proper intel on anything. He didn't like surprises. He went to great extremes to keep that kind of shit under control. And this bony blonde had wild card written all over her. He'd talk to Wilcombe about it in the morning. Details mattered, and someone had dropped the ball regarding this woman. Bracken prided himself on never being the guy that dropped anything. He didn't understand why no one else did. He stayed secluded in the dark office until the security cameras showed both Nails and the woman get into a dark four-door sedan and drive away. It took a while. The girl wasn't making it easy on him. McKenna struggled to get her into the car. Bracken sighed and thought about something his father told him right before he partnered their MC with The Englishman. *"If Oscar Wilcombe ever said something would be easy, it wouldn't be—but the money will make it worth it."* So Bracken dealt with the headache. Wilcombe's money bought a lot of Tylenol. He watched the dark sedan finally leave the parking lot.

Once Nails and his companion were off the premises, Bracken came out of the office, made his way down the small concealed staircase, and pushed open the door leading to the bar. He took a seat at one of the middle stools with the intended purpose of not talking to anyone. He just needed a beer. Without asking, the bartender, one of the MC's new prospects—a scrappy fella named Romeo—set an ice-cold pint of Newcastle down in front of Bracken. He wasn't even bothered that one-third of the glass was foam. His worries ran deeper, so he stuck a finger into the glass to let the oil from his skin help the suds level out. He stared down into the amber liquid.

"Bracken," a voice called from a few stools down on his left.

The president hung his head. So much for not being bothered. Bonner was another one of Wilcombe's necessary evils. He was a scumbag pimp, and Bracken didn't care much for him or his opinion.

"Your friend," Bonner said. "The big man with the clubbed hand. There is something wrong with him, yeah? He's a bit touched in the head?"

"I'm not sure what his fucking deal is, Bonner. But he's not my friend. He's my job."

Pinky took the stool to Bracken's right, and now the big man wished he'd forgone the beer and never left the office. Romeo, behind the bar, set another frosted pint in front of Pinky as well, a glass of bright yellow horse piss. Miller Lite. Pinky's go-to. Bracken looked at it, disgusted. *How do people drink that shit?*

"You think he's going to take the offer, Boss? Bonner is right. I think he's a tard."

"Watch your mouth, Pinky. That man is inner-circle with the Burroughs family and he'd snap your neck for calling him that . . . and I'm not sure what that guy is going to do. I just know that either way, it's going to get messy before we can call it a wrap. And who knows for sure what anyone is going to do when there's a woman involved. Touched in the head or not."

Pinky and Bonner exchanged a glance.

"Does he know?" Bonner whispered to Pinky.

Pinky shook his head slightly to get the pimp to shut up. He knew better than to give Bracken more to be concerned about.

"Pinky, take the van and keep an eye on him. There's a mobile phone in the glove box. He heads out of state, you let me know."

Pinky nodded, hammered his beer, and headed out the back door. Bracken held up his empty glass and Romeo set down another one in its place, identical to the first, except this time, there was barely a half inch of head on top. Bracken grinned. The kid learned fast. He'd be one of the good ones.

Chapter Forty-One

During most of the ride back to the motel, Dallas insisted on blaring the music from the tape deck and singing along at the top of her voice. After the first few times that Nails tried to lower the volume, she'd just yell louder and sing over everything he tried to say, so he finally gave up. She yelled every word to a Tracer's Bullet song out the window into the cold night air until eventually the obnoxious drunk began to fade into the regretful, quiet drunk. She laid her cheek against the cool metal of the window ledge and let the wind rush her face. Nails turned the volume off and this time he didn't get an argument.

"Are you going to be sick?"

"Yes."

"Do you need me to pull over?"

"No, I can make it if I don't close my eyes. Just don't stop. The wind feels good."

A few minutes later, Nails pulled the Honda into the parking space in front of their motel room. He hadn't even cut the ignition before Dallas had her door open and began to spray half-digested cheeseburger puke all over the asphalt. Nails raced around the car to make sure she didn't fall out. An open plastic traveler bottle of vodka fell onto the ground from the floorboards. That explained how she was already drunk before she walked into the club. He remembered the car that had pulled in behind Pinky's van at the liquor store. He should've been paying attention. He should've recognized the car and then none of this would've happened. He held her by her shoulders, careful to stay out of the puddle of vomit, or the possibility of more to come. Some Good Samaritan in a tank top and flip-flops, carrying an ice bucket back to his room, began to walk toward the Honda, more curious than concerned. "Y'all good over here? Lady, you good?"

One brief glance at Nails was answer enough for the man, who quickly left, deciding to leave well enough alone. Nails waited for a break in the projectile sickness and then lifted Dallas out of the car, surprised at how much frailer she seemed to be than he expected. It amazed him how some-one who could command an entire room the way that she did could also shrink down into such a tiny little creature. He carried her into their room. The minute her feet touched the floor, she broke away from him and made a bee line for the bathroom, dropping to her knees in front of the toilet for round two. Nails crouched down beside her and held her stiff hair out of her face as she spat yellow bile into the commode. He thought about how he used to do the same thing for his mother when he was younger. After her treatments. While Satchel sat on the couch with his feet up, drinking beer. He wasn't trying to have a memory like that right now, so he just sat on the floor as Dallas went limp and melted around the cold porcelain. Once he was sure there was nothing left in her to come out, he lifted her up like a child and laid her on the bed, covering her with clean white sheets and the motel comforter. She pulled the linens in tight around her and curled into a ball. Nails wet a washrag in the sink and sat on the edge of the bed. He cleaned the dried sick off her face as she fought to keep her eyes open.

"Get some rest," he said and went to stand.

"Please don't leave."

"I'm not going anywhere. Just to the couch."

She put a hand on his knee. "No, just sit here with me for a little while. If I close my eyes the room starts to spin. It helps to talk. Just for a few minutes."

"You want to talk?"

"I know you're mad at me."

"I am mad. I don't understand why you did all this. Why you followed me there. Why you acted like that."

"I didn't mean to get this messed up."

"But why did you even come there. I told you it was dangerous."

"I was scared." She nuzzled the sheet and pressed part of her cheek into his leg.

"Scared of what? You were safe here. I told you that."

"Scared of losing you."

It took a long time for Nails to respond to that. He was getting jumbled up. "You're drunk."

"So? It doesn't mean it's not true."

"I said I'd be back."

"People say a lot of things they don't mean."

"I don't."

"Everyone does." She was fading. Nails could see it. He began to stand up again, and again she stopped him.

"Wait, whose turn is it?"

"Whose turn is it for what?"

"To ask a question?"

"Dallas, I don't want to play this game. You need to sleep, and I need to think."

"So it's my turn, then."

"Dallas . . ."

"Tell me something I don't know about you. Tell me something no one knows."

"Dallas, I told you I don't want to do this."

"Please. Just talk to me." She cuddled in around him some more, but it didn't make him as uncomfortable as it should have. She felt warm. He liked it. He also didn't know why he said anything. Maybe it was because of the bathroom, holding her hair while she got sick, the same as he had done for his mother. The words just flowed out as he thought them. "My father killed my mother."

Dallas lifted her head slightly and looked up at him. "What?" Even in her semiconscious state, she wasn't expecting to hear that.

Nails felt disconnected from the moment again, as if he wasn't the one talking, like he was just bearing witness to a stranger using his voice. "She got cancer when I was a kid. She smoked. A lot. Every day. I hated it. I always asked her to stop. But she didn't, and it made her sick. It got bad, and she'd get these treatments. That only made it worse. She stopped going after a while and just stayed in bed all day. Sometimes I'd stay in the bed with her. Sometimes Satchel wouldn't let me."

"Who's Satchel?"

"My father," Nails said, but those two words felt like broken glass in his throat. "He's my father," he said a second time more to himself.

Dallas put her hand on his knee again. Nails didn't even notice. "The hospital put machines in our house. Machines that helped my mom with her pain. Nice nurses would come by sometimes but eventually the machines were the only thing keeping her alive." Nails stopped there. He wasn't sure why he was telling her any of this. He was only keeping her awake when she needed sleep, but she pressed him.

"Keep going," she said. "Tell me."

"One night Satchel told me to sleep in my own room. I did. I had to. I was little. I couldn't fight him yet, so I had to do what he said. Mama had stopped talking, too. She hadn't said anything in days. So I did what he said. I just went to bed. The next morning I came out of my room to go to school and Satchel was on the couch, drunk asleep. And mama was dead. He'd turned off the machines. He kicked me out of her room and turned off the machines and then drank it away like she never existed."

"That's horrible."

"She was cold when I touched her. Some people came and got her. They put her in a bag. I never saw her again. I never got to say good-bye. He took that from me. That's what he did. And now Mr. Burroughs wants to take everything from me, too."

"Who is Mr. Burroughs?"

"It doesn't matter. But you're right. People never mean what they say. And I don't think I want to talk anymore."

"I'm so sorry, Nails."

"Nelson, my real name is Nelson." Saying that out loud surprised him more than the story he'd just told her. He hadn't spoken his given name since the day Gareth Burroughs had started calling him Nails. Nelson didn't fit him anymore. It was a name for someone else. It felt foreign in his mouth. Like a stone under his tongue.

"I like that name," she said, "Nelson," and she slid away from him on the bed. At first, he thought she was repelled by what he told her. But she wasn't. She was just moving over to make room. "Lay down with me, Nelson." She rubbed her hand over the empty space between them.

"I can use the couch."

"No, you can't," she said, her voice all dry and groggy. "Lay down."

Nails didn't argue. He kicked off his boots and lay down next to her. Dallas nestled her head on his shoulder, and he adjusted her pillow for her.

"Does my breath stink?"

"Yes," he said immediately, and she pushed on him with all the strength of a peacock feather. "You really don't know how to lie, do you?"

He didn't answer her. He was thinking about Mexico now. Being alone in a place like that. "Are you still awake?" he asked her.

"Yes."

"If you could go anywhere. Anywhere in the world. Where would you go?"

"Alaska," she said, without a second of hesitation.

Nails glanced down at the top of her head. "Why Alaska?"

"Because it's cold there. And I am so damn tired of the heat." She added, "We could start over."

Nails lay there silent and still for a long while, with Dallas's warm breath on his neck. It smelled like sour milk, but he didn't care. He didn't want to move. He stared up at the popcorn ceiling of the cheap motel room and thought about his family, about never really having one, and about how hot it must be in Mexico. He bet it was hotter than Florida—or Georgia. He didn't even know where Alaska was. He was lost in his head when Dallas tugged gently at his shirt.

"Are you going to be sick again?"

"No."

"Then what's the matter?"

"Do you want to hold my hand?" she asked, in a voice that sounded light-years away.

He did, but he said, "No."

"It's just my hand. Holding it won't kill you."

"Yeah, I think maybe it will."

Chapter Forty-Two

Around midnight, Clayton checked into the Sunshine Inn, a squat little motel located twenty miles outside Jacksonville city proper. He stood behind his Bronco in a completely empty parking lot. Not a single car. Not a single light on in any of the rooms. He doubted the place had more than thirty to begin with and he also doubted, now that he was here, that the Comey brothers had been honest with him about where he needed to go. The kid working behind the counter of this bright orange and white dump told Clayton he was the first customer they'd had in over three days. So he was either lying, showing discretion toward their *esteemed clientele,* or worse, he was telling the truth, which meant that Clayton's newfound sleuthing skills had just come to a screeching halt.

A single streetlight by the road lit the parking lot with hazy blue light that cast a long shadow from a dumpster on the corner. It smelled of overcooked fish, hot sauce, and swamp water. He grabbed his backpack from the truck, matched the number on the keychain in his hand to the correlating orange door, and entered his room for the night. The heat inside the room overtook the heat outside and blasted Clayton with a thick wave of stale air. He felt on the wall for a light switch, pressed it, and moved from the fluorescent blue light of the sidewalk into the dim yellow of the room. *This is the Sunshine Inn,* he thought, *presented in every form of light except sunshine.*

After turning on the A/C unit under the window and adjusting the slider from red to blue, he dropped his bag on the bed. Fuck it. He'd slept in worse. He'd spent the night in a cow pasture once, while his older brother Buckley and Scabby Mike rooted out psychedelic mushrooms. If he could handle sleeping on a bedroll surrounded by cow shit and tripping idiots all night, he could handle a rat-trap motel. As long as he kept a light on to keep the roaches at bay.

After he washed his face and brushed the fur off his teeth from the seven-hour drive, eating nothing but Slim-Jims and Combos, he sat down on the bed and picked up the phone. He hit zero.

"Front desk."

"Yeah, hey. I got two questions."

"Room number, please."

Clayton paused. "Um. It's me. Clayton Burroughs in room 23. I thought I was your only guest tonight?"

"Right. Mr. Burroughs. How can I help you?"

Clayton shook it off. "How do I make a long-distance call from this phone?"

"Oh, that's no problem, sir. If you provide me with a credit card, just dial nine and then one, and then the number you want to dial. The charges will be added to your room fee."

"I checked in with a credit card. Don't you have an imprint of that already?"

"Oh, right. Then you're good to go."

"So nine, then one, and dial?"

"Yessir."

"Okay, second question. Is there anywhere decent to eat around here that is still open?"

"Um, I know that the Huddle House closed at midnight. And I think Pizza Hut has stopped delivering."

Clayton waited for more. There wasn't any more, so he clarified. "I'm asking about anything close by that *isn't* closed yet."

"There's a Krystal's right up New King's Road. I think they're open all night. But it's about a half-hour drive."

"And that's it?" Nothing about a sackful of stomach grenades sounded tempting at all.

"We've got a vending machine right outside the office. If you need change, just knock on the office window."

Clayton hung his head and scratched at the back of his neck. "All right then, thanks."

"Will there be anything else, Mr. Burgess?"

Clayton closed his eyes and sighed. "No. No, that's it. Thanks."

"You're welcome, and thank *you* for being a guest of the Sunshine Inn."

Clayton held the phone loosely in his lap long enough for the dial tone to kick in before he hung it up. He dug into his backpack and took out the cigarettes he'd bought back in Franklin. He lit one up, but this time he toughed out the coughing fit of the first drag and took another. Bad habits of this caliber took determination. He tipped his ash into the flimsy tin ashtray on the nightstand, poured himself a cup of water from the sink, and returned to the bed. He thought this must be what prison was like. Four walls, water, a pack of cigarettes, and a lot of self-loathing. He was hungry, but real food would have to wait until the morning—on his drive back home.

He smoked the Camel down to the butt and lit up another. He kicked off his cowboy boots and socks and waited for the sweat to dry from his feet before he lit up his third smoke and grabbed the phone again.

Nine.

Dial tone.

One.

Dial tone.

And after a quick review of the clock on the wall, he punched in Kate's number. It rang quite a few times before she answered. He knew he was waking her up, but right before he began to set the phone back in its cradle, he heard her sleepy voice.

"That you, cowboy?"

"Yeah, baby, it's me. You up?"

"I am now." She yawned out her words. "I didn't think you'd call me this late. Are you in trouble or just horny?"

"Neither, ma'am, but if you decided to talk dirty, I wouldn't stop you."

"Clayton, I love it when you're charming and all, but I *just* got to sleep. So tell me what's going on."

Clayton looked back up at the clock. "Why were you up so late?"

"Well, I was up till eleven-thirty grading papers for both me and

Chloe since she's been out, and I've got a brand-new aide shadowing me all week who has never worked with middle school kids a day in her life. So I stayed up a little later to make her a few cheats for tomorrow."

"You're pretty thoughtful, Miss Farris."

"Oh, I know. I'm a peach. Did you make it to Florida?"

He leaned on his thighs and quietly took a drag of the Camel. "Yeah, I'm here now, a place called the Sunshine Inn, but I'm sorry, Katie. I think this whole thing is a bust. I actually got lucky around Franklin. You would've been proud of me. I found a trail to follow. It turned out that Jacksonville was on the money but that's about it. Oh, and Nails is traveling with some girl."

"A girl? What girl?"

"I don't know, but apparently she's with him of her own free will, and they knocked over a gas station together on their way down here."

"Are you kidding me?"

"Nope, it's a long story, but the point is, I'm pretty sure that all of it led me to right here, which is nowhere. I've officially reached a dead end, baby." Clayton took another drag and tamped the cigarette out in the ashtray. "If he was here, and I don't think he was, he's already long gone and I—"

"Clayton?"

"Yeah?"

"Are you smoking?"

Clayton sat up straight and waved his hand around in the haze of smoke, as if she could smell it through the phone. "No, baby. Of course not. Why would you ask me that?"

"It sounds like you are smoking."

"Well, I'm not."

"Okay, Clayton. If you say so. But listen, before you left here you said you had no idea where to even start looking for Nails, and now you tell me you found a trail and was able to follow him to where you are now. That's a big jump. So just believe in yourself. Maybe there's another big jump right around the corner."

"I don't know, Kate. The longer I stay out here, the dumber I'm going to feel coming home empty-handed, you know? And Deddy. When he finds out what I'm doing, he's going to wig the fuck out."

"Don't worry about your father. That's the one blessing that comes with having the name Burroughs in this town. It makes you the only truly safe people in the whole state."

"I don't know about that, Kate. He threatened to throw me off my own roof yesterday. That's why I called you from the diner. In case he has my phone at the cabin bugged. I swear he knows everything."

"Well if that's the case, then he already knows where you are and what you're doing, so you might as well keep doing it. And the roof thing? He threatened you. Again. Big surprise, baby. That's what he does. He's threatened you at least twenty times over since I've known you. That's nothing new. He intimidates people for a living. You know that. But you're his son. He'd never really hurt you."

"Like I said, I don't know if I believe all that, but honestly, it's not me I'm worried about."

There was a long pause before Kate's voice came back over the phone. There wasn't a hint of sleep in it now. Clayton knew she'd have trouble falling back asleep. He shouldn't have woken her up in the first place.

"Clayton, listen to me. I love it when you feel the need to be my hero. I really do. But I can take care of myself. The place is my home, too, and I'm not a delicate flower that needs protection."

"I know, but—"

"Your father also knows damn well that even threatening me would be the final wedge between you two, and there would be no coming back from that, so as crazy as I might think your father is, he's not that stupid. So just stop. Okay. I'll be fine."

Clayton leaned back down on his thighs. "I hope you're right, Kate."

"I'm always right. So put all that business out of your mind and do what you went down there to do. Just give it one more day. If nothing comes of it, we both can say we did the best we could. And that's what matters."

He reached for the cigarettes but thought better of it. He knew she'd be able to tell. "Okay. I'll give it another day."

"Also, my mama always told me that when you have a problem, or you hit some kind of wall, just sleep on it, and you'll be surprised by what a little sunshine can do."

Clayton looked out the window at the *Sunshine Inn* logo on the sign outside by the road. "Your mama is a smart woman, Katie, but it's a different kind of sunshine down here."

"I'm sure you'll figure it out, Clayton. Now try and get some sleep."

"Okay, baby." He stood and closed the curtain to block out the neon glow of the sign. "Hey, Kate? One more thing before you go?"

"Yes?"

"What color are your panties?" He twirled the phone cord around his fingers.

"Is that a trick question?"

"No, why?"

"Because you know I'm not wearing any," she said, and hung up.

Clayton smiled as the phone clicked in his ear. That woman owned his very soul.

Chapter Forty-Three

Once the snoring began, and Nails was convinced that Dallas was fully asleep, he carefully slid his shoulder out from under her cheek. He'd lain in that bed staring at the ceiling long enough. If he was going to do this, he needed to do it now. He knew full well what the ramifications would be. He knew the danger he'd be putting her in, but he also knew that no one had ever looked out for her. Just like him, not in any way that mattered. He'd been exploited his whole life. And he wasn't going to let that happen to her just because she made him feel good about himself. She deserved something better. He'd been the one to make the decision to lose his shit at Freddy's place, not her, and he wasn't going to let her fall down the rabbit hole with him any further. If he did, then all this—the past few days, all the mistakes he'd made—would remain just that—mistakes. It would all have been for nothing. He might as well just have stayed in his seat that night at The Chute and let that dirtbag Robbie do whatever he was going to do to her. She was Nails's responsibility now and trying to sneak her into some Mexican hellhole with him, forcing her to live this life he'd brought on himself, just wasn't the right thing to do. But, maybe tonight, with a little luck, he could right the ship.

He cautiously eased off the bed, walked softly to the bathroom, and used a wad of toilet paper from the counter to wipe off the drool that Dallas had left on his T-shirt. He unbuttoned his jeans, pulled them down to his knees, and recleaned the wound on his leg, using up the last of the fresh gauze they'd stolen back in Franklin. He also ate a few more pills. As he was about to stand up from the edge of the tub, he saw something on the floor. A few things, actually. He leaned down next to the toilet and picked up a fold of one-dollar bills, some lip gloss, a business card for some consulting firm, and a Georgia driver's license. He set the money, the lip gloss, and the card down on the counter and studied the ID. It had a picture of a blond woman that clearly wasn't Dallas—but close enough to pass inspection by a doorman at a bar or club. The date of birth listed on it—he used his fingers to count—would've made her thirty-one. This was obviously Dallas's fake ID, and it must've fallen here on the floor when she was sick over the commode. *Mae McNally* was the name of the woman on the license and her address was listed as *960 South Dunham* in—*Dallas, Georgia*. Nails allowed himself a small smile before he set the ID down on the counter with everything else. He liked being in on the secret.

He gently put his weight on the doorframe as he buttoned up his 501s and listened to Dallas—or whatever her real name was—sleep. He honestly didn't care what she called herself as long as she was around for him to hear it. After he carefully tugged his boots back on, he crept across the room to the dresser next to the TV and quietly opened her handbag, swiveling his head back to look at her every ten seconds or so. He felt guilty about going through her things without her knowledge, but he just piled that onto the rest of the guilt he felt for getting her involved in his life to begin with. At least this was a step toward making things right.

The bag was a soft quilted fabric held closed by a drawstring, so it opened easily enough. The first thing he saw was the silver ring with the blue stone Dallas claimed she'd stolen from Robbie. He didn't like that she'd kept anything of his but he also wasn't comfortable being jealous of a dead man either. He put it back and pushed aside the cheap plastic sunglasses and disposable camera, the medicine bottles, gaudy costume jewelry, and the endless amount of lip gloss and makeup. Then he found what he was looking for. He gently lifted the red leather wallet out of the bag and kept his eyes on Dallas as he undid the snap. She didn't move. She just continued to snore and drool on the pillow where his shoulder had been. The wallet didn't have much in it, a credit card made out to someone named Kenneth Stone that had expired in August 1995, most likely stolen, a Radio Shack rewards card with just a customer number but no name, a pharmacy prescription discount card, again with only a member ID number and no name, and a ton of coupons for makeup cut from various mailers and magazines. No other IDs or anything with an address on it. But there was a picture, beneath a plastic window, that he had to struggle with to remove. A picture with the gold *Olan Mills Photography* logo in the bottom right corner. The glossy finish had faded, but the two faces were easy to make out. One was a man in a dark blue shirt with shaggy dark hair and matching muttonchop sideburns. Nails assumed him to be Dallas's father because he stood with his arms around a blond woman who was unmistakably Dallas's mother. She was also dressed in blue. The picture must've been taken ages ago, before the couple had any kids, but it was all Nails had to go on, so it was going to have to do. He tucked the photo in his back pocket, along with the roll of the cash she had, and grabbed his .45 and the motel room key off the nightstand. The digital clock read 2:14. He stood with his eyes closed and took in a long, deep, final breath before he opened the door and eased it closed behind him.

Chapter Forty-Four

Pinky parked the van at the Whataburger across the highway. He watched as Nails walked to the motel office, spent a few minutes inside, and then got into the Honda. Pinky snatched the new mobile flip phone that Bracken had given him and punched in a number. He couldn't wait to try it. It was the first time he'd used one. The club was getting high-tech these days. Bracken answered on the first ring.

"Pinkerton?"

"Yeah, yeah, it's me. Listen. I think our boy is on the move. I'm pretty sure I just watched him check out of the motel, and he's pulling out of the lot as we speak. I'd say that's a pretty clear indication that he's about to jump ship."

"Was he alone?"

"Yeah, he's leaving by himself."

"So the girl wasn't with him?"

"Nah. Just him."

"Did he have anything with him, a bag, a duffle, anything to indicate long-term travel?"

"Um, no. Not that I could see."

"Then I'd say that's not a clear indication of anything other than he's going out. He might just be hungry. Your job isn't to draw conclusions. Your job is to monitor him. So do your job and follow him."

"Right, right. I'm on it." Pinky set his can of Miller Lite in the cup holder and cranked up the van.

"Pinkerton, I don't need to remind you how dangerous that man is, so keep your distance and if it looks like he is indeed headed out of state, call me back and let me know, and then I'll forward that information to Oscar, but I'm not going to call the man to tell him that McKenna went out for a pizza. Clear?"

"I got it. I'm on him. I'll hit you back."

"Also be aware that every time you use that phone it costs the club money."

"I know, I know. But you gotta admit it's worth it. No more pager and pay phones. No more scrambling for the right location. These things are badass."

Pinky kept talking into the phone while he drove for a solid five minutes before he realized that there was no one listening on the other side.

Chapter Forty-Five

Clayton's eyes popped wide open and he sat up straight in the bed. He looked at the clock on the nightstand. 3:31. What did he say to Kate on the phone? It was something dumb. He said this place had a different kind of sunshine. Shit, why didn't he think about that before he settled in here?

He pushed back the sheets and jumped out of the bed. He pulled the drawer of the nightstand open and felt a surge of pain run down his arm. His shoulder started to throb. *Goddamn.* It must've been from when Jack Comey whacked him with that shovel, but whatever. No time to worry about it now. The drawer only had a small Gideon Bible in it. He left the drawer open and searched the rest of the room for what he needed. He found nothing, so he grabbed the phone, this time a little more gently to avoid aggravating his shoulder any further. He tapped the zero key. It rang and rang and rang. He hung it up and tried again. Still nothing. He let it ring long enough for it to revert back to a dial tone. He slapped it back down and paid for the impulse with another bolt of lightning down his arm. He carefully pulled off his T-shirt and examined his shoulder in the vanity mirror. The bruising looked bad, all yellow and dark purple, but he figured if he could raise his arm above his head then nothing was broken, and he'd just have to deal with it. He ran some cold water over his face and new beard, sniffed at his armpits, and decided he wasn't foul enough to shower. So he put on a clean shirt and a fresh pair of socks from his bag. He pulled on his jeans and boots from the floor, ignoring his shoulder pain, slapped his hat on, and scanned the room. He hoped he wasn't forgetting anything.

Ten seconds later, Clayton was hoofing it down the breezeway, his backpack over his good arm, and heading toward the motel's office. He was still tucking his shirt in behind his belt buckle as he tried the door, locked. He jiggled at the handle and looked for a buzzer. There wasn't one. Next to the door was a large plate glass window. He held a hand up to the glass to look in between the blinds. It was obvious to Clayton now why the kid working there wasn't answering the phone. The ponytailed teenager was passed out cold in an office chair, reclined back with his feet kicked up on the counter. The smell of weed wasn't evident outside where Clayton was standing, but he could only imagine that it had to be inside. He rapped his knuckles on the glass and the kid shuffled a bit, but just readjusted himself and crossed his arms. Clayton banged on the window and then banged again. This time the kid jolted awake. The chair tipped backward, sending the young man straight to the floor. He looked as if he had no idea where he was, and Clayton called out to him. "Hey, buddy. Out here."

The kid stumbled to his feet and quickly slapped the lid closed on the cigar box full of weed, rolling papers, a set of hemostats, and a ton of seeds. He scrambled to use a stack of tourist pamphlets and magazines to cover a large ashtray filled with cigarette butts and whatever else. When he was done, he stood with his arms out to his sides as if God had just spoken to him. "Hello? Who's there?"

"Out here, man. It's Clayton Burroughs from 23. I tried to call you."

"Who?"

Clayton sighed and yelled slower. "Clayton Burroughs. Your guest in room 23."

"Right. Mr. Burroughs. What's going on? Do you need some change?"

"No, I need a phone book. Can you let me in? The door is locked."

"Yeah, no can do, man. The rule is to lock up after one o'clock."

"Well, can you make an exception? I really need to get at a phone book."

"Yeah, I hear you, but I'm not really supposed to unlock the door for anyone after one in the morning. That's the company policy." He began to slide all his dope paraphernalia into a drawer in the desk as if Clayton couldn't see him doing it. In fact the kid hadn't even looked his way yet.

Clayton took off his hat and pressed his forehead on the glass. "Look, man. I don't care at all about what you're doing in there. I really don't. And I'm sorry I woke you up, but I just need to look at a phone book. If you've got one in there and can just hand it to me out the door, that would be great. Really. That's all I need."

"Again, sir, I hear you, but I'm really not allowed to open the door for anyone. I could get fired, dude. And I need this job, you know?"

Clayton reseated his hat and paced back and forth in front of the window. He stopped and looked at the vending machine on the other side of the window. "What if I needed change? You asked me if I needed change. What if I did? How are you supposed to get me change if you can't unlock the door?"

The kid pulled a string inside, raised the blinds all the way to the top edge of the window, and finally looked out at Clayton. He pointed down to a small rectangular piece of metal in the brick. It was a drawer that operated from the inside. "You just put your cash in that, and I'll swap it out for you. How much do you need?"

Clayton looked at the kid sideways. "I don't need any, man. I need a phone book. Can you just stick one in there and let me borrow it for a second?"

The kid mulled it over, shrugged, and retrieved a thick Southern Bell phone book from a cabinet next to the desk. He opened the sliding metal drawer that accessed the outside and struggled to fit the book inside. "It ain't gonna fit, sir."

"Okay." Clayton was losing his patience, but he knew exactly how this kid would react to anger. The blinds would go down and that would be that. He'd probably call the police. He thought about just getting in the Bronco and searching out a phone book somewhere else, but he gave the kid one more shot. "Look, man. Just tell me, do you know if this is the only Sunshine Inn around here?"

The kid looked over Clayton's shoulders and out into the lot, as if Clayton were asking if there was another motel behind him. "In Jacksonville," he clarified. "Is there another place called the Sunshine Inn located in or around the city of Jacksonville?"

"Um, I'm not sure. Maybe?"

"That's why I need the phone book, brother."

The kid suddenly looked pleased with himself, as if he'd just figured out the answer to a riddle. "Well, shit, man. I can look that up for you."

"That would be great, thank you."

Clayton watched as the chubby kid in deck shorts and a black sleeveless T-shirt flipped through the yellow pages in the back of the book. When he got to what he thought was the right page, he leaned down, only inches from the paper and used one finger to search out the names.

"I don't see another Sunshine Inn listed but there is a couple other sunshine places, like there's *The Sunshine Camper and RV Park*, and *The Sunshine Palace*, and *The Sunshine Villas Resort and Spa*. But no other Sunshine Inn."

Clayton rubbed at his sore shoulder. "All right, man, listen. I know this is asking a lot, but do you think you could write down those addresses for me? I'll be happy to pay you to do it."

"My man, I'll do you one better." The kid pressed down on the phonebook and carefully ripped out the selected page. "Will this work?"

"Hell yes. That will work."

The kid folded the flimsy page of yellow paper in half and then in half again before tucking it into a small steel bowl connected to the inside of the receptacle drawer. Before he closed it, Clayton asked, "I don't suppose you have any Advil or Tylenol in there I could buy from you?"

The kid cocked his head and squinted his bloodshot eyes. "Are you a cop, man?"

"What? No. Is it illegal to buy Tylenol in Florida?"

"Nah, man. I'm just saying, I might have a little something-something for you, a little better than Tylenol, if you know what I'm saying. Cheap and on the ready."

Wow, okay, Clayton thought. "No thanks, I appreciate it, but no. All I need is that page and some Tylenol if you have it. If you don't, I'm all good."

"You sure, bro?"

"Yeah, I'm sure."

The kid opened another drawer of the cabinet, pulled out a large generic bottle of acetaminophen, and shook a few tablets into the steel bowl along with the yellow page. He pushed the drawer open, and Clayton swiped everything up. He dry-swallowed the pills, slid a five-dollar bill from his wallet under the bowl, and pushed the drawer back through.

"Thanks, dude."

"No worries. I appreciate your help."

"Yeah, man. Anytime. And if you're ever in the market for you know—the killa—then stop on by. I'm here every night after six. The name's Taco."

"Right on . . . Taco," Clayton waved back over his head as he walked toward the Bronco.

"Yeah, man. For real. See ya. And like . . . good luck with . . . like . . . whatever the fuck."

Clayton tossed his bag on the front seat of the truck and watched the blinds go down on the office window. He got behind the wheel, turned on the overhead light, and looked at the listings on the page. He used a little deductive reasoning to remove the Camper/RV Park and the resort with a spa from the list of potential places to check out and decided that the best option was another motel that, according to his map, was a little over forty miles away in the heart of the city. A place called the Sunshine Palace.

Chapter Forty-Six

Pinky kept the van at least two car lengths behind Nails as he followed him down the highway. He turned off on Exit 12—Edmond Hicks Road— to a town called Petty Branch. Pinky had been through here before. It was a little upscale for his taste. Both the beer and the women were small-batch and exclusive—much too expensive for him. The two vehicles took a left at the next light onto SR 14. Pinky tried to stay as far behind the Honda as possible, until Nails finally pulled into a bar called Taillights. It looked like a RaceTrac truck stop dressed up as a TGI Fridays, and the parking lot was packed, even at this hour. Pinky passed by the lot after Nails turned in, but circled back around and parked on the far side of the building just in time to catch Nails walking in the front door. Once Pinky was settled in with a fresh Miller Lite from the cooler between the seats, he considered using the mobile phone again to contact Bracken. But the big man said only to call him if McKenna headed toward the state line, not if he went to a bar. Pinky wasn't sure why he chose this particular bar, as there were plenty of late night watering holes closer to the motel, but he didn't give it much more thought than that. Maybe McKenna knew some-one out here. Maybe they had two-for-one drinks for the handicapped. Pinky laughed at his own joke. He'd acquired a nice little beer buzz from this bullshit baby sitting assignment. He still didn't quite understand why the MC, or The Englishman, had gotten into bed with these rednecks. Pinky had met Gareth Burroughs several years ago, him and one of his monkey enforcers. He wasn't impressed then, and he wasn't impressed now. But his link in the chain of command didn't require him to understand those decisions. His job was to kick back under the umbrella of his fast-approaching retirement and be happy with all the cash flow that arrangement afforded him. He was just biding his time and doing what he was told. Bracken might be a sanctimonious asshole sometimes, but he was still the kind of brother that someone like Pinky wanted on his side. So with that thought, he slammed his beer, pulled another from the cooler, and waited.

It turned out that he didn't have to wait long to see the big Georgia Boy come back out. But McKenna didn't leave. He just returned to the Honda and sat in the car. Something was rotten in Denmark and Pinky thought about checking in with Bracken again. But for what? He was sure the president would just tell him to wait it out. And so that's what he was going to do. He finished the beers in the cooler as the time passed. All but one. The last one spilled all over his lap and floorboards a few hours after he'd fallen asleep. By the time the wet crotch woke him up, most of Taillights' parking lot was empty, and there was no sign of the Honda. Nails McKenna was gone.

Chapter Forty-Seven

After tipping one of the bartenders twice the cost of the juice he ordered, Nails was quickly able to find out who the owner of Taillights was. A man named Gary Sinclair, and luckily, he was working that evening. In fact, he was just a few tables away, talking to a group of young women. The bartender pointed him out. "He's right over there. He doesn't normally come out of the office just to comp a bill, but for a bunch of honeys like that, it looks like he made an exception."

"Right," Nails said. Gary Sinclair. Gone was the dark shaggy hair and the muttonchops, replaced by a tight gray ring of stubble and a well-manicured beard. He was older for sure, but it was still definitely the man from the picture. Strangely though, he didn't look anything like the devil Nails had pictured in his mind. If anything, he looked normal. Boring. Nothing like the kind of man that Dallas had made him out to be. But Nails knew that meanness came in all shapes and sizes. This was no different. Nails didn't even bother to pull the photo out of his pocket for comparison. That was him. That was Dallas's father. And according to the bartender, Taillights didn't close until four a.m. He'd have to wait. He thanked the bartender again, laid a ten on the bar, and left. He looked back at the balding old man with his pants hiked up way too high, the man laughing it up with a table of girls the same age as his daughter, and he felt a stone form in his stomach. *See you in a few, Gary,* he thought, as the door closed behind him.

Nails half expected to see the skinny man with the mustache or even a group of those bikers waiting for him by the car. He saw the van following him here as soon as he'd left the motel, but there was no one outside waiting. He guessed they were just keeping tabs on him, and if they were going to intervene, they would've done it by now. So he got in the car, sparked the ignition wires under the steering column to start it but left it in park. He listened to Dallas's cassette in the tape deck on low as he waited for Gary Sinclair to call it a night and lead him right where he needed to go.

Sinclair, he thought, and then said the name out loud a few times to himself. Finally, he knew something real about Dallas. He knew her name. Part of it at least. The part she didn't want anymore.

By four-thirty in the morning, most of the patrons and staff had gone home. Nails had listened to both sides of Dallas's mixtape. He watched the bartender he'd spoken to earlier be one of the last ones to leave with a pretty redheaded girl on his arm. Just then, Nails had a terrible thought. He remembered what Dallas had said about her father staying at this bar until all hours of the night. Sometimes not coming home at all. He hoped that tonight wasn't one of those nights. He wouldn't have this chance again and he wanted to be back to her before sunup—before she woke up—and that was only a couple hours. Luckily, that thought faded as the neon lights that rimmed the roof of the club clicked off, one section at a time. He could see Pinky's van clearly now that the parking lot had emptied out. He couldn't tell for sure from that distance, but the silhouette of the driver, backlit by the streetlights, looked slumped over behind the wheel. Whoever it was looked like they'd fallen asleep. Someone was going to have to pay for that. Nails let a small smile slip out. That was getting easier to do lately.

Not long after the bar lights went dark, Nails's target finally showed. Gary, along with two big bruisers in black T-shirts that read STAFF across their backs, came out the front door. Gary was holding a briefcase in one hand and a set of keys in the other. The two bouncers surveyed the parking lot, while Gary locked up and set the alarm. All three men walked to a silver Buick Regal and Gary got in. When the headlights came on, the two men went their separate ways, and the Regal started to roll out of the lot. Nails counted to ten before he followed. With the Regal ahead of him, he checked the rearview for the van. It hadn't moved and he shook his head. That was a distraction he wouldn't need to be worried about during whatever came next.

It was a short ten-minute ride through town before the Regal turned into a subdivision. The car came to a complete stop at every sign and took a series of turns before it reached its destination, a steep driveway leading up to a split-level house. It was a nice house. Nails wasn't expecting the place to be as nice as it was. He honestly didn't know what to expect. There weren't a lot of homes like this back on the mountain where he grew up. It looked like a difficult place to run away from. But children didn't run away from houses. They ran from the people inside them. Nails passed the drive and parked a few houses down. He cut the headlights and made his way back to Gary's on foot. Nails watched him as he held the storm door open with his foot and searched his keys for the right one. When he found it, Nails moved up the drive like a whisper. He pressed his .45 against the small of Gary's back.

"Don't move. Don't turn around. Don't speak. Or I will shoot you in the spine."

Gary didn't move. He didn't turn around. And he didn't speak. But he did piss himself. The smell of urine on the welcome mat didn't surprise Nails at all. Guys like this always pissed themselves. He stifled a sneeze before he spoke. "Now I'm going to ask you a question. And you're going to answer me—quietly. Nod if you understand."

Gary nodded.

"How many people are inside?"

"Just my wife. Please don't hurt us. I have money. I have some—"

Nails thumped him on the back of the skull with the barrel of the gun and then shoved it into his kidney. He wasn't gentle about it. "I said quietly, Gary. Whisper. Use one-word answers. How many people are in the house?"

"One."

"Your wife?"

"Yes."

"Is she usually asleep when you get home this late?"

"Yes."

"Do you have an alarm on the house?"

"Yes."

"Okay, good job. Now listen close, Gary. This is a .45 caliber revolver I'm holding to your back. And I will kill you if you don't do exactly what

I tell you to do. And it will be loud. Your wife is going to hear it. She's going to wake up. And she's going to find you sitting in your own guts on the front porch. Now nod if you have a clear picture of that, Gary."

Gary nodded the best he could through his new case of the shakes.

"Good. Now, if you do what I ask when I ask, no one will get hurt. I'll only be a few minutes. Then you can go wash the piss off yourself, okay?"

"What do you want?"

Nails smacked the revolver into Gary's temple, and he dropped the keys.

"I want you to stop talking," Nails growled through his teeth. "And that's the last time I'm going to tell you."

Gary was shivering now, and Nails was pretty sure that he'd started to cry, too.

"This is your last chance. Bend over slowly. Pick up the keys. Open the door. Turn off the alarm. In that order. Quietly. Do nothing else. If I think you're doing anything hinky with the alarm, or if you yell to your wife, I'll kill both of you. And it's going to be a big mess. Are we good?"

Gary sucked at the snot running from his nose and nodded once more.

"Okay. Then get to it."

Nails took a step back to give the man room to move. It took Gary a moment to get his convulsions under control enough to squat and pick up the keys but he managed. He stood up and slid the right key into the lock. He clicked the deadbolt and then slowly turned the same key in the door-knob. Nails pressed the gun harder into his back and took the keys away from him with his left hand. When Gary saw the deformity he flinched and made a whirring sound.

"Now open the door, Gary. And turn off the alarm."

Gary turned the knob and pushed the door open into the darkened house. A chirping noise and a blinking red light came from a small unit on the wall to their right. Nails used the gun to push Gary toward it. Doing his best to stop shaking, he pushed a sequence of numbers into the keypad. The chirping noise continued, and the light remained red. Nails shoved Gary again. "I'm trying," he whisper-sobbed and punched in the numbers again. This time the light turned to a solid green. Nails moved Gary forward, deeper into the house, and flipped the switch on the wall next to the alarm to cut off the porch light. There were no other lights on in the house, but enough moonlight shone through the windows of the living room to make out the interior.

Gary sat his briefcase down in the middle of the foyer and put both hands in the air. "Wh . . . what now? I told you I have money. I can get it for you."

Nails brought the gun down hard into the side of Gary's head. He collapsed into a heap on the thick Flokati rug. "I told you not to speak, stupid." Nails stood over Gary's unconscious body, gun still drawn, as he listened for any movement. There were stairs to his left and he imagined the master bedroom—and the wife—would be up there. He stood, soaked in the moonlight for several minutes, until he was convinced that no one had been disturbed by the noise, and the alarm had been permanently silenced. Gary was out cold, but Nails kicked him like a sandbag just to make sure. He waited a little longer to listen for sirens just in case the prick had triggered a silent alarm or someone outside had seen them on the porch. When he finally felt confident that he could move freely, he took a breath, tucked his gun into his jeans, and began to make his way around the house.

He maneuvered through the shadows of the wide-open living space, purposely keeping his distance from the huge windows facing the street. The sectional couch looked like real leather, expensive. A velvet painting of a matador fighting a bull hung above it and a modest-sized TV built into a carved wooden cabinet sat against the opposite wall. Abstract art hung above a recliner that sat in the corner. Adjacent to the living room was what looked like a dining area that no one ever used. Cloth napkins were folded into fancy tents and arranged at every place setting. Everything seemed clean, polished, and absent of dust. The rooms horseshoed around into a kitchen lined with dark wooden cabinets and a kitchenette table half covered with a spread of paperwork and documents. The whole kitchen smelled of onions and beef stock, like a roast had been slow-cooked that night. Nails stopped in the middle of the kitchen floor. The house seemed ordinary enough and it would have been if it weren't for the absence of two things that Nails assumed he would've seen by now. There weren't any pictures. No framed photos on the walls, no school pictures of the kids, no family portraits, nothing—and secondly—there wasn't a piano. Nails rubbed at the back of his head. He had a brief and horrible thought that he'd gotten it all wrong. Maybe these people—this house—wasn't Dallas's house at all. Maybe Gary Sinclair wasn't her father. Maybe her father sold Taillights to someone else, and this was the new owner's house. Maybe she'd lied about it. Maybe he should've compared the photo. But he was so sure. Goddamn, did he fuck this up, too?

The kitchen allowed moonlight in from twin windows above the sink, so he was still able to see, but right before the entranceway back into the foyer where Gary was laid out was another short set of steps leading down into a den of some kind. That room had no moonlight to move through. It was full dark. He'd need to turn on a light to see. He slowly crossed the cool Mexican tile of the kitchen floor to the carpeted steps. He tried to let his eyes adjust but the downstairs area remained pitch-black. He glanced over at Gary, who still hadn't moved, and he took the first step. The creak in the board made his heart race. He braced himself on the railing, slid his foot across the step closer to where it met the wall, and waited to hear any other movement in the house. He heard nothing but his own rush of blood. He took another step down, careful to keep his boots to the sides of the stairs. He took two more before the railing ended and he was on the carpeted floor—swallowed up by the darkness. He brushed the back of his hand lightly over the wall to his left, searching for a light switch. When he found it, he clicked it on, and there it was. A beautiful white baby grand, just as Dallas had described. It took up most of the room. But it wasn't the sight of the piano that sucked all the air out of his lungs. It was the plush sofa to the right of it, where a woman in her late forties sat, wrapped in a comforter staring directly at Nails in wide-eyed horror.

Then she screamed.

Chapter Forty-Eight

Nails held his hands out. "Stop. Stop screaming."

The woman only got more hysterical, screaming for help, screaming for Gary. Screaming like a siren.

Nails tried to overpower her tone so he could be heard. "Please stop. I'm not going to hurt you."

The woman pressed herself into the far arm of the sofa and wailed. Nails drew the .45 out of instinct. "Please," he said again, louder but not aiming the gun at her. He moved toward her when another voice bellowed in from behind him.

"Drop the gun, you son of a bitch."

Nails swiveled to look back at Gary, standing on the steps, blood oozing down the side of his head, holding what looked like an antique hunting rifle. "Drop that gun or I swear to almighty Christ . . . I'll blow you away."

Nails suddenly felt like he was swimming in molasses. The woman had stopped screaming and was now hyperventilating.

"Who's in charge now, motherfucker? Who's the man in charge now?"

Nails was thinking in slow motion and couldn't speak.

"You think you can break into my house? Threaten me? Threaten my wife? Drop that gun on the ground, boy." Gary took the steps slowly and moved closer, keeping the rifle aimed at Nails's face. When he got his first good look at Nails, he tilted his head. "What the hell? Are you some kind of retard or something?"

Nails didn't think. He just moved. Gary had gotten too close and put the rifle within reach. Nails swung and grabbed it by the barrel. He heard the empty click as Gary pulled the trigger. The damn thing wasn't even loaded. Nails yanked on it with all his strength, but Gary held on, and Nails sent him crashing into a coffee table in front of the sofa. Nails stood there for a moment holding both the rifle and the .45. Gary held his broken mouth, bleeding onto the floor in the center of the busted table. The woman on the couch was just staring blankly at the whole scene as she struggled to breathe. The room fell completely silent, as if the universe had hit pause. Finally, Nails tossed the rifle up and over the railing and it slid across the kitchen floor. He thought it might have been some kind of replica and not even a real gun. But regardless, it was now out of play. He came back to his senses. The woman began to cry.

"Just stop," Nails said, coming down from the rush of almost being shot in the face. "I'm not here to hurt you. Either of you. Just calm down." When he realized he was pointing the .45 in the direction of the sofa, he lowered it and tucked it away. "I know you're scared. I scared you. But I'm not here to hurt you. I'm not."

"Then what the hell do you want?" Gary said, holding his bloodied mouth.

"I'm a friend of . . . I know . . . Just wait . . ." Goddamn it, not now. This wasn't the time to get all jumbled up. He squeezed his eyes shut for a second and opened them. *Just put it together, Nails, and say it.*

"I came here for Dallas."

Both Gary and his wife just stared at him as if he'd just said something in a foreign language.

"Wait. Wait. I know . . . that's not . . . That's not her real name. But that's how I know her."

"Know who?" Gary blurted out from the floor. "What the hell is all this about?"

"Your daughter," Nails finally managed to get out. "I'm here because of your daughter. That's all. I came to get something for her. Just let me get it and I'll go."

Gary pushed himself up to his knees and went from being angry to indignant. He was still afraid, but something in his expression changed. "You've got the wrong place, asshole. We don't have a daughter."

"Gary," the woman said. It was the first time she'd spoken without sounding like she was being murdered. Nails held Gary's stare. He was confused. There was a piano. This had to be the right place. These had to be the right people. The woman on the couch was the woman in the photo from Dallas's wallet.

"Don't fuck with me, old man. I know all about you two. She told me everything."

"Sharon, go call the police."

"Gary," she said again.

"I said, go call the police. Right now."

Nails drew the .45 again. And he aimed it at Gary. "You're not calling anyone. If you try to, then I'll use this. But if you both just calm down and let me get what I came here to get for your daughter, I'll be gone. You'll never hear from me or her again."

"I told you, we don't have a daughter."

"Stop lying to me, Gary." Nails pulled the picture of Gary and his wife from his back pocket and held it out. "This picture is of you. So stop trying to play me for a fool."

What happened next made Nails feel like he was going crazy. Gary, still bloodied and sitting on the floor, started to laugh. Just a chuckle at first and then a full-on belly roll. "You think *I'm* playing you for a fool? That's fucking rich. I'm sorry to tell you this, pal, but you're the one who got played. You got it all wrong. We don't have a daughter. Never have."

Nails felt himself start to spiral again. This broken-faced fat man was staring at a stranger, pointing a gun at him, in his own house—and he was laughing? The confusion spread like static through Nails's entire body, making his fingertips tingle. He shifted his eyes to the woman that Gary had just called Sharon. She was still crying but she wasn't hysterical anymore. Her chest wasn't heaving. She'd gone from being terrified—to looking almost sad? Could that be right? Everything felt upside down.

Nails glanced around the room. He looked at the piano. A copper plate with several candles burned down to various lengths sat on top of it next to a small five-by-seven framed photo. He focused on the picture more intensely, and then moved toward the piano and picked it up. It was a picture of Gary and Sharon—and Dallas. She was younger, but it was her. Her summer-sun blond hair was cut much shorter in the picture than it was now. But she looked just like her mother. And she was smiling that smile that took up her whole face. He'd recognize it anywhere. These people almost had him convinced that he had it wrong—that he was crazy, but there she was in living color. Nails held the picture out at Gary. "No daughter? Then who's this?"

Gary just glared at him and spit blood on the carpet, so it was Sharon who answered. "That's a picture of us with our only child. His name is Riley. That's our son."

Chapter Forty-Nine

Dallas didn't want to get out of bed. She still had the spins, and she was far from sober, but she had to pee so bad. She rolled over and swept an arm across the side of the bed where she expected to find Nails. It was empty. The sheets were cold. "Nails?" she said into the dark and didn't get a response. She sat up and repeated his name but still didn't get an answer.

She got up, clicked on the overhead light, and made her way to the bathroom, holding her throbbing head. She peed and splashed some water from the sink on her face before she noticed some of her things on the counter. She slipped her hand into the left side of her padded bra, the last place she'd kept her fake ID and cash. She must've dropped it all on the floor when she was sick. Nails must've found it. She picked up the business card and vaguely remembered the man who'd given it to her back at the biker bar. *Bonner.* Bonner Broome, according to the card. He could pass for handsome but what was up with the spray-tan—gross. She flipped the card over and saw there was something written on the back. *Anything, Anywhere, Anytime.*

Yuck, she thought, and tossed the card back on the counter. *Where was Nails?* She hoped he was out finding them some food. She was starving.

She poured a plastic cup of water from the sink to wash the taste of cat-shit out of her mouth and then refilled the cup and looked around for her bag. She needed to take her pill. And she was sure she had some aspirin or some Motrin in there. She spotted it next to the TV and immediately knew something was wrong. The drawstring was undone, and the top flap was wide open. She could see her wallet lying on top from across the room. "What the fuck?"

She set the water down next to the bag and snatched up the wallet. Why had he gone through her things? And where the hell was he? She looked around the small room but didn't know why. It's not like she just didn't see him. He was kind of hard to miss. She knew she was alone. She held the wallet in her hand and dug through the bag some more. The roll of money was missing. She closed her eyes and took a breath. There was a rational explanation.

He needed money to go buy some food. He knew I'd be hungry. He was thoughtful that way. That's why he went through my wallet. But then he found the money loose in the bag, so he took it and he left, but he'd be back soon. Any minute now. That's what happened. That's what must have happened.

She hadn't left anything about who she was in her bag for him to see. She'd been careful about that, nothing with her name or address; she was a ghost—a ghost named Dallas. She'd been thorough about all that ever since she left home—even before Robbie. She thought about the ID on the counter. She'd found it at a bus station near Helen. All that would tell Nails was that her name wasn't really Dallas, but he knew that already. He'd even said as much. She squeezed her eyes shut. She was sure he still didn't know. Even when he saw her getting dressed in the bathroom. She was sure then he didn't know. And would he leave her if he did know? She opened her eyes. *Of course he would.* But that's not what was happening. She was overreacting.

She opened the wallet again and looked through the contents. It took a minute before she noticed it was missing. The picture of her parents. She didn't even know why she'd kept it. Her heart started racing. *"Why would he take that? He wouldn't know how to find them if he . . ."* She closed her eyes again. She'd told him where they lived. Where she grew up. She'd even told him the name of the place her daddy owned. She opened her eyes back up and stared at the empty plastic window in the wallet where the picture had been—right before she threw it at the wall. "Fuck," she yelled and pushed her handbag off the dresser along with the VHS tapes and the cup of water. Everything went sailing and rained down on the carpet. If he didn't know already, he would soon enough. She pictured him sitting at the bar at Taillights having a nice little chat with Gary. "Fuck," she yelled again. Nails wasn't coming back here. She'd never see him again. And why should he? He'd told her his darkest secrets. He'd even told her his real name. And all she'd given him were lies.

The tears started. She couldn't stop it. She sat on the edge of the bed and sobbed into her hands. The motel checkout was at eleven, and now she had nothing, no one, and nowhere to go. She swung at the lamp on the nightstand, knocking it to the ground, and then ripped the clock out of the wall by the cord and threw it. It shattered into pieces against the wall. Why hadn't she just told him? Maybe he would've been different. Maybe if he'd heard it from her. She paced the room, crying and cussing, and crying some more. Her head was pounding, and her heart felt as broken as the busted alarm clock scattered all over the carpet. This was her life. This was always going to be her life.

She stopped pacing when she heard a car pull up outside. The headlights cut ribbons of light through the drapes, forming bright stripes on the wall. She realized she'd been holding her breath and so she allowed herself to breathe. He was back. He was different. He did understand. She fucking knew it. She ran to the door, swung it open, and smiled wide before her heart sank. It was a car she didn't recognize. A couple she'd never seen before were opening the door to the room next to hers. The man was old and wore a suit two sizes too big, his tie undone. His companion was more girl than woman. She wore a terrible black wig and fake eyelashes. They stopped laughing at whatever they'd both found amusing when they saw Dallas standing in the open doorway of her room. She must've looked insane. She felt insane.

"You all right, darling?" the girl in the wig asked. Dallas crossed her arms over her chest, suddenly aware of how bare she was and how exposed she felt.

"I'm sorry. I thought you were someone else."

"Your date stiff you on the cab fare?" the creepy old man asked. The girl in the wig slapped playfully at his arm. "Oh stop it, Sal."

"Fuck you, old man," Dallas growled and shot him a bird.

"Oh my, kitty got claws."

The girl in the wig winked at Dallas before they disappeared into their room and locked the deadbolt. Dallas's arms fell into a tight hug around her abdomen as she slid down the stucco wall. She sat on the concrete breezeway and cried. After a few minutes of sobbing and self-pity, she wiped at her face and got to her feet. She straightened out her dress and looked out at the empty parking space where the Honda had been. She saw all the dried vomit, and then a little closer to the curb she saw the plastic traveler of vodka. She picked it up, shook the contents—over half full—and went back inside.

After thirty minutes of sitting on the bed, hoping to hear another car pull up outside, and draining what was left of the vodka, she stood up, wobbled a little, and gathered most of her things from the floor. She picked up the sapphire ring and wondered how much she could get for it at a pawn shop. Her headache was gone, replaced by a fresh new drunk. She stuffed the ring and most of the contents from the carpet back into her bag and then stumble-walked back to the bathroom.

The couple next door made no effort to hide what they were doing in there. The sound of a creepy old man enjoying himself mixed with the sound of a hooker pretending she was. Dallas considered waiting outside for the couple and bashing the old man over the head. She could rob him and possibly make a new friend of the hooker, but decided not to. She didn't want to fall into that shit again. She swore she never would, and she wasn't ready to break that promise to herself. She needed another way out, now that Nails had abandoned her. So, she did her best to ignore the noise from the next room, took a shower, and dried off. After she put on her makeup, she picked up the ID and business card from the counter. She was glad she hadn't thrown the phone. And despite how late it was, she opted to take this Bonner guy at his word. The note on the card did say *anytime*. She hated it, but what other option did she have? She'd ruined everything. She tapped the nine key and then punched in the number from the card.

"Pick up, man. Please. Please, pick up."

After a few rings, the man with an accent answered. "Hello?"

"Hey there, you."

"I'm sorry, who is this?"

"It's Dallas. From the bar? Earlier tonight. You gave me your card? Is this Bonner?"

"Right. Right. Of course. You're calling a little late, yeah?"

"Honestly, handsome, I haven't the slightest idea what time it is, but you wrote on this card anytime, anything. So were you just flirting, or did you mean it?"

"Of course I meant it, Miss Dallas."

"Well, then. This is the time and I'm the thing." Just saying those words made her want to vomit. "So how about you come and pick me up."

"What about your friend? The big fella from the club?"

"He left." She did her best to keep from crying again. "Turns out he's not really my friend after all."

"I'm sorry to hear that."

"Don't be. I'm not. So can you come get me or not?" She held her breath during the pause on the line.

"Of course I can. I'll send someone to pick you up right now. Just tell me where you are."

Dallas exhaled. "The Sunshine Palace. Room one-two-nine."

"I'll have someone there within the next half hour. My driver will be in a black Tahoe."

He has a driver, she thought. *Maybe this wouldn't be so bad. Maybe he's not so bad. Maybe he'll just give me a place to crash just until I figure out what to do.* "Thank you, Bonner. I'll be on the lookout."

"See you soon."

"Yes, you will." It made her stomach clench trying to sound flirty with this man. He ended the call and Dallas was instantly filled with dread. What if she'd just made a colossal mistake and jumped the gun? What if Nails was coming back? She really thought there might be something this time—something real—something better than this. She grabbed the traveler bottle and chugged the last of the liquor. No, this was her life. She'd always get left behind. People would never want her for longer than what they could get out of her. And nothing ever lasts. And it was better to put on a smile for this asshole than to be booted to the curb with nothing in a few hours. She stood by the window and although she prayed to see a stolen Honda, she eventually left in a brand-new Tahoe.

Chapter Fifty

"Watch where you're going," Clayton yelled out the window and jerked the steering wheel hard to the left. If he hadn't been wired from the White Crosses and Jolt Cola he'd bought on the way there, that big black Chevy would've T-boned his truck as it pulled out of the parking lot. "No one can drive in this state, I swear to God."

He calmed down and parked in front of the office of the Sunshine Palace. It wasn't the Ritz Plaza, but it was definitely a step up from Taco's roach motel, home of *the Killa*. Clayton was only four hundred miles from home, but he felt like he was in another country—a country made of neon lights, concrete, and bad decisions. He cut the engine, killed the rest of his soda, and got ready to talk to the next character on this wild-goose chase.

The office door made an electronic chiming sound when Clayton pushed on it, but no one was at the desk, and no one came running. He banged the bell on the desk a few times and figured he'd give it a minute. After all, it was pretty late. He scanned a shelf of VHS tapes while he waited. *Jackie Brown. Face/Off. The Devil's Advocate.* He picked up a copy of *Chasing Amy*. He loved that movie. He normally wouldn't watch that kind of thing, but Kate made him rent it one night, and he really liked it. The guy who played the lead was going to be a big star someday. Clayton was sure of it.

"Can I help you?"

Clayton turned to see a woman trying to smile at him. She'd clearly been asleep just seconds ago. He put the movie back on the shelf. "Yeah, hey. Sorry to wake you, but I was hoping to find out if a friend of mine was staying at this hotel."

"It's a motel. Hotels have their doors on the inside. This one has its doors on the outside. For easy access. To motorists. Hence, motel." The woman never lost her sleepy smile.

"Um. Right. Okay." Clayton took off his hat and pushed his hair back. "So I was wondering if a friend of mine was . . ."

"Name?"

"What? Oh, right. My name's Clayton Burroughs."

The woman's smile loosened but still kept its shine. "Not your name, sweetie. The name of the friend that might be staying with us."

Clayton reset his hat. "McKenna. His name is Nails—I mean Nelson—Nelson McKenna."

The woman rested on a stool and typed into a computer on the desk. "No McKennas in the system, sorry."

"Yeah, he might be using a different name."

The woman behind the counter just stared at Clayton as if she was wondering what she was supposed to do with that information.

"Look, my buddy is a big fella. He's bald and he might be traveling with a young woman. A blond girl."

The woman kept staring at him. "Are you po-lice?"

Clayton shook his head. "No. Why does everyone keep asking me that?"

"I don't know, the hat maybe?"

Clayton rolled his eyes up to the brim of his stiff Cattleman and took it off. "No, I'm not a cop. I'm just looking for a friend. That's it. Does anyone staying here fit that description?"

"Look, fella. I'm not tryin' to get myself involved in anything crazy. Are you trying to start up anything crazy? I've got three hours left on my shift and I'd rather you just save the crazy for after I leave."

Clayton leaned on the counter. "No crazy. I promise."

The woman gave Clayton a long once-over. "Well, there ain't no McKenna staying here, but a fella named Wayne is that fits that description."

"Wayne?"

"Yeah, a Mr. Bruce Wayne and his lady friend, Vicki Vale."

Clayton laughed into the side of his fist. "Yeah, that sounds about right. You wouldn't happen to be able to give me Mr. Wayne's room number?" Clayton put on his best charming Southern boy smile.

The woman sighed. "One twenty-nine, young man. They checked into room one twenty-nine."

Clayton straightened up and slapped his hat back on. "I could kiss you. Thank you."

The woman warned him again about "no crazy" and Clayton promised. She started to say something else, but Clayton had already started to hustle down the breezeway toward room 129. The sun was about to come up and he couldn't believe he'd done it. He'd found him. He couldn't wait to tell Kate. He banged on the door. Nothing. He banged again and tried to look through the window, but the curtains were drawn. He banged a third time. There weren't any cars parked in front of the room, but that didn't mean anything. Nails probably had to ditch his car after that robbery. Finally, he walked back to the office. The woman behind the desk appeared to be waiting for him.

"Are you sure that's the right room? One twenty-nine? I don't think there's anyone in there."

"Well, that's what I was trying to tell you, hotshot, before you high-tailed it outta here. The big fella left around three a.m. Looked to me like the girl he was with had a little too much to drink. She puked all over my parking lot. So you can tell 'em thanks for that when you see them. But anyway, I reckon he put her to bed and then headed back out. I haven't seen him since."

"But the girl. She might still be in there?"

"Might be. She looked pretty wasted. Your buddy had to carry her inside. Probably in there sleeping it off. Dead to the world."

"Any chance of you letting me in there to check?"

"Nope. That I can't do. Rules are rules. But if you come back at eleven, you can sneak a peek in there with housekeeping."

Clayton leaned against the door. All the excitement of the moment expelled from him, and he felt like a deflated balloon.

"Is there anything else I can help you with, sugar?"

Clayton slowly peeled himself off the doorframe. "I reckon I should get a room?"

The woman turned a clipboard of paperwork around to face Clayton and he filled it out.

"I'll put you in one thirty-two if it's just you. No foldout. Just the one bed."

"That's fine."

"Will there be anything else?"

Clayton had no idea how tired he was until that moment. He'd only slept a couple of hours, and he still hadn't put his eyes on the prize—and he was starving. "Any chance of finding decent food close by this early?"

The woman pointed a thumb behind her. "Cues. Right next door. Best biscuits and gravy south of the Mason-Dixon."

Clayton doubted that, but it made his mouth water all the same.

Chapter Fifty-One

"I don't understand," Nails said, lowering the gun.

"Of course you don't, young man. Neither do we. These things aren't natural. They aren't meant to be understood." Sharon Sinclair pushed the fluffy comforter off her and took a tissue from the box on the table. She wiped at her face and offered another one to Gary. He pushed her hand away.

"You need to go upstairs and call the damn police. This . . . this . . . person just broke into our home and assaulted me—assaulted us."

"Please, Gary, I believe this man has clearly been taken advantage of by Riley, the same way he took advantage of us. I think God would want us to lead him down the righteous path and help him understand that he is as much a victim here as we are, and we shouldn't turn him away."

"He nearly cracked my skull, Sharon. I'm bleeding. He has a gun. This isn't Bible study, and he isn't—"

"Shut up," Nails said. "Just shut up for a minute." Nails tucked his gun back into the waistband of his jeans and held the picture back out to Sharon. "This is not your daughter?"

"No, that is most definitely not our daughter. That is our son, Riley. I have that picture there, on the piano that he used to play so beautifully for me, as a reminder of him, and how what happened to him has left a hole in our family that will never be filled."

Nails set the picture back on the piano. "You're talking as if she's dead. I just left her. Not even thirty minutes away from here."

Sharon smoothed out the front of her nightgown and rose off the couch. It was unsettling to Nails how much she looked like Dallas. She sat next to him as if he were some long-lost member of the family and not someone who'd just brutally attacked her husband and forced his way into her home. The skin around her eyes and cheeks was puffy and blotched, red from crying. Her left cheek looked bruised and yellowed. But her eyes—the blue—were the same faded denim color. They were Dallas's eyes. Warm and inviting. He couldn't stop staring at them. And she didn't seem nearly as afraid of him as she did—or still should be. She laid her hands in her lap. "What is your name, young man?"

"My name isn't important."

"All right, I understand. But you need to understand, too. Riley is not the person you think you know. Someone like you? So easily misled. You have no idea just how deeply the devil had rooted his seed in Riley. Look at everything you've done here. Tell me it isn't because of my son's manipulation. He lied to you. Used you. And I understand how upset you must be. Now that you know the truth."

Nails stood up. The pain from his knife wound shot straight into his hip. The pills were wearing off but he ignored it. "You're wrong. I do know her."

"Whoever you think you know, buddy," Gary said through bloody teeth, "it ain't my son. It's an abomination."

Abomination.

That was a word Nails was familiar with. He'd been called that several times by his own father. He looked at Sharon, searching for any glint of empathy against that kind of horseshit talk, but all he saw in her face was complete and total agreement. He'd known people like these two his whole life. People who clutched Bibles instead of each other. People who prayed for him to be "healed" of his affliction, too. The same people that prayed for Satchel to find the strength to deal with having an abomination for a son.

"It wasn't up to her," Nails said. "It wasn't her job to explain it to you. To help you understand her. She was a kid. You were her mom and dad. It was your job to protect her. To keep her safe. No matter what. She needed you because she had no one else. But she wasn't what you expected—" He slapped the golden plate of melted candles off the piano and chunks of wax flew all over the room. Sharon tried to get up, but Nails blocked her. "So you made her believe she wasn't worth anything.

You made her afraid of telling anybody the truth. You taught her how to lie. Not some goddamn devil. Now you just sit around here and act like you're the victims." Nails pointed toward the couch. "Get up and go sit over there."

Sharon moved to the couch but Gary rose to his feet. "How dare you come in here and judge me, you son of a bitch."

His wife begged him to sit down, but he ignored her and got louder. "*My* son, stealing my *money*—and his own grandmother's estrogen pills?" He pushed a finger into Nails's chest. "If he was standing there instead of you, I'd beat the queer right out—"

Nails was done listening. He swung his left fist like a sledge. It connected to Gary's jaw with a wet smack and knocked him over the couch. By the way he lay against the wall all mangled, Nails thought he might've just killed him. He wasn't sure, and he felt nothing either way. He just wanted what he came for so he could get back to where he belonged.

He looked at the wreck he'd made of the room. "You," he said, and nudged Sharon with his boot. She was afraid to look up at him. "Where is Dallas's music? Her piano music. That's what I came here for. Where is it?"

She pointed a slim and shaky finger at the piano bench. Nails lifted the lid and saw stacks of sheet music and composition notebooks. He pushed the papers around but couldn't make head or tail of it. "Get up and get me a trash bag."

She got up and moved toward the steps to the kitchen.

"If you touch anything else up there, including that rifle, your husband is a dead man—if he ain't already."

Sharon came back down with a kitchen trash bag and shook it out.

"Put everything from that bench in the bag."

She did it without argument and handed Nails the bag full of papers.

"Now go sit on the floor."

She did that without a word as well.

"Now this is what's going to happen next." Nails was seeing clearly. Anger channeled his clarity. "I'm going to leave now, and you will do nothing. You won't call anyone. You won't tell anyone about what happened here. You won't even talk to each other about it. Eventually all this will just be a bad dream. But it will be a dream you lived through. You will never see me or your daughter again. Ever. We're just going to vanish. And you're going to let that happen. Because if you don't . . ." Nails focused hard on Sharon. He really wanted her to understand what he was saying. "All I have to do is pick up a phone and give this address to any one of the killers I know that will do anything I ask them to. You could be in your bed or at the grocery store. You could be walking to your car after work and then that's it. You'll meet that God you love so much. The choice is all yours. Sit here and pray. Forget I exist. Forget Riley. Or call the police the minute I leave and hope that they catch me before I can make a phone call of my own. Even if they do catch me, I'm still entitled to a phone call from jail. Do you know who I'd call, Sharon?"

"Someone to hurt us?"

"Smart lady."

Nails walked up the steps into the kitchen and ripped the phone off the wall. He smashed it on the linoleum floor next to the toy rifle. He was positive there was another phone upstairs or somewhere else in the house if they were hell-bent on using it, but he was betting that the lie he just told about knowing a bunch of hit men that would come and kill them in their sleep would have the effect he wanted. He didn't take anything they wanted. And Gary's jaw would heal. Nails would get back to the motel and wake up Dallas. He'd give her the music she missed so much. She'd be happy to know she was never going to be alone again. And the two of them would finally be done looking for a place to belong. Everything was going to be fine.

Chapter Fifty-Two

Nails tossed the bag of papers and notebooks over his shoulder and unlocked the deadbolt to the motel room. He hadn't beaten the sunrise, like he'd hoped, but it was still early by Dallas's idea of time—by anyone's really. And even if she was up, he knew she'd be thrilled to get this stuff back.

And the rest of it didn't matter. She'd be worried about what he'd found out in Petty Branch, but he'd show her it didn't matter. He knew it would be all right. She'd accepted him without hesitation from the start, so she'd have to get used to feeling accepted, too, no matter how uncomfortable it was. If she could do that for him, he could do the same for her. Everything seemed a little brighter this morning—newer—more important somehow. As if something cold and dark had been cut out of him and left on a stranger's floor in a neighborhood, replaced with something different. Something that started today. With this sunrise. Nails didn't fully understand this odd feeling vibrating deep in his bones, but he was learning. And it started with her. It was the tug of optimism—like seeing colors for the first time after twenty-six years of monochrome. His mind was calm. He knew this time that his words wouldn't get gummed up. He'd get it right. They'd get it right together. He opened the door.

The first thing he saw from the doorway was the smashed lamp on the floor. The bed was a mess but empty.

"Dallas?" The door clicked closed behind him and he dropped the trash bag of loot on the bed. He opened the curtains and flooded the room with light, and then kneeled and picked up a shard of plastic from the carpet. The alarm clock was busted to hell. Some of Dallas's lipstick and makeup was scattered on the floor as well, but her handbag was gone from the dresser. "Dallas," he called out again. The bathroom was wrecked as well, but also empty, and then he saw the liquor bottle on the nightstand. The same bottle that had fallen out of the car the night before—but now it was bone-dry. "Goddamn it, Dallas. What did you do?" He felt at the small roll of cash in his fanny pack. He'd taken all their money with him when he left, but he didn't expect her to need it before he got back. He tried to think. She was from around here, so she must know some people, someone she could have called, but no one she'd mentioned, other than the two he'd just left. "Fuck." He sat on the bed. "Where did you go?"

Like an answer to his question, someone knocked on the door. He didn't even bother with the peephole. He pulled the door open, fully expecting to see Dallas all wound up and pissed at him for leaving again, but it wasn't her, and suddenly everything went foggy again. The buzzing in his brain came back. A rain cloud of confusion choked out all his newfound serenity. He could only get one word out of his mouth.

"Clayton?"

Chapter Fifty-Three

"Hey, buddy." Clayton held his hands out to his sides. He had a napkin tucked into the neckline of his white T-shirt and specks of gravy in his beard from his second visit to the restaurant next door. Nails felt at the small of his back for the gun and Clayton backed up. "Whoa, big fella. I come in peace. I'm a friend, remember?"

Nails leaned his seven-foot self down and poked his head out the door. He scanned the parking lot and saw Clayton's Bronco parked a few doors down. He'd driven right by it and hadn't noticed. "What are you doing here? Did Mr. Burroughs send you?"

"Shit no. You know I don't work for my father. I'm here looking for you. And I gotta tell you, I am amazed. Seriously. I can't believe I found you."

Nails didn't take his hand away from his back and Clayton made sure his hands stayed where Nails could see them. He repeated himself, slower, with gravel in his throat. "Then what are you doing here, Clayton?"

"Can I come inside? I'll explain everything. I swear."

"Tell me from right there."

"Nails, this is important. It's not a sidewalk conversation. Please, man. I'm not your enemy. I'm here to talk to you. Me and Kate and Amy . . ."

"Amy?"

"Yeah, Amy. Amy Silver. Believe it or not, she's the main reason I'm out here looking for you."

Nails spoke as if he were trying to form a sentence out of chewed bubble gum. "Is—is—she—Amy—is—she all right?"

"Yes, man. She's fine. But you're not. So I've spent the last three days trying to track you down. Just let me in and I'll tell you everything."

It took Nails a beat, but finally he stepped aside and allowed Clayton in. He lowered his hands, took off his hat, and looked around at the trashed room. "Jesus, what happened in here?"

"I don't know. But tell me why you're here."

"Okay, but this is a lot to digest. So do you want to sit?"

"No."

"Nails, I swear to God, I'm not here to hurt you, man. Just relax. Please."

Nails slowly took a seat on the bed. Clayton Burroughs had always been a friend. He'd never been mixed up in Gareth's shit. He was maybe the only person Nails knew who wasn't. Clayton took a seat at the table opposite the bed. He realized he still had the napkin tucked in his shirt, so he pulled it out, wiped his face, and tossed it on the table. He started at the beginning, by telling Nails about Kate and Amy coming up to the house on the mountain. He laid out everything they said. He explained that they all agreed that Nails was unwillingly walking into an unmarked grave, sentenced by the very man who sent him there to *save* him.

"My father, Nails. He doesn't just let people who work for him retire. Not people like you—people that know things about him. Things that could potentially be a threat to him down the road. He just doesn't let it happen."

"I'm not a threat to him."

"I know that. Everyone who knows you knows that. Everyone but him. Nails, he's my father, and I know him better than anyone else on this planet. So, believe me when I tell you, he thinks *everyone* is a threat to him."

"So why didn't he just kill me at Freddy's? Why go through all this? Why send me here?"

"Optics."

"I don't understand."

"He didn't kill you immediately after what happened because, as deranged as he is, he does operate under *a code*. If you want to call it that. I know it sounds ridiculous, but he has rules. He isn't going to kill someone in his own family. It's not a good look and it's bad for business. But that's how he sees you, Nails. As kin. Like a son. A better one than me. But you're not blood, and that's important, too. So to handle you, he found a loophole."

"A loophole?"

"Yes, a loophole. I know how it sounds, but I also know my father. So, for him, all this shit he's put you through makes perfect sense."

"I still don't understand."

"Nails, my deddy farmed you out. He got you as isolated as he could from him and anyone else who knows you—or cares about you—so that you disappear—into a hole somewhere. And it never blows back on him, so he doesn't have to take responsibility."

"But no one has tried to kill me here either, Clayton."

"Really? So, what did they offer you, a condo on the beach?"

"No." Nails stopped looking through the open curtains that had been distracting him through the whole conversation and finally stared at Clayton. "He wants me to go to Mexico. Tonight. On a cargo ship. Alone."

Clayton let Nails's own words hang heavy between them and spell out what he'd been trying to say the whole time. He leaned down on the table. "That sounds pretty isolated to me, Nails. And since no one will ever be able to know he ordered it, in some twisted way, he'll feel like he's not responsible for pulling the trigger. So, all the men back home who lick his boots for a living will continue to think he's a saint who doesn't murder his own people—his own kin."

Nails turned back to the window. "Humph."

"That's it? *Humph*. Do you not believe me, Nails? You think I came all this way on a hunch?"

"No. I believe you. I figured as much anyway. It just doesn't matter."

"Of course it matters. How can you say that?"

"Because I'm not going to Mexico. I have my own plan."

"And what is that? To run? Nails, there are probably people watching us right now. Do you really think he can't get to you, or that girl you're with? Before you even hit the state line?"

Nails glared at Clayton before he rushed him. He pinned Clayton to the wall with a massive forearm across his neck. "What do you know about her? Did you do something to her?"

Clayton could barely breathe, much less speak. "No," he wheezed. "Stop it . . . Nails . . . stop it. I'm your . . . friend. I'd never . . . hurt you . . . or a woman . . . you know that . . ."

Nails finally let go, and Clayton fell forward, grabbing at his throat and gasping for air.

"Jesus Christ, Nails. Not . . . cool."

"How do you know about her?"

"Damn, man, have you not been listening? You need to focus here. I told you I tracked you down, starting with the robbery of that gas station back in Franklin. That led me here. And the woman in the office at this motel confirmed there was a girl with you when you checked in. And oh . . ." Clayton pulled the bank deposit bag out of his jeans from under his shirt. "Those two assholes in the Mustang that ripped you off? The ones that jacked your bankroll?" He tossed the bag on the table. "They regret it. You're welcome."

Nails picked up the cash and set it back down. "I'm sorry, Clayton."

"Yeah, apology accepted. Damn." Clayton picked up his hat and sat back down, still rubbing at his neck and trying to catch his breath. "Who is she, anyway? She's the only part of this I don't understand."

Nails sat back down on the bed. "That kid. Back at Freddy's. The one I . . . that I killed. I didn't mean to do it."

"I know that. Everyone knows that. But who's the girl?"

"She's the one I did it for. That punk was doing things to her. I couldn't let it happen."

"So how did she end up with you?"

"Long story. It's not important. But now she's gone. I don't know where and I don't know what to do. Everything I try to do, I fuck it up. And I keep fucking up. And now she's gone."

Clayton eased back in his chair. This wasn't the same Nails he was used to talking to. This was who he used to be—the kid who'd gotten absorbed into the persona of *Nails* that Clayton now felt responsible for. This was the friend that Kate and Amy had asked him to come find. He hadn't seen this version of Nails in almost a decade. In fact, this wasn't Nails at all. This was Nelson. He looked different now. He was still big and angry. But there was something in his voice that reminded Clayton of who he used to be. The kid who put his own life on the line for Amy when no one else could. Clayton got up and sat down on the bed next to him. "Okay, man. I get it. But maybe it's better that she's not here."

"Why?"

"So we can unfuck the situation you're in."

Nails sounded defeated and broken. "What would you have me do, Clayton?"

"I thought you'd never ask."

Chapter Fifty-Four

"And they call me the stupid one."

"Man, you're not listening."

"You want me to turn myself in?"

"To Sam Flowers, yes. Tell him your side of the story. Tell them all it was self-defense. Freddy will back you up. If what you're saying is the truth, anybody who was there will back you up. Think about it. And if you don't mention his name, my father won't touch you. He can't kill his own just out of paranoia. He'll lose his grip on everything. His own twisted code works against him. Hell, Nails, even if you had to do time, and I doubt you will, there's no one on earth built to handle it better than you."

"Thanks, Clayton."

"Okay, maybe that's not the best selling point. But this way, no matter what happens, you get to go home. And you'll have me, and Kate, and Amy, right beside you every step of the way. We can leave now and be back home by nightfall. All of this can be over. No more running."

Nails had been holding the plastic bag full of Dallas's papers and notebooks while he sat on the bed, running his hand over it as if it were a living thing. "You really believe all that is possible, don't you?"

"I do. I won't let anything else happen to you, Nelson." Nails's real name slipped out of Clayton's mouth with such ease it surprised them both. But Nails just tossed the bag on the floor, stood up, and looked back out the window.

"No."

"No what?"

"No, I'm not going anywhere."

Clayton ran his hands through his hair. He'd done what he thought was impossible by even finding this man in the first place, but he'd also known in his gut that this would be how it played out. No one was going to tell Nails McKenna what to do, and no one would change his mind once it was set. Clayton studied the way Nelson was looking out the window. He looked worried. No one in McFalls County had ever been able to get through to the real person inside Nails, but clearly someone out here did. The one person who was absent from the equation. A wild card that no one would have seen coming.

"It's her, isn't it? You don't want to leave her, do you? You know what I'm telling you is the right play, but this is about her. You don't want to leave without her."

"It's not about what I want to do, Clayton. It's about what I'm not going to do. And I'm *not* going to leave her. I've already broken my promise too many times. I'm not going to do it again. I won't."

Clayton put on his hat. "Okay then, brother. Let's find her."

Nails turned from the window. "How?"

"I found you, didn't I?"

Chapter Fifty-Five

They began to scour the room.

"What is this?" Clayton picked a business card from out of a small trash can next to the TV stand. He read the typeface aloud. "Bonner Broome Consulting."

"I don't know," Nails said as he walked out of the bathroom after looking for something, anything, that might let him know where Dallas had gone. "I found that with her ID on the floor before I left last night."

Clayton flipped it over and read the handwritten note on the back. He handed it to Nails. "None of that means anything to you?"

Nails mulled over the name on the card. He'd heard it before but couldn't remember where. "Where was this?"

"In the trash over there by the TV."

Nails had found it in the bathroom where Dallas had dropped it. He didn't think anything of it at the time, but it was with her ID and the couple of bucks she had on her at the time and everything else was gone—but this card had made its way to the trash. She didn't take her handbag into the biker's club with her last night, so she had to either have this card with her when she walked in, or it was given to her while she was there. The revelation hit him hard. "The tan man. Bonner. Don't call him Boner," he said.

"What?"

Nails looked at Clayton as if he'd just walked into the room. "Bonner. He's the tan man from the biker bar."

"I need more than that, Nails. Who is he?"

"I don't know." He picked up the phone and looked back at the card.

"Wait, Nails. Stop."

The anger was setting in quickly and Nails's face flushed with red. "Why?"

"Just hold on a minute. Have you used the phone since you've been back?"

"No."

"Then stop. Think. We don't want to lose a lead, in case that wasn't the last number she called. So try redialing first, and if this Bonner guy answers, we'll know she called him. He won't be able to deny it."

"I don't know how to do that shit."

"Here, give me the phone."

Nails was reluctant. But Clayton was smart. Smarter than him. So he handed it over. Clayton read the dialing instructions on the base of the phone and typed in the sequence to redial the last number called. A man with a thick southern California accent answered.

"Broome Consulting."

"Yeah, hi. Um, listen." Clayton hadn't thought far enough ahead about what he'd say when someone answered. He stumbled over his words. "I'm, uh, just wondering, what kind of consulting y'all do?"

"I'm sorry, friend, may I ask who is calling?"

"Oh, right. Yeah. My name is . . ."

Nails was done listening to Clayton fumble, so he pushed him aside and took the phone. "My name is Nails. Where is Dallas?"

"Dallas? I'm sorry, are you asking me about our affiliation in Texas?"

The voice was all Nails needed to hear to know that he was talking to the same man he'd met at the bar. The man who'd been sitting with Dallas. The heat coming off him was palpable and his grip on the phone tightened. His knuckles white. "We met last night. At the biker bar. You don't want to fuck me around. Where is the woman you gave your card to?"

"Again, I must apologize. I don't know what you're referring to. I run a private consulting firm and I'm afraid you've mistaken me for someone else."

"You are right to be afraid. I know she called you from this phone and—"

The line went dead.

Nails looked at the earpiece and the corners of his vision went white. He resisted smashing the receiver against the nightstand. Instead, he dialed the number again. It rang three times before being put through to an automated voicemail. He stood still for a moment and then hung the phone up. Clayton had seen Nails act like this before. The man was scary when he was in a rage, but he could be downright terrifying when he went blank—like this. "What's the move here, Nails? Who is this guy?"

Nails stood still for a long time before he opened his fanny pack. He unzipped it and took out a slip of paper with a phone number written on it. He dialed.

"Wilcombe Exports, how may I direct your call?"

"Put the fancy man on the phone."

"Can you repeat that, please?"

"Put Wilcombe on the phone. Tell him it's Nails."

"Of course. Please hold."

It only took seconds for Oscar Wilcombe to pick up. "Mr. McKenna, I'm ecstatic to hear you've decided to accept our proposal."

"Can you hear me, Wilcombe?"

"Yes, of course. I can hear you just fine."

"My voice is coming through okay?"

Wilcombe hesitated before he answered a second time. "I can hear you, Nails. Please say what it is you would like to say."

Nails looked down at the business card. "Bonner Broome. Tell me who he is and how I can find him. Tell me now, and don't lie. I know he's friendly with your people and I know you can tell me where he is."

"Mr. McKenna, if you can tell me what the issue is, I'm sure we can find a remedy."

"You said you could hear me. So I'm not going to repeat myself. And if you play this the other way and you send your bikers at me, they better not miss."

There was a long pause on the line. When Wilcombe finally spoke, all the jubilation was missing from his voice. It was overcast and cold. It was the sound of the real man running things. The man who *owned* the dog pound. This was the man Bracken Leek referred to as *The Englishman*. "Bonner Broome is a man I sometimes do business with out of necessity, but he is of unsavory character. I can also tell you that he is protected and well-guarded. The sort of business he runs requires it."

"What sort of business?"

"The business of procuring women—men—boys—whatever. For the purpose of sale."

"He's a pimp."

"At the very least. Yes."

"And this pimp is protected by you and your attack dogs?"

"If you are referring to the Jackals MC, then no. While my affairs do often overlap with Mr. Broome's, they are separate entities. I will tell you what you want to know, but it's vital that you understand me when I say that it means your exit strategy is off the table. I can't be seen as a man who plays both sides. You do understand that. You will be on your own."

Nails felt like he was about to spin off the earth listening to this ass-hole's long-winded answers. "I don't care."

"Our friend from Georgia will not be pleased."

"The only friend I've got from Georgia is standing right here next to me. And I'm running out of patience."

Wilcombe went quiet for a moment and then recited the address. Nails repeated it to Clayton, who'd been waiting with pen and paper.

"One last thing, fancy man. If you feel the need to tip off Broome that I'm coming, when I'm done with him, I'll come for you next." Nails hung up the phone and took the address from Clayton.

"Who the hell was that guy, now?"

Nails ignored him and immediately went to work collecting what he needed. He checked his gun, swiped up all the cash from the table, and stuffed it all into the trash bag with Dallas's music.

"Nails, talk to me. How are we doing this?"

Again Nails ignored him. He opened the door and walked out. Clayton followed him to the Honda and Nails popped the trunk.

"C'mon, man. What is happening right now?"

Nails paused. "Go home, Clayton. This isn't your problem. Go home to Katelyn."

"No." Clayton got indignant. "Hell no. I didn't come all this way to find you so I could just go home and let you get yourself killed."

"You're going to get *yourself* killed if you stay." Nails tossed the trash bag in the trunk.

"I'm not leaving, Nails. Wherever you go—I go. So you can tell me what's happening, so we have a better shot at surviving it. Or you don't, and I follow you anyway." The two men locked eyes. "I'm not walking away, Nails. I'm not."

"Do you even have a gun, Clayton?"

"No."

Nails took a deep breath and reached into the truck. He pulled out the shotgun he'd taken from the two bigot rednecks back in Valdosta. He held it out to Clayton. "Can you shoot this?"

"Nails, that's a scattergun. Anyone can shoot one of those."

"Fine. Then take it."

Clayton did.

"Now, you drive."

Chapter Fifty-Six

Oscar Wilcombe set the phone back in its cradle. When he'd moved to this country from Great Britain with his daughter, he'd expected an easy life that would keep him even-tempered and young. Yes, he'd gotten somewhat rich, but his hair had begun to thin. The lines on his face were getting more pronounced, and with every new but lucrative dealing came a deep fatigue he had yet to grow accustomed to—a weariness brought on by phone calls like this one. The job was supposed to be a simple exportation—and then a quiet disappearance. A problem that would only take a few days to handle and would become a favor he'd carry in his pocket for future use. Now, it had become a headache that would most likely cost him money and become a bloody mess within the hour. He took off his glasses and pinched the bridge of his nose before using the intercom to call for Bianca. The only true and steady thing in his life. "Bianca, where are we this morning?"

"Your first appointment is already here, sir."

"Please apologize on my behalf and let them know I'll be just a few more minutes."

"No problem, sir."

Wilcombe reached into the bottom drawer of his desk and removed a mobile phone. He powered it on and flipped it open. This phone was only used to call a single number. It only rang twice.

"What do you need, Oscar?"

"Gareth, my friend. I'm sorry to tell you this, but your package has gone rogue."

"And how do you know this?"

"From the mouth of the lion himself, I'm afraid."

"He told you personally to fuck off?"

"Not in such colorful language, but yes. Just now. He called to let me know he was turning down the offer."

There was a pause on the line. "So be it, then. Let it ride. I'll get to it when I get to it."

"Of course . . . but Gareth, your man also said something to me that I found to be quite troubling. And I think you should know."

"Yeah, what's that?"

"When I mentioned to him that our *friend from Georgia* would not be pleased, he countered my point by telling me that the only friend he had from Georgia was standing there in the room next to him. Are you aware of such company?"

Another pause on the line and then a muffled crash. Gareth didn't hide the anger in his voice. "I wasn't sure until right this minute, but I'm aware now."

Another loud crash came over the phone with some stifled cussing. "Gareth, are you all right?"

"I'll be fine."

"Is this *friend* your man spoke of also outside the span of what I can offer?"

"I wish you'd talk like a goddamn normal person, Oscar."

Wilcombe eased back in his chair and ignored the jab. "I'm simply passing on information, Gareth. Do with it as you will."

Gareth breathed heavy in the phone. "Do you have children, Oscar?"

"I hardly see why that's relevant to our relationship, Gareth."

"It's a simple question, Oscar. We've known each other a long time. So, yes or no."

Wilcombe didn't see the harm in sharing basic information, so he answered. "Yes. Yes, I do."

"And what lengths would you go to in order to keep them whole?"

Gareth's questioning resembled a threat, but Wilcombe wasn't seeing the point. "Gareth, I suppose there is quite literally nothing I wouldn't do to keep my child out of harm's way."

"Well then, I hope you're hearing *what I'm asking you for* here."

Oscar straightened up in his chair. "Ahh. I see. McKenna's friend is one of your children. Your youngest, I suppose—"

Gareth cut him off. "No more talk on the phone. I'll put people on it, but I need you to keep him out of the line of fire, Oscar. That's priority one. If you can pack him up, I'll handle his ass myself when he gets home."

"Of course."

"Priority one, Oscar. I'm serious."

"I understand. Family first."

"Yeah, that's what they say." And with that, the line went dead. Wilcombe turned off the phone. He replaced it in the bottom drawer of the desk and pushed the call button on the intercom. "Bianca? Please send our guest back now."

"Yes, sir."

Chapter Fifty-Seven

Alex Price entered the office, set his briefcase on the floor next to a plush leather chair, and sat down. The Englishman began to stand but resettled, seeing that his guest had already taken the prerogative. He put his glasses back on. "Mr. Price. I'm sorry to have kept you waiting, but I must say that I am very intrigued by this visit from someone such as yourself."

Alex crossed his legs. "So you know who I am?"

"Of course. I have to warn you that I'm not a religious man by any means, but your father and your family are quite well known. Even here in Florida. I think it's wonderful that you and I have something in common."

"We do? What would that be?"

"Why, motorcycles, I would presume. We have many prestigious clients such as yourself that come searching for the perfect custom yet elegant ride." Wilcombe arranged some catalogues on his desk to face Alex while he spoke. "I'm sure you've done your research and I can assure you that you've absolutely come to the right place."

Alex popped a stick of gum in his mouth from his shirt pocket and rolled the slip of foil into a ball between his fingertips. He offered a piece to Wilcombe.

"No, thank you," Wilcombe said, and jumped back into his pitch. "What type of bike are you interested in? Ducati? Benelli? Guzzi? A Triumph, maybe? That is my personal favorite. I own a Trophy 1200 myself. It's a pristine work of art from the ground up. But I suppose I'm a little biased to the U.K. I'm positive that we will be able to help you find the perfect fit."

Alex chewed his gum and set the balled-up foil wrapper on the edge of Wilcombe's desk. Oscar peered at it over his glasses as if a bird had just flown overhead and shit on the mahogany. He put a quick stop to his rambling.

Alex uncrossed his legs and shuffled his chair closer to Oscar's desk. "Mr. Wilcombe, I've never driven a motorcycle before in my life."

"Well, my friend, it is never too late to learn."

Alex shook his head. "No, I mean, I'd never want to, either. Do you know how many people die every year driving one of those things? The stats are off the charts. No thanks. I'll stick to four wheels and an airbag."

Wilcombe sat back, removed his glasses, and tossed them on the desk. "My apologies, then, Mr. Price. Considering your stance, I'm afraid that leaves me at a loss as to why you're here."

Alex reached into the same pocket he'd taken the gum from and removed a photo. It was the same photo he and Michael had shown Freddy Tuten back in Georgia. He held it for a moment while he spoke. "You said when I walked in here a minute ago that you knew who I was and were familiar with my family. With our ministry."

"I did and I am."

Alex laid the picture on the desk on top of all the colorful motorcycle catalogues. "I'm familiar with you, too. And I was told you might be able to help me. Do you know who the people in this picture are?"

Oscar returned his glasses to his face and looked down. "No, I'm sorry. I do not."

"That's my younger brother, Robert, and a friend of his. This picture was taken two months ago in Atlanta, but he was killed in a bar fight a few days ago in a place called McFalls County. It's in the Blue Ridge foothills of North Georgia. Are you familiar with that place?"

"No," Wilcombe lied. "I am not. But I am sorry for your loss."

"Thank you. I've been able to keep this information out of the media this long. That's why you hadn't heard about it yet, and my presence here today, I suppose, is a fishing expedition to see if I can find the man who killed my brother—and possibly find this woman." Alex pointed to the blond girl in the photo. "Are you sure you've never seen her before?"

Wilcombe didn't even look a second time. It was true, he didn't know the man in the picture. Gareth hadn't told him the dead man McKenna left in Georgia was quasi-famous before sending him to Florida. He would've bumped his fee if he'd known. But he did know the woman in the picture was the same woman McKenna had just called and threatened him about. He'd seen the security video at Bracken's bar. "Why are you here, Mr. Price, in my office, asking me about things that have nothing to do with me or my company?"

Alex rested his elbows on his knees. "Listen, I'm not here to cause you any trouble. I'm not. I found out my brother was killed, and I went there to identify his body. I found out the name of the man who did it, and it led me here, to Jacksonville. I probably don't need to tell you that I am a man of vast resources, so I tapped into a few of them and found out that you are also a man of many connections. You apparently know this city better than anyone, and the man that killed my brother was told to come here. I have more than just an interest in the man himself; I also need to find this woman. So here I am, taking a shot in the dark that you might be able to help me. And I am willing to pay you handsomely for it."

Alex lifted the briefcase into his lap and undid the latches. He spun it around to face Wilcombe. It was filled with freshly wrapped bills. "This is twenty-five thousand in cash. It's for you. All I need in return is the location of that girl. That's it. I don't care about anything else. And if I find her, there's a second case, just like this one, in your future."

Wilcombe considered this man and his offer. Fifty thousand dollars to give up two people he assumed would be dead by the end of the day anyway. The problem would be dealt with. No blowback. And possibly a new friend in this incredibly wealthy televangelist. He really had nothing to lose, if it weren't for the faint echo of Gareth Burroughs's words still drifting in his ears. Asking him about *children*. And McKenna's *friend* being *"priority one."*

"I'm sorry, Mr. Price, but you were ill informed. I don't know anything about any of this. If I could help, I would. But sadly, as it stands, I cannot."

Alex nodded and closed the case. "Well, thank you anyway for your time." He stood up to leave. Oscar stood up as well.

"But leave the case—and a contact number." He handed Alex a pen. "Because one never knows the difference a day might bring."

Alex smiled at the crack in Wilcombe's stony exterior and set the briefcase back on the floor. He wrote his number down on the back of a Wilcombe Exports business card.

"No. I suppose we don't."

Chapter Fifty-Eight

It took Nails and Clayton about forty-five minutes in morning traffic to reach their destination—a secluded road past an industrial park and lumberyard right outside the city. After circling by the address Wilcombe had given them, Clayton parked the Bronco a little ways down a road lined on both sides by chain link fencing. It led to a brownstone-type two-story building. It looked more like a tax attorney's office than a brothel. Clayton cut the engine.

"You know they're probably waiting on us in there, right?"

"Probably."

"And your plan is to walk right in the front door."

"Yeah."

"And you think they are going to just let you in?"

"Probably not."

"But you're going to do it anyway?"

"Yeah."

"Nails, is this girl worth it?"

Nails didn't answer that. He didn't think he had to. "You can still walk away, Clayton."

Clayton didn't answer *that*. He didn't think *he* had to.

Nails flipped out the cylinder in the .45, inspected the load, and clicked it back in place. Clayton inspected the shotgun as well—five shells. Nails got out of the truck and started to walk down the street, keeping to the edge near the fencing. Clayton made his way through a hole in the fence to the woods on the other side. He disappeared between the trees.

A man, much smaller than Nails, stood at the entrance to the building. He wore a dark blue suit and a white button-collared oxford. His hair was cut into a high-and-tight with military precision. Nails guessed the guard was wearing his gun in a shoulder holster, with a backup on his ankle. If Wilcombe had tipped off these assholes, he didn't do a very good job of conveying the threat, if this was the only guy they put on the door. Nails walked directly up to the brick steps leading to the porch and just stood there, his hands in his pockets. He would have whistled a tune if he knew how.

The man in the suit finally caved. "Can I do something for you, buddy?"

"No. I'm good."

"Then keep walking, chief."

Nails kicked a little dirt off his boot on the sidewalk. "No. I said I'm good right here."

The man in the suit pulled back one side of his jacket to show off the Glock he had tucked into the shoulder holster under his arm.

I knew it, Nails thought. *Douchebag.*

"I'm not asking, sport. Now take a walk."

Nails took his right hand slowly out of his pocket and rubbed the back of his neck. "You know what? Maybe you can do something for me."

"Oh yeah, and what's that?"

"Sleep."

The doorman didn't have a second to think about it before Clayton crept up from behind and brought the stock of the shotgun down on the back of his head. He tumbled into the bushes. Nails hammered a fist into his face to make sure he was down for the count and then he took the Glock. Nails also fished the .22 caliber Smith & Wesson off the guard's right ankle holster and handed the small handgun to Clayton, who tucked it into his jeans. Clayton pointed up and to the right of the door at a security camera. "If they didn't know we were coming before, they do now."

Nails didn't seem to care. He pulled open the door to the building and swung the Glock 17 inside. It was just a typical office, a receptionist's desk front and center, an impressionist print on the paneled wall behind it, and a few leather chairs up in front. There was one set of double doors to the left and a staircase leading up to the right—but no people. The front room was empty. Nails used the gun to motion toward the double doors. On a silent count of three, Clayton kicked them in and both men swung their guns inside. It looked like a boardroom. A massive, polished oak table that took up most of the area, surrounded by chairs on casters, and more bad art. But again, empty of any people. They moved across the blue-and-yellow-striped carpet to the stairs. Nails took them first, and Clayton backed him up, keeping the shotgun pointed behind them. If they were expected, this would be the choke point, from above and below.

Nails took the stairs in stride, but Clayton stumbled a bit, dropping the small .22 down several of the stairs, causing unwelcome noise. Nails stopped and shot him a curt look. Clayton nodded. He understood. He quietly picked up the gun, and they continued up to the landing. They crept around the divider wall and ascended to a second-story hallway. One door on the right, another one further down on the left. A young woman standing in the hall surprised them. She wore teal lingerie, a sheer camisole, and six-inch heels. She slow-walked toward them, using the wall for balance. From the faraway look on her face and her zombie-like movement, it was clear she was stoned out of her mind. Nails bent his elbow to point the Glock at the ceiling and pushed the barrel of Clayton's shotgun downward. He held a finger up to his lips. The woman mimicked him by holding one to her lips as well. She was too gone to care who was creeping around in the hallway. She floated by them like a phantom. Clayton stopped and watched her pass; the idea of her made his heart hurt.

Nails tapped him softly on the knee and motioned to the door on the right. Nails moved to the hinged side of the door, staying low, and Clayton tried the knob. Unlocked. He pushed the door open, and then almost gagged. Nails whipped the Glock around and pointed it inside. In the center of the baby blue room stood an obese, hairy man, with his pants around his ankles, his sagging pale ass on full display. Clayton could see a girl—a very young girl—on a daybed in front of the naked man. But before he could do anything, or the man could turn his head around or make a sound, Nails rushed inside. He grabbed the side of the fat man's sweaty face and bashed it through the drywall. It happened so fast. One second Clayton was trying to process what he was looking at, and next, a disgusting human pendulum was hanging from a hole in the wall by its neck, like a side of butchered beef. The girl on the bed was even younger than he thought. She was naked, her arms mapped with track marks, barely lucid. Clayton tasted bile in his mouth as stomach acid burned his throat. He lay the shotgun on the ground, pulled a thin sheet over the little girl's body, and then started to pick her up. Nails grabbed his shoulder and turned him around. He shook his head.

"I'm not going to leave her here," Clayton whispered in a voice far from calm.

"She's not who we're here for."

"I don't care. Look at her. She's just a little kid."

"We'll come back for her."

Clayton wasn't having it and turned to pick her up again. Nails pulled at his shoulder with more force and spun him back around. "Clayton, I need you. We will come back for her. You have my word."

Clayton turned again and looked at the frail outline under the sheet and the face of somebody's daughter. How was something like this even possible? "I'll be back," he whispered to her. "I promise. I'll get you out of here." He reached down and picked up the shotgun. His hands were shaking, but he followed Nails out of the room, leaving the girl behind. They moved back into the hallway, still staying low, and arranged themselves around the other door. Nails turned the knob and pushed in the door. Clayton swung the shotgun inside the darkened room, but this time something fast came down and knocked the gun from his hands. Then something else blurred and jetted out from inside the room. It caught Clayton in the temple and he went down. Nails moved into the room, looking for something to shoot at in the dark but only felt the cool metal of a gun pressed against his head from the hall. Stupid. He and Clayton hadn't been lucky so far. They'd just been lured further in. And he hadn't heard anything. He'd let it happen. And now Clayton was down. Nails didn't move.

"You think you can crash my party without an invitation?" Broome said from somewhere inside the room. A man in a suit came out of the dark. He stepped over Clayton's body on the floor and pointed his gun directly at Clayton's head. A tattooed man in a white tank top and chinos cut on the lights. He held a handgun the size of a small cannon. "Drop the piece, ese."

Nails felt someone pull the .45 out from the back of his jeans. He had no other option. He looked down at Clayton, who hadn't moved, and lowered the Glock. He dropped it to the floor. Next came a blinding burst of pain that erupted from the back of his skull and turned into a piercing white light—and then everything went full dark.

Chapter Fifty-Nine

His head ached from the hit he took, but the pain proved Nails was still alive. His vision was blurry, and it took a moment for his eyes to adjust to the light. He couldn't move. His hands were bound to the arms of a chair. His feet were bound, too. His left hand throbbed like hell. He spoke with a mouthful of chalk, saying the first thing that came to mind. "Clayton?"

"Ahhh," Broome said. "Frankenstein's monster has returned to the land of the living." He stood directly in front of Nails. "Wakey wakey, you ugly motherfucker. Check it out. Me and the fellas couldn't get a zip tie around that big-ass mitt of yours so we fucking nailed it to the chair. Get it? We *nailed* it." Broome laughed, but no one else did.

Nails looked down at his deformed hand to see two shiny silver nail heads sticking out.

"But you didn't even flinch you goofy fuck. I thought for sure you'd at least groan, but nothing. It was fucking weird."

Nails didn't have time to respond before Broome sank a six-inch blade through the flesh and bone of his left hand deep into the wood of the chair. This time Nails did flinch. He wasn't ready for the pain. It was blinding. His whole body seized and he screamed. Now all the voices around the room erupted into laughter.

"He felt that shit, though. Didn't he fellas?"

Nails felt like he was spiraling. He managed to stifle his scream while he bucked against his restraints.

"I'm sorry. Did that hurt? My bad. Here, let me straighten that out for you." Broome wiggled the massive knife side to side between the knucklebones. He yanked it out of Nails's mangled hand. This time Nails didn't scream. He wasn't going to give this bastard the satisfaction again. He ground his teeth and took it. Then he heard Clayton.

"Stop it. Leave him alone," he yelled. Nails turned his head and could see Clayton zip-tied to a chair of his own.

"Oh no," Broome said. "I absolutely am not going to leave him alone. But I can start in on you now if you want." Broome wiped the blade across Clayton's T-shirt, smearing it with Nails's blood.

Clayton didn't say anything else. He was trying to be hard, but Nails could tell by his eyes that he was scared to death. Nails let out a muted, "Don't touch him."

Broome backed off and leaned against a table in the middle of the room. He wore a tan blazer, with a black V-neck T-shirt underneath. The tattooed man in the wife beater was pacing the floor behind him, still holding the .44 Magnum, and two other men in suits were standing to the left, behind Clayton. He should never have agreed to let Clayton come here. It was stupid. But that wasn't a surprise. Nails's entire life had been filled with stupid. Now he was about to die stupid, and he'd dragged one of his only friends right down into the stupid with him.

Broome scraped the tip of the blade lightly across the polished tabletop. "So what exactly did you think was going to happen here, big fella? Did you think you and the ginger here were just going to bust up in my place like a couple of cowboys and rescue the damsel in distress? Are you really as stupid as you look? Pepe, look at this guy. How do you think he even got out of kindergarten being this fucking stupid?"

"No clue," the tattooed man said.

"No clue. That's what you look like right now, big boy. Like you got no fucking clue. And guess what?" Broome came off the table. "You don't." He grabbed Nails by one side of his face and slid the knife down his right cheek. The skin split and blood poured from the wound, but he still didn't scream, or cry out, or even blink. He held Broome's eyes until he moved back and looked away. Then he pointed the knife. "Oh my," Broome said. "What is that about? You got an Ouchy?" A bloodstain had begun to spread across Nails's jeans. Broome brought his fist down on the wounded leg. More white bursts of light flashed in his vision. He winced in pain, but still didn't scream.

"Oh, c'mon, big boy. You're really not going to let me have any more fun listening to you holler?"

Nails let his vision clear, found Broome's eyes again, and tried to let himself be amused by the man's spray-tanned face. "I'm going to kill you, Boner."

Broome chuckled. "You hear that, boys? He's gonna kill me." He hammered another punch into the cut on Nails's cheek. And then another. He brought the hilt of the knife down on his wounded leg. Then again on his ruined left hand. Clayton yelled out again for Broome to stop. Nails just spit blood in his face and tried to keep conscious. He could take it. He had to. He wasn't done yet. He needed to keep the focus on him, and why he was there. *Dallas*. He was there for Dallas. "Where is she?" he asked.

"She?" Broome laughed. Pepe did, too. "She . . . is in the back. We've been having a right good time this morning." He wiped his knife on Clayton's shirt again. "She—and I use that term loosely—is a rare beast, yeah? I was lucky to find her. I can understand why you'd want her back. The things she can do with the right persuasion. I—how do I put it? I took *risks* with that one."

Nails struggled against his restraints, and this time, for a moment, Broome and his people tensed, thinking he might break free. But he didn't.

Broome screamed into Nails's face. "She came to me, you bald fucking inbred. I want you to remember that. I want you to remember you gave up your life, and the life of Howdy Doody over there, for a whore who came to me *willingly*. You really are as stupid as you look."

"I'm going to fucking kill you, Boner."

Pepe giggled at the insult, but after a curt look from Bonner, he stifled it immediately.

Broome put his hands on his hips. He was getting frustrated. "Playground insults, huh? Now I think you really are retarded." He moved over to Clayton. "I wonder if the ginger here is just as immune to pain as you are?" He held the knife up to his ear and Clayton struggled to move his head away from the blade. Bonner ordered one of the suits to hold him steady. One of them put Clayton in a headlock and exposed his ear to the blade.

"I'll start with this," Broome said. "But the nose—man, that is really the best part to take off. People look fucking insane without a nose. It's crazy, man. But you'll see. I'll save that for last."

Clayton tried to break free but couldn't. Broome grabbed a handful of his hair and held the knife to his ear. But a new voice thundered into the room, interrupting the cut.

"Put the knife down, Bonner." It came from the door behind Nails. Broome turned to look as the man holding Clayton's head let go. He drew his gun. The other man in the suit did, too. What happened next only took seconds. But for Nails, it felt like an eternity. Automatic gunfire deafened everyone and filled the room with a blue haze. Pepe fell to the floor to keep from being mowed down. He dropped the .44. He decided to leave it. Clayton made himself as small as possible as the two men behind him were cut to ribbons. Chips of paneled wood and brass shell casings bounced all over everything. Nails thought the gunfire would never stop. But it did, and the room fell silent. All but the ringing in his ears. Broome had hit the floor as well and had his face covered. He must've dropped the knife, nowhere to be seen. He slowly took his hands away from his eyes as half a dozen men in black hoodies filed into the room. Some of them wore jeans and sneakers, some wore black tactical pants and boots, but all of them wore balaclavas or bandannas over their faces. All of them had their hoods up. And all of them carried automatic rifles.

"What the fuck is all this?" Broome said.

The biggest one in the group answered him. "If you don't say my name out loud, Bonner, I won't have to kill you. Are we clear."

"All right. All right." Bonner looked around the room at the hooded men. "But what is this shit? I'm within my rights here. These men broke into my place. This is a personal matter that doesn't concern you people."

"Well, apparently it does." The leader motioned to one of the hooded men. "Cut them loose." Then he pointed at Pepe, still flat on the floor. "And find Pepe's gun." He looked closer. "Goddamn. Is that a .44 Magnum? It might take two of you to hold it."

Nails watched a man with a hood pick up the huge gun from the carpet and try to figure out what to do with it. Another hooded figure was kneeling, trying to cut through the zip-ties around his ankles. The hooded man didn't look up at Nails but he whispered. "I'm doing you a solid here, McKenna. So don't rat me out for falling asleep in the van the other night. You just shook the tail. Cool?"

Nails nodded—and that confirmed who he thought these voices belonged to. Pinky cut his right hand loose, and Nails ripped his left hand free as if he felt nothing and stood. He used his shirt to wipe at the blood streaming down his cut cheek. One of the hoods handed him a bandanna. He used it to wrap his wounded hand.

"What the hell is going on here?" Broome said again but he stayed on his knees. Everyone ignored him while two other hoods freed Clayton.

The leader of the group lowered his rifle and looked at Nails. "You should go."

There was no mistaking those stone-gray eyes. "Your boss said I'd be on my own here."

"Yeah, well, you still are."

"I don't understand."

"I wish I could say this was about you, McKenna, but it's not." Bracken turned and pointed to Clayton. "It's about him."

Clayton had managed to stand but his legs were shaky. He coughed out his words. "What's about me?"

"You're a VIP, son. Your presence here has some important people concerned. We're here to get you out safe and get you home."

"Some important people? You mean my father?"

"Does it matter?"

Clayton looked at Nails. "No. I guess it doesn't, but it does matter that we find Dallas."

"Look kid, I said you were a VIP, not that you have any say-so about what happens. We're here to remove *you* from harm's way, that's it. So, let's go."

Clayton didn't look terrified anymore. He looked emboldened. As if he now had some kind of leverage. He reached down and picked up one of the dead men's handguns at his feet. Six automatic rifles went up and trained on Clayton. All of them except Bracken's. He didn't flinch. Clayton didn't aim the gun at anyone in particular. He just swung it around. "Man, whoever you are, I appreciate the save. I really do. But you can tell whatever *important people* you answer to that I'm not leaving this place until that man over there finds who he came here to find."

"Put the gun down, Burroughs."

They knew his name. He'd called it right. These were people who knew his father. They had to be. "I will, but something tells me that no one in this room is going to take the chance of shooting me and having to answer for it. So just let us find the girl. Please."

Bracken stood quiet and stared at Clayton, studying his resolve. He finally held up a gloved hand and then slowly lowered it. Every gun in the room lowered with it. "Okay, son. Do your thing."

Nails took that as a license to move. He stepped toward Broome and yanked him to his feet.

Broome looked to Bracken. "This is bullshit, man. You can't let this happen."

Bracken just backed away and Nails pulled the pimp in close. "Tell me where she is."

Bonner looked at Bracken again, who rested his assault rifle over his shoulder. "Tell the man what he wants to know."

"Tell me, now," Nails screamed, spitting blood into Broome's face.

The tan man pointed at the wall. "She's in there."

Nails couldn't see anything. "In where."

"There. It's a room. Just press on the wall."

Nails looked again, and this time he could see the faint outline of a door. He dragged Broome across the floor and pushed it open.

Chapter Sixty

Dallas was lying on a filthy mattress on the floor. She was on her belly, covered in bruises. Her black dress was ripped into thin strips of elastic fabric, and she wasn't moving. Nails growled at Broome, lifted him into the air, and smashed him into the doorframe. Something cracked inside him and he screamed as he slid to the floor. Nails left him and dropped to his knees. He took off his jacket and tossed it over Dallas. A leather works kit sat open on the floor next to the bed, a burnt spoon, used syringes, and a scattering of little balloons filled with black tar. Nails gently turned Dallas over. He could see the fresh pinholes in her arms. Her eyes were open, but the color had drained from them. They were glossy and gray, her pupils huge black voids.

"Dallas? It's me. Dallas?" He shook her. "Dallas, please wake up." Her eyes rolled back in their sockets as he tried to hold her upright. "Please, Dallas, wake up." He shook her harder. Nothing. Her lips were dry, waxy, and cracked. Her hair felt like straw and the room smelled like sweat, vinegar, and death. Nails buried his face in her neck. Her skin felt cold and clammy on his face. The tears started to come, and they stung the gash on his cheek. "I'm sorry I left. But don't do this. Please don't go. Please wake up."

Foamy white spittle leaked down her cheek. Out of the corner of his eye, he saw Broome inching his way into the main room. Nails gently laid Dallas down, spun around, and grabbed him by the hair. "No," he said and raised Broome off his feet. "I told you I was going to kill you, Boner." He bashed Broome's face into the doorframe. Blood splattered all over the wall. "I told you I was going to kill you for hurting her." He bashed his spray-tanned face into the wood again. And that's when he heard her. He heard Dallas cough.

Nails dropped Bonner again and rushed back to her side. She was trying to focus her eyes. She was trying to speak. Nails leaned in as close as he could.

"Don't," she said. "Don't kill him." She coughed again. "That's not who you are anymore. You came for me. That's all that matters. Don't be"—she hacked again—"who . . . they want you to be."

Nails had already forgotten the man on the floor behind him as soon as he heard her voice.

Chapter Sixty-One

Nails folded his jacket in around her like a blanket and picked her up. He stepped over the mangled garbage at his feet that he'd already forgotten about and made for the exit. "She needs a hospital, Clayton," he said as he rushed through the room. Everyone let him pass.

Clayton turned to Bracken. "There's a girl," he said. "A little girl. In the room across the hall. She's only . . ."

"Say no more." The big man pointed, snapped his fingers, and two hooded men hustled out into the hall. "We'll get the little girl to a hospital, and we'll look for anyone else. You have my word."

Clayton couldn't make out the man's face, but he could see his eyes. Clayton had looked into the eyes of a killer before. And this man was definitely a killer. But there was something else going on in there. Honor, maybe. Clayton was grateful for it. "Thank you," he said. "I'm going to take Nails and that woman to the hospital we saw on the way here. I know you're here because of my father. And if he wanted me out of harm's way, I am. You did your job. Have me followed if you want to but I need to go. I'm not going to go anywhere I can't be found. So, are you going to try and stop me?"

"No," Bracken said. "Go with McKenna. We'll clean this up like it never happened."

Clayton nodded and headed downstairs.

Once he was gone, Bracken pulled the balaclava from his face. All the other hoods unmasked themselves, too. Bracken picked up the .44 Magnum from the table and dumped all the bullets from the cylinder into his palm. He helped Pepe Ramirez to his feet and handed him the gun, handle first. "It looks like you're running this show now. But under my rules. No more kids, girls—or boys—and no more dope unless it's cleared by me. If I hear you broke any of my rules after today, nothing will keep me from ending you."

Pepe pointed at Broome's mangled body on the floor. "What about him?"

Bracken unshouldered his rifle, walked over to Broome, and fired two rounds into his head and heart. He stepped back to Pepe. "There is no him. So do you understand?"

"*Si, lo entiendo.*"

"Good. Now clean all this shit up. Pinky? You and Romeo stay and help. Burn what you can't bury. The rest of you? Let's go home."

Chapter Sixty-Two

Clayton drove as fast as he could. They both knew they were losing precious time by the second. Nails cradled Dallas in his lap and spoke to her the whole way. He wiped the drool from her face and pushed her hair back out of her eyes. She'd broken into a sweat while they were driving and was shivering now, but Nails took that as a good sign. She was alive. He was careful to keep her covered with his coat, despite no one being around to care. He didn't expect for her to talk to him, but at some point, she did. He didn't hear her first words over the rush of wind through the windows, so he leaned in closer.

"Dallas, I'm here. I'm right here. We're taking you to a hospital."

Her voice was like thirty-grit sandpaper rubbing against her throat. "What happened to your face?"

"It's nothing. I'm fine. Don't try to talk. We are almost there."

Of course, she didn't listen. "You came back."

"I never left, Dallas. I only . . . wanted . . ." *Goddamnit, brain, not now. Not now.*

"I'm sorry."

"No. Don't say that. I'm sorry. I should've told you where I was going."

"No," she coughed and spit up more foam. He wiped it away with the bandanna wrapped around his hand. "No," she said again. "I'm sorry for all of it. From the start. I picked you." Her words sounded like they were being filtered through gravel. Clayton and Nails both rolled up their windows to be able to hear her better.

"I picked you, too."

Clayton glanced over at them, and again, he was looking at Nelson McKenna, not Nails. This wasn't the thug his father spent years turning into a weapon. Not anymore. This was who Nelson was always supposed to be. A protector.

"No. Listen," Dallas said. "I mean I picked you. I saw you outside that night." She spoke in bursts between coughing fits. "I saw you get out of your car . . . and break that guy's arm . . . But then you were kind to him . . . I flirted with you on purpose . . . I danced for you . . . so you'd notice me."

Nails wiped more drool from her cheek as she shivered.

"Because I needed . . . you. To save me . . . from Robbie. I used you, Nelson . . . I'm not a good person."

Nails didn't care at all about her confession. He rested his forehead on hers. "Neither am I," he said. "But together—we can be better."

Clayton plowed into the emergency lane at St. Vincent's Riverside Hospital. He screeched the truck to a stop, nearly sending everyone through the windshield before he got out and ran to open the passenger side door. Nails carried Dallas though the huge sliding glass doors. "We need a doctor," he yelled. Dallas's body began to seize up in his arms as he shouted. She became rigid and started to convulse.

"We need a doctor, please," Nails continued to yell across the waiting room.

Several nurses rushed to them, and soon Dallas was out of the canvas jacket wrap and covered in a sheet on a gurney. Nails tried to answer questions on the fly, but he couldn't. He tried to stay with her, but Clayton had to hold him back. The big man stood in front of the one-way doors that said ESSENTIAL PERSONNEL ONLY for a long time. After a few more minutes of pacing the fluorescent waiting room, a nurse finally came back out with a clipboard. "Excuse me, sir?" she said to Nails. "We have administered Narcan to the patient to try and combat the apparent overdose, but—oh my God." The gash on his cheek surprised her. "Sir, you need medical attention yourself."

Nails lowered his head. "Just help her. I'm fine."

"But sir."

"I said I'm fine. Leave me alone."

"Okay, well your friend is still in critical condition and is suffering from internal bleeding. The doctor needs as much information as possible about what happened. Can you help me with that?"

Nails looked directly at the nurse. She realized then that he was different and shifted her tone to a honey-coated voice reserved for a child.

"Are you any relation to the patient?"

"No."

"Can you tell us the patient's name?"

"Dallas—No—Riley . . . I think."

"Do you have a contact for his next of kin? Or do you know his blood type?"

"No."

"And can you tell me your name, sir?"

"No."

Clayton stepped in and tried to take over, but Nails pushed him back. "No, Clayton. You've done enough. I can do this." Nails took a breath and tried to center himself. "My name is Nelson. Nelson McKenna. My friend's name is Riley Sinclair. She doesn't have any other family. And she needs you in there more than I need you out here."

The nurse took a moment to write what she could on the clipboard. "Can you tell me what happened, Mr. McKenna? Or what specific drugs *she* is on? Which narcotics or medication?"

Clayton stepped in again. "I think she was given a large dose of black tar heroin."

"Okay. And was this a domestic altercation? I can see that you are also wounded."

"Oh. Right. No. This isn't what it looks like. Mr. McKenna's friend was attacked. He tried to help and that's how he got hurt. The attackers left. And I brought them here. That's really all we know."

"Are you related to the patient, sir?"

"No. Honestly, I don't know her at all."

"And your name, sir?"

"Clayton Burroughs." He spelled it out for her as she wrote it down.

"Can I ask you both to take a seat and fill out some paperwork for us." She handed the clipboard to Clayton, not Nails. "Just do the best you can. But I'd ask that you please not leave, considering your friend's condition, I'm sure the doctor will have some additional questions for both of you."

"We'll be right here, but do you think I could possibly get a clean rag or something for my friend's face?"

"I'll bring you some gauze."

"Thank you."

It took some time, but Clayton was able to convince Nails to sit. He flopped down in one of the plastic seats lining the glass wall. A man in a Marlins baseball jersey sitting next to him got up immediately and left. Clayton took the vacated seat. He leaned down on his elbows and spoke under his breath. "You need to leave. Here, take my keys, get in my truck, and go."

Nails shook his head. "I'm not going anywhere."

"Listen to me, man. You are already wanted for the thing back home and maybe the gas station robbery, too. And we both look like we just walked off the set of a horror movie. This shit does not look good. And that nurse? She's about to run both our names and call the police. I can buy you some time here but you've got to go." Clayton tried to tuck the keys to the Bronco into Nails's hand. He refused.

"I'm not leaving her, Clayton."

"They are going to fucking arrest you, Nails. And on top of everything, they'll probably blame you for all this, too."

"I'm not leaving her."

"You do understand the difference between turning yourself in to Sam Flowers for something you did in self-defense and being arrested in another state for a bunch of other shit, right?"

"I'm not leaving her, Clayton. And I thought you told me you came here to let me make my own choices. Not to be told what to do."

Clayton hung his head. Nails was right. This was his decision. "Okay," he said and leaned back in the chair. "I'll be right here."

It took less than ten minutes after Clayton's warning for the police to show up. Neither of them was surprised when they saw the blue lights outside reflecting off the glass. The sliding doors opened, and there was a parade of local, state, and federal agents. The nurse who called it in motioned toward Clayton and Nails. The officer in charge, a brunette, with her hair pulled back into a tight bun, announced herself and drew her side arm, as did a half dozen other cops, all training on Nails and Clayton.

"Nelson McKenna and Clayton Burroughs. On the floor. Now. Both of you. On the floor and hands behind your heads. Down, now."

Nails and Clayton both complied and lay down on the cold tile floor of the ER waiting room as the police scrambled to cuff them both. It took them some time to deal with Nails's left hand. Clayton and Nails were only inches away from each other. Their cheeks pressed hard into the smooth tile. The lead investigator kept her distance but addressed Nails directly. "You're McKenna?"

Nails strained to look up from the floor. "That's my name."

"You are wanted for questioning in the state of Georgia involving the murder of Robert Price. These officers are now going to lift you up and read you your rights. Do you understand?"

He looked across at Clayton. "This is what you wanted, right?"

"Not like this, buddy. But don't worry. You're not alone. I got you."

"Do you understand?" the female agent said again, much louder.

"Yes." It took several of the officers, all dressed in tan, blue, and black, to lift Nails to his feet. Every other cop in the room took a step back when Nails finally got to his full height, but Nails didn't fight them. He didn't offer any resistance at all. He even stopped listening to them. He just looked back at Clayton, who'd been lifted to his knees by a pair of county deputies.

"Don't leave her, Clayton."

"I won't."

"Promise me. It doesn't count unless you promise."

"I promise you, Nelson. I've got this." He watched as they walked Nails out of the hospital ER and put him into the back of a Duval County patrol car. Clayton wasn't sure if this was the right thing or not, but he was sure that no matter what happened, he'd keep his word.

One of the deputies asked Clayton to stand and turn around. The sheriff of Duval County instructed the deputy to remove the handcuffs. "Those won't be necessary."

The deputy removed the handcuffs and was curtly excused.

"Clayton Burroughs?"

"That's me."

"You're free to go, son."

"I am?"

"We'd appreciate it if you stuck around for a few days all the same, in case we have any questions for you, but yes, you're allowed to leave." The sheriff handed Clayton his card.

Clayton took it and stuck it in his back pocket without looking at it. "So I'm not under arrest?"

The sheriff chuckled. "Just call my office in the morning, son, and let me know where you'll be staying. If we need a statement, then we'll call you in."

Clayton wasn't about to argue. "Okay. Will do."

"And if I can do anything for you. Anything at all. You just let me know." The sheriff winked.

"Um, okay. Thanks."

The sheriff tipped his hat. "And tell your deddy I said hello."

Chapter Sixty-Three

Clayton made the call to the Duval County Sheriff's Office to inform them he could be found at the Sunshine Palace motel where he'd extended his stay, but no one ever reached out to him in return. He was never called to come in or asked anything pertaining to the incident at Broome Consulting concerning Nails or Dallas or anyone else. There had been nothing about it in the papers or on the news either. The men who helped them had told Clayton at the time that it would be like it never happened and that was exactly how it felt. Except for the damage done to Nails and his friend Dallas.

He split his time between watching VHS movies he checked out from the lobby of the motel and sitting at St. Vincent's hoping to hear some good news about Dallas. That good news never came. So far he'd learned she had suffered a fractured hip, several broken ribs, a broken wrist, massive internal bleeding, and torn ligaments in her shoulder. But the worst of it was the overdose. Her seizures had caused respiratory failure and cut off the supply of oxygen to her brain until the doctors were able to get her back. She was now lying in an induced coma—one Clayton was told she might not wake up from. There was nothing left for Clayton to do now but hurry up and wait. So that was his plan—to wait. He'd given his word.

He checked in with Kate every night for the first few days. She told him that Nails had been transported back to McFalls County but now he was sitting in a jail cell somewhere in Fulton County awaiting an indictment hearing for the killing of Robert Price. Kate said it looked possible that the charges would be kicked down to manslaughter. But the whole thing got complicated once everyone found out the dead man was the son of a famous TV preacher. He was one of those late night *buy your way into heaven* types, just by calling in your credit card number. Clayton wasn't a fan.

On the fourth day after Dallas had been hooked up to a ventilator, Clayton sat alone in a small waiting area at the hospital watching the news on a TV mounted in the top corner of the room. The volume was down, but the ticker scrolling across the bottom of the set mentioned the passing of that very same popular televangelist. His name was Tyson Price. He'd suffered a massive stroke several months ago, according to the closed captioning. Clayton reckoned the death of the preacher's youngest son had caused the last thread tethering the old man to this world to finally snap. Clayton imagined if there was a God, that old Tyson Price must be having to answer for the con game he'd played in life that made him rich off the backs of the faithful. At least Clayton hoped that was the way it was going down. The preacher's older son had been on the TV a lot as well, talking about God's plan or some other teleprompted cardboard shit. Every network also plastered Nails's mug shot every chance they could. The picture looked doctored. They made him look like a monster. The con artist and his dead son were made out to look like American royalty, but Nelson McKenna was made to look like a crazed murderer. Clayton got sick of hearing it pretty quick.

He got up and turned the channel to *The Andy Griffith Show* and sat back down. About fifteen minutes into the second episode of a marathon, a doctor by the name of Swann came into the waiting room and slumped down in the chair next to him. The doc had a round sweet face and looked entirely too young to be a seasoned ER doctor, but today she looked hollowed-out and dry. She sat for a minute and stared blankly at the television before she let the gentle hammer fall on Clayton.

"I'm afraid all I've got is bad news."

"Well, then all you can do is shoot it straight, Doc."

"Are you sure that Riley's parents don't want to be here for this?"

Clayton still wasn't used to hearing Dallas referred to by that other name. "I've tried several times, Doc. So have the police. They aren't interested. She's over eighteen, so no one can make them." Clayton *had* tried to contact her parents, but they just kept telling him to leave them alone. They told him that Riley was already dead to them. They also sounded afraid to even talk about it. He eventually gave up. "I can't understand people like that, but it's how it is. So, as sad as it may be, I'm all she's got right now."

"So you wouldn't know if Riley has a DNR order in place?"

"Do you know any healthy nineteen-year-old kids that do?"

"Right. I suppose not." Dr. Swann rubbed at her eyes and yawned against her will. She also looked hesitant to say anything else and Clayton felt lucky he didn't have to do this woman's job.

Clayton broke the silence and got right to it. "Is she dead, Doc?"

"Technically no. But the ventilator is the only thing keeping Riley alive. We have no idea how long her brain went without oxygen, so even if she were to come out of the state she's in, we have no way of knowing the full extent of the damage. Her quality of life moving forward is what we should be thinking about now. And without any next of kin to claim her, she'll become a ward of the state." She finally looked Clayton in the eye. "Unless you apply for guardianship, but that could take a while and time is not on our side."

Clayton took off his hat and held it in his lap. He rolled the brim in his hands. "You've seen this kinda thing before?"

"I have. Too many times to count."

"So what are her chances? No bullshit. Is it possible she could be okay?"

Dr. Swann whistled out a long exhale. "Anything is possible. But it's a hundred to one that she even wakes up. And like I said, that might be the beginning of the worst part."

Clayton shook his head. "I've heard of folks coming back from some pretty crazy odds, Doc."

"I admire your optimism."

Clayton stood up and reseated his hat. "Do I need to do anything right this minute or do I have a little time to sort some things out?"

"Take all the time you need, Mr. Burroughs."

Chapter Sixty-Four

Clayton was about to open the door to his Bronco when he heard someone call his name from a few cars over. He turned to see Alex Price walking toward him. "Mr. Burroughs. Excuse me. Can I get a minute of your time?"

Clayton scanned the parking lot out of habit. His father had taught him to always be conscious of his surroundings. If someone was calling your name to the left, then look to the right. But all he saw was a thin Black man wearing a dark gray henley and slacks, leaning against the side of a blue BMW several cars away, smoking a cigarette. That wasn't uncommon since there were new rules these days about smoking near hospitals. Alex eventually made it over to the truck and held out his hand. "Mr. Burroughs, my name is—"

Clayton ignored the hand. "I know who you are. I've seen you on TV."

Alex tried to appear modest. "Yeah, I think they've been playing that press conference on a loop. I'm not used to being so recognizable."

"Why are you here, Price?"

"Just to talk."

"To me? I don't have anything to say about your brother. I wasn't there. But I can tell you that Nelson McKenna did nothing but protect people that night."

"I'm not here to talk about my brother."

"Then what do you want?"

"I want to talk about his friend, Riley—or Dallas if you prefer."

"I don't prefer. She does. And from what I heard, she and your brother weren't exactly friends. In fact, I hear tell that your brother was an abusive rapist sack of shit." Clayton could tell his words burned, and for a moment he could see the shark swimming right under the skin of Alex Price. Clayton liked that he rattled his cage.

"I told you. I'm not here about that. I know who and what Robbie was. I don't give a damn about Robbie."

Clayton tilted his head. That was a cold thing to say, coming from the man's own blood. It intrigued him, but not enough to waste any more time. "Look, buddy. I know you've had a tough week with your family and all. But I really don't have anything to say about any of it. Nelson is a friend of mine and you and me being all chummy ain't really a good idea." Clayton turned to open the door of the Bronco.

"She took something," Alex blurted out. "Dallas. She took something from my brother."

Clayton held the door handle and listened out of courtesy.

"She took a piece of jewelry from him. A sapphire ring. It's not that valuable or anything, just a trinket really, but it's important to me. It's important to my family. It belonged to my father, and I'd just like to have it back, that's all."

"And you think I have it?"

"Possibly—if you happen to have the girl's personal effects. I can't get any information from the hospital."

"Not my problem."

"Listen, I know that my brother probably deserved what happened to him. I'm not arguing that. He's always been a stain on my family's name. But if you've seen my press conference, then you know I haven't spoken an ill word about your friend McKenna. I'd just like to get back something that she should never have had in the first place."

Clayton studied the man. Price seemed desperate. But his brother was dead, and he'd just lost his father. Regardless of who a father was to his son, it was still an understandable loss. Who wouldn't feel desperate? "All right," Clayton said. "I've got a few things to do before I head back to my motel. But I can meet you there in about an hour or so. If this *trinket*, or whatever it is, happens to be with Dallas's things, you can have it. But then I think it's a good idea that we don't meet again."

"Okay. I'm fine with that. Thank you."

Clayton nodded and Alex stuck a piece of gum in his mouth. "So I'll see you back at your room in an hour then?"

Clayton agreed and watched Price walk all the way back to his car before he got in the Bronco. He watched him drive away in a silver Audi and then watched a blue BMW follow him from the lot. Clayton had intended to go and pick up some food and visit the Duval County sheriff to take him up on that favor he offered the day Nails was arrested. But now all that could wait. Clayton thought it was odd that this Price asshole hadn't asked him what motel he was staying at. Or why he felt the need to bring a backup man *just to talk*. Clayton looked around inside the Bronco to see if anything had been touched. Nothing seemed out of order. He looked at the back floorboards of the truck where he'd stuffed a large trash bag full of papers he'd taken from the stolen Honda before the police impounded it. He pulled it out, opened it, and stared at Dallas's handbag. He set the trash bag back down and cranked the ignition. There was a change in plans.

Chapter Sixty-Five

It took Clayton a lot more than an hour to get back to his room at the Sunshine Palace, but it only took about ten minutes before the inevitable knock on the door came. He'd had more than enough time to place everything where he wanted it. He answered the door and invited Alex inside. This time Price had brought his backup man with him instead of stashing him a few cars away. The man in the gray henley wasn't holding a gun, but he walked around the room with the arrogance of having one. He poked his head in the bathroom to make sure they were alone as Clayton retook his seat in a chair next to the wall.

Alex leaned on the front door. "This would already be over if you'd just told me you had what I needed in your truck at the hospital."

"Too bad I came out of the ER before you could break into it, like you and your buddy there did to my room while I was gone."

"What gave us away?"

"Does it matter?"

Alex smiled. "I suppose not. Now tell me where her things are."

Clayton had no intention of lying. He knew he'd been watched as he carried it all in from the truck. He pointed toward the bed. "Right over there. On the floor next to the nightstand."

Alex didn't waste any time hustling across the room and snatching the handbag from the floor. He dumped the contents onto the bed and shuffled through the makeup and loose change, the medicine bottles, and jewelry. He even tossed away the bank bag full of cash, growing increasingly irritated as he spread the things out over the bed.

"What?" Clayton said. "You can't find what you need? Your family heirloom isn't in there? Your invaluable trinket?"

"Stop fucking around, Burroughs. Where is it?"

"Where is what?"

"Okay. That's enough. Michael, this redneck wants to play games. Show him exactly who he's playing with."

The silent man *was* holding a gun now as if by magic. He took a step toward the chair, but instead of pulling out the small .22 caliber pistol he'd stuffed down in the cushions, Clayton put his hands up—both of them. "Okay. Okay. Take it easy. No need for all that. Put your pit bull on a leash, Price. What you want is right there on the table." He pointed to the silver ring sitting on top of an orange and white photo envelope with a *Kodak* logo on it.

Alex glared at him before picking up the ring. He held it in his hand for a minute and squeezed it. Clayton smiled as Alex tossed it on the floor like garbage and picked up the envelope full of photos. He flipped through the four-by-six pictures inside. This was what he'd really come for. This had been the whole point. The pictures were all of Robbie and Dallas—and Alex. And they weren't flattering. They were the kind of pictures a man like Alex Price couldn't allow to be seen by anyone. The kind that ruined people and took down empires. Especially an empire that called itself a church. Clayton leaned back in the chair and politely asked Michael to put his gun away for the second time. The man seethed and looked to Alex for instructions. Price conceded, and Michael holstered his gun.

"I found Dallas's camera. That's what you really wanted, right? That's what all this is about. You made up that whole story of wanting some fucking heirloom. You just didn't want the world to find out that your holier-than-thou scam is really run by a bunch of predator dirtbags. Did your deddy know?"

"Fuck you, Burroughs."

"I'm guessing he didn't."

Alex was coming unglued, and Clayton was counting on his being irrational. "What's stopping me from taking these and having Michael put a bullet in your head right now?"

"Nothing. Except if you do that, all the other copies I made at Kinko's and sent to a few friends of mine back home will hit every newspaper in the country. What do you think I've been doing for the past few hours? But sure, you could kill me and at least you'd have that set right there— you know—to remember the good times." Clayton smiled a smug, shit-eating grin. Alex had been outfoxed but this Michael asshole looked smart. He was the one to worry about. The Nigerian man pulled Clayton out of the chair by his shirt, but he broke free and held out the .22. "Touch me again, motherfucker, and you're going to see a whole different kind of redneck. Do you know who my family is? You don't want to walk this road, I promise you."

Michael took a step back.

"I'm holding all the cards here, dickhead. Hell, I could shoot you both for breaking in here and threatening my life. And after the cops get a load of those photos, who wouldn't believe me?" Clayton kept the small gun aimed at the Nigerian. His heart felt like it might burst out of his chest. Michael tensed, but Alex finally yelled for him to stop and pulled him back. Clayton was counting on that and let himself relax a little.

"All right. Stop this. Just tell me what you want. Money? How much?"

"I don't want your fucking money."

"Then what?"

"First, I want you to fund Nelson McKenna's legal defense. Your family got him into this shit and your family is going to get him out. I don't care how you do it or how many people you are removed from it, but *he's* going to need your money and you're gonna make that happen. And then you're going to use that same family money to make sure that not one single thing happens to him if he ends up in prison over this shit."

"That it?"

"And then you're to go away. Disappear. Don't step foot in my part of the world. Ever. I want you and your bodyguard here to just walk away. Leave and crawl back into whatever sick, depraved hole you came out of. And I also want you to stay as far away from Dallas as possible. Leave her be. Leave us be and you'll never hear from us again."

"And that's it?"

"That's it. You leave my friends and family alone and I don't ruin your life. You leave us alone and those pictures never see the light of day. It's a better deal than you deserve."

The tension in the room eased and Alex picked up the pictures. "How do I know I can take you at your word?"

"You don't. But what choice do you have?"

"Why the hell are you even doing this? Why do you even care? My brother is already dead. I'm just trying to fucking end this. And the girl, Dallas—she's . . ."

"*She's* the *why*, you sick fuck. How about the two of you look at those pictures again. Look at her face. Look at her face and tell me . . . does she look like she's having any fun? You and your brother look like kids at Christmas, but does she? Do you think that's what a woman having a good time looks like? You're lucky I don't shoot you both in the kneecaps and throw you in a fucking river somewhere."

Alex almost looked remorseful. "It wasn't like that."

"Like you'd know the difference. Now get out. There's nothing left to say. You and this asshole get in your fancy cars and drive away to your fancy lives, pay your debt to McKenna, and don't look back."

Alex handed the stack of photos to Michael, who made them disappear into his pocket without looking at them. He stepped back from Clayton. His blood boiled and he felt helpless. Being helpless wasn't something he was used to. But there was no other play. He nodded and motioned to Michael, and then walked out the door.

Clayton leaned on the closed door and exhaled. He had just put on an Oscar-worthy performance, and he felt like he could finally breathe. He took the roll of negatives out of his pocket and squeezed them. He hadn't made any copies. And even if he did, he wouldn't know where to send them. All he had were those negatives that he had forgotten to take out of his pocket. A simple frisk, and the whole charade would've been over. But he sold it. And it felt good.

Chapter Sixty-Six

Clayton crossed the line into McFalls County around six-thirty p.m. and drove straight to his small cabin on Bull Mountain. Kate was there waiting with the first real food he'd had in over a week, along with a hug he could've crawled into and lived in forever. After he wolfed down his own weight of corned beef, stewed potatoes, and cabbage, he lay his head in Kate's lap on the sofa, and that was it. He was out. She let him sleep and that's exactly what he did. He slept like the dead. But he also knew he wouldn't be sleeping late. He had one more thing to handle to make everything right. And that would happen at dawn—on the mountain.

The sun hadn't come up yet as he wheeled the Bronco into the gravel drive of the house on Cripple Creek Road. He'd expected to be the first one there, but his father's old side-step was already parked outside and the work lights in the house were on. The generators were humming, and the churning of crickets mixed with the sound of warm machines. The barn door was open and electrical cords were dropped all over the porch. The beams from his headlights showed him that the roof shingling had been finished as well. It looked as if his father hadn't missed a day of work on the house since Clayton left. He wondered before he got out of the Bronco if the house was even going to be for him anymore. He hung his head and steeled himself for what was coming next, but he knew he was being watched, so he grabbed the thermos of coffee that Kate filled for him and a pair of leather work gloves off the seat. *Well. Here goes nothing,* he thought, as he climbed down out of the truck and headed inside. He corrected himself as he walked. *No. Here goes everything.*

Gareth was in the great room trying to maneuver a full-sized sheet of drywall into place by himself as Clayton entered the kitchen. The interior of the house had a strong smell of disinfectant. Enough to sting his eyes. He didn't know what that was about, but he put his gloves on anyway and set the thermos down on the counter. Gareth carefully set the sheet of drywall down and turned to his son. "Well, come on, boy. You going to just stand there or are you going to help me with this?"

That wasn't the greeting he'd expected to get after everything that had happened over the past week, but he went with it anyway. He grabbed one side of the plasterboard and Gareth grabbed the other. They shifted it into place next to the others that Gareth had apparently already hung by himself.

"Hold it steady."

Clayton did, pressing the sheetrock firm against the support beams as Gareth picked up the nail gun. Clayton knew his father could easily start to hammer nails directly into his back if he wanted to, but he didn't turn around. He stayed in place and waited. Gareth slid a small stepladder over to the left of Clayton and began to nail the drywall in down the stud. He did the same on the other side and set the nail gun back on the floor. He went to retrieve another sheet from the stack and Clayton stopped him. "Deddy. Don't you think we should talk?"

Gareth stopped, turned, and caught Clayton's eye. "I reckon we will when you're ready."

"I'm ready now."

Gareth spit on the floor and his voice got colder to match the morning. "You right sure about that? You sure you're ready to own up to your bullshit?"

"No, Deddy. I just want to talk."

"Talk about what, exactly? You wanna talk about what a goddamn disappointment you are?" He crossed the kitchen, leaned on the marble, and scratched at the back of his neck. "Maybe you want to talk about how much money you cost this family to cover your self-righteous road trip. Or how many favors I had to call in just because you couldn't leave well enough alone."

Clayton took his gloves off. "Yeah, Deddy. That's exactly what I want to talk about. Disappointment and family."

"Boy, you don't know jack shit about family."

"You're wrong. I'd say I learned quite a bit about it over the past few days."

Gareth slowly moved toward his son and stood just inches from Clayton's face. They might've been the same size, physically, but Gareth had the presence of a grizzly, and Clayton still feared him. But now wasn't the time to show it. Gareth spit on the plywood flooring again. "Let me tell you what I learned first, boy. I learned that no matter what I say, you're going to do whatever the hell you want. Even if it hurts your own kin. And you do it without thinking about a goddamn soul but yourself." Gareth spit again. "How did it feel, Clayton? Tell me. How did it feel to have to have your deddy come and pull your ass out of the fire? How does it feel to know that you'd be a dead man right now if it wasn't for me?"

"I appreciate your help down there."

"Oh, do you now? Well, let me ask you this. How does it feel to know that you did it all for nothing? How stupid does a son of mine have to be to not know the extent of my reach? Do you really think you saved anyone? Are you really that dumb?"

"Nails isn't anyone. He grew up right down the road from us. He's like family to me—like family to you."

"But *like* family—*ain't* family. He's only a threat to my family, now. He lost control and turned himself into a threat to everything we have up here, and you're just too damn fool to know it." Gareth took off his hat and threw it. Clayton thought he was about to swing on him, but that didn't happen. He watched his father allow himself a moment to calm down. "The point is this, boy. I had to chew up a lot of resources to keep your dumb ass alive and you still think you saved your buddy." He moved in a little closer and spoke a little softer. "I've got just as many people on the inside as I do on the outside. McKenna is still going to end up a dead man, and you—you are still exactly what I always thought you'd be—weak."

Clayton waited for the old man to finish preaching from his pulpit before he moved to the countertop in the middle of the kitchen. He unscrewed his thermos, took two Styrofoam cups from a sleeve, and set them down on the marble. Without looking up, he said, "Deddy, I love you"—he poured some coffee—"but if you take one more shot at my character, then today is going to be the day we do more than talk."

Gareth cocked his head and nearly smiled at Clayton. "All right, boy." He took a sip of the coffee. "I think I agree. Today is the day we do more than talk. Today's the day you earn your place in this family. Come with me." Gareth took off his gloves and grabbed one of the work lights hanging above him. He pulled at the orange cord to give himself some slack and walked down the boards in the hall, leading to what Kate had come to call the "baby's room," for when and if a baby ever came. Gareth pushed open the door and went inside. The thick, acrid smell of disinfectant, along with the rank odor of blood, piss, and shit, flooded out into the hall. Clayton covered his mouth and nose. He didn't want to see what his father had stashed in that room, but he followed him in anyway. Gareth hung the light from a paint-speckled folding ladder. Clayton stood in the doorway. The room that he and Kate had imagined painting pink or sky blue one day now had protective plastic tarps stretched all over the flooring. Shiny black pools of congealed blood covered the clear plastic in nonsensical patterns, and an overturned five-gallon bucket of feces and whatever else was spilled in the far corner. Flies buzzed around it in a feeding frenzy. A roll of excess plastic was folded in half and tucked up against the wall. This was now what Clayton would imagine every time he came into this room. This was the filthy scene that would be burned into his brain forever, and the idea of putting a baby—his baby—inside a kill box made his stomach turn. He was positive that was why his father had done it. To strip him of that feeling of innocence. The room was dark and rancid despite the newly hung light, but as Clayton's eyes adjusted, he realized that the roll of excess plastic near the far wall wasn't just some inanimate object. It was moving. It was breathing. *Jesus Christ. It was alive.*

Clayton crossed the plastic-covered floor and each step got stuck in the pools of black jelly and peeled up from the sticky surface. The person on the floor lay in a defensive fetal position—clothed—but busted up and broken. Every ragged inhalation sounded like a buzzsaw blending in with the generators.

"What the hell did you do, Deddy?"

Gareth sat on one of the steps of the ladder and adjusted the work light to give Clayton a better view. "I didn't do nothing. He did it to himself."

"Who is this?" Clayton said, as he squatted down to get a look at the mangled face below him.

"That right there is what a threat to our family looks like, son. When it's handled the right way."

Clayton didn't recognize the man, but he saw something on the ground next to him that filled in the blanks. He picked up the floppy tweed hat. "Stan? Stan Moody?" Clayton stood and spun around to his father. "What the fuck, Dad? Why? Why did you do this?"

Gareth let go of the light and walked over to his son. "What? You're shocked? Is that it? You're goddamn confused? You just don't understand?" Gareth spoke as if he were talking to a child. "The humanity of it all? How could I be such a monster, right? Why, Stan Moody was a good man. He was an honest worker. Hell, he was born right down the road from you. You've known him your whole life. He was—what did you say a minute ago—he was *like family*." Gareth laughed right before he went cold and blank. "He's also the point. The part you never seem to figure out, son." He gestured down at Stan, who hadn't moved. He'd just gurgled blood and moaned. "That sack of shit sold you out. Not only did he run his mouth to your high school little girlfriends that put you on this fool's errand, but he also gave up Nails just because the price was right. He gave up his own people and put *my* son in the crosshairs for one grand in small bills. That's it—a measly thousand dollars. That good man. That friend of the family. Right there. On the floor at your feet. If it wasn't for him, you would never have had to face what you did down there. You wouldn't have had to have me put a stop to it." He moved in closer to Clayton. "You would've been here—with your family. And Nails wouldn't be locked up like an animal right now. It could've been done clean. He wouldn't have felt any pain. And none of this would've happened, but it did. And it happened thanks to him." He pointed down to Stan.

Clayton looked down at the pile of ground beef in a corduroy jacket. Amy Silver's foolish, drunk uncle. "Why didn't you just kill him then, Dad? Why is he here? In this house? Right now?"

"Because it ain't my debt to pay. I've been waiting for you."

Clayton felt the cold steel of his father's Colt Python revolver being pressed into his hand.

"Take it, son. I kept that piece of shit alive for you. Now, show me there's some of my blood in your veins and that you finally understand. A threat is a threat. And blood is all that matters. Not money. Not land. Goddamn, not love. Just blood. Our blood."

Without thinking, Clayton took the gun and held it. He'd always dreamed of feeling the heft of his father's Colt. Ever since he could remember. As a boy, it was all that mattered. The gun was a gift from his mother, Annette, to his father before she abandoned them. The silver nickel plating gleamed in his hand, glowing like something alien in the electric light of the work lamp. He felt the urge to shoot every single round in the gun straight into the center of the earth and blow up the world—himself included. But what would that accomplish? Kate was part of this world. Amy, Nelson, and now Dallas were a part of this world. *He* was still a part of this world. And this—was just a gun. It was just a tool created to decimate whatever crossed his path, born of destruction. But Clayton didn't need a gun. He needed a compass, born of direction—and that was something his father couldn't give him. He'd need to find that on his own.

As he gripped the gun, he couldn't stop his eyes from swelling with tears. He knew his father would be disgusted. But his tears were filled with the same acid and rage his father was made of. His father had meticulously but unknowingly taught him how to feel that way. He dropped the silver Colt to the ground. He didn't want to blow up the world. He just wanted to go home.

Gareth didn't bother to pick up the gun. He knew as soon as it hit the floor that he'd failed. And there was no redemption left for his youngest son. He leaned back on the ladder and said nothing. He just pulled some moist tobacco from his pouch and set a plug in his cheek. Clayton straightened himself out. He knew he couldn't help Stan. Gareth would kill the man before Clayton even tried to help him. And begging would just make it worse. But he did dry his face before he turned around. "Is this how it's done, Deddy? Is it?"

Gareth tucked the pouch back in his jacket. Talking was over, now. Everything concerning Clayton was over now.

"Is this how you got Nelson to buy into this shit back at Burnt Hickory? By making him believe it was about family—and not about murder, guns, and money? Is this how you turned him into Nails? Just to toss him out like trash when you were done with him."

"It's time for me to go, son. The talking is over. We—are over. I'm done trying to help you."

"Trying to help me?" He pushed his anger down, despite how sideways it felt in his throat. "It is time for you to go, but hear this, old man. Loud and clear. You're not going to sic any of your thugs on Nails while he's locked up, and he's never going to utter your name to anyone. Because he does think of you as *real* family whether you do or not. It's called loyalty, and you could take a lesson from him."

"Is that right?"

"Yeah, that's right. And the best part? I have Stan Moody to thank for that. Okay, he ran his mouth. Sure. And you must mean he *sold out* Nelson and Dallas to that asshole Alex Price and his people, but guess what? I turned that around. Nelson will be protected if he goes to prison by the Price family's money because I used my goddamn brain instead of a gun to figure it out. So do your worst, old man. Please. Try. Because when it comes down to dollar for dollar? You'll lose. And you can thank me for that."

"And you're willing to bet your family's whole life up here on that, son?"

"My family is Kate now, Dad. My family is made up of the people that want what's best for me. Not of *relatives* who want me to kill old men in cold blood for making shitty decisions. You have Halford and Buckley for that. So, pack up your tools and your shit, and get the hell off my property. I'll finish it alone. We're done."

Gareth leaned over and picked up his gun. He held it loosely in his hand, and Clayton thought he might use it. He didn't doubt his own father would shoot him in the back. But for the first time in his life, he didn't fear it. It was now or never, and none of it slowed his step or his tongue. He walked out of the room, down the hall, and stopped at the front door. He turned and faced his father for the last time. "You know something, Deddy? All of this?" Clayton motioned to the house, but he alluded to much more. "All of this is going to burn one day. It doesn't have to. But doing things your way makes it inevitable—and so it will, I promise you. One day I'll be holding that Colt in my hand, but the *right* way, and all this? It's gonna burn—to the ground. And don't be surprised if I'm the one with the match."

Gareth just sighed and spit on the floor as if he hadn't heard a word. Clayton turned and hopped off the porch. He got into his Bronco and cranked the engine. But even the roar of the 302 big block wasn't enough noise to muffle the shots that Gareth put into Stan Moody. One in the head. One in the heart. What Clayton's father called *insurance shots*. He'd come back in the morning, and he was sure that nothing would be left. Stan's body would be gone. All traces of blood and shit would be cleaned up. The room might even be painted, and the smell of death would be covered up. He also knew his father would never come back. But at least Kate would never know. Clayton would never tell her. He had just become a man who kept secrets from his wife. He could call himself a liar now, a parting gift from his father.

2007

Bonus Tracks

Chapter Sixty-Seven

Raymond "Sting Ray" Lewis rolled the book cart through the second-story corridor of the USP Federal Prison in Atlanta. He stopped at every cell but not everyone wanted or needed to see him. The old man did, however, enjoy his visits to cell number B-61. He stopped there every Tuesday afternoon at two-thirty after chow, like clockwork. He looked forward to talking with the big man that took up that ten-by-twelve space.

"Today is the big day, huh, Nails?"

Nails was gathering all the books he'd checked out from the prison library to give back to the custodian. "Yeah," he said, and held each book out to Ray, one at a time through the bars. "I suppose so." Not every inmate was as conscientious about returning books to the prison library. Most of the pages from the paperbacks that were allowed to be in the cells were used by the inmates to burn into ashes—fodder for tattoo ink—or for extra toilet paper. But Nails always returned what he borrowed, un-damaged. And he never took anything he didn't read.

"You don't sound too excited about it," Ray said as he gently placed each of the books in the cart. *Leaving Las Vegas, The Old Man and the Sea, The Collected Stories of John Steinbeck.*

Nails took off his thick black reading glasses. "It's been a long time since I've been out there, Ray. I'm not sure what to think."

"You're going to be fine, Nails. Just fine. You just remember ol' Ray when you get where you're going. You remember my commissary number?"

Nails smiled. "Yes, I do, old man. And don't worry. How could I forget the guy who helped me get my GED, or turned me on to Elmore Leonard?"

"You did that yourself, big man. All I did was file the paperwork."

"That ain't true. But thank you anyway, Ray."

"You know, I don't say this very much to the young bucks that come and go through here, but I'm going to miss you, Nails. Some of these boys deserve every bit of the time they get, but you? You done earned what's coming to you today. I wish you the best. I mean that." Ray smiled through the bars, showing off a bright white set of dentures.

"It's been good knowing you, too, Ray." When he was through sliding the books through the bars, he stuck out his right hand and Ol' Stingray cupped it with both of his. He shook it and nodded. And that was it. Ray pushed his cart forward to the next cell and the next, and Nails went back to getting his things together. Earlier that morning at roll call, one of the guards had dropped off an empty cardboard box and Nails had spent the morning filling it with all his possessions. He peeled a few photos of classic Ford muscle cars that he'd cut from magazines off the walls and carefully stacked them in the box. He didn't know why he was keeping them. It wasn't like he had a place to go that he'd be able to hang them back up. This cell had been his home for some time now, and even leaving prison, Nails still felt like he was getting tossed out of his life when the timer was up. He folded a Parker Brothers chessboard in half and slid all the plastic pieces into the box.

He took a moment to look at the empty top bunk in his cell, where his cell mate for the past six years, a man named Jimmy Thorne, had slept. Jimmy had been serving an eleven-year sentence for holding up a pharmacy in Decatur, using a paintball gun. He'd also taught Nails how to play chess. Jimmy called Nails a natural. Jimmy was dead now from a hotshot of horse tranquilizers, and no one ever came to replace him. That was three months ago. Nails sat down on the lower bunk and slid a desktop tape deck out from under the bed. All the guards knew he had the tape player, but they also knew that Nails received special treatment. He had people with money—big money—on the outside looking after him, and important people from all the tribes inside watching his back. He never gave anyone a problem anyway. He'd been a model prisoner during his incarceration. He kept to himself mostly and barely even spoke unless spoken to.

Nails tossed some earbuds into the box, along with some papers from under the mattress. Utah Marvin, the guy who smuggled Nails his current tape deck and kept him hooked up with a once-a-month supply of C batteries, tried to keep him up to date by telling him that no one listened to cassette tapes anymore. iPods were the thing now, whatever the hell those were, but Nails preferred the tape player. Utah Marvin wouldn't understand. He hit the eject button and the lid popped open. He removed the white cassette with the faded gray Sharpie marks on it. Clayton had somehow gotten it in to him a few years back and Nails could still make out the words *R's Mixtape*. He'd had to operate on that damn cassette several times to keep it alive over the years, but it still worked. And Nails knew every word to every song. He held it in his hand for a minute, turning it over and over like a silver dollar before he gently placed it in the box as well. He had a few books of his own that he tucked in the box, but he left the tape deck itself on the bed. He knew someone on the block would get better use out of it. He didn't need it anymore. It had served him well.

After packing up, Nails sat on his bunk, rubbing the scars on his knuckles for another hour. At three-thirty, two guards filed into view outside his cell. The taller one yelled out to the monitor, "Open Cell Block B, number 6-1. Inmate number 0-7-1-3-2." Steel began to grind on steel and the cell door cranked its way open. Nails took his glasses from the desk and tucked them into the shirt pocket of his jumper. "Step on out, McKenna."

Nails stood up, grabbed his box of belongings, and walked into the corridor. One of the guards entered the cell to inspect it and held up the tape player. "You leaving this?"

"Yeah, give it to one of the boys."

"Will do, McKenna."

"And don't barter for it, Culpepper. Just give it to someone who can use it. Don't make it about you."

"Understood, Nails."

The other guard, Stevens, a short and husky fella who walked with a hitch in his step, chimed in. "Finally going home, huh, Nails? How's it feel?"

"Home." Nails chewed on the word like he didn't know the definition. "I don't know yet."

"Well, I know we're gonna miss you at chess club." It was a dumb thing to say to a man on his first afternoon of freedom after nine years of being locked in a cage, but Nails answered anyway.

"Thank you, Officer Stevens." They walked. Following the blue stripe painted on the floor.

It took less than an hour to process Nails out of prison. They handed him a large plastic bag with a pair of jeans, his socks, a bleached but still bloodstained T-shirt, his boots, and a canvas jacket. He used a small changing room that could barely accommodate his size to get dressed and then he handed the extra-large jumper and his size thirteen jellies to one of the guards. After having to sign his name on a bunch of forms, he was handed a second plastic bag filled with the rest of his personal effects. One blue bandanna—washed, one black leather fanny pack, one wallet—empty, and a large roll of duct tape that no one could explain. He didn't bother to argue about it. He just took it. He unzipped the fanny pack, and other than the tattered copy of a James Cain novel and a stubby pencil, there was also five grand in hundred-dollar bills stuffed into it. No one bothered to explain that either, and again he didn't argue. He just took it. He assumed the money had come from Clayton. Or whoever Clayton had looking out for Nails these past nine years. Clayton never told him who. And Nails never asked. He just attached the strap of the fanny pack to his waist and slid it around to the small of his back.

The guard behind the glass window gave him copies of the paperwork he needed to bring to his assigned parole officer, and Nails tossed his jacket over his arm. Five minutes later he was standing in front of a sixteen-foot gate topped with razor wire. He was aware of it opening, but he focused on the blond woman leaning against an SUV on the other side.

"Good luck, Nails," the guard said. And that was it. He was free. The sun was high and hot, and the dark red SUV shimmered like a mirage. He walked toward it and tried to block the sun from his face. "Dallas?" he thought, as he and the woman got closer to each other. He'd thought it out loud and he felt foolish for letting his mind play tricks on him like that. He leaned down to let Amy hug his neck. "Sorry, Nelson. It's just me."

"Don't be sorry. Thanks for coming."

"I wouldn't have missed this for the world."

Nails straightened out and looked around. "I figured Clayton would be here."

"He wanted to be. But he's busy doing sheriff stuff back home. You know he's the law in McFalls now, right?"

"Yeah, I heard."

"He'll be waiting on you when we get back."

"Okay," Nails said and tried not to stare at her, but he couldn't help it. He hadn't seen Amy since they were teenagers and it felt bizarre. But it was much more than that.

"I look like her, don't I?"

Nails felt a buzzing in his head that he hadn't felt in almost a decade behind bars. "You do—a little. I'm sorry. I don't mean to stare."

"It's totally fine, Nelson. I understand. You ready to get out of here?"

"Yeah, I think so."

"Well, c'mon then. There are a lot of people back home who can't wait to see you."

Nails just stood there looking down on this older, but just as beautiful as he remembered, version of his high school crush, not really knowing what to say.

"I know it's a lot to take in, Nelson. I mean, I don't know, but I know it's . . . oh, hell, let's just get out of here." Amy took Nails's box of belongings and put it in the backseat. "C'mon. I left the A/C running and put the seat all the way back for you." She started to open the passenger side door of the burgundy Explorer.

"Amy?"

"Yeah?"

"Do you mind if I drive? I kept my license valid through the mail. So it's legal."

Amy smiled. "Of course." She handed him the keys and she got inside. It took him a few minutes to configure the seat and the wheel to accommodate a man his size, but with Amy's patient guidance, he eventually got himself settled in.

"Do you know how to get there from here?"

"I think so. But do you have a map?"

"I'll type it in my phone." Amy tapped an address into the *Maps* app on her iPhone and a voice over the stereo told Nails which way to go.

"You've got a map on your phone—that talks to you through your car?"

"Oh, baby boy—" Amy gently slapped his thigh. "You missed a lot. I'll tell you all about it on the way. Head out of that gate over there and turn left. That should bring us to 85 North."

Nails followed Amy's directions and watched the prison get smaller and smaller in the rearview mirror. He also felt his life expanding, getting bigger and bigger, to the point that he felt like he might explode.

Chapter Sixty-Eight

The drive from Atlanta to Hillcrest Cemetery in Waymore Valley took about two hours. During that time, Amy explained to Nails all about how her iPhone worked. How it was a game changer, and she couldn't live without it. She told him about her husband, Parker, and how they met at her job, working together at a newspaper in North Carolina, but also how the internet was slowly choking out the newspaper business, and how she'd probably be writing a "blog" at some point in the future. Nails didn't know what a blog was. So she told him all about that, too. He didn't remember Amy being so talkative back when they were kids, but he didn't mind. He liked listening to her talk. He liked how happy she sounded. She wasn't traumatized by what happened to her when they were kids. She wasn't frightened of him. If she had been once, she wasn't anymore. She'd moved on. She was a successful young woman. With a family. And a life she enjoyed. Good for her.

After they crossed the county line, she told him to take a left on White Bluff Road.

"I know where it is from here, Amy." He sounded colder than he intended.

"Right. Sorry. Of course you do. I'm just all caught up, you know?"

"I know, it's okay."

They drove a few more miles in silence, and eventually, Nails turned into the cemetery entrance. He knew right where to go. He hadn't been out here in well over twenty years, but a man never forgets where he buries his mama. He pulled the SUV over to the shoulder of the road and he and Amy got out. They made the long walk over the winding breezeway. He stopped in front of two matching gravestones. One that belonged to his mother and the other to Satchel. The old man died five years ago and Nails had been denied the opportunity to attend the funeral. He didn't care that much, though. He doubted there was much of a turnout. And seeing how the old bastard had decided to be buried here, spoiling the earth right next to his mother, the same way he'd spoiled her life. It wasn't something Nails wanted to be a part of anyway. He kissed his fingers and laid them on his mother's grave before walking a few feet over to a smaller one. A more recent one. One that read *Riley Sinclair 1979–1998*. The only other thing carved into the granite was the word *FEARLESS*. Nails didn't know where the money came from that made all of this possible, just like the mysterious wad of cash currently in his fanny pack, but Clayton had done exactly what Nails had asked of him, and the gravestone looked just like he hoped it would.

Nails knelt down but he didn't cry. Amy put a delicate hand on his shoulder. "I'm sorry, Nails."

"It's okay. Thank you for keeping all this so nice."

"Don't thank me. This is all Kate's handiwork. She handles everything out here. She's been out here once a month like clockwork since, well, since it happened. We had a small service. But I'm sure you know all about that."

"Yeah, I heard. Clayton kept me informed. But he never told me if her parents showed up. Did they come?"

"No. Clayton tried to convince them, several times, but they didn't agree with her being buried out here. They thought she should've been buried in Florida. But if they really cared, they didn't show it. They didn't fight for it at all."

"That's my fault."

"No, Nelson. No it's not. Don't say that."

Nails didn't push it. Instead, he picked up a few chunks of white rock and put them on top of the slab of granite. He and Amy stayed still like that for a moment before Nails finally stood. "Okay," he said. "We can go now."

Chapter Sixty-Nine

Amy was supposed to bring Nails to Freddy's bar when they left the cemetery, but he insisted that she drop him off by Burnt Hickory. She explained how she would be leaving town to go back to North Carolina the next day, and Nails understood. So did she. It was too much, too soon. They said their goodbyes and Amy Silver went back to her life.

It took a few days of being alone in the woods, camping, with the feel of the packed dirt under his bedroll, hearing the nightbirds and the rushing water of Bear Creek, for Nails to find his bearings. He walked along the overgrown train tracks that he used to follow when he was a kid. This was his home, but it didn't feel that way anymore. It never really had. So much had changed, but so much stayed the same. His trailer was gone, demolished, so he visited Satchel's house. The place had been abandoned since his death and fallen into disrepair, so Nails didn't spend much time there. There was nothing in that box of ghosts that interested him. It was just a time capsule of bad memories and fresh anger that he'd spent the past nine years trying to clear from his system. He didn't want to be there. Honestly, nothing about McFalls County felt welcoming or brought any sense of comfort except the sound of the woods at night and the smell of the damp clay. He'd missed that more than he thought was possible.

It was his fourth night of freedom before he decided to go see Freddy. The Chute was a two-hour walk from Satchel's house, but Nails didn't mind making it. The night air cleared his head of cobwebs and phantoms. He arrived at the familiar shoal-covered parking lot and looked at the same neon signs that had lit up most of his Friday nights over a decade ago. The place hadn't changed much at all. It was a snapshot of a different time. Walking through the front door of the bar was the first true feeling of belonging he'd felt since he'd been back. He didn't know the kid at the door and so he just walked by. The kid didn't bother to stop the giant, either. He didn't get paid enough. The inside of the bar hadn't changed much either. There was a DJ booth now instead of a jukebox, but otherwise it was the same as he remembered it. The massive disco ball still twirled overhead and the whole place was drenched in the same red light. He looked at the empty room where a girl named Dallas stole his heart and then took a seat at the bar.

Freddy, dressed in a pink bathrobe and wearing the brightest blue eyeshadow money could buy, was behind the bar. The Chute's proprietor had aged and gotten fragile, but not fragile like fine China. He looked more like a glacier that was steadily losing huge chunks of ice into the sea. A frosted mug of apple juice sat on a bar napkin in front of Nails before he even settled into the stool.

"I was beginning to wonder when you were ever going to show. All the balloons done fizzled out and the cake is probably stale by now."

"It's taken a little getting used to," Nails said. "I'm sorry if I messed up the welcome home party." He downed the juice and Freddy poured another, fresh mug and all.

"Don't worry. I get it. I figured if I had to wait nine years to see that chrome dome of yours that a few more days wasn't gonna hurt my feelings too much."

"I should've come by sooner."

"Forget it. Did you get the commissary money I sent?"

"Every month like clockwork."

Freddy just smiled.

"Thanks, man."

"Not a problem." Freddy put two fingers in his mouth and whistled. Another kid that Nails didn't know appeared from back in the kitchen. "Gavin, I want you to meet a friend of mine. Nails McKenna. We go back—way back."

The kid stuck out a hand for Nails to shake. He took it. "Nice to meet you, sir."

"Call me Nails."

NOTHING BUT THE BONES ▪ 309

"Cool. Always good to meet a friend of Freddy's."

Freddy scuffed the back of the young man's neck as if he were his grandson. "Listen, I want you to go to my office and call our friend the sheriff. Tell him our prodigal son has finally decided to grace us and to get his ass out here, pronto."

"You want me to call Sheriff Burroughs out here—on purpose?"

"Yeah. Now get."

Gavin disappeared back through the door he'd come out of, and Freddy watched him go.

"He's a little young for you, yeah?"

"Nah," Freddy said. "I'm just a little too old for him. But it keeps me sharp, you know? You only live once."

"I guess so, Freddy."

People were coming in the door now, and as early as it was, Nails could tell the night was about to crank up. People much younger than him were filing in and they were playing music he'd never heard before. He sipped at the second mug of juice and Freddy took the next hour or so to catch him up on the mountain gossip. The biggest news was about Gareth Burroughs. "He got himself blown up in a meth lab fire," Freddy said. "At least that's the story being sold to all of us. But the truth is, no one really knows what happened. Clayton's big brother, Halford, is calling the shots on Bull Mountain these days and he's as big a bear as his father ever was. Maybe bigger. And can you believe that Clayton Burroughs is the county sheriff now?"

"I can, Freddy. It makes sense. Clayton is solid. I think he'll make a good sheriff."

"Well so do I," Clayton yelled from across the room. Everyone turned to look. He stood at the door in his starched tan shirt and silver star. The whole room got quiet until Clayton unpinned his badge and stuck it in his pocket. A moment later, Kate Farris, now Kate Burroughs, joined her husband at the door and they crossed the room holding hands. Nails thought the hug Kate gave him might almost snap his neck. She eased back. "Welcome home, stranger."

"It's good to see you, Katelyn."

"It's good to see you, too, Nelson." She moved aside for Clayton to share the next hug. They bumped shoulders. The way men do.

"We expected you a few days ago. We had a cake."

"Yeah, Freddy told me. I'm sorry. I just needed to get my head right."

"Well, you're here now. That's all that matters."

"Yeah."

A man in a bright yellow T-shirt barked at Freddy from the far end of the bar and waved an empty beer bottle in the air. "Who've I got to blow to get a beer in this dive?"

"Fuck off, Earl," Freddy barked back. "I'll be there when I get there." Freddy opened a couple of beers for Clayton and Kate, and they all toasted to the return of their friend. Nails felt good and hollow at the same time. He couldn't explain it. He wanted to be here but still felt out of place. But he did notice the way Freddy and Clayton kept looking at each other. Prison had taught Nails to pay attention to body language. You needed to be able to read the signs before something popped off. And there was clearly something going on here that he wasn't aware of.

He put a stop to it. "Does someone want to tell me what's going on?"

Clayton nodded to Freddy, and the old man went to work on the combination safe. "We would've told you what was going on four days ago if you hadn't decided to go all *Kung-Fu* and wander the earth first before coming to see us."

"Cut him some slack, Freddy," Kate said. "The man just said he needed to get his head right."

"Yes ma'am," Freddy said, as he opened the safe and removed a large yellow legal file.

"I don't need any more money, Freddy."

"Good, because I'm not about to give you any." Freddy tucked the file under his arm. "Why don't we head into my office."

"I think that's a good idea," Clayton said.

"What is this about?"

"Just hang on a second, Nails."

Gavin reappeared from the kitchen door.

"Gavin, would you go handle Earl over there?" Freddy pointed at the shiny yellow man at the end of the bar. "And work the bar for a little while. I've got some shit to handle."

"No problem." Gavin crossed the bar, and the group of friends picked up their beers. Nails left his juice where it sat. Freddy headed toward his office in the poolroom and everyone followed.

Once they were all inside, Clayton closed the door. Freddy lay the file down on his desk. He stepped over stacks of loose paperwork and boxes of clutter to get into his closet. He took out a black canvas duffle bag. He tossed it on the desk next to the file. The duffle had a layer of dust on it so thick that Freddy had to wipe it down with some paper towels from a roll on the desk. "We've been holding on to this for a long, long time, man." Clayton took a seat in one of the chairs opposite Freddy's desk and pushed the bag toward Nails.

"What is it?"

"Open it and find out."

Nails sat down in the other chair, found the pull, and unzipped the bag. It was stuffed with notebooks and papers. It didn't take long before it all started to look familiar. It was hers. Her music. Dallas's music. Nails shot Freddy a look and then stared at Clayton and Kate. He'd thought this stuff had been lost forever. "How did you get this?"

"I've had it the whole time," Clayton said. "Although I never really knew what most of it was until after you were sentenced. I took it from the trunk of that car you stole back in Florida before it was impounded. And it sat in my closet at the house for years collecting dust. Then, when I got elected sheriff, Kate and I went through it all. When we realized what it was, we put it in that bag, where it sat in the closet of my office downtown until four days ago when I brought it here."

Nails rummaged through the bag. He still didn't understand a word of it, just a bunch of bars and symbols. But for a moment, just a beat, he could feel her—and it all came flooding back.

"Clayton wanted to bring it to you at the prison, but I told him that was a bad idea." Kate leaned on the edge of the desk. "I didn't know if it would be taken away from you in there, and I thought it was best if we just safeguarded it for you until you were released."

"Thank you, Katelyn."

Seeing the pages of music brought Dallas back to him like a hard rush of blood to the head. It also brought back all the mistakes he'd made. The biggest one being the night he left her to retrieve all the stuff in this bag.

But his friends didn't know that. They thought this was a good thing. They didn't understand. They were trying to be his friends. But that bag was just a huge reminder of what he'd done wrong. It was just paper. It wasn't worth it. All he wanted to do that night was impress her. Make her happy. And it cost her everything. Nails began to tuck the notebooks and papers back in the bag and then zipped it up. "Can you hold on to it for me a little longer? Until I find a more permanent place to stay?"

Freddy smiled. It was a mischievous smile. Nails hadn't seen the old man ever look like that before. "What's that look, Freddy? What is it?"

Freddy pushed the bag to the side and focused on the file lying on his desk. He laid a callused hand on it. "Now I need you to listen to me before you open that. Clayton and I kept this part from you for a damn good reason. So don't go getting shitty about it. Let me explain first."

Kate pulled a third chair away from the wall and sat down next to Nails. She put her hand on his knee.

"Freddy's not being entirely truthful, Nails. He did want to tell you. I was the one that insisted we didn't." Clayton rubbed at his beard. "But just hear us out."

"Hear what out?" Nails was getting agitated at all the cryptic nonsense. "Just tell me what is going on."

"Just show him," Kate said.

Clayton picked up the file from the desk and handed it to Nails. After a bit of stink eye, he opened it. Inside were several eight-by-ten black-and-white photos. He held up the first one. It was taken from a long-range camera, and it showed a picture of a woman, a blond woman, slender and smiling, wearing a T-shirt, sunglasses, and jeans. She was walking down an unfamiliar city street holding a cup of coffee and talking on a cell phone. Nails looked at it for a long time before it set in. It was the smile. It was almost too bright to look at. He glanced up at Freddy, who looked practically giddy. Nails couldn't form any words. So Freddy did.

"She goes by Rachel now. Rachel Sinclair. She's a piano teacher in a small town north of Richmond, Virginia. She also runs a Narcotics Anonymous meeting every Wednesday night at the Baptist church up the road from her house. Her address is written on the back of that photo."

Nails flipped it around and read it. He turned it back over and looked down at the other pictures. All of them candid, all of them taken by a professional. "H . . . How?"

Clayton took the volley. "What happened to the two of you down there left her in really bad shape. The doctors told me she would likely never wake up from the coma she was in, so that's what I told you. But before I left Jacksonville I asked the sheriff of Duval County to keep tabs on her. He's a good man and he kept his word. It turned out the doctors called it wrong. Riley did wake up. They got in touch with the sheriff, and he got in touch with me. I called in another favor and he had the hospital fudge her paperwork. Then we had her transferred to a rehab facility under the name Rachel to keep her clear of the armed robbery and grand theft auto charges that *Riley* would be facing if she ever woke up. If the sheriff down there hadn't worked his magic like he'd done, she'd be locked up right now. I had to keep it all on the down low to avoid her going to prison, too. Riley Sinclair had to die in order for Rachel Sinclair to have a chance at living. I was going to tell you once she was back on her feet, but then it all went sideways. Kate and I were footing the bill for her physical therapy for a while, anonymously of course, but then one day I get a call and find out that she just up and checked herself out. No forwarding address. No nothing. I tried to track her down, but the girl is good, and the trail went cold. Not knowing what happened to her only made not telling you feel more like the right thing to do. I didn't want to give you any false hope. I didn't know if you'd end up doing the whole fifteen years or not. And hope can deal the hardest blows."

Nails flipped through the pictures. One by one. Soaking them up. Every detail. She looked amazing. She looked happy. "So, what is all this, then? You finally found her?"

"No, brother. That was all Freddy."

Freddy leaned forward on his desk. "After your parole hearing went through last month, Clayton finally told me everything he just told you. I wanted to tell you. But first, I figured what the hell, maybe I could try and find her myself before you got out. I made some calls. I found some guys in Atlanta named Cobb, a couple of fellas that Scabby Mike recommended. They're professional trackers known for finding people that others can't. I asked them to see if they could find her. It took them less than a week."

Nails felt his hands shaking. She was alive. Dallas was alive. That information danced across his brain like a fresh fire. But the flame was already beginning to die out. He'd nearly gotten her killed before. He wasn't going to do that again. He was a convicted felon now. She was free of him. He wasn't bringing his shit into her life. He wasn't making that mistake again. Not ever. He started to put the photos back into the file. Freddy looked confused.

"You don't look all that happy, Nails. Your girl is alive. You can go to her. You've had too much of your life taken away already. You don't need to waste the rest of it on this mountain. What's the problem?"

Nails looked around the room at the faces of his friends. "I'm not going to ruin her life again, Freddy. She doesn't deserve it. Look at these pictures. She looks happy. I'm not going to fuck that up."

"Well, in that case, let me buy you a lottery ticket."

Nails looked confused. "A lottery ticket?"

"Yeah. To win a John Deere tractor."

"What do I need a tractor for?"

"To pull your head out of your ass. Because thinking you might be bad for that woman might be the dumbest thing you've ever said."

"Take it easy, Freddy." Kate moved her hand from Nails's knee to his shoulder and leaned in to look him directly in the eye. "Nelson, maybe you're right. I don't know this woman, so I can't speak on her. Maybe she doesn't deserve it. But I *do* know you. And nobody deserves it more. There's so much love in you for everyone else. For me and Clayton. For Freddy. For Riley. But none for yourself. Don't let that happen. At least take that bag back to its rightful owner and find out. It's public record that you've been released. She might be waiting."

Nails shook his head. "Even if that were true, nobody is going to accept it. Her and me. The world ain't built that way."

Freddy laughed. "You've been gone a long time, buddy. The world is a different place these days. People love who they love. Nobody gives a shit about that anymore. You're running out of excuses, Nails. And you're running out of time. Life is too short."

Nails's mouth was dry, so he sipped from Clayton's beer. Then he downed it. "She's probably got someone, Freddy. It's been nine years."

"Oh, she does."

Nails stared at him. That was a cruel response.

"Take a look at the last picture again." Nails slid it to the top of the stack. It was a picture of Dallas—or Rachel now—sitting in a playground sandbox, holding up a toddler. "She's got him," Freddy said. "Those Cobb brothers told me that she adopted that boy two years ago. He's her son." Freddy leaned down and looked at the photo again. "I can't tell what nationality the kid is but I'm guessing Cubano. Them Florida girls love their Cubanos."

"That's racist, Freddy."

"Yeah, well, I'm old. And you're just sitting there getting older."

Nails stared at the pictures, flipping through them again and again, until he landed back on the photo of her with the little boy. He stared at it for a long time.

"Go, Nails. Take that duffle bag and go, and don't look back. You can take any one of the cars I've got in the back lot. I suggest the Monte Carlo. She's a beast on the open road."

Gavin poked his head through the office door. "Hey Freddy, you really should get out here. It's getting kinda rowdy."

Clayton stood up and went to fish his badge out of his pocket, but Kate got up and stopped him. "No way, cowboy. You're off duty tonight. So, you can buy me another beer if you want, but if you pin that thing to your shirt, you can look forward to sleeping on the couch tonight."

"Yes, ma'am." Clayton held his hand out to Nails and the big man took it. "Whatever you decide. I've got your back, Nelson. That's a promise." Nails nodded. Kate gave him another hug, and soon he was in the office alone. He sat there for a while before tucking the file under his arm and grabbing the keys to the Monte Carlo from a hook beside the door. He stepped out of the office and saw Freddy behind the bar. The two men locked eyes and that was all that needed to happen. Freddy went back to work and Nails left through the side door.

He tossed the duffle bag in the backseat and got behind the wheel of the Monte Carlo. He turned the key in the ignition and the voice of some cereal box evangelist filled the interior of the car. Nails shut the man up by mashing the cassette tape from his pocket into the tape player. The familiar songs from *R's Mixtape* took its place.

As he sat in the car, it occurred to him that almost a decade ago, he'd found himself alone in a parking lot, holding a stack of a cash and a phone number. He remembered the feeling of being ejected from his life—lost and unwanted. Now, he was in that same parking lot with another wad of cash in his pack and an address. But this time he didn't feel like he was being cast out of where he belonged. He felt like he was about to go and find it.

Coda

Chapter Seventy

He took his time making the trip to Virginia. He drove during the day so he could take in the country and stopped whenever he got tired. Along the way, he treated himself to a few decent hotels and more than a few hot showers. He bought himself some new clothes and a new pair of boots. He even got himself a prepaid cell phone and took the time to learn how to use it. He knew he still needed to deal with his parole officer but being a good friend of the new sheriff of McFalls County gave him all the time he needed.

It was late afternoon on a Wednesday when he arrived in the sleepy town of Big Island, Virginia. He thought it was an odd name for a place nestled in the rocky landscape of the Blue Ridge Mountains—nowhere close to the sea—and he still wasn't sure showing up here was a good idea. But he took the hairpin turns and narrow roads into town anyway. He double-checked the address written on the back of the photo, although he didn't need to. He'd memorized it before he'd even gotten out of Georgia. The sun was low behind the hazy backdrop of mountains and the skyline burned, painting the world with shades of pink and yellow. He could feel his own heartbeat as he pulled up in front of the simple stick-framed house and sat for a minute to try and calm himself down. The house was blue. The shutters on the windows were bright white, red-tipped azaleas lined the yard. The brick porch was covered with various potted plants and ferns. Children's toys were everywhere. The front yard had two Japanese maples and a green plastic sandbox shaped like a turtle. When Nails spotted the little boy sitting in it, holding a small shovel and a bucket, he

almost drove away in a panic, but he didn't. He cut the engine, rubbed
the sweat from his palms on his jeans, and got out of the car. The little
boy watched him curiously as Nails slowly walked up the pavers to the
house. He was sure the kid would be frightened of him, but he held up his
good hand anyway and said, "Hello."

The little boy waved back but looked unsure of the big strange man
walking across his yard. Nails could feel it in his bones that any minute
now the kid would scream. This was a bad idea. He had no business here.
Disrupting lives and scaring children. It had been too long. Dallas had
come out here for a reason. To get away. For a fresh start. Nails would
just be a reminder of the horrible past she'd hidden herself away from. He
was bringing the trauma right back to her doorstep. He shook his head
and closed his eyes. "No," he said under his breath and turned back to
the car. He'd only taken a few steps before he heard the creak of a screen
door open behind him. He froze when he heard a voice—her voice. A
sound that crushed his chest.

"Nelson? Come inside."

Nails must've heard that wrong. He heard what he wanted to hear.
It had been nine years. She wouldn't just invite him to come inside as if
she'd seen him yesterday. He knew he should just keep walking, but he
couldn't get his legs to move. He couldn't turn around, either. He didn't
know what to say. He didn't know how he was supposed to act. How
could he be so stupid to bring all the horror of what they'd gone through
back to her doorstep?

She repeated herself. "Nelson, come in and get cleaned up for dinner."

Hearing that confused Nails even more. It had only been four days
of her life—nine years ago. And now here she was saying his name like
she talked to him every day since. That couldn't be right. He found the
guts to face her. She stood tall on the front porch as beautiful as he remembered. Even more so. The girl he knew was gone. The woman she'd
become left him weak. Her hair was longer now and the color of summer
wheat in the sun. Her cotton dress pressed against her legs in the breeze,
and he couldn't speak. He hadn't had that problem in years but there he
was, standing in front of the one person he'd spent every day of the last
nine years thinking about and now he was a mute fool all over again.
There was no way this could end well. She didn't need this. She came to

this place to hide from him. To hide from the past. She didn't want anything to do with him. The little boy waved at Nails again before running up the steps toward his mother. "Do as I said, Nelson, and I'll be right in." She rustled the kid's hair as he went inside. Nails felt his chest go tight. He had it wrong. The child's name was Nelson. If she came here to hide, it wasn't from him.

Once the boy disappeared into the house, Dallas took the steps, slowly at first, in her bare Grocery Store Feet. She walked toward him but gradually began to run. Before Nails could react, she jumped up and grabbed him. She hugged his neck, her feet dangling several inches above the grass. She was as light as paper-mache. Nails put his hands on her hips, careful not to hold her too tight. Still afraid she might vanish in his arms like some trick of the light. But she was no illusion. She was real. He wasn't going to seize up this time. He would hug her back. He closed his eyes as she squeezed him tighter, and instantly everything else in his mind faded away. All his mistakes. All the violence. All the constant noise in his head. It all went quiet. All the pain he'd ever caused or endured. It all gave way under the weight of this moment.

"If this is all I get. Just this. Just this one last snapshot in time. It would have to be enough. It would have to make it all worth it."

Without loosening her grip around his neck, or letting her feet drop a single inch toward the grass, she leaned in closer to his ear. With breath that smelled like honeysuckle, she said, "You know you just said that out loud, right?"

He didn't know that. And he laughed. Hard enough to hurt his belly.

She hugged even tighter. "So are you going to stick around this time?"

"Yes."

"Do you promise?"

"With all my heart."

"Well, then come in the house, handsome. Because there's someone I'd like for you to meet."

Acknowledgments

Yeah, I know. I am fully aware that this novel is not what most of you thought would be coming next. But I reckon that was the point. If you made it to this page, then you are clearly willing to walk through fire with me—burns be damned. So, thank you. The world has enough bleakness in it right now. And there are plenty of writers out there happy to provide that if you want it. For me, I found myself, while writing this book, yearning to share a little hope. Hope that exists even in the darkest corners of the Deep South.

Love, the South, and crime are often interlaced. And in the end, all three might kick the shit out of you, but it's still love that conquers all. I've yet to find anything that can compete. So thank you to the readers that stuck with me through this story. Because without you, I'd be talking to myself in a padded room.

I'd like to thank Judith Weber and Nat Sobel for not giving me an inch of ground to mess this up. For helping me make this one count. And of course, thank you to my editor, Kelley Ragland. Because without her, I'd be typing this into the ether, instead of the back of a published novel. I love you, Kelley—madly. You deserve the accolades because you're a fucking queen.

This book isn't like the rest of my catalog. It's a story I felt like I needed to write. A love story for people who have suffered at the hands of ignorance, bigotry, and intolerance since I was a little kid. Before we knew how to see the differences in people as a good thing. It's a story for people who could use a leg up in the world. People who wake up every day and think they are alone. This book is a little over three hundred pages of proof that you're not. It's for everyone who thinks they are at the end of something, when maybe it's only the beginning. Being lonely is part of life. But being alone doesn't have to be. It's curable. By reading. By going outside. By answering the phone. By making the call yourself. This book is for you—because I get it. Because I am one of you.

Thank you to Jason Sheffield and Dan Adams for being constants without questions. Thank you to James Anderson, GP Gritton, David Hutchison, Steven Uhles, Peter Farris, Meagan Lucas, Jennifer Finney Boylan, Viet Thanh Nguyen, Sarah and Jimmy Quick, and Julie Cross. Thank you to Kate Lynn Moss for constantly telling me the unvarnished truth—for being my true north. Dallas owes you a great debt of gratitude as well. Thank you to Jennifer Panowich, who showed unconditional support of this hard-left turn I took. And hey, Lindsey Wallen, keep writing and us proud.

But lastly, and most importantly, thank you to the two most incredible women I know. Talia and Ivy Panowich. (Yes, they are both named after Batman villains.) Thank you for not just granting me the gift of being your father, but for helping me navigate a world that now belongs to you. My plan was always to leave the world a better place than I found it. Mission accomplished by handing you two the wheel. To say I'm proud of you would be an understatement. You taught me that sometimes I'm the one in the room who needs to sit down, shut up, and listen. So I can learn and understand. So I can be part of your world—a better world than mine.

I should also mention how important it is that everyone listen to Ethel Cain's music. Or Morgan Wade's. Or to read both Charles Bukowski and Pablo Neruda. But don't get stuck inside one or the other. Be open to all of it. And eat food you can't pronounce. Listen to people that don't look or sound like you. Do it slowly. Enjoy it. And be grateful.